The
Catch

JENNA MILES

DEDICATION

For C, A, and L
"So I don't ever want to see you settle for anything less than everything. Just do me a favor, and believe that you deserve it."

And for Uncle Ed
1951-1994
You wrote about me, so I wrote about you.

CONTENTS

ACKNOWLEDGMENTS

I have so many people to thank for their generous time and attention in helping me to sound as if I know what I'm writing about:

Elizabeth Bernstein, editor at EBC Books, for her invaluable feedback on my manuscript, and for suggesting the title of the novel.

Travis Corby, attorney at Shernoff Bidart Echeverria Bentley LLP, for his insight into medical insurance rescission cases.

Geniveve Ruskus, attorney at Lakin Spears, LLP, for answering questions about family law.

Larry Collins, President of the San Francisco Community Fishing Association and of the San Francisco Crab Boat Owners Association, for information about the San Francisco fishing industry; fishing boats and their layout; and the life of a commercial fisherman.

Rod Moore, Executive Director, West Coast Seafood Processors Association, and **Susan Chambers**, Deputy Director, West Coast Seafood Processors Association, for information about the fishing and fish processing industries in San Francisco and Alaska and about the life of a commercial fisherman; for connecting me with Caito Fisheries; and for treating me to lunch!

Jeanette Caito of Caito Fisheries, for allowing me to tour Caito Fisheries' processing plant and answering questions about its operations.

Angel Cincotta of Alioto-Lazio Fish Company, for insight into the San Francisco fishing and fish processing industries and their history.

Maureen Hanhan, for insight into what it was like to grow up in the Outer Sunset in the 80s and 90s.

Jon Greene of Scoma's Restaurant, for insight into the cooking profession in a seafood restaurant.

Scott Lenhart of Great White Shark Expeditions in San Francisco, for insights into the whale watching industry.

Professor Mark Carr, Department of Ecology and Evolutionary Biology, University of California, Santa Cruz, for his idea of what question a marine biology student would ask her T.A. during office hours.

Andy Touhy, instructor at Writing Salon, and the participants of his writing workshop for their feedback on sections of my novel.

Sarah Hansen of Okay Creations, for her amazing cover art.

All of the beta readers who generously gave their time and feedback on the various iterations of my manuscript.

Pull down the screen
Wrap me in copper thread
Sing me down in scales
End me in velvet coral
and opalescent foam
Don't raise the alarm

2012

The fog was as much a native of this neighborhood as Julia was. But it was January, so this morning she had a clear view out the window of her old bedroom to the houses on the next block. Beyond that, across the Great Highway, the ocean would be glittering all the way to the horizon.

Julia hadn't slept, which wasn't all that surprising since it was her first night back in her parents' house. But also, her conversation with her sister the night before kept running through her mind. So did the name of the person they had talked about for the first time in over five years.

"He's doing that whale watching thing," her sister had told her. "It worked out."

Julia's kids would wake up at any minute. She let the curtain drop and tiptoed through the shadows, silently closing the bedroom door behind her so she wouldn't wake her daughter. She padded through the living room of her parents' house and descended downstairs.

In the in-law unit, she flipped on the light and opened the bedroom door a crack. After confirming that her son still slept soundly, she went to the computer, booted it up, and opened a browser window.

She had restrained herself from doing this for the past several years. She doubted the wisdom of what she was about to do, and did it anyway.

She typed "William Quinn whale watching" into the search engine, and hit enter.

Boom, she thought. The very first result was a whale watching company based out of San Francisco. The meta description underneath it contained his name.

Steeling herself, she clicked on it. There it was, the business she had imagined with William all those years ago, fully realized. She searched the navigation bar on the left. There was a link to "The Vessel" and one to "The Naturalists," but none for "The Captain."

So she clicked on "The Vessel," and read the description of the catamaran. Her stomach flopped when she saw its name – The Albatross. This definitely had to be it, but still no sign of him anywhere.

Then she scrolled down.

True to form, he had hidden himself far below the information about the vessel itself, refusing to devote a whole section of the web site to himself.

Well, she thought. This was what I came all the way down here to see.

She allowed herself one final look at him, standing casually on the deck of the boat. He had grown a beard again, as he had in Alaska, and his face showed new signs of wear and tear. A hat covered his hair. But the eyes told her it was him.

She moved the cursor to where it said "The Naturalists." Here's where she might have been, had she not made the choices she did. Who would she find there, in her place?

She allowed the cursor to hover, without clicking on it. Then she closed the browser window and sat motionless in front of the screen a while.

It didn't matter anymore. She had made her choices. What had her sister told her just last night? "Do something for yourself, for a change."

So Julia opened two new browser windows. In the first one, she typed, "Castro Aquarium Service." In the second, she typed, "How to write a business plan."

1993

Julia's first job at the restaurant was washing dishes. After she broke six dishes and flooded the pot room, her father assigned her to one of the prep cooks. Three batches of over-softened compound butter and one batch of wilted salad later, he decided her talents might lie with greeting the guests.

At the same time, her mother discovered that Julia could be of some use to her. Julia learned to place orders, and one morning her mother said, "I'll need you to go to Cardone's to pick up a load of salmon that just came off the boat."

So Julia followed her sister Alison down the pier to the fish processing plant that overlooked the bay and the fog-shrouded Golden Gate Bridge. Bustling behind the counter of the plant's tiny storefront, Ann Quinn paused long enough to wave a friendly hello to Julia and Alison. Her face had deep lines and sharp angles, but her smile was quick and warm, with straight white teeth that did not quite match her rough face.

"Afternoon! They let her out?" she called to Alison in a husky voice, jerking her thumb at Julia. Without waiting for an answer, she burst through the door that led into the plant, barking, "Will! Dunphy's order!"

Moments later, a figure emerged, slinging a tote of salmon around the counter and dropping it onto the rolling cart they had brought. He straightened, his eyes lingering a moment longer on Julia's unfamiliar face before dashing around the counter again without a word.

"Thanks, William," Alison called, and he lifted his hand once before disappearing into the plant again.

"Who was that?" Julia whispered as they wheeled the cart back onto the pier.

"William Quinn." When Julia drew a blank, Alison prompted, "The son?"

Julia looked back at the door he had gone through. "Ann and Jim's son?"

"He goes to Holy Cross, you know. He's in your class."

"Really? I've never seen him."

"You probably never noticed him because he looked like a new person every year. A couple of years ago, he grew about a foot. Then he spent another year or two looking like a stick insect." Alison eyed Julia suspiciously, and grinned. "But I guess he's worth noticing now?"

"I guess so."

"You know he lives only three blocks away from us, right?"

"No, I didn't."

"A very easy distance for a late-night booty call."

Julia smacked her. "Speak for yourself."

The next afternoon, Julia pulled the cart into the plant by herself. Ann Quinn, behind the counter again, called out, "On your own, already? Well done!" Then, over her shoulder, "Will! Dunphy's!"

William appeared with the tote and dropped it onto Julia's cart. She halted his retreat by saying, "I hear we're in the same class at Holy Cross."

He turned a pair of blue eyes on her with a directness that Julia imagined some people would find unsettling. He said nothing, so she persisted. "I'm going to be a senior next year. What about you?"

"Yeah." He stood his ground, with none of the shuffling or shoe-gazing of most guys her age.

"I can't believe we've never had a class together before."

"We've had two classes together."

"No way. When?"

"Earth Science, in ninth grade. And French, in tenth."

Mortified, Julia said, "Oh, I'm surprised you even recognize me from back then. That was when the guys used to call me Horsey Face, and Mosquito Bites.'"

The corners of his mouth turned up slightly. "You held your own pretty well."

"Even so, I did run right out and get braces as soon as I could. And I'm saving for a boob job."

He still smiled faintly but said nothing more, so she said, "See you tomorrow."

"Okay," he replied, and dashed away.

The next day, as ever, William rounded the corner with the tote, but stopped when he saw Julia and her cart.

"Is that all you brought?" he said. When Julia nodded, he asked, "Didn't you bring anyone else with you?"

"Why?"

"You've got a lot more today than you did the last two days. That cart won't cut it."

"Get the dolly and take it over, Will," barked his mother.

Within a few minutes, Julia and William carried five totes of fish back to the restaurant, one on Julia's meager cart, and four stacked on William's hand truck. Walking alongside him, Julia had to crane her neck to look up at him.

"Do you work here every day?" she asked.

"Yeah, either at the plant, or on my uncle's boat."

"Your uncle's boat." It dawned on her. "You mean a fishing boat?"

He nodded.

"You help unload when he docks?"

"Yeah, and I go out with him sometimes too."

"Go out. You mean fishing?"

Again, there was that almost imperceptible turning up at the corners of his mouth. By now, they were at the restaurant, and they had no more time to talk in the bustle of unloading the carts. He slipped out of the restaurant before she knew he was leaving.

One morning, while setting places with an excellent view of the pier, Julia spotted a familiar figure ascending from one of the boats. She recognized him when he lowered his hood and pulled the hat from his head, rumpling his wavy light brown hair even more than usual. William hoisted totes full of shimmering fish up to the pier. He and the older man he worked with were close enough that she could hear their voices shouting to each other.

The older man must have been his uncle. He was a stocky, middle-aged man with a weathered face, a mustache, and dark hair well-streaked with gray. He bore a definite family resemblance to William's mother. Even from all this distance, she could hear him swearing and see him spitting over the deck.

William was cut more finely than the rest of his family, his manners less brusque, and Julia could not help but wonder what forces had shaped him differently. Besides, she had a weakness for the tall, lean types, and he combined that with such surprising strength that she found herself riveted to the window, watching him work.

The next day, though William slung a tote of salmon onto her cart in his usual rush, she took advantage of the one sidelong glance he cast her to flash her friendliest smile. He hesitated, and she said, "Where do you go when you go on the boat with your uncle?"

He stood still and faced her for a moment. "It depends on the day."

"Okay, so where did you go yesterday? When I saw you working on the boat?"

His eyes widened at her revelation that she had been watching him without his knowledge. But in a steady voice he replied, "Yesterday, out by the Farallones."

"Really? How often do you go out there?"

"Pretty often. I always try to go with my uncle when he's heading out that way."

"I've only been out there twice. The first time was when I was twelve, and my Uncle Rob took my sister and me. That's how I became interested in being a marine biologist. That, and overdosing on too many episodes of Nature on PBS."

"Will!" Ann Quinn's sharp bark made them both jump. "Those fish won't clean themselves!"

William turned to go, but his striking eyes lingered on Julia for one moment longer. Julia was alarmed at just how peeved she felt with Ann Quinn at that moment.

The Fourth of July found Julia working the hostess station in the lobby of the restaurant. She had an excellent view through the floor-to-ceiling windows to the outside, where the throngs assembled in the distance for the fireworks. As light retreated from the sky, the stream of hungry patrons slowed to a trickle.

Through the window, Julia saw a figure approaching which had become all too familiar to her. William spotted her through the glass even before opening the door.

She smiled her usual bright smile that warmed her whole face. "Table for one?"

"I was just coming by to say hi."

"Are you here all by yourself?"

"No," he admitted. "I left my parents and sister back at Aquatic Park."

He had cleaned up after his shift at work, and looked completely different in a plaid flannel shirt, jeans, and Doc Martens. After a moment's hesitation, he ventured, "What time are you stuck here until?"

"Technically until ten, when we close. But I don't think we're going to get very many more customers today."

"Think you can get away to watch the fireworks?"

"Not with the general in charge."

"The general?"

"My dad. But you can see the fireworks pretty well through the windows here, assuming the fog doesn't ruin them as usual. And I can probably get away with stepping outside for a few minutes, too."

He shoved his hands into his pockets and glanced around. His eyes settled on the huge, brightly colored tropical fish tank behind her.

"That's nice. I've never had the time to really look at it before."

"Thank you! I have a smaller one just like it at home."

He looked at her in astonishment. "You put that together?"

"Yes, I'm afraid I must accept all the blame."

"Do you get any help from anyone else?"

7

"Not unless you count books and my former boss, who taught me how."

He surveyed the aquarium again. "I hear those are pretty hard to take care of."

"That would be an affirmative. But I had a really great teacher. I spent the last two years working for Castro Aquarium Service."

"Why don't you work there anymore? Seems like it would be the perfect job for you."

"Because my boss died. Of AIDS. The shop closed down after he died. And the only reason I got the job in the first place was because my boss's partner was my Uncle Rob. He's too sick to work anymore, so he lives at home with my grandma now."

It took him a moment to realize her uncle was not merely her boss's business partner. "Oh. I'm sorry to hear that. Are you very close to your uncle?"

"Yes, very. Along with my grandmother, he and Tim practically raised me and Alison, since our parents work all the time. He's responsible for the weirdo you see before you today. With an Irish grandmother and a flaming queen as parental figures, you can hardly be surprised that I turned out a little different."

As usual, he gave a half-smile but said nothing. She blurted, "Wait here," and ran off to the kitchen.

She found Alison plating panna cotta, and cleared her throat. "Excuse me."

"Mm." Alison did not look up.

"I'm going to take some panna cotta, okay?"

"Is this for a customer?"

"William Quinn is in the lobby."

Alison smirked, but waved her assent. With no eye for presentation like her sister, Julia slapped two helpings onto the first plates she could find and hurried back to the front. She found him still sitting patiently on a bench, gazing at the aquarium.

"Since we're stuck here, we may as well make the best of things," she declared. She handed him his portion and sat beside him on the bench. "So, what bizarre, hidden talents do you pursue in your spare time?"

"Compared to your aquariums, nothing interesting."

She waited for him to elaborate. "Okay, I get it. Me first. I know it looks like I was born in a thrift store in Bohemia, but the truth is, I make almost all of my own clothes. My Uncle Rob is responsible for that, too. He taught me to sew, and then I taught myself to knit and crochet."

To her surprise, he reached out, touched her crinkled scarf and the crocheted flower on her hat, and said, "What about these?"

"Not the scarf or the hat. Those really are thrift store finds. But the flower on the hat? That's my special touch." When he still said nothing, she added, "I'm also an incurable reader. A classics junkie. The Janes, all the way."

"The Janes?"

"Austen and Eyre. But I like it all. To Kill a Mockingbird. I Know Why the Caged Bird Sings. Did you know part of that takes place in San Francisco?" She nudged him with her elbow. "What about you? Do you read?"

"Sure."

"Okay. Still too soon, I get it. Oh! Did I ever tell you that I read the entire novel Gone With the Wind when I was only thirteen? It almost turned me into a flaming racist. My uncle rented the movie version for me. I was so disappointed that they cut it back to only four hours. It would have been much better as a miniseries." When he still refused to respond, she insisted, "Okay, it really is your turn now. I asked if you read and you said, 'Sure.' So what do you like to read?"

He picked at his panna cotta. "I'm not much of a fiction reader."

"*Fisherman's Digest? Penthouse Forum?* Come on, give me something to work with here."

He shifted in his seat, cleared his throat. "I used to read a lot of poetry."

She realized too late that the shock had registered on her face, plain for him to see. He set aside his half-eaten plate of panna cotta and turned to stare out the window.

"I'm sorry," she gasped. "I'm so sorry. It's just – if you had told me that you were a lizard disguised in a suit made of human skin, I could hardly be more shocked."

He cast her a sidelong glance. "Wasn't that the plot of a TV show?"

9

"Yes! See, that's just what I like about you. You're weird enough to know what I'm talking about."

"Is it really so shocking that I would read poetry?"

"No, I'm just trying to reconcile my previous concept of you with this new information. You know, only sensitive boys read poetry, and all that stuff." She lifted a spoonful of panna cotta halfway to her mouth, then lowered it again. "You're not gay, are you?"

He only smiled.

"Oh, my God. You're gay."

"I'm not gay," he laughed.

She had a moment of relief, then said, "Are you bi?"

He laughed again, shaking his head.

"I'm so glad. Not that there's anything wrong with either of those things, mind you. It's just, it would have been tragic."

He reddened and looked out the window again, and she realized what she had just admitted. Quickly, she said, "So you *used* to read poetry. Do you still?"

"Sometimes, when I have time."

"What poets do you like best?"

"I kind of like it all." For a brief moment, it occurred to Julia that maybe he had made the whole thing up just to impress her. But then he said, "Everything from Coleridge and Whitman, to Kerouac. Maya Angelou writes some poetry too, you know."

"I know; I have a volume of hers at home, right alongside my copy of *I Know Why*." It still felt surreal to be talking about this with him. The working class boy and the poetry buff would not coexist in her mind. "Did you ever write any of your own?"

"I messed with it a little, when I was younger."

"Why did you stop?"

"I wasn't really any good." He dug back into his panna cotta again, and she sensed that he didn't really want to talk about this anymore. After a while, he said, "I also like photography."

"Really? What do you take pictures of?"

"Whatever strikes me. Mostly landscapes and cityscapes. Sometimes people."

"Do you ever take pictures while you're out on the boats?"

"Sometimes."

"Can I see them?"

To her surprise, he said, "Sure. Are you working at the restaurant all summer? I can bring them up here sometime."

"Yeah. Well, except for next week when I'm going to marine biology camp."

"There's a whole marine biology camp?"

"Yep. My parents couldn't help me much with the cost of it, so this is pretty much what I've been working and saving for the past two years. I'm hoping it'll help on my application to UCSB. I'm so psyched; I get to go out on the boat and help document whale fecal plumes. For me, it's a dream come true."

She stopped talking because he hid his mouth behind his hand, and his eyes crinkled up in a way she had never seen before. At first she thought he was crying or about to sneeze, but then it dawned on her.

"You're laughing at me!"

He removed his hand from his mouth, confirming her suspicions. It was a silent laugh, but a laugh nonetheless.

"Why are you laughing at me?" she demanded, snickering a bit herself. It was impossible to mind the transformation that laughter brought to his face.

"I'm not laughing at you. I'm just laughing at the idea of anyone getting that excited about whale fecal plumes. But it's great."

She beamed her brightest smile and leaned toward him. "You *are* laughing at me. But it's okay, I don't mind. I know you think I'm strange; everybody does."

"I don't think you're strange."

"But I *am* strange. Do you know, when I was thirteen years old, I converted to Islam for two days?"

He laughed out loud now, and she laughed with him.

"It's true! Our church had a lending library with books about all of the world's major religions. I read about each one, and somehow I got hung up on Islam. I stole a little rug from the hallway for my prayer rug and put it in my room facing toward Mecca, or at least I just faced it toward the east."

"So why did it only last for two days?"

"It was a pain in the ass to pray five times a day."

They both burst out laughing so loudly that the diners seated closest to them turned to stare.

"I'm just picturing you at school, trying to find excuses to go pray," he said after a while.

"Exactly! Though it could hardly have made them think I was any weirder. I really didn't have a lot of friends in those days. I used to shut myself up in my room, looking at atlases and encyclopedias all day. I looked at them so much that they finally fell apart, and I had to keep them together with a giant rubber band. I think my parents and sister thought I was masturbating in there, and just left me alone."

He fell back in his seat laughing again, and flushed bright red. She watched him with pleasure, thinking first of all that he was way out of her league. And second of all, that in spite of that, she would be surprised if he didn't ask her out by the end of the night.

The fireworks began. They stepped out into the chill and watched the show from just outside the front door of the restaurant. Julia clapped and cheered during the best parts of the show, but William stayed silent next to her. When the grand finale erupted overhead, the flashes of light caught his eyes as they turned away from her and back to the sky.

The sky went black again, and though her pulse slammed in her ears, she was determined to face him. This was it. If it was going to happen, this was the moment.

She glanced furtively at William and found him already looking at her. An awkward silence ensued, broken when William said, "I have to meet my parents at the bus stop."

"I've got to go back inside to help close the restaurant," she heard herself say.

He nodded. "See you tomorrow."

"Yeah," she said, and he turned to go without another word to her.

What had she been thinking, talking to him about masturbation? Obviously, when he flushed red, he was just embarrassed. Sometimes she thought it was true what her parents told her, that she had no filter between her brain and her mouth.

She made up her mind to never let herself imagine things about him again.

Talk of her uncle got Julia thinking about a promise she had made. The day after returning home from her marine biology summer camp, she pushed her cart of aquarium supplies five blocks down the street. It was one of her favorite things to do, taking this walk through the fog that muted the sounds of the neighborhood like cotton in her ears. The fog didn't depress her the way it did her mother, who was forever lobbying her father to move them to a different part of the city. It centered Julia, and lately Julia needed centering before seeing Uncle Rob.

When she arrived, she used the key on her chain to let herself in. The house smelled like potato soup. Julia found the source, and her grandmother, in the kitchen.

"Oh! You startled me, love," exclaimed her grandmother, turning from the stove. Her voice still bore traces of her native Ireland.

"Sorry, Gran." Julia went to kiss her. "How's he doing today?"

"Today's a good day," said her grandmother. "He's been up all morning, and he's keeping down pureed foods. You'll find him in the living room."

"Can I bring him his soup?"

Her grandmother spooned it into a bowl. "Let it cool a while before you give it to him, though. If it's too hot, it comes back up."

Julia carried a tray with the soup and a cup of water into the living room. She found him in the easy chair in his pajamas and robe, gazing idly at the aquarium in the corner of the room.

He turned to smile. "Julie."

"Hi, Uncle Rob." She set the tray on the coffee table and came to kiss his cheek.

"So it's potato soup again, is it?"

"Gran says you've been able to eat today." They shared the same copper hair, freckles, and quick metabolism, but he was looking more gaunt than ever lately. His temples looked sunken, a new development since the last time she had seen him.

"The old bat supposedly hung up her nursing uniform fifteen years ago," he said affectionately.

"She says it's been a good day. What have you been doing with yourself?"

"I managed to get a little writing done this morning." He gestured over to the desk in another corner of the room. A half-filled sheet of white paper stuck out of the top of an old manual typewriter. A small stack of filled pages sat alongside the machine.

She set up his TV tray and placed the bowl and cup in front of him. "Can you manage it?"

He lifted the spoon. It was shaky, but the soup made it to his mouth. He set it down again to smile at Julia.

"So what brings you all the way over here? Not to watch me eat, I hope."

Julia gestured to the aquarium. "Maintenance."

"I can't tell you what a comfort that thing has been to me. And an inspiration," he added, looking over at the typewriter again.

"Inspiration?"

"I'm writing a novel that takes place on a tropical island."

"I'm glad you've started writing again."

"Me too. I'm just surprised I can still do it after all these years. So what about you? How was your camp?"

"Awesome! Even though I didn't get to document whale fecal plumes, after all."

"Such a pity."

"But I did get to conduct an otter trawl for plankton. And we got to set up our own aquariums in the dormitories."

"Let me guess who got top marks on *that* project."

Julia laughed. "In the end I kind of took over as the unofficial instructor. You wouldn't believe the total amateur they had in there. Just some marine biology grad student who happened to keep aquariums as a hobby on the side, and not even saltwater aquariums. Poor Kevin. He was still using techniques from the 1950s and he couldn't get anything to survive in those tanks. But I straightened him out."

"And wound up on a first name basis, I see."

"Well, at first I think he kind of resented me. But by the end of the week, he was coming to me for advice on all kinds of things. And on the last day, he gave me his phone number and told me to look him up if I ever get into UCSB. He said he'd try to hook me up with an internship."

"Oh, honey. Kevin wants to hook you up with more than an internship."

Julia threw a napkin at him. "Stop."

"You mean you don't return his good opinion?"

"Not in that way. The main reason we clicked was because he seemed so familiar somehow. Then finally, about halfway through the week, I figured it out."

"What?"

Julia went to the fireplace mantelpiece to retrieve a framed photograph she had known all of her life. It was a very old photo, the colors all fading to red. A very young Rob, with a very young Tim looking over his shoulder. Smiling, the both of them, their whole lives ahead of them. The water at their backs.

Julia brought the photo to Rob and pointed to Tim. Someone had snapped the photo long before Tim had grown portly, when he still possessed a full head of curly black hair, a full beard, and outmoded browline glasses.

"Kevin could have been Tim's long-lost twin," Julia said.

Rob smiled and touched the image of young Tim. "Well, you could do worse."

She gestured to his soup. "Now, it's time for you to focus on that. I'm going to get started."

While he ate, she conducted the weekly water tests, scraped the algae from the sides of the tank, and replaced the filter carbon. By the time she finished, Rob's bowl sat half-empty.

"Just like Tim would have done," said Rob as she turned from the aquarium.

"I should think so. He drilled it into me enough. I'm still terrified to deviate from his instructions."

Rob gave a shaky laugh. "He had that effect on people."

Julia nodded toward his bowl of soup. "How's that sitting with you?"

"Great, so far. I'll finish the other half in a bit."

When her grandmother returned to the living room, he looked cheerful again, and the bowl of soup was empty.

"Why don't you two engage in another Skip Bo battle to the death?" suggested her grandmother as she cleared away the dishes from Rob's tray.

When she was gone, Rob leaned his painfully thin frame forward in his chair and whispered, "Poor choice of words."

"You're telling me. I'm a goner, for sure."

Julia reached into the cabinet for the battered pack of Skip Bo cards. He leaned back in his chair and watched her shuffle the pack.

"Where's Alison today?" he wondered.

"She's working today, like every day. I don't think she's going back to culinary school this year, though."

"That must be a disappointment to your dad."

Julia dealt the cards. "Between you and me, I think she's going to try for her own cake decorating business."

"You mean open her own shop?"

"No, I think she's going to ask Mom and Dad if she can bake from home for a while."

He played a hand. "The market is saturated."

"I don't know anything about that. But she has a real gift for it, you know. I think if anyone can break into it, she can."

He discarded, and watched her draw three new cards. "So for you it's marine biology at UCSB, then?"

"All the way."

"I think that's great. You know exactly what you're doing and where you're going. I had a good run, but I got off track a bit."

"What are you talking about?"

He perked up and waved his hand dismissively. "Oh, I don't mean to sound morose. I don't regret a day I spent at that aquarium business. But I do regret putting my writing on hold for so long. You sure you wouldn't consider reviving the old place one of these days? You have such a gift for it, same as Tim did. Almost seems a shame for you to not make a living out of it."

"You mean the aquarium company?" She smiled, thinking of William. "You're the second person to ask me something like that in the past couple of weeks."

"Oh?" He sat up straighter, his curiosity piqued. "And who is the first, pray tell?"

"A friend of mine."

"Oh," he said, smiling. "A friend."

She played her hand.

"Admirers coming out of the woodwork," he ventured.

"He's not an admirer; trust me," she said drily.

"Well, dear, if marine biology is your true passion, then don't ever let me see you put that on hold. Not for anything. Not for any*one*."

She did not know how to respond to that, so she discarded. He played the last card in his stack, and won the game.

Julia said, "My fish at home are feeling jealous."

Rob sat back in his chair and smiled at her. "Yes. Thank you for coming."

She came forward and gave him a hug and a kiss.

"Love you, Julie," he said.

"Love you too."

He leaned the easy chair back and closed his eyes, and she followed her grandmother downstairs.

"Thank you for coming to see him," her grandmother whispered as Julia gathered up her cart.

"Does anyone come to see him these days?"

Her grandmother looked somber. "You and Alison, and your parents when they can. Sometimes your Aunt Kathleen, and Holly. The others... they won't even let their kids come over here anymore."

Julia frowned, but only said, "I'll be here again next week."

"It really lifts his spirits. He feeds off it the whole week."

Julia hugged her goodbye. On the way home, she glanced furtively down William's block, turning her uncle's counsel over in her mind.

Early the following Sunday morning, Julia sat yawning in the restaurant office over the day's inventory when the doorbell rang at the back door.

"Will you get that, dear?" her mother said without looking up from her books. "I am not getting up from here until I figure out where this extra sole is coming from."

"Gladly," said Julia, springing to her feet. When she flung open the back door, there stood William, bracing a dolly with a crate of fish against his side.

"Special delivery," he said. "A load of sand dab, right off the boat this morning. My dad wanted to see if your dad was interested."

"Normally probably so, but I warn you, we got a less than glowing review in the *Chronicle* this morning."

"Oh. What did it say?"

"Well, it compared our cioppino to something from a can of Chef Boyardee, for one thing. And it said something about the restaurant being apparently past its prime, like its owner and head chef."

"Ouch."

"Yep. Of course, I think my dad is the only one around here who's surprised by any of this. I remember all too well the time at school when I overheard a guy ask who I was. Someone told him that my father owns Dunphy's, and he said, 'I hate that place. It smells like old people in there.'"

William smiled but said nothing, so Julia led him to the office, where her father sat uncharacteristically idle at his desk, the newspaper spread out before him. It took him a few moments to notice them standing there, but when he spotted William, he dragged himself to his feet to shake his hand.

"William. How are you? I hope you had a great birthday dinner here with your family the other day."

"We did, thanks. The food was great," William added kindly.

Her father sank back into his seat. "William, let me ask you something. You had the cioppino the other night. What did you think of it?"

Poor William, thought Julia. He shifted his weight and glanced back at the load of sand dab he had brought with him, considering. Then, to Julia's amazement, he looked her father in the eye and said, "I've had better."

Julia watched outrage and mortification wage battle on her father's face. William had literally stunned him to silence for a few moments, an unprecedented feat in the history of this kitchen. When he finally recovered his powers of speech, Julia's father spluttered, "Oh really? Where?"

"My grandmother's."

Her father nodded, spying an opening. "We all like best what we're used to."

William said nothing, and Julia's father was all too happy to move on from the subject. "Well, what can I help you with? You came here; you obviously wanted to see me about something."

18

William mentioned the sand dabs, which Julia's father inspected, managed to find fault with, and dismissed brusquely.

The restaurant was closed on Monday, but on Tuesday, William appeared again at the kitchen door, ostensibly with another special delivery for Julia's father. But on top of the box of fish sat a round container. After Julia accepted the delivery, William turned to Julia's father.

"I also brought you some of my grandmother's cioppino."

Ballsy, thought Julia. At least he had the wisdom not to do it in front of any of the kitchen staff. Her father accepted the container and gave some chilly response that Julia didn't quite catch. After William left, Julia's father carried the container to a trash can.

"Oh come on, Dad; we've got to at least try it," Julia pleaded. "You can't throw away his whole container, anyway. It's probably his grandmother's."

"You go right ahead," he said, thrusting the container at her. "Make sure it gets back to him."

When lunch time rolled around, Julia poured the stew into a pot and warmed it. Everyone in the kitchen gathered around to taste. The silence and knowing looks that went around the room told Julia that it was her job to deliver the news.

"Dad, you won't believe this. This is the worst cioppino I've ever tasted in my life!"

The irresistible prospect of making William eat crow lured her father to the stove. He accepted the spoon Julia handed him, tasted, and shot her a quizzical look. The laughter that burst from the staff gave away her ruse. Glowering, her father hurled the spoon into the nearest sink and stormed away.

William made sure to return later that afternoon on some trumped up business. Julia handed him back his clean container and whispered, "It was amazing."

Spotting him while slicing leeks, Julia's father said cooly, "Give my compliments to your grandmother."

"I would, but she's dead."

The knife slicing the leeks slipped, and Julia's father narrowly avoided amputating his own fingertip. "You said it was your grandmother's cioppino."

"It's her recipe."

"Who made this, then?"

"I did."

"Bullshit."

Minutes later, William stood in the kitchen in coat and hat with Mark, the sous chef, who frowned and sniped. Mark had tried unsuccessfully for the last two years to convince Julia's father to scrap his cioppino recipe and start anew. But Mark's resentment cooled quickly under William's humility. William either did not know or pretended not to know certain little tricks and seasonings that Mark obligingly filled in for him, and in short, William played the part of the grateful student. By the end of the afternoon, they had a pot of cioppino that was superior even to what William had brought in.

To his credit, Julia's father had a respect for raw talent and gumption that superseded even his ego. "You said your grandmother taught you this?"

William nodded. "I mostly learned by watching, then doing. The whole family cooks together, when we can."

"And your grandmother was Italian?"

"Her parents were from Sicily."

"What else can you do?"

"Pretty much anything my grandmother could do. Or at least three quarters of it."

By the time William left that night, he had a new part-time job as a dishwasher at Dunphy's. Considering it offered only the vaguest promise of leading to prep cook in the future, and that William would have to give up much of his work at the plant and on his uncle's boat, Julia was surprised he took it at all. As he tossed his jacket in the hamper, Julia leaned up against the wall.

"I thought you said you have no hidden talents."

"If I told everyone about them, they wouldn't be hidden," he replied. He smiled slightly at her, and rounded the corner to leave.

On the first day of their senior year, Julia and her cousin Holly filed into the AP Biology classroom and took seats next to each other. After Julia spread her books and notebooks on her desk, she took in the infamous Dr. Benson's legendary classroom, chock-full of Lord of the Rings paraphernalia.

Holly poked her. "Don't look now."

Julia followed Holly's gaze behind them. William leaned back in his chair with his legs stretched out, tapping his pen nervously on the desktop. He looked strangely out of place in his school uniform of khaki pants and a blue knit sweater with the school logo. When she turned, his eyes flickered up to meet hers.

She smiled, and he gave her one of his half-smiles in return. She marveled at how, in the past three months, it had not once occurred to her that she might share a class with him this year.

The instructor came in, a stark woman who introduced herself as Dr. Benson, with emphasis on the Doctor.

"Fair warning: this course will challenge you. There will be no curve. I will not hold your hand. Not all of you will pass, but those who do will go on to be doctors, engineers; in short whatever you want to be. The highest universities will come calling for you. This school, and my course, are held in the highest esteem on the West Coast."

After a dramatic pause, during which Julia exchanged mocking self-important faces with Holly, Dr. Benson unceremoniously drilled down the syllabus.

"We waste no time here. Our first lab will be today. The laboratory is next door. I will allow you to choose your lab partners, so choose wisely. You'll be stuck with them for the rest of the year."

She stopped, and everyone waited for her to continue.

"That means now, by the way, so chop chop."

Julia gathered her lab workbook and pen and filed through a door into an adjacent room. She claimed the nearest empty lab table, spread her belongings on the black table top, and turned to find herself staring not at Holly, but at a shoulder. Startled, she looked up, and up some more at William's face.

He spread his books on the table top as if this were the most expected development in the world. Disoriented, Julia searched frantically for Holly, and finally found her directly across from her on the other side of the lab table. Holly had settled for their friend Michelle as a lab partner, and the two of them tried, mostly unsuccessfully, to stifle their snickers at Julia's expense.

Julia's first thought was that Holly had orchestrated this somehow, but William would have had to participate in Holly's conspiracy, and she found that unlikely. She opened her mouth, but closed it again when she realized she had no script for rejecting him as a lab partner. There was nothing left but to accept it, at least for the day.

Resigned, she grinned up at him and said, "Ready to play with flies?"

"After handling fish guts all summer, it should be a piece of cake."

Before she had time to think further, Dr. Benson called them all to task. While she drilled them in safety equipment and lab protocols, Julia found her attention wandering back to her unexpected lab partner.

She had never stood in such close proximity to him for so long. He was well over six feet tall, and she was alarmed at the way her body responded to it.

She jumped at Dr. Benson's sharp voice beside her. "Am I straining your attention, Miss...?"

"Dunphy," she croaked when she had recovered her powers of speech.

"Miss Dunphy, if you find me unworthy of your attention, regular biology is just down the hall. Perhaps your lab partner has a longer attention span. Mr. ...?"

William shifted his weight. "Quinn."

"Mr. Quinn. Do *you* know the difference between diffusion and osmosis?"

Julia didn't even know she had ever asked a question. Unfortunately, William didn't make her look any better with his answer. In a low voice, he replied, "Diffusion is the movement of molecules down a concentration gradient. Osmosis is movement across a permeable membrane."

Dr. Benson looked almost disappointed not to have tripped him up. "A *selectively* permeable membrane. And don't forget the part about it moving from a region of higher concentration to a region of lower concentration. Perhaps you'll be the brains of the outfit, Mr. Quinn."

When Dr. Benson moved away, Holly smirked across the table at Julia. She, at least, could probably guess the true source of Julia's distraction.

This was not going to work out. To pass Dr. Benson's course, she needed total focus.

After lab, Julia snatched Holly by the arm and pulled her into the hallway.

"Switch lab partners with me. Tell him you can't stand Michelle. He can have her."

"I don't think so. You should have seen the way he practically sprinted across the room to beat me. Besides, he's super smart. Why wouldn't you want him? For a lab partner, I mean."

Julia dropped her arm, and stalked away.

On Thursday morning, William said, "I've been thinking, it might be helpful if we form a study group."

Julia raised an eyebrow. "A study group?"

"For weekends, or even weekdays when we're not working. Maybe the four of us," he said, gesturing to Holly and Michelle as well as Julia and himself.

"Oh, I see what you're up to! You kinky boy." His face turned almost purple, and she laughed at him. "Good God, relax. I think it's a good idea. Where should we do it?"

"Well, I was going to say in each other's homes, but I'm afraid you'll hit me over the head with some more innuendo."

"Oh, I would find a way to do that, regardless. Holly, Michelle, did you hear that?"

Holly's be-goggled face popped up from across the lab table. She had attempted to pin back her unruly, frizzy brown mane, but numerous wisps escaped confinement and stuck straight up, giving her the appearance of a mad scientist.

"Hear what, Jules?"

"We're forming a study group. First meeting's at William's place. What day, William?"

He shifted his weight, drummed the table top with his fingertips. "I – we can do it in the library instead."

"Oh no, I'm not missing a chance to see you in your element."

"Okay… what about Saturday in the afternoon?"

"No go," Holly replied drily. "Gotta work."

"So do I, you know," said Julia.

"Oh, yeah. And I have to work on Sunday," he mused.

"What about today?" asked Michelle.

No one claimed any prior engagements, so Julia poked William in the arm and said, "I sure hope you cleaned house."

That afternoon, while the others spread their books and junk food on the coffee table, Julia glanced surreptitiously around William's house. It had basically the same floor plan as Julia's, but someone had long ago covered over the hardwood floors with lava-orange shag carpeting. Wood-framed furniture upholstered in avocado green sagged in the living room. Dingy polyester drapes filtered mustard-yellow light from the windows. Julia snooped at the numerous family photos on the wood-paneled walls and found one of the whole family when William was about five years old. All of William's siblings bore more of a resemblance to Ann, and therefore to the Italian side of the family, than William did.

They were already well into their review of diffusion and osmosis before the rest of his family began trickling in. Curious at the unfamiliar voices in their home, his parents peered into the living room.

"Well, hello," said Ann, wide-eyed.

"We're studying," explained William.

"Fantastic," she replied. "There's sodas in the fridge."

His father merely cast them all an amused sidelong glance, but said nothing. Julia couldn't help noticing that William had inherited all of his mustachioed father's height with none of his barrel-chested girth.

A while later, a teenage girl rounded the corner, wearing only a soccer uniform, a dark brown ponytail, and no make-up.

"What are you guys studying?" she demanded unceremoniously, and Julia's eyes were drawn to her muscular calves.

"Diffusion and osmosis," said Michelle.

"Better you than me." The girl stole a handful of potato chips from their stash and left the room without even introducing herself.

"Bye, Kelly," William shouted after her. To the rest of them, he explained, "That's my sister."

"Where does she go to school?" asked Julia. She knew she had never seen her at Holy Cross.

"Lincoln," replied William. "She could have gotten an athletic scholarship to Holy Cross, but her grades weren't good enough."

But Julia was no longer listening, because halfway through his speech an aberrant figure had exploded into the living room. This figure sported black hair sculpted into a faux-hawk, multiple facial piercings, and colorful tattoos that crawled up like vines from under the collar of his leather jacket to strangle his neck.

He reminded Julia somehow of an incubus.

"Holy shit," the incubus blurted with a grin, lighting a cigarette and leering impishly at all three girls.

"Mike," William chided. "Be a gentleman."

It seemed impossible that Mike and William could have sprung from the same genetic material, until Mike proclaimed, "Righteous, little brother."

"Well, I think we've established one fact for certain," said Julia when Mike had disappeared around the corner. "This is an unusual occurrence in the Quinn household."

"Studying of any kind is unusual in the Quinn household," replied William.

"I wasn't talking about studying," Julia teased him, and felt her stomach flutter at the way his face reddened.

Holly rolled her eyes and observed, "I think we've done enough damage for one day." Shoving her books into her bags, she added, "I have to get to the library and start figuring out this project for history class. Do you have any ideas what you're going to do it on, Julia?"

"I think I'll try prostitution."

"What the heck are you talking about?" Michelle demanded.

"It's a major research project due by the end of this semester," explained Holly. "We have to research an occupation or industry of historical significance to San Francisco. The premise being that these industries are rapidly fading into the history books."

"Well, that rules out prostitution, then," Michelle pointed out. "Alive and well."

"Damn. That would have made for some interesting research," said Julia. While she waited for everyone to finish gathering up their stuff and file toward the front door, she found her attention wandering back to the old family photo on the wall. She had met two of William's siblings, but as she gazed at the photo, she blurted, "Oh, you have another brother?"

From the look on William's face, she realized she had said something very wrong. But William only replied, "Yes."

Seized with embarrassment, Julia turned back to the photo and tried to gloss over whatever mistake she had made by saying, "You were blond!"

Holly came to the rescue. "Isn't it a drag how blond hair always darkens when you get older? Except Alison's. That's totally real, of course."

Julia tugged the copper hair beneath her knit beret. "I would like to state for the record that I came out of the womb this way. I swore I was going to dye it as soon as my parents would let me. But once I got old enough to do that, I realized I kind of liked being different."

"You would," said Michelle, unleashing a hiss of carbonation from another bottle of soda.

As they passed the kitchen, Ann called out, "Will, we're eating soon."

"I'll be back," he said.

Once outside the house, Holly and Michelle went one way toward the bus stop, while Julia headed toward her house, pulling her jacket tighter against the fog and the chill. When William didn't turn back, Julia realized that he was going to walk with her. Typically, he could find nothing to say.

"I'm sorry," Julia said after a moment.

"For what?"

"About your brother. Whatever it is."

"Jimmy's in prison. He was a mechanic, like Mike and everyone else on my dad's side of the family. But boosting cars was more of his thing."

"Well, there's one in every family."

"There's a convicted felon in your family, too?"

"Probably. There's bound to be one in there somewhere, between my dad's prolific Irish family and all the Okies on my mom's side. Nevertheless, point taken. Perhaps I should have said there's a black sheep in every family."

They lapsed into silence for a while, until Julia blurted, "I can't stand the suspense anymore. I have to know, how did you get to be the academic genius of the family?"

"I'm not a genius."

"Modesty noted. Now answer the question."

William considered. "I was never much good at any of the things my family liked. I'm no mechanic. I'm not great at sports. And I was never any good at making friends, so I had plenty of time for reading and studying."

"I didn't make friends *because* of all my reading and studying. At least at Holy Cross, everyone is a nerd."

"My grandmother supported me," William said. "She found out about the scholarship to Holy Cross."

"But no one else did," she said.

"Did what?"

"Support you."

He smiled a bit ruefully. "You saw that old family photo. I think everyone already figured I was the mailman's kid."

"Well, for what it's worth, I like you exactly the way you are." She held up her fist. "Comrades in nerdhood."

He gave a short laugh and humored her with a fist bump.

At her house, she said, "See you tomorrow."

"Julia."

She turned, and felt her heart lurch at the look on his face. She waited, frozen in – what? Fear? Anticipation? But he only peered at her a moment.

"See you tomorrow," he said.

He backed away, shoved his hands into his pockets and turned to go. She watched him walk down the street, away from her.

During her break from work the next day, Julia found William leaning against the side of the building, staring off at the water and the boats.

"How's it going?"

He jumped at the sound of her voice, but he said, "Half the guys back there are stoned out of their minds."

"It's practically a requirement of the job. When I didn't see you in there, I was afraid my dad had already fired you."

"Thanks for the vote of confidence."

"So, how are you holding up?"

"Fine," he said. Typical William. Had she really expected him to complain?

"What do you do out here all by yourself on your breaks?"

"Look out at the boats and wish I was on one of them."

She followed his eyes to the boats in their slips. "You could be."

"Could be what?"

"On one of them."

He said nothing, and she felt her mouth curling into an involuntary smile as a new thought occurred to her.

"Why did you take this dishwashing job, anyway?"

He shrugged. "It's a stepping stone to a cook position."

"That's no guarantee, especially with my dad. Is that really something you want to do? Be a professional cook?"

"Sure," he said, but he still refused to make eye contact, and drummed his fingertips on the railing of the pier.

She decided to have mercy on him and change the subject. "What's the furthest out you've been on a boat?"

"I've been as far as 150 miles off shore, during albacore tuna season. That's where the warm water edge sits at the beginning of summer, so that's where you find the tuna."

"Do you make it back in the same day, or do you have to spend the night on the water?"

"That time, it was a three week trip."

"Holy crap! When did you do that?"

"Last summer."

"And your parents let you do that? Isn't that dangerous?"

"I made a lot of money off that trip."

Julia shook her head. "One hundred and fifty miles. I've never been that far out on a boat."

"It's farther than I've been by land."

"You're kidding."

He laughed, shook his head. "When would I ever have a reason to go that far?"

"I don't know. To visit family? Go to Disneyland?"

"All of the family we know well enough to visit are right here in the Bay Area. And when do my parents ever take vacations?"

"Don't your extended family ever take you anywhere with them?"

He shrugged.

Julia was stumped. "So what's the furthest you've ever been by land?"

"Maybe fifty miles."

"You're joking."

"When you live and work here," he said, gesturing out to their view of the Golden Gate Bridge, "why would you ever need to go anywhere else? Unless it's sailing out the Gate onto the open ocean."

"I hear you. I've asked my parents for another trip to the Farallones for my birthday this year, but it's not looking good. Those excursions are expensive."

His eyebrows raised. "When is your birthday?"

"It's in October."

"That's good. You might still see blue whales then."

"That's my dream. Have you ever seen one?"

"No, but my uncle has." He hesitated a moment. "Speaking of which, I was thinking about your history project."

She gave a short laugh. "What does any of that have to do with my history project?"

"You could talk to my uncle about what he does. My mom's family has been fishing out of San Francisco for almost a hundred years."

Julia considered a moment. "That's a good idea."

"I think it meets all your requirements. Holly said it has to be something that's going the way of the history books. Plus, it used to be that nearly all the fishermen here were Italian, but that's not true anymore."

"You're right; it's perfect. Can you put me in touch with your uncle?"

"We could go out on my uncle's boat one day before the salmon fishery closes at the end of September. You could interview him then. It would kill two birds with one stone."

"How's that?"

"My uncle's boat would take us right by the Farallones. An early birthday present."

She felt her pulse quickening in spite of herself. And not just at the prospect of going to the Farallones after all, but because he had thought of it for her birthday.

Until she remembered.

"My parents would never let me go. Not on a boat, by myself, with two men. I'm sorry, but they're from another century."

He thought for a moment. "They can come too, if they want. Or maybe they'd accept my mom as a suitable chaperone?"

She smiled. "They might agree in the name of my education. I'll ask them tomorrow morning."

After a while, he glanced at his watch. "I have to get back inside."

"What time do you get off work?"

"When the job is done. Maybe around 10:30."

"You must be exhausted when you get home. How do you get your homework done?"

He shrugged. "I don't need a lot of sleep. That, plus lots and lots of coffee."

"Do you have to take the bus home, or does somebody at least pick you up?"

"I drive home."

"Really? You have a car?"

He shook his head. "A motorcycle."

"You're joking."

He beckoned her around the corner of the building to where he had parked a motorcycle quite illegally against the back of the building.

"Jesus Christ. I don't even know what I'm looking at here," she admitted.

"It's a 1985 Yamaha V-Max."

"Like I know what that means."

"My brother would say it's a Shelby Cobra without the training wheels."

"Yeah, you're still speaking in code. How long have you had this thing?"

"My family gave it to me for my birthday. Actually, it was mostly Mike's doing. He found it and fixed it up for me. It was practically ready for the scrap pile before that."

"How obliging of him to give you something to commit suicide on for your eighteenth birthday."

He smirked. "Have you ever ridden on a motorcycle?"

"Me? No."

"Do you want to go for a ride?"

Her heart leaped into her throat. "What, now?"

"I can take you home tonight. I brought an extra helmet."

"I'd catch hell on earth from my parents if I rode with you on that thing. Especially at night."

He raised an eyebrow. "Okay."

"Oh, Jesus. You either think I'm a prig or I'm trying to brush you off."

"Are you?"

"Which one, a prig or brushing you off?"

"Either."

"Definitely a prig."

He checked his watch. "Break's up."

She groaned. "Fine, I'll do it. Meet me at your bike after close. I'll come up with some cover story for my parents, but if you're out of a job tomorrow, don't blame me."

He smiled slightly, and watched her go back inside.

"Bye," Julia called breezily to her parents as she passed the office after close. "I caught a ride home with someone."

"With who?" her father demanded.

"Holly was passing by on the way home from her job. She's waiting outside."

Julia didn't wait for more questions or for them to detect what a bad liar she was. She strode down the hallway as fast as she could, carrying all of her belongings, and burst out the back door.

She found him already waiting there, leaning casually against the wall, neither concerned nor in any hurry.

"Let's go," she said breathlessly.

He took his time opening the saddlebag and flinched as she practically hurled her belongings in there.

"We'd better hurry," she explained.

"Is there a problem?"

"No, I just don't want them to see us."

"Who?"

"My parents."

The threat of her parents did not add any urgency to his pace. He handed her a helmet and said, "Put this on."

She fumbled with it, and said, "How does this thing work?"

He smiled and came toward her. Turned the helmet 180 degrees from the way she had it, and lowered it onto her head. Hovering just over her, he buckled the strap and tightened it under her chin.

Then he put on his own helmet and mounted the motorcycle. At her bewildered look, he said, "Put your foot on the footpeg here, and swing your leg over."

She complied gingerly, suddenly shy at sitting so close behind him, straddling him with her legs.

He turned his head back and said, "Hold on to my waist."

Overcome with embarrassment, she touched his waist with her fingertips.

"You're gonna need to hold on tighter than that."

She half-suspected he was trying to take advantage of the situation. But with the deafening blast of the engine a second later, she squeezed him around the waist as tight as she could.

"Jesus Christ."

The sound of her own voice did not reach her ears. Before she knew what was happening, the motorcycle roared down the alley and onto the street.

At first, she held on for dear life and stared straight ahead at his back. But after a few minutes, she felt confident enough to relax and look around a bit. She had a feeling that he was holding back for her sake, and frankly, she was thankful for it. She was also thankful that he took the direct route home.

She had to admit, it was even a little bit fun as they roared through the Presidio, down through Golden Gate Park, where she could smell the eucalyptus trees in the park in a way she never could in her father's car. William's loud pipes turned heads wherever they went, and she did not know whether to feel embarrassed or, perhaps, a tiny bit thrilled.

When they finally blasted into the Sunset and pulled up in front of her house, he killed the engine. The sudden silence hurt her ears almost as much as his engine had at first. He turned to look back at her, and she realized he was waiting for her to hop down from the bike first.

She performed the task as delicately as possible, and then he swung himself off deftly and removed his helmet. She removed hers as well, and handed it to him. He opened the saddlebag and handed over her belongings.

When she could finally hear herself think again, she said, "Why does it have to be so loud?"

"It was Mike who tricked this thing out for me. And I keep it that way because if other drivers can hear me, they might also see me."

"Right, that's why." At his bemused expression, she added, "Don't try to convince me it doesn't turn you on."

A flash from the front window of the house caught their attention, and they watched the curtain drop.

Julia's face burned. "My sister is spying."

He backed away toward his bike. "See you Monday."

"Thanks for the ride."

"Any time."

"It was fun, but I'm afraid this will be the first and last time. Unless you're done working for my dad."

He said nothing, and she didn't get a read on his expression because he dropped his helmet over his head. She made her way up the walkway, and as she opened the front door of the house, she heard the engine blast. When she turned to look, he was already gone.

Alison was there as soon as she walked through the door. "Was that who I think it was?"

"Probably. Oh, and thanks for spying, by the way. It scared him off good and proper."

Alison covered her mouth with her hands, but her eyes were laughing. "Sorry."

Julia brushed past her toward the staircase, but Alison stopped her with a hand on her arm.

"Hey, don't be mad at me. I heard those pipes and thought a biker bar had opened across the street. If I had known it was your man, I wouldn't have looked."

"He's not my man."

"Well it sure as hell looked like it, the way you two were making eyes at each other."

"I know this may be a different concept for you, but a girl can talk to a guy without fucking him."

"Well then, why was he bringing you home?"

"He offered to bring me home. What do you want me to say?"

Alison touched her arm again. "Jesus, don't be so defensive. Come on; come in here with me. Let's catch up."

Reluctantly, Julia followed her into the in-law unit and took a seat beside her on the sofa. "Do you like him?" asked Alison.

"Of course I like him."

"You know what I mean."

Julia's heart, mind, and body had been a riot of conflicting feelings all day long. "Yes."

"Great. And he obviously likes you."

"Why do you say that?"

"Because he wouldn't waste his time if he didn't at the very least want to get in your pants. So what else has been going on with you two? Is it just lust, or is it something more?"

Julia told her about his idea for both her history project and her birthday.

"Julie, you know he wouldn't go to this much trouble unless he was really, seriously into you. He comes to the restaurant on July fourth just to see you. He takes a job as a dishwasher at the restaurant for no other discernible reason than to be near you. He forces himself upon you as a lab partner. And now this. What are you waiting for, an engraved invitation?"

Julia had to finally admit that she was probably right. "Why doesn't he just say something, or do something?"

"He *is* doing something. But he obviously doesn't feel confident making a run for first base. You're going to have to do it."

"I don't know if that's a good idea."

Alison threw up her hands in disbelief. "Why not?"

"Uncle Rob told me that he regretted putting his dreams for himself on hold in order to be with Tim. I don't want to have to choose."

"Why does it have to be a choice?"

"Did you know William has never travelled beyond fifty miles from home? He would no more fit in in Santa Barbara than he would in Uzbekistan. Besides, he's going to get a scholarship somewhere else. We'd have to live far apart for at least four years. A decade, if I get my doctorate. The odds of that working out in our favor are slim."

"Take a piece of advice from your sister, who has much, much more experience than you do. It almost strains credibility, how sweet he is. In fact, I'm not really sure I buy it." She took Julia's hand. "Enjoy it now, for whatever it is. You still have your whole senior year to finish. Worry about the future later."

"I don't think I can operate that way."

"Suit yourself. But you're over-thinking it." Alison rose from the sofa, still holding Julia's hand. "Come with me a minute."

Julia allowed Alison to lead her to her bedroom. Alison gestured for her to close the door, then opened a dresser drawer and handed Julia a sealed packet of birth control pills.

"Just in case," Alison said.

Julia gaped at them. "You just have these lying around?"

"I'm taking the shots now. Start them right now. After a week, you're good to go. Then you'll have to get your own prescription." She went to her desk, retrieved her wallet. Handed Julia a card. "Go to this clinic. If you need money, let me know."

Julia held the packet and the card by the corners, as if they were contaminated.

Alison put her hand on her arm. "It'll probably hurt the first time. And you may bleed."

This was all just too surreal. Julia fled upstairs to the sanctuary of her room and her aquarium.

Saturday morning, Julia and Alison got up early and loaded a cart full of aquarium supplies, soft food, blankets, CDs, books, and whatever else they could think of that might be of comfort to their uncle.

Their grandmother took them aside in the entrance and said, "Just to prepare you, he looks a bit odd. The doctor says he has fluid on his abdomen because of the cancer on his liver. It makes it harder for him to eat."

They steeled themselves for anything. Uncle Rob leaned back in his easy chair in the living room, thinner than ever, yet with his stomach oddly swollen. But he smiled brightly when they wheeled their cart in.

"What's all this?"

"A Dunphy-sized care package," said Alison cheerfully. "Books, CDs, videos, everything your heart could ever desire. And food. Lots and lots of food."

"I'm afraid most of that food will go to waste," mused Rob.

"We'll just see about that," Julia's grandmother said cheerfully, taking the containers of food and carrying them with her into the kitchen.

"Good God, woman; there you go again, force feeding me like a goose," Rob called after her. When she was gone, he added to Julia and Alison, "Not that I have much liver left to pâté."

They cringed at his gallows humor. To hide her face, Julia began gathering up the aquarium supplies.

Sensing her discomfort, Rob tried a change of subject. "You have a big birthday coming up soon. Any crazy plans?"

Julia forced a perky tone of voice. "Nothing crazy. Alison has threatened to take me to a club of some kind. And I'm going out to the Farallones."

"Oh, I'm glad you found a way to pay for it, after all."

Julia shook her head. "A friend of mine has an uncle who's a fisherman, and we're taking his boat."

Rob's eyes widened. "Is that safe?"

"It's no more unsafe than any other trip out there."

Rob considered for a moment, then shrugged. "Well, it's nice of your friend's uncle to take you all on his boat, just for that."

"I got the impression that his uncle will be working at the same time."

Rob looked confused, then smiled slightly. "*His* uncle. Oh."

Julia gave him the stink eye. "He's just a friend."

"He'd love for it to be something more," grumbled Alison, "but Julia's not going to do anything about it."

"Why on earth not?" asked Rob.

"She claims you told her she should not let love get between her and her goals in life."

"I'm sure I said no such thing."

"Not exactly like that," sighed Julia. "You said something like you wished you had not put your own dreams on hold for so long."

"I also said I didn't regret a single day I spent in that aquarium shop with Tim. And it's true." Rob took Julia's hand.

"Don't be afraid of love. And don't compromise. If it's meant to be, the details will work themselves out."

"That's exactly what I told her," said Alison, "pretty much word for word."

"I don't know if I believe in 'meant to be,'" Julia mused.

Rob seemed to consider something for a moment. "Julia, you know where my crystal collection is, don't you? Will you go and get it for me?"

Inside a cabinet in his bedroom, she found a small case with numerous little drawers. It was heavy for its size, but still manageable. She carried it out to the living room and set it on the table, next to all of his bottles of prescriptions.

He opened the drawers and picked through them. After a minute's search, he pulled out a small, colorful object.

"Watermelon tourmaline," he said. "That ought to do the trick."

He waved Julia over and placed the small, polished cross section into her palm. She immediately saw how it got its name. It had a pink inner section, surrounded by a circle of white, surrounded in turn by an outer ring of green. Just like a slice of watermelon.

"How is this supposed to do the trick?" she wondered.

"You make your own magic. This will help."

Julia was used to her uncle's eccentricities. He kept a cauldron in his bedroom, for instance. But she carefully wrapped the stone in a napkin and placed it in her pocket, anyway. She would put it on the knick-knack shelf in her room. If nothing else, it would remind her of him when he was gone.

Rob turned to Alison. "What about you? How's your love life?"

"Swinging as usual."

Rob smirked because he knew she meant it more or less literally. "Who's the latest iteration?"

"His name's David. He's a waiter at the restaurant. But I'm bored with him." As if for emphasis, she yawned. "He works all the freaking time, and now that I don't work there anymore, he calls to check up on me about ten times per day."

Rob raised an eyebrow. "I don't like the sound of that. Why is he checking up on you?"

"I guess he knows I have a short attention span." At the look on Rob's face, she added, "Don't worry, Rob. You know me. Guys are like wild animals – they have more to fear from me than I do from them."

Rob's brow still furrowed with concern, but he knew as well as Julia did that her boast was not far from the truth. Rob reached out for both of them, and they each took one of his hands.

A keen energy radiated through the over-large eyes within his shrunken face. "You're not off the hook just because I give up the ghost. You know me; I'll find some way to come haunt you. So I don't ever want to see you settle for anything less than everything. Just do me a favor, and believe that you deserve it."

Tears stung Julia's eyes. To hide them, she buried her face in Rob's shoulder. He put his hand on Julia's back and said, "Good God, girl, don't develop a flair for melodrama now. I really *will* feel like a failure."

Julia and Alison both gave shaky laughs. Rob pulled Julia away from his shoulder.

"Hang on to that stone. You won't lose it, will you?"

Julia shook her head. "I promise."

The last Saturday in September was one of those Indian summer days when it was 85 degrees in the city. Anxious to take advantage of what would probably be the last decent beach day of the year, Julia begged her parents for the day off.

Afternoon found Julia surveying herself critically in the mirror in her new pink bikini. Alison gave a wolf-whistle as she rounded the corner into Julia's room.

"I think it looks even hotter on you here than it did in the fitting room!"

"Well, if it doesn't, it's too late now. It took half the morning just to find one with a top that doesn't fall off of me."

Alison, who could not commiserate with a lack of curves, grinned and rumpled Julia's hair. "Are you ready to go? People will be showing up by now."

Julia nodded.

"Bring some warm clothes," suggested Alison. "We're staying past dark and building a bonfire."

Julia held up her beach bag, already packed with warm clothes. "But I don't know how late I can stay. I'm supposed to meet William at his uncle's fishing boat at four o'clock in the morning. What about David? Is he coming?"

"No, he has to work. Bastard."

Julia put on her swim cover and sandals, and together they headed the few blocks down to the beach. Alison skipped ahead of Julia a few feet, child-like, her peroxide-blond hair bouncing along with her, before waiting for Julia to catch up. Crossing the Great Highway and climbing the dunes, the powerful waves rose into view, crashing with less violence than usual onto the shore.

It was a rare tolerably warm day on the beach, and the water glimmered all the way to the horizon. Bodies packed the sand. It took a long time for them to spot Alison's friends and then to find an open spot of sand nearby to spread their belongings.

"Where's Holly?" Julia wondered, looking around for their cousin.

"Are you kidding? She's not slummin' it down here with us," replied Alison. "She's up at Pacheco Beach."

Without any further ado, Alison ripped off her swim cover and, in some masochistic ritual, ran to plunge her body in the frigid water. She surfaced with her arms outstretched and a scream of pure joy, and her friends followed her lead, as people were inclined to do.

Safely installed on her beach blanket with no one to talk to, Julia contented herself with people-watching. Surfers in abundance rode the waves. A group nearby played an impromptu game of beach volleyball. Children dug for buried treasure and built sand castles. In the distance, hang-gliders floated in the air, having launched from Fort Funston. She watched them lazily for a while.

"Look who's here." Her sister's voice jarred her from her reverie.

Julia's eyes followed to where her sister pointed. It took a few moments, but she gave a start of recognition. Only a few blankets away sat William, his knees drawn up to his chest, engaged in a similar game of solitary people-watching. She had not recognized him at first because he sat with his back to her, and because an enormous black tattoo spanned his shoulder blades.

"Is that really William?" She would never in a million years have imagined him with a tattoo of any kind, let alone of that size.

"Go see for yourself."

Julia looked suspiciously at her. "Did you invite him?"

Alison laughed. "If I could take credit, I would. But everybody and their dog is here today."

Julia sprang to her feet and sneaked up behind him.

"What is this?"

He turned and looked startled to see her. She had the awkward sensation of watching his eyes flicker involuntarily down her body before he forced himself to look away.

"What is what?" he mumbled.

"You have a tattoo?"

"Oh."

"Well, you are just full of surprises, aren't you? What is that, a seagull?" She knelt down for a closer look. "Oh no, it's an albatross, isn't it?"

He nodded.

"An albatross in a cage. What's that all about?"

"If I told you, I'd have to kill you."

"Oh! Well then, tell me and kill me quickly."

"My brother drew it."

Julia dared to tap it with her finger. "Your brother drew *that*?"

"He's very talented."

"And you let him do it to you?"

"I didn't let him ink me. I'm not suicidal."

She looked at it again. It was very finely detailed; she could see the feathers on the albatross' wings and the hinges in the cage. And now that she was really looking, the cage looked more like a jail that the bird struggled to escape. The head was turned in profile with the beak open and the wings outstretched between the bars of the cage.

"When did you get this?"

"About a year ago."

She feigned shock. "That sounds dubiously underage to me."

"This is my brother we're talking about here. He has connections."

She grinned facetiously at him and said, "You are a very bad boy."

He looked both amused and embarrassed, and clearly had no idea how to reply.

"We're sticking around on the beach until after dark, building a bonfire," she said. "I'll need someone to keep me company while everyone else smokes pot. Don't tell me you have something better to do."

"Are we still going on my uncle's boat tomorrow?"

"Why wouldn't we?"

"If we do this, we'd be lucky to get a couple of hours of sleep, at the most."

"That's what God created coffee for."

He smiled a bit. "I don't have any warm clothes with me. I'll have to go home first. And I'll only stay if I can keep my brother with me."

He looked in the direction of the impromptu volleyball game, where for the first time she noticed his brother, nailing a serve and leering at every woman under the age of fifty who passed. For that matter, his sister Kelly was there, too. She wondered why she hadn't noticed them earlier. Mike certainly stood out with his shirt off, with most of his torso and both of his arms wrapped in brightly colored tattoos.

"If you must," Julia conceded. "But if you don't return, I'll come hunt you down."

He got up to go talk to his brother. Free to stare unobserved as much as she liked, she watched his bird in a cage disappear into the distance.

"That is so fucking hot," said Alison when he was out of earshot. "I felt sure you two were going to drop right there on the sand and bump uglies."

"Jesus, Alison, I'm blushing."

"What? I would have done it myself if I weren't so conscientious of our sisterly affection. Looks like we're not the only ones, either."

Julia looked around. It was true; a lot of other girls were watching him.

"He has no idea, does he?" mused Alison. "That's so refreshing. He hasn't been hot long enough for it to go to his head. You're a lucky girl."

"Why am I a lucky girl?"

41

"Oh, come on. Don't tell me you didn't notice. He had to carry his towel in front of him when he stood up."

"You're vile."

"You're the one panting over him like a bitch in heat."

"Oh my God, I can't take it anymore. His brother is over there; go talk to him. I think you're soul mates."

Alison looked over at Mike, as if really considering it. "Very well. But remember, Julia; if you want this to happen, you're going to have to make the first move. He's not going to do it."

She bounded away to insert herself into the volleyball game beside Mike. Julia resumed her seat on the beach blanket and tried to watch, but her mind and body were occupied with other feelings. To clear her head, she decided to get up and join her sister and Mike on the side opposite Kelly. William's sister was an intense competitor, but Julia had length of bone to her advantage. After she spiked the ball over the net to win the game, Mike high-fived her and Kelly seemed to look at her with new respect.

She scanned the beach behind her, and to her surprise found William had already returned with all of his stuff. He sat on his towel, watching them. She flashed him a smile and waved him over, but he shook his head, so she went to kneel down beside him.

"Come play; your sister needs another teammate."

"I'm not much of a joiner."

She gave him the stink-eye. "What does that even mean? You joined our little beach bonfire party."

"You'd just make me look bad," he said mildly.

"Are you in?"

Julia jumped at her sister's voice beside her. Alison gestured toward the volleyball net. "The next game is about to start."

"No thanks; I think I'll keep William company."

Alison didn't try to argue, even though it meant certain defeat for her side of the net. She bounded away again, and Julia and William sat together in silence for a while, watching the others play.

"I get it now," she said.

"Get what?"

"The Rime of the Ancient Mariner. You said you liked Coleridge. The Rime of the Ancient Mariner is about a sailor who kills an albatross and curses his ship. He has to wear the albatross around his neck." She gestured to his tattoo. "Your albatross is in a cage. You're trying to contain a curse, and it's about to escape."

"It's a good guess."

"Oh, come on. I don't know about any other girls, but you're not going to score points with me by being mysterious."

"I'm not trying to score points with you."

"Oh, now that's a tough one. I could act nonchalant and pretend not to care. Or I could stomp off in a huff. Or I could just come right out and say, 'What's the matter? Aren't I worth scoring points with?'"

He smiled and said, "I just mean it's kind of private."

"If it's so private, then why do you have it on display for the whole world to see?"

"Ninety-nine times out of a hundred, it's hidden."

"Well, I guess today is just my lucky day." She rose to her feet. "If you're not going to play fair, then I'm going to rejoin the volleyball game. At least maybe they will."

By the time she had played another few games, it was getting cooler on the beach, and the crowds were thinning out. People had started pulling out their warmer clothes and putting them on over their swim suits. After the sun set, some of Alison's friends built a bonfire, burning pallets stolen from the Safeway store, and Julia spread her towel beside William on the sand.

Somebody had brought a jam box and popped in a Pavement CD. Forties emerged from previously hidden caches. Someone even produced a guitar, which Mike commandeered and began tuning. Julia was surprised when he played quite competently and sang "I Want To Be Sedated" in a good tenor voice.

After struggling to sing the first stanza over the roar of the ocean, Mike put his hand over the strings and called out, "Will, help me out here!"

William shook his head.

"Oh, come on!" cried Mike. Looking at Julia, he added, "You wouldn't know it, but this loser here has a great singing voice. Used to write songs all the time." Turning back to William, he goaded, "What's the matter, Will? Do I make you feel inadequate?"

"I used to wish I could sing, until I heard you. Now I just wish *you* could sing," retorted William.

Mike grinned at him before plunging back into the song again. His energy was infectious. The rest of the group began singing, then practically shouting along as they really got into it. When the song was over, everyone cheered and begged for more. Mike plunged into his rendition of Sweet Home Alabama. Julia joined in too, and nudged William by leaning into his arm. William smiled, but still declined to contribute his voice.

Alison, sitting on the other side of Julia, threw a handful of sand at William. "Jesus, dude, you're a freaking stick-in-the-mud!"

William flushed red and stared into the bonfire. Alison scoffed and went to flop down beside Mike. Julia would have felt sorry for William, but his inexplicable reticence bemused her as well. She turned her back on him and plunged into the chorus of Sweet Home Alabama with more gusto than ever.

After a while, William said, "I'll be right back." Julia watched him retrieve a couple of bottles of beer from the previously hidden source. When he came back, he held one up and raised his eyebrows by way of offering one to Julia.

She smiled and accepted. He opened it, handed it to her, and sat down beside her.

"Cheers," she said, clinking her bottle against his. They each took a swig.

"So you sing and write songs, too?" she asked when Mike had finished Sweet Home Alabama.

"Used to."

"You used to do a lot of things. Are you sure you're not still sneaking around, writing poems and songs and singing when no one's looking?"

"I do still, sometimes."

"Ah! The truth comes out."

Mike had moved on to "Blister in the Sun" at the request of Alison, who knelt behind him and hung about his neck and shoulders. Julia turned to William and said, "I would like nothing better than to hear you sing right now."

But still, William shook his head. She shrugged and turned back toward Mike, singing badly at the top of her lungs. When she glanced back occasionally at William, she found him staring down at the sand, digging little trenches with a stick.

She was all but ready to scrap any plans she may have had to make a move on him tonight.

Mike exhausted his repertoire and the jam box took over again. Somebody passed around a joint. Julia declined, and he offered it next to William, who also declined.

"Would you have done it if I hadn't sworn you to be my comrade in sobriety?" she asked when the joint-passer moved on.

"Probably not, honestly. I've been trying to stay away from it for a while now."

"Oh, so not only have you tried it, but you're a reformed pothead."

"With brothers like mine?"

"O, ye of little resistance."

"I've resisted a lot of what my brothers have offered me." He poked her on the arm with his beer bottle. "What about you?"

"You mean have I tried it? No, I really haven't. I'm so allergic to cigarette smoke, I'm afraid to even try. So don't scorn me; it's just pure self-preservation that's kept me on the straight and narrow."

He took a swig of his beer. "It's probably all a load of bullshit, but the whole gateway drug thing panned out in my brothers' case. Of course, they probably would have gone on to the harder stuff even if pot never existed."

"The harder stuff?"

"My brother Jimmy is a meth head. That's the real reason he started stealing cars."

"Really?" Julia sat stunned for a moment. "Did Mike ever have a problem with drugs?"

"He at least messed around with it quite a bit. For now, his passions seem to be alcohol and tobacco. And tattoos. And women. We're an addictive family. If it's not a substance, it's work, or something else."

Julia shook her head. "You and him – brothers? It doesn't compute."

He peered sharply at her. Looked away again, and took another swig of his beer.

"Out with it, man," she prompted.

"He's not as bad as you think," he said. "I watch his back these days because he watched mine once."

Her eyebrows lifted. "What do you mean?"

"He and Jimmy used to run together. For the longest time, Mike did whatever Jimmy told him to do. But the older Jimmy got and the more addicted to meth he became, the meaner he got. Mike has never been one to run away from a good fight, but it's just not in his nature to be cruel, any more than it is in mine."

He stopped here. Gently, she prompted, "What happened?"

He stared ahead into the bonfire. "When I was twelve, I was pretty much a little shrimp who liked to write poetry and songs, and cook, and play with cameras. It just didn't quite jive with what Jimmy thought a guy should do, and he beat the shit out of me all the time, even though he was twice my size. Called me a fag, and a little cunt, and told me he'd better not catch me at it again. So I kept on doing my thing, but I learned to hide it. Periodically he'd come pick on me, knock me around a little bit. It went on like that for two years. Then, when I was fourteen, he finally caught me at it again. Dragged me out of the house by the hair and tore a chunk right out of my scalp. I have no idea what he was going to do to me, but he was tweaking so bad he was out of his mind. Mike saw it happening. By then he was big enough to stand up to Jimmy. He found my dad's gun and came after us. He kept him off me from that point forward."

Flabbergasted, Julia pulled her knees up to her chest and wrapped her arms around them. "Why didn't you ever tell me this before?"

He smiled wryly at her. "Why would I have ever told you a thing like that?"

Julia considered. "Fair enough. But it sure would have explained a lot about you." She felt guilty for having judged him earlier. This sudden, intimate revelation unleashed a renewed flood of tenderness, even admiration. "How did you find the courage to keep doing your thing at all?"

"Sheer stubbornness. It's a Quinn family trait," he said with a rueful smile. "Plus, my grandmother. She supported me when no one else did. All of my mother's family are very musical. I think the poetry and songwriting is just an extension of that."

"Who put this grunge shit on?" Alison's voice tore through their solitary confidences and brought them back to the group. She jabbed a button on the jam box, silencing the music and popping open the CD player.

"Damn straight," called Mike. "Here, put this on."

"The Replacements? You've got to be kidding me." She flung aside his offering and said, "From now on, it's DJ Alison, no requests taken." She slammed another CD in and pushed play on Bjork.

"I kind of like grunge," said William mildly after listening for a while. "I like The Replacements, too. But I guess they're not my favorites."

"They're better than hairspray metal. I'm so glad that's over now," said Julia. It dawned on her to wonder, "What *is* your favorite?"

"I guess Led Zeppelin is probably my go-to for the moment. That, and Pink Floyd."

Julia did not particularly like or dislike those bands. Come to think of it, she had never really paid them much attention.

"I like all kinds of music," she decided to reply. "Except, apparently, hairspray metal. But other than that, when I say I like all kinds of music, I really mean it. Not a lot of people who say that really mean it."

They listened to "Human Behavior" soaring out of the jam box. It was a fitting soundtrack to this stage of the night, when everyone was high or tipsy or both. The bonfire mellowed as well, and she found herself shivering. She stood to stir it a bit, and when it roared again, she flopped down beside William, as close as possible so that their arms pressed against each other. He did not flinch or try to pull away from her.

She turned to look at him, and he met her gaze a bit shyly.

"It's pretty late," he observed quietly.

She nodded, and knew they would have to part ways soon. But she was not ready to part ways with him, sleep be damned. She remembered her sister's words, and decided to take a leap of faith.

She let her fingers wander. Let them crawl across the sand to brush against his fingertips.

He did not try to take his hand away. Though she looked straight ahead into the bonfire, she was blind to it. She let her hand slide across the top of his a bit more. Dared to stroke it with the tip of her thumb.

His fingers wriggled loose, then came to rest again, loosely intertwined with hers.

She dropped her eyes down between their bodies. Took in the proportions of his hand, the knuckles, the skin that was browner than hers, the nails trimmed short. Her pulse slammed in her ears at an unprecedented pace. She willed herself to look up into his face. To kiss him, if he would let her.

She heard tittering all around them, and snatched her hand away. When the tittering didn't stop, she glanced around for the cause. Several people stared off to the left of where Julia and William sat. There, she spotted her sister. With Mike.

Apparently Alison had taken Julia's suggestion about Mike a little too much to heart. They sat a ways off by themselves, but made no attempt to hide their passionate making out. As Julia watched in horror, Mike's hand reached up Alison's shirt.

Julia sprang to her feet and, without thinking, bolted to where her sister and Mike sat.

"Alison!"

Her sister either did not hear or ignored her, so Julia seized her by the arm and jerked her to her feet.

"What the hell?!" screamed Alison.

Julia dragged her sister away from Mike, ignoring the laughter that followed them from all sides. "You might want to get a rubber before you go any further with that one," she whispered fiercely. "For that matter, you might want to gargle with Listerine a few minutes, too."

"How the hell is this any of your business?" hissed Alison.

Julia dragged her back to her spot next to William and snatched up her belongings and Alison's as well. William sat rooted to the ground, apparently incapable of action. Julia dared not look him in the eye.

"We're going home," snapped Julia.

"I am not!"

Julia whirled on her. "What about David?"

Alison glared.

Julia shoved Alison's belongings into her arms and pulled her away. When they were a safe enough distance from the group, she said, "That guy has probably been inside more vaginas than a gynecologist. What is wrong with you?"

"Right, Saint Julia; I should make Mom and Dad proud and be a frigid cocktease like you."

"Better than getting a direct injection of the clap."

"I know you're sexually frustrated, but it's your own fault. How many different ways does he have to throw himself at you? Pretty soon he's going to figure out he's a sex god and move on. Meanwhile, don't take it out on me!"

Alison stalked back to the bonfire, and Julia fled the other direction, toward home. She could not decide whether she was angrier at Alison or herself. She looked back long enough to see William give Mike a shove and to hear Mike's cretinous laugh, like a jackhammer.

And then she heard William's footfalls shuffling across the sand, and he was shouting, "Hey!"

She did not stop or turn around. He caught up, and his hand was on her arm, spinning her around.

"I want to go home," she protested, snatching her arm away.

"Okay," he said, his hands in the air. "I just…" He gave a huff of frustration. "I made him leave your sister alone."

"It's fine, William," she said. "Nothing and nobody can help my sister."

She turned to go, but he touched her arm again. "Will I still see you tomorrow?"

Amid everything else, Julia had almost forgotten about their planned excursion on his uncle's boat the next day. But she said, "Quit trying to get out of it."

A trace of a smile played at his lips, and she turned to go.

The next morning, Julia's father drove her to the pier and walked her through the dark to the slip that William had directed them to. They spotted it in short order because it was one of the few slips with human activity on it.

The boat was less than fifty feet long, and looked even smaller up close than it did from a distance. William and his mother were already on board, helping to make bait. William wore his yellow foul weather bibs over a gray sweater. They spotted Julia and her father, and Ann beckoned them with a wave and an easy smile. Then she shouted into the cabin, "Frank!"

William's uncle emerged a moment later, and they all ascended the ladder to meet Julia and her father.

"Paul, Julia, this is my brother, Frank Cardone," said Ann. "He's the captain."

"Pleased to meet you," said Frank. "Welcome aboard."

"Thanks for letting me come with you today," said Julia.

Frank grinned at Julia's father, who peered back apprehensively. "We'll take good care of her."

Ann slapped Frank on the back. "I trust my own son with him."

"We'll be back by sunset," Frank said, descending the ladder again. "Will, come on down and let her hand her stuff down to you."

William complied, descending the ladder onto the deck. Julia dropped her backpack down to him, and he said, "Now come down the ladder."

Julia's father supported her while she got her footing on the ladder, and a moment later, she found herself accepting William's offered hand of support as she stepped down onto the deck. Both his eyes and his hand lingered just a moment on hers before he turned to go help his uncle.

Her heart fluttering, she looked back up at her father, who said, "You be careful. Listen to Frank and do whatever he says."

Julia gave him a reassuring smile, and then he was gone.

She spotted Ann nearby and asked, "Can I help with anything?"

"I think it's best if we just stay out of the way. Bring your stuff inside. Have a cup of coffee."

Sheepishly, Julia grabbed her bags and followed her into the main cabin. Ann led her to the galley in the back of the cabin. She found two mugs in the cabinet and poured a cup of coffee for each of them, then gestured to the table in the middle of the cabin. Julia took a seat on one of the benches.

A few minutes later, Frank came into the cabin. "Are you girls ready?"

"As ready as we'll ever be," said Ann.

Frank took his seat in the captain's chair. Julia got up and watched out the front of the cabin as William untied the boat from

50

the piling. Frank put the boat in gear, and pulled away from the dock.

William returned to the cabin and pulled on his hat and foul weather jacket. "Do you want to come out now?"

Julia put on her own hat and jacket, and followed him onto the deck. Ann, she noticed, lingered not far behind, obviously determined to faithfully execute her chaperone duties.

It was five o'clock, and a faint light glowed in the east. Frank, however, steered the boat west toward the Golden Gate Bridge. Julia, William, and Ann stood on the bow of the boat and watched the bridge approach.

Julia had never gone under the bridge at night. It glowed against the black western sky, and she watched in awe as it loomed nearer, the cars crossing it. It rose over their heads, and she craned to see the underside of it. When it passed over the top of the boat, William said, "Do you want to go see it from the stern now?"

Since there was nothing but black ocean ahead of the boat, she agreed. William led her along the starboard side of the boat, and Ann followed. Behind the main cabin was a ten foot tank, set into the deck, with ice in it. William saw her peering into it and explained, "This is where we put the salmon when we catch it. Or you can put live crab in it during crab season."

He led Julia and Ann around the tank and down into the gaff hatch at the very end of the stern, where they could watch the Golden Gate Bridge and the city slowly fade away behind them. The sun rose, and the lights of the city slowly winked out by the time land disappeared over the horizon.

"Do you want to go up to the top drive?" asked William.

"The what?"

"Up there." He gestured to a set of steps that led up to what looked like another cabin.

"Sure." She followed him up there, shadowed by Ann, and remarked, "There's another whole steering station up here."

"That's why it's called the top drive," William explained. "You go up here for better visibility, like when you're driving onto crab pots, or when you're driving into the harbor."

"They used to call this Dago Heaven," laughed Ann, "because of all the Italian fishermen that worked out of San Francisco, and because up there you're closer to God."

William cast Julia a sheepish look, but relaxed into a smile when she returned it with a good-natured laugh. She stood at the steering station and looked out across the water from this higher vantage point. After a while, she spotted a smudge on the horizon.

"There's the islands," she said. "My binoculars are in my bag."

The cold wind whipped around them now and the water was much choppier out here. For extra warmth, they pulled their hoods up over their heads and descended the stairs to the deck again. Julia went inside the main cabin to retrieve her binoculars. William and Ann followed close behind.

"What's the plan, then?" Frank asked William.

"We'll do our sightseeing when we get out there," replied William. "Give me a couple of hours. Then I'll help you."

Frank nodded and turned back to the front. William went to get his camera and pour himself a cup of coffee, then joined Julia on the bow. To Julia's surprise, Ann stayed inside the cabin. She guessed Ann could adequately supervise through the windows, anyway.

"I'm sorry about my brother," William said finally.

"Actually, after the story you told me last night, I have a whole new appreciation for Mike. Though not quite as much enthusiasm for him as Alison has. You'd better warn him."

He looked embarrassed, unsure how to respond. He started to turn toward the islands and lift his camera to his face.

To hell with it.

She put her hand on his arm and nudged him to face her. Reached up to touch his face, and accidentally jabbed him in the eye with her finger.

"Ow," he said, flinching.

Her stomach fluttering, she laughed and held him steady with her hand on his arm. Reached up more carefully this time, and caressed his cheekbone with her thumb.

His eyes widened as he realized what was happening. He took her hand and led her to a part of the deck where there were no windows through which his uncle and his mother could spy on them.

Bits of hair escaped from her hood, blowing wildly around her wind-chapped cheeks, straying into her mouth. He pulled her close to him. Slowly, one by one, he tucked the wisps of hair up underneath her hat. The unexpected, tender gesture surprised her with a flood of warmth that radiated from her chest through the rest of her body.

Looking at him felt a bit like staring over the edge of a cliff. If the look on his face were any indication, he was just as woozy. She remembered the electricity of her fingers brushing against his. How it kept her awake the rest of the night, thinking of it.

He clasped her face in his hands and gently touched his lips to hers, and all her layers of clothes were suddenly much too warm for her.

She had long since fallen over the cliff, and was dead gone.

He broke away and looked a moment at her face, as if to ask permission to do more. She smiled up at him encouragingly. Felt her pulse pounding in her throat. Felt slightly drunk. He closed his eyes, kissed her again. Put his tongue in her mouth.

She nuzzled the hair on the back of his head, pressed his mouth into hers. Gave him her tongue willingly.

When he broke away, he still held her face in his hands, and said, "Wow."

"Yeah," she laughed.

"I don't want to go home after this," he whispered. "I want to go somewhere else with you."

It was hard to summon enough breath to answer him. "Where?"

He brushed his hand across her cheek. "Anywhere."

A shuffling sound on the deck triggered her reflexes, and she sprang back from him. Frank emerged from the cabin, with Ann close at his heels. It was impossible to tell from the look on their faces whether they had seen anything. By silent agreement, Julia and William returned to the railing to pretend they had been looking out at the islands all along.

Frank clapped a hand on William's back. "What's next?"

Shooting a desperate look at Julia, William replied, "Can you bring the boat right up to the island and drop the anchor? Then we can have an early lunch and I can take some photos while we're there."

Frank nodded and returned to the cabin, but unfortunately, Ann came to stand between Julia and William. Reaching for Julia's binoculars, she asked, "What am I looking at here?"

"Don't you need to get lunch ready?" William tried.

"What's to get ready? We all brought sack lunches."

Ann lifted the binoculars to her eyes and peered out at the islands. Across her, Julia and William exchanged a long, woeful look.

Please God, Julia thought. Make her go back inside. Leave us alone.

"What am I looking at here?" repeated Ann, thrusting the binoculars at Julia.

Resigned, Julia accepted them. Every nerve ending in her body still scintillated, but there was nothing for it now. Now they were close enough that she could make out a colony of seabirds and sea lions, though they were still tiny specks, even in her binoculars. Not much was happening on the water at the moment, either. She heard herself talking, trying to provide interpretation to Ann, but she had no idea what she said.

"Let's get a little closer to the islands first," William suggested to Julia after a while. "Then I'll ask Frank to stop so we can eat and you can ask him your questions."

Julia nodded. They got close enough to really see the individual birds and sea lions through the binoculars, moving around, packed close together on the rocks. William picked up his camera again, and they went back onto the bow and gazed out, Julia through her binoculars, William through his camera. They were steering toward a sheltered cove, scattered with sea lions on the guano-strewn rocks. They were so close that Julia could hear their noises now. William snapped away, until Frank killed the engine and came out onto the deck.

"There you go," Frank said. "Close enough to throw a can at the furbags."

They really were just about that close. Frank looked at William and pointed to the anchor winch at the bow. "You want to do the honors?"

William dropped the anchor, lodging them in place. The noise and the smells of the animals assailed them now.

"We'd better go in the cabin to eat," Frank observed.

Reluctantly, Julia followed them inside, where they washed their hands and retrieved their lunches. While they sat around the table, Julia pulled out her list of questions. For the next hour, Frank and Ann regaled Julia with tales of their hundred-year family history in San Francisco's fishing industry, from their grandfather who arrived from Sicily in 1891, alone and penniless; to the first fishing boat he bought less than ten years later; to the fish processing plant his fourth son Frank Senior opened on the pier in 1947. William chewed his sandwich and listened quietly, but from the way his eyes shone, it was obvious that he himself took no small pride in the familiar stories. She liked him all the more for it.

After cleaning up from lunch, Frank turned to William and said, "Well, shall we get to work? Let the lady see what it's all about?"

William raised the anchor, and Frank turned the boat back out to sea. Then William helped Frank bait the hooks and lower the outriggers. Six lines trolled through the water as they cruised along, mimicking a school of fish. Julia watched out the rear windows of the cabin as William and Frank took their positions in the gaff hatch and waited.

Soon, the springs on top of the outriggers bounced, signaling a catch. As soon as they gaffed a fish, they slammed its head against the gaff hatch to kill it, ripped its gills out, and bled it. Then they gutted it, cleaned it, and dropped it into the slush tank. It was a brutal, bloody business, but they had it down to an art. It was a noisy business too, as the gulls were having a field day overhead.

There was only so much that Julia could watch before it strained her attention. So she went back onto the bow to peer through her binoculars. She spotted Pacific white-sided dolphins and Dall's porpoises, but not a single whale. For Julia, who had seen plenty of dolphins and porpoises in her time, it was turning out to be a disappointing day on the water.

When there was finally nothing left to do, and the boat was on its way back to shore, William cleaned up and joined Julia on the bow again with his camera.

"I hope you weren't too bored out here all that time," he said. "Or too grossed out by watching us work. I forgot to warn you."

"You're going to have to work a lot harder than that to gross me out. But I have to confess, I think you would do well in slasher films." She could not help but laugh out loud at the incongruity of him ripping the gills out of those hapless fish.

"Do you want me to take a picture of you here?" William asked. "A souvenir?"

"Okay."

He positioned himself in front of the cabin. She stood at the bow, the vast expanse of the ocean and the swooping seabirds serving as her backdrop.

"What do you want me to do?" she asked.

He looked through the viewfinder. "Just act natural."

"That's impossible."

"Then act unnatural. That should come naturally to you."

She laughed. The camera clicked, and he lowered it from his face.

She waited. "That's it? Aren't you going to try for a second one, just in case the first doesn't come out?"

"No, I think that pretty much did it."

She opened her mouth to express her skepticism, until she noticed him squinting off into the distance behind her.

"That's a big one," he said. "What kind of a whale is that?"

She followed his eyes, and her jaw dropped. For a few moments, no sound escaped her throat.

"Blue!" she finally yelped. "It's a blue whale!"

His eyes widened at her, and she practically shouted, "Take pictures!"

But he had run out of film, so he sprinted back inside to retrieve more. He emerged from the cabin moments later, already snapping photos from across the deck. His mother followed close at his heels, and even Frank came out to admire the creature for a moment.

William stood at her side now, snapping photo after photo as the whale approached. Growing alarmed, Frank went back into the cabin in case he needed the steer the boat away.

It was yards away from the boat now. As they watched, the whale blew a powerful jet of spray thirty feet into the air, then dove into the water, its enormous fluke lifting above the surface. A moment later, its U-shaped head resurfaced, then it sprayed again. It repeated this pattern several times before plunging one last time into the sea, its giant fluke lingering one long moment as if waving goodbye.

Julia remained at the rail for a minute longer, waiting, hoping for one more glimpse. But the creature had plunged into the deep, and was gone. It was a once in a lifetime experience, and she knew she might never see it again.

"That," she said finally, "was the best birthday gift I have ever received."

William's camera, which snapped non-stop while the whale remained, was still now, and so was he. He said nothing, so she turned to look at him. The wisps of hair that he had tucked up under her hat earlier had escaped and once again blew around her glowing cheeks. She beamed her pure joy at him.

His mother still lingered nearby, so William stepped closer to Julia, close enough that his fingertips touched hers. It was all the encouragement she needed to weave her fingers through his, to press her palm against his. He caressed her hand with his thumb, and Julia was insensible to everything except her body's acute response to his physical presence and the relentless pace of her own heart.

After a minute, William whispered, "After my mom and I drop you off, I'll come back over to your house."

He hadn't said where they would go or what they would do after that. Her plan for that night had been to finally start her admission essay to UCSB. If he asked to come inside the house, would she let him?

He was waiting for an answer from her.

"Okay," she whispered.

Ann's car, parked behind Cardone's, was a remarkably well-preserved brown Oldsmobile Cutlass from the late seventies with an eight-track player in the console. The whole way home, Ann prattled on about how Jimmy and Mike had kept the Oldsmobile alive and running all these years. Had viewed it as their own private laboratory, in fact. But Julia did not care about Jimmy or Mike or their mechanical prowess. She felt William's eyes boring into her from the back seat.

When he came over later, would she even put up a token resistance? Try suggesting that they go out somewhere, instead?

She would not. In fact, the first thing out of her mouth would be, "Do you want to come inside?"

She burned with the anticipation of it. And why not? Hadn't she been taking Alison's pills, just for this eventuality?

She had no condoms.

Surely she could find one in Alison's room. If William was smart, he'd bring one of his own. Of course, what did it matter? She felt fairly certain he was a virgin, too. His reserve had never put her off, but that was probably exactly why he liked her — she didn't give up on him like all the other girls did.

An unfamiliar, flashy yellow sports car, tended with obvious love, was parked in front of Julia's house. Julia tried to place it, but she couldn't.

As Ann steered the Oldsmobile to the curb, she said, "Hey, isn't that Mike's Camaro?"

From the back seat, William said nothing. Why was Mike's Camaro parked in front of her house? There was no one home except —

"Alison."

Julia clapped her hand over her mouth. Watched Ann and William exchange significant looks.

"Oh my God," she said, out loud again.

The car stopped in front of her house now, and she scrambled out of it. At the front door, she stopped.

What, exactly, was she planning to do? Barge in there and pull him off of her?

Julia turned and stalked back to the sidewalk. Hesitated long enough to see the wary looks on Ann and William's faces, still inside the car. Bolted down the sidewalk, headed she knew not where.

Ann's passenger door squawked open, and her voice shouted after William. But the door slammed shut again, clattering the window, and Julia heard his footsteps running after her.

"Julia."

He caught up to her in a moment and slowed to walk beside her. Thankfully, he didn't try to say anything yet.

Back at home, Alison — David's girlfriend this time yesterday — lay on her back getting humped by Mike Quinn, reigning horndog of the Outer Sunset.

Who was she to judge? Had she not just been prepared, hours after her first kiss, to lose her virginity?

William's voice tore into her solitary brooding. "He's not as bad as you think."

She held up her hand. "I don't want to talk about it."

Another long stretch of silence ensued before he said, "Let's stop in here. Get something to eat."

They were standing in front of the 46th Avenue diner. She nodded, and he held the door open for her. He sat beside her in the booth, and after placing their orders, she leaned back in her seat and stared out the window.

After a while, his hand slid across hers. She didn't draw away, but she faced him and said, "I have a lot going on these days."

"What do you mean?"

"I was going to work on my essay for UCSB tonight. I haven't even started on the application yet, and it's all due by mid-November. And my grades... for the first time in my life, I'm not making straight A's. That's probably fine for most people, but not for someone trying to get into UCSB. I can't put my mind to any of it lately."

His fingers laced through hers, and he stroked her hand with his thumb, as he had on the boat. "I can't stop thinking about you."

He didn't add the word "either" to the end of his sentence, but he didn't have to. How did he know exactly what she was talking about? And why did her heart and her body pull her so tenaciously in one direction, while her mind stubbornly anchored her in another?

He touched her chin, lifted her face to his. Leaned into her, and she yielded to the soft brush of his lips against her top lip, then her bottom one. To the slightly rough fingertips on her face. To the more angular lines of his own face, with its day's worth of stubble, against her fingertips and her chin. As it had so many times that day, heat radiated downward through her body, and she was all but ready to take his hand, to lead him back down the few blocks to her house.

Where they would meet Mike and Alison on their way out.

She gently nudged him to break the kiss.

"This isn't the best time for this."

He searched her face for some clue to her meaning. "We can go someplace private after this."

"That's not what I meant."

"Then what?"

She faltered, unsure how to explain this to him in a way he would understand. "You know how I told you my Uncle Rob and Tim practically raised me?"

He nodded.

"Well, Rob has always been gung-ho about education. He actually gets excited about touring college campuses. When I was fourteen, he took Alison and me down to SoCal for a week during summer, and we stopped along the way at UCSB. Alison yawned through the whole tour, but I decided right then – *that's* where I'm going. And that's been my one single focus ever since then."

William waited for her to continue. When she did not, he prompted, "Okay...?"

She dropped her eyes down to their hands clasped together on the booth seat. "I have so many things I need to do between now and the middle of November. I can't let myself lose focus any more than I already have."

"I won't get in your way."

"This is going to take all of my time for the next month and half. You'll never see me outside of work and at school."

He let go of her hand and frowned down at the table top a moment. "This is all just because of Mike and Alison, isn't it?"

"No, not all because of them. They just brought me back to reality."

"What reality?"

"I was ready to cast aside every other part of my life, just for you."

"*Just* for me?"

He waited a moment for a reply that never came. Abruptly he scooted out of the booth, pulled some cash out of his wallet, and dropped it on the table top.

"Are you leaving?" she asked incredulously. "We haven't even gotten our food yet."

"I'm not hungry."

"Will. I didn't mean it the way you took it."

Will. His expression softened. He stood frozen a moment, staring out the window at the traffic on the street without really seeming to take any of it in.

"Will," she tried again. "Sit down. Listen for a minute."

Slowly, he resumed his seat beside her. She took his hand again and said, "Just give me a month and a half."

The waitress brought their food then. William picked at his burger, and Julia shifted the French fries around on her plate. He leaned back in his seat and said, "Your uncle reminds me of my grandmother."

"A gay man and a Sicilian grandmother. Not an analogy I would have concocted off the top of my head."

William slid his arm around her shoulders. Picked up a French fry off her plate and inspected it. "Right before she passed away, she connected me with Father Molloy, at the church. He's been trying to get me a full-ride scholarship to USF here in the city."

Though Julia wasn't sure if it was wise, she asked, "When did your grandmother pass away?"

He dropped the French fry back onto her plate. "A year ago."

Julia rubbed his back where the caged albatross – the one he had gotten a year ago – spread its wings underneath his clothes.

One Thursday in October, William touched Julia's hand behind the cover of the lab table.

"Happy birthday, tomorrow," he whispered. "Are you coming to our study session at my place today? There's something I want to give you afterward."

Her heart soared briefly at the prospect that he had actually gotten her a birthday present, but it promptly sank again. "I have so much homework piled up, on top of my application materials."

He squeezed her hand. "It's okay."

"Will, I'm sorry."

"Don't worry about it."

But she did worry about it. After class, as she exchanged her books at her locker, she felt a hand on her shoulder.

"I brought it today, just in case," he said, handing her a 5x7 photo envelope. Then he quickly walked away.

Suspense got the better of her. She ripped open the envelope, reached inside, and flipped through photo after photo that he had snapped of the blue whale they had seen together on his uncle's boat. The images were crisp and vivid, the colors even sharper than the reality.

She flipped through some more and found the photo that he had taken of her on his uncle's boat. She had completely forgotten about it. She looked at it, and leaned against the locker for support.

It was quite possibly the best photo ever taken of her. And in the background, he had captured the blue whale. He knew he got it in only one shot. He didn't even have to see it.

There was something else in there. She reached inside and pulled out a CD in a thin jewel case.

Inside the front cover of the jewel case she found a small, folded piece of paper, which she opened. A handwritten note read, "Listen to it all the way through. The whole thing."

Where and how could she listen to it here at school? She couldn't, not without skipping lunch.

Lunch period found her in the library with the headphones on, listening to all surreal twenty three and a half minutes of her introduction to Pink Floyd, beginning with, "Overhead the albatross..."

That evening at the restaurant, Julia sought William out on his break from work and found him, as usual, on the pier.

"How's prep cook going?"

He jumped at the sound of her voice. "Pretty good. Much better than washing dishes."

"My sister and I are going to a Halloween party at Holly's house. It's not entirely legal."

"What does that mean?"

"It means alcohol will be served to minors."

"And her parents are okay with that?"

"My aunt and uncle will be in Hawaii, blissfully ignorant of the proceedings."

He considered. "Halloween parties aren't really my thing."

"What?"

"I don't do the costume thing."

"Oh, come on!" She beamed her brightest smile at him; but even as she said it, she realized that she could never picture him in a Halloween costume. "Well, you know where Holly lives, in case you change your mind."

He looked down at her apprehensively. Wondering, she knew, whether she had listened to his message yet.

"We were in French together in tenth grade," she said.

His eyes widened. She knew he understood.

"It's amazing what you can re-learn during a lunch period in the library, Monsieur *poète maudit*," she added. "You're not so esoteric as you think you are. I had just blocked Baudelaire and his sad captive albatross out of my memory, that's all."

She reached for his hand. Held his fingertips in hers for a few moments. But the restaurant patrons looking out on them through the floor-to-ceiling windows prevented her from doing more.

He took her hand and led her back around the corner, to the alley behind the restaurant. He turned, and cupped her face in his hands. Kissed her, on the lips at first, but soon his lips traveled up her jawline to her earlobe, her neck. Hot and cold electric shocks reverberated through her body. His mouth, his tongue found their way back to hers. His hand nuzzled the small of her back. Slid down a little further, and pressed her hips into his. He touched and stroked her hair with his fingertips, as if it were something he had wanted to do for a very long time.

"Don't go," he whispered into her ear when her break was over.

"I have to," she replied. "So do you. You're late."

He kissed her again. "When can I see you again?"

"I'm off tomorrow and Saturday."

He shook his head. "I'm working."

"Sunday's the Halloween party," she said ruefully. "I'm busy all that day, too."

The look he gave her was pained, but he kissed her one more time. She smiled up at him, and held his hand until they got back inside.

The day of the party, Julia and Alison rode the bus to St. Francis Wood. Many other past and present Holy Cross students streamed into the house, which thumped all the way from the corner of the street with bass music from a Halloween party soundtrack.

"I predict an early crashing of this party by the cops," Alison said cheerfully.

Julia and Alison filed inside and laughed at Holly, dressed as Rose from So I Married an Axe Murderer. They compared costumes with the other revelers they knew, couldn't believe River Phoenix had died that morning either, and located the jello shots as quickly as possible. Sufficiently warmed, they made their way to the impromptu dance floor in the living room.

Somebody came up to Julia and said, "Some guy is looking for you out there."

"Oh my God, it's William," said Alison, seizing Julia's arm.

"Where?"

"I don't know where. But what other guy would be looking for you here?"

Julia smacked her and craned her neck to look for him. "Come with me," she said to Alison, afraid of losing her in this dark, thumping, teeming mass of costumed humanity.

They went back together to the hallway, where she spotted him, hanging back, looking ready to escape out the front door. She beamed and waved, working her way through the crowd until he finally spotted her. When he did, his eyes gave another one of those involuntary flickers down her body.

"Ariel!" exclaimed Alison, gesturing like a game show hostess at Julia's mermaid skirt and clamshell bikini top.

"I'm not Ariel," Julia protested. "I'm just a mermaid."

"Ariel," insisted Alison, tugging on Julia's copper hair. "No wig needed."

William remained frozen in place, his eyes riveted to Julia, apparently incapable of speech.

"I think he approves," Alison observed aloud.

Reddening, William looked then to Alison, in her black wig with fringed bangs. "What are you?"

Alison whipped a kitchen knife and fake penis out of her waistband. "Lorena Bobbit?"

He cast her a dubious look, and turned back to Julia. At first she didn't think he had come dressed as anything at all, but then she noticed the uncharacteristic black leather jacket and boots.

"I give up," she said.

He opened his arms out to the side, as if to give her a better look. "Biker."

Julia and Alison gaped a moment, then collapsed in a fit of giggles.

"That is the worst costume I've ever seen!" laughed Julia when she recovered her powers of speech.

He looked distinctly uncomfortable, and Alison exclaimed, "Oh, poor William! You conned him into coming here, and then you laugh at him! There's got to be some way we can help him."

Julia thought for a moment. "I have an idea, but it's a long shot. Come with me."

She took William by the hand and led him through the gridlock of bodies toward the kitchen. When she looked back, she realized that she had lost her sister. Or, more likely, Alison had dropped her, quite deliberately.

It was less crowded and much quieter in the kitchen. Julia let go of his hand and rummaged through the ample cabinets.

"What are you doing?" asked William.

"Like I said, it's a long shot," was all the reply she would give. But after a minute or two, she located what she was looking for: a can of Crisco. "Bingo. Now for part two. This is even more of a long shot." And yet, after a moment or two more, she found a set of food coloring. Beaming triumphantly, she held them up for him to see. "My sister is obviously not the only baker in the family."

He eyed her warily. "What are you going to do with that?"

"Relax," she said, cradling her finds in one arm and grabbing his hand again. They plunged into the masses, working their way through to the other side of the house, where she found the small bag she had stowed under a bench in the entry hall. Up the staircase she led him, past the bodies lining the darkened stairs, to what she knew was a guest bedroom. She opened it; it was occupied already.

"Oh, sorry," she gasped, slamming it shut again. Jesus, why didn't they use the lock? That's when she realized what this must look like to him, and felt herself redden.

"Let's do this in the hallway," she suggested. There weren't very many people there. She found a small desk in the hallway with a chair and pulled it out for him.

"Sit."

He obeyed remarkably well, apparently too stunned to put up much resistance. She opened her bag, pulled out her eye shadow applicators. She used one to blend together a dab of Crisco with some black food coloring.

She brought the applicator toward his face. He pressed himself as far back into the chair as he could and demanded, "What are you going to do with that thing?"

"Impromptu Halloween face paint. *You* are going to be the biker from hell."

He tried to clamber out of his chair, but she steadied him with a hand on his shoulder.

"Will you just relax?" she pleaded. "You are looking at an accomplished Halloween costume and makeup artist of many years' experience. How do you think I came across this costume I'm wearing? You won't find another one exactly like it."

"That's true," he conceded, sinking back into his chair.

She snickered, and he watched as she came forward, her face hovering inches away from his. His eyes locked on hers, wide like a startled animal, and intensely blue. They flitted involuntarily down her body, at the clamshells, her trim waist, the aqua mermaid skirt hugging her slender hips.

She cupped his chin in her hand and lifted his face. "Look at me."

His eyes snapped immediately to her face. She came forward even closer with the eye shadow applicator, and he knocked her arm aside with his hand. She flinched, and he broke into nervous laughter.

"Oh, come on!" she laughed.

"There's no way I'm letting you do that to me."

But she was having too much fun watching him laugh. She came toward him again, and once again he blocked her. She tried switching hands, but he blocked that one as well.

By now they were both flushed red with laughter and exertion. When she reached toward him again, his hand closed around her forearm and held it there. So she reached out with her other arm, took the eye shadow applicator from her trapped hand, and brought it toward his face. He seized that forearm with his free hand and held both of her arms there.

Though he still smiled, he wasn't laughing any more. Her laughter came only in spurts while she waited for his next move.

"Drop that thing," he said, shaking her hand.

"No," she said with a nervous laugh.

"Drop it," he repeated, shifting himself forward in his seat. His hand crawled its way up her forearm to her hand. He pried open her fingers, and the eye shadow applicator tumbled to the floor.

Still, he held both of her arms there, his eyes flickering down her face to her mouth. He pulled her even closer, between his legs, and his lips were on hers. He let go of her arms, and put his hands on her rib cage.

After a moment, he broke away to look into her eyes. She put her forehead against his, and he stroked the side of her face. Kissed her lips again, and again.

Her heart was pounding now, and he pulled her down into his lap. It didn't matter anymore that people milled all around them; she let him crush his mouth into hers, kiss her deeply. Let his hands slide along the bare skin of her torso, her arms, her shoulders.

"Let's go into one of the rooms," he whispered into her ear. She shook her head, and he whispered, "I just want to lay down with you."

Her mouth twisted into a wry smile. "Will, I'm sitting in your lap, and I can tell that you don't just want to lay down with me."

With a mortified look, he said, "I'm sorry."

But she stroked his hair and laughed so good-naturedly that he couldn't stay embarrassed. He touched her lip with his thumb, and she opened her mouth and let him skim his tongue over hers again. He rested his forehead against hers, and his fingertips traced the line of her bikini top, along the curve of her breast.

"Jesus," he whispered.

She lifted his face to hers. Saw the wolfish sort of look in his eyes. Wondered if it would really be so bad if she just went to lay down with him.

"There you are," gasped a voice on the staircase behind Julia.

Julia scrambled to her feet, wrenching herself from William's grasp. He looked as startled as she felt by the breaking of the spell.

"We have to go," came the voice again, and Julia turned. How had she not recognized the voice as her sister's? She managed to mumble something incomprehensible even to herself.

"Uncle Rob is dying," Alison said.

"What?" She had Julia's full attention now. "How do you know?"

"Holly told me. Aunt Kathleen just called here on the phone."

"Let's go," said Julia, springing forward.

Alison stopped her with a hand on her arm. "He's not at Gran's."

"Where is he?"

"Marin General."

"You mean Marin County?"

Alison nodded.

"What the hell was he doing there?"

"Somebody found him at Point Reyes. Apparently he decided to take an impromptu road trip."

"Do Mom and Dad know?"

"Somebody probably called them at the restaurant, but you know Dad can't leave. Maybe Mom can."

"We have to get there," said Julia desperately.

"I'm trying to find someone here with a car who can drive us."

"I can take Julia." Behind her, William's voice startled Julia. She had almost forgotten he was there.

Julia turned to face him. "How are you going to take me?"

"On my motorcycle, of course. I wouldn't have been much of a biker without a bike."

"You don't have any other clothes," Alison pointed out to Julia.

It was true. She couldn't exactly hop on the back of his bike in a mermaid skirt and bikini top. Even if the skirt would let her mount the bike, it was getting colder, and it was going to rain.

"We'll have to call a cab," Julia said.

"I don't have that kind of cash on me," Alison despaired.

"We're in a house. Maybe you can scrounge around and find something to wear?" William suggested.

Alison looked at Julia. "Borrow something from Holly."

"I'll stay here," William shouted after them as they ran past.

"I'm so sorry," whispered Alison, gripping Julia's arm when they were safely past him. "But I was afraid you'd be angry with me if I didn't tell you. Please tell me I made the right call."

"Of course you did," murmured Julia, flipping the lights on in Holly's room. "You were just in time."

Together, they rifled through Holly's closet. Holly's clothes were still two or three sizes too big, and the pants were too short for her legs. But with the help of some belts, it might do the trick. Julia wriggled out of her mermaid skirt and yanked on the smallest pair of jeans she could find. Too big, but only just. She threaded a belt through the belt loops, tightened it to its tightest setting. They stayed up.

Alison handed her a long-sleeved T-shirt, a fleece sweater, an all-weather jacket to go over that. Mittens, a scarf. A fleece hat. A pair of rain boots, too big, but it hardly mattered until she got to the hospital and needed to walk again. She would bring her sandals with her.

While Julia braided her hair down her back, Alison peeked out the door into the hallway. "Look at him out there, still sitting in that same chair. I should go out there and talk to him. Help him think less about Ariel, and more about Lorena Bobbitt."

Julia tied off the braid. "How will you get there?"

"I'll just have to see if I can find a ride." Alison touched Julia's arm as she started to brush past. "Be careful."

Julia ran back to the hallway and found William in his chair still. She gathered up her bag and headed for the staircase.

"Let's go."

He got up and followed her downstairs wordlessly. The crowd was almost impenetrable now. He took her hand, assumed the lead, and sliced through the crowd like an ice breaker.

Out the front door they spilled into the chill night air. Still he held her mittened hand and led her to his motorcycle parked on the corner. She watched as he silently pulled on his gloves, zipped his jacket. Then he took his own helmet and lowered it onto her head.

Confused, she looked around him for the second helmet, and saw none hanging on his bike. Her heart sank a little. Clearly, he had not been thinking of taking her anywhere tonight.

"I can't do this," she protested. "You can't take me all the way to Marin on your motorcycle with no helmet."

He said nothing, just fastened the strap under her chin and tightened it as far as it would go. She tried to back away, but to her shock, he lifted her and put her on the back of his bike himself. A fleeting image of Viking abduction passed through her mind as he mounted the bike in front of her, until the roar of the un-muffled engine blasted the thought from her mind.

Great, she thought. I've gone from Viking conquest to biker bitch in one turn of a key.

"Hold on as tight as you can," he shouted over his shoulder at her.

She tightened her grip slightly.

"Much tighter. Trust me on this."

She squeezed him around the waist as tight as she could. With a blast of the engine, he peeled away from the curb, jerking her head back with the force of the acceleration.

She hardly knew what happened after that as she held on to him for dear life. She had a vague awareness of winding in and out of streets she didn't know, rolling through stop signs, flying up hills and down again. They were both lifelong residents of the city, but she couldn't guess how he knew his way around these streets when she didn't. She recognized Taraval as they crossed it, but then the unfamiliar side streets swallowed them again. She was beginning to wonder if maybe he wasn't such a hot shot, maybe he was lost too, when the side streets dumped them out onto 19th Avenue.

They split lanes and swerved around stopped traffic, making record progress through the Sunset, Golden Gate Park, Richmond. Roaring through the Presidio, onto 101.

The Golden Gate Bridge loomed ahead of them. The rain system had not arrived, not yet shrouded it in clouds. The air changed, blasting through William's hair, and she realized that he must be freezing to death with no helmet. She wondered why he hadn't worn a hat, and realized that the wind probably would have blown it off, anyway. Nothing for it now. They accelerated onto the bridge. She gripped his waist tighter, hoping it would somehow keep him warmer, and turned her head to watch the city lights and Alcatraz glowing on her right. To her left spread the black expanse of the open ocean.

On the Marin side, her head jerked back again as he blasted the engine. They drove another fifteen minutes or so, then exited the freeway. It wasn't much longer until the hospital loomed before them.

He found a parking spot and silenced the engine. Her ears rang as she leaped off the back of the bike and took off the helmet. She waited as patiently as she could while he removed his gloves, jammed on his hat, and fumbled with his helmet.

His whole body shook with cold.

"Let me do that," she said, taking the helmet from him and hanging it herself. The deed done, she added, "Let's run. It'll warm you up, anyway."

They sprinted into the hospital building as fast as her too-big boots would let her and found somebody at a desk to direct them to her uncle's room. She jammed the elevator button repeatedly, but it didn't come fast enough, so they bounded up flights of stairs and burst breathlessly onto her uncle's unit in front of the nurse's station.

The nurse at the station looked up wide-eyed at them.

"I'm looking for Robert Dunphy's room, please," Julia panted. "I'm his niece."

The nurse gave her the room number and pointed her in the right direction. "But first, let me find his nurse so she can fill you in on what to expect. He's stable for now, so there's no urgency."

A few minutes later, the nurse arrived at the station. "He's lucid at the moment, but when he arrived he was disoriented. His kidneys are failing."

"Do you have any more information on how he ended up here? All I heard is that he was at Point Reyes."

"Yes, some passers-by found him collapsed there. He's got a fair knot on his head. I don't know any more than that." She touched Julia's shoulder. "Have you seen him lately?"

"A week or so ago."

The nurse nodded. "I just wanted to make sure you knew what to expect."

The nurse led them in the direction of the room. They slowed their pace as they approached, and Julia went inside. Her uncle's eyes were closed, his mouth open. His appearance was nothing short of skeletal. A large white bandage covered part of his forehead, presumably where he hit it. She went forward and clasped his hand in her own. It was so bony, she was afraid of breaking it if she gripped it too tightly. His sunken eyes opened, and he smiled in recognition.

William hung back in the doorway, halfway hiding behind the door jamb. She looked back and saw him reeling a bit in shock at her uncle's appearance.

"I'll be in the waiting room," he said in a low voice.

She nodded, and watched him go.

"Your friend is cute," her uncle offered when she turned back to him.

"He's not just my friend."

He summoned enough strength to give her hand a faint squeeze. After a moment, he asked, "What are you doing here, Julie?"

"I should be asking you the same thing."

"I needed to see it one more time."

"See what?"

"Point Reyes."

"Why?"

He turned his face back toward the ceiling and closed his eyes. "Tim."

She wondered if he was getting confused again. She stroked his hand, waited. After a moment, he turned back to her and said, "They could have just left me there. I really didn't want to die in my mother's house, but I guess that would have been preferable to here."

She did not know what to say. She couldn't tell him he wasn't going to die here. She was afraid he would be embarrassed if she told him everyone was coming. So she stroked his hand and said, "Alison dressed as Lorena Bobbit for Halloween."

A slow smile played at his lips. After a moment's consideration, he said, "That's not far from the truth."

She laughed, and his body shook a bit with silent laughter.

"I don't know why you're here, but I'm glad you came," he said after he recovered. "How did you get here?"

"William brought me. My boyfriend."

He looked serious now. "I'm sorry I scared him off."

"You didn't. You heard him; he's in the waiting room."

He squeezed her hand with as much strength as he could muster. "Follow your heart."

He turned back toward the ceiling and closed his eyes once again. She stroked his hand again, but he seemed to be asleep. She paged the nurse, who examined him.

"It will probably be tonight," the nurse said gently.

An hour later, her uncle lay with his mouth open, his breathing labored. Julia leaned forward, pressing her forehead against the hand she clasped in her own.

She heard a noise behind her, and turned to see William disappear behind the door jamb. Swiping at her tears, she sprang to her feet and ran into the hallway to find William heading back in the direction of the waiting room.

"Will."

At the sound of her voice, he returned to meet her halfway.

"I'm sorry," he said quietly. "I wanted to make sure you were okay."

She buried her face in his shirt, and he wrapped his arms around her. He held her there, rubbed her back and allowed her to wet the front of his shirt with tears.

Julia heard a shuffling sound behind her, and a voice cried, "William!"

William sprang back from Julia at the sight of her mother and grandmother.

"What on earth are you doing here?" her mother asked him.

In a low voice, he replied, "I brought Julia."

"You brought – Julia," she repeated. "You brought *Julia?*"

"She wanted to be here. When she heard."

Julia's mother looked at him as if a sudden new thought had entered her mind – he had been with Julia. She didn't know that. She looked him up and down, in his black leather jacket and boots, and said, "Well, thank you for your help, William. We can get her home safely."

He looked to Julia, who smiled and nodded. He reached out as if to touch her, then, remembering himself, jammed his hands in his jacket pockets and turned immediately to go. On his way to the elevator, the doors opened and Alison emerged. She recognized him and waved. In fact, she was trying to say something to him, but he turned and bolted for the stairwell.

Alison watched him go, then jerked her thumb back in the direction he fled. "Where's he going?"

Julia frowned at her mother. "Mom, why did you have to scare him off like that? He got me here in time for Rob to know that he wasn't alone!" Julia's grandmother appeared wobbly, and Julia caught her around the elbows. "He's still with us, Gran; don't worry. He's just going in and out."

Julia's mother glowered. "Well then let's not lose any more time arguing."

When they had all gathered around Rob's bedside, with Julia's grandmother and Alison each clasping one of his hands, Alison asked, "Do any of you know why he was at Point Reyes?"

"He was feeling better than usual," Julia's grandmother explained. "I felt comfortable leaving him alone while I got some work done around the house. When I came back to check on him, he was gone. The car was gone, and so were the keys. I had no idea where he had gone until the police called to tell me where they had found him."

"But you don't know *why* he went there?" asked Alison.

Julia said, "He was lucid a little while when I got there. I asked him about that, and he just said, 'Tim.'"

Julia's grandmother smiled a bit, and went to dig around inside of her purse. She pulled out the small framed photograph that Julia and Alison had known all their lives, the one that always sat on her mantelpiece. A very old photo, the colors all fading to red. A very young Rob, with a very young Tim looking over his shoulder. Smiling, the both of them, their whole lives ahead of them. The water at their backs.

"I thought he might like to have it here with him," Julia's grandmother explained.

She opened the frame, pulled out the photo and turned it over. Handed it to Julia.

"Point Reyes," it said on the back in Rob's handwriting.

Now Julia knew.

Like a message from the hereafter. "Don't be afraid of love." Even with all of the regrets and lost opportunities, Tim was still the last thing he thought of; Point Reyes was still the last place he wanted to visit.

Julia buried her face in her free hand and wept openly. Her mother and grandmother both enfolded her in their arms.

Julia swiped at her eyes. "I'm sorry. I didn't mean to make everyone feel worse."

Her grandmother put a hand on Julia's shoulder and said, "What were his last words?"

"They're not his last words," Julia balked. But her grandmother fixed her with misty gray eyes, and Julia knew – they probably were. She thought for a moment, and with a flood of awe, she remembered them.

"Follow your heart."

They lapsed into silence, too stunned and emotionally spent to respond.

Julia tried then to decide what those words meant for her, personally. Her mind travelled back over that night. The way that William had come to the party after all, even though he didn't like Halloween parties in general. The look in his eyes as he put his hands on her. The way he gave her his only helmet, risking his safety, freezing himself halfway to death to get her where she wanted to go.

And yet, he had not brought an extra helmet. He had not planned to take her anywhere that night.

The regret she felt at this told her more about her feelings than anything else could. If her uncle wanted her to follow her heart, then her heart had never loved another human being more than it had grown to love William.

When Julia returned to class with Holly two days later, William already sat at his desk, tapping his pen as usual. Immediately his eyes locked on hers.

She could not stop the almost giddy smile from spreading across her face. Reddening, she looked away and bolted straight to her chair. She smiled down at her desk top, not daring to look at him again.

At their lab table, Julia looked up at William and whispered, "Can I talk to you after class?"

His eyebrows raised. "Yeah."

Somehow they slogged their way through the day's lab. After class, he followed her out the door, and she said in a low voice, "Come with me to my locker."

He followed her silently, and when they reached her locker, she opened the door and stood in front of it. It would hide her from at least half the hallway.

He stood very close to her, leaned against the lockers. "Your uncle?"

She shook her head.

He put his hand on her arm. "I'm really sorry."

Her eyes stung ominously. She reached into her backpack, slowly shelving a book or two in her locker. After a moment, the hand on her arm nudged her, and he gathered her up. She wrapped her arms around him in a hug, blinking back tears, and pressed the side of her face against his chest. Felt the nubbly texture of his blue uniform sweater against her cheek and heard the quick pace of his own heart. Smelled the spicy, masculine scent of his soap. He rubbed her back gently with his hand, put his nose in her hair.

A teacher's throat cleared beside them, and instinctively they pulled away from each other. Julia resumed exchanging books in her locker, and the teacher eventually moved away again.

After a moment, she said softly, "Thank you. For the other night."

"You're welcome."

"Will," she ventured, "why didn't you bring a second helmet with you to the party?"

When it finally dawned on him what she meant, he explained, "You told me you would never ride with me again."

Her heart pounding, she considered her options. Kissing was strictly forbidden at Catholic school. Their manner toward each other had not escaped notice; several people stared in groups, whispering. Teachers stood all around, outside their classroom doors.

To hell with it.

She slid her arm around his waist. He started a bit, then pulled her into him willingly enough. She reached up and splayed her fingers along the side of his face. Caressed his lips with her thumb. A few guys nearby wolf-called in support.

"Don't make me enforce it," came a voice beside them. Julia's English teacher, a young guy in his twenties.

She let go of William, smiled impishly up at him, and she could tell he was trying not to let his own smile overtake his face too much. She finished exchanging the books in her locker, and slammed the door. Cast him one more impish look before turning to go.

He caught her by the arm and whispered, "When can I see you?"

"Maybe after school."

He shook his head. "I have to go straight to work."

"At work, then." One more coy look before dashing away. He loosened his grip just enough to let his hand travel down the length of her arm as she walked away, ending with his fingertips on hers.

She carried the phantom sensation of his fingertips all through her next class period. To her surprise, when the class ended, she found William waiting in the hallway for her.

"Come with me," he said.

He had that wolfish look again. He took her hand and she followed him silently, unquestioningly, through the halls into a little-used corridor. Out a long-forgotten back door, into an empty alley.

He was kissing her almost before she knew what was happening. She wrapped her arms around his neck and felt his hands sliding under her sweater, against the bare skin of her waist. While his lips traveled over her face and neck, his hands strayed up her torso. He wrenched her bra up and closed his hands over her breasts.

She gave a little exhale of pleasure, and at the sound of it, he did too. He lifted up her skirt and slid his fingers between her legs. She drew her breath in a quick gasp, and he took her hand and pressed it against the crotch of his pants so she could feel his erection.

She realized that if they carried on at this pace, they were going to have sex, right there in that alley. Her instincts propelled her onward; and yet, it was far from what she had always imagined. She didn't even know how they would accomplish it. Standing up? He was so much taller, she couldn't imagine how that would work. Lying down on the cold pavement?

Her sister's warning drifted through her consciousness. "It'll probably hurt the first time. And you might bleed."

Reluctantly, she pushed his hand away and stepped back. Unable to look him in the eye, she yanked her clothes back in place and whispered, "We can't do this right now."

He froze, and she dragged her eyes up to his. For the second time in less than two days, he looked as if the spell had broken.

"Not in an alley behind school," she explained. "I really don't want it to happen this way."

She flung open the door and fled back inside.

Julia kept her head down for the rest of the day, terrified of seeing William again. At work, she managed to avoid him until after the restaurant closed, when she spotted him in the break room at the lockers. She stopped short and turned to retreat, but he had already seen her.

"Julia."

Reluctantly, she turned to face him. He came to stand in front of her and said, "Will you come outside for a minute? I just want to talk."

After a moment's hesitation, she moved toward the back door. He followed her outside into the alley, where no one would see them.

After an awkward silence, he said, "I'm sorry. I swear, that's not what I had in mind when I brought you outside today."

"It's okay."

"I really—" He seemed to be struggling with what to say. "I really like you. I don't want you to get the wrong impression."

She gave him a bemused look. "I like you, too."

He frowned. "No, that's not what I meant. I meant exactly the opposite. I *really* like you. I don't want you to think that all I want from you is—" The word sex stuck in his throat. He peered intently at her, allowing her to fill in the blank.

She smiled. "I really like you, too. And I don't want you to think that all I want from you is sex, either. But I also really want to have sex with you."

He gave a short, incredulous laugh, and reached for her. Put his hand on her arm, and stroked her hair with his other hand.

He was beautiful. Stunning, actually. His blue eyes, his face, his tall lean body. His heart that never gave up on her.

She reached for his hands, took them in her own. Kissed the tops of them, each in turn. Turned them over, kissed the palms as well.

He took her face in his hands and put his lips on hers, lingering there for a long time. When at last he broke away, his face was all joy, with no trace of the anxiety that had been there moments before.

She took his hand and led him back inside to the break room. She moved silently to her locker and gathered up all her belongings. Guessing her intent, he quickly did the same. She put on her coat and gloves and followed him out the back door, past her parents, past everyone. Let him lower the spare helmet onto her head, tighten it under her chin for her. Climbed on the bike behind him. Held on tight as he roared away.

His driving was hardly less urgent than it was the last time she was on his motorcycle. When he finally parked, she got off the motorcycle and he lifted the helmet off of her head. Pulled off his own helmet and touched her tumbledown hair. Kissed her mouth repeatedly. She opened her mouth, accepted his tongue.

When he pulled away again, he had that wolfish look that she knew all too well by now. She looked around. They were in front of his house.

"Why are we here?"

He touched her face. "Come inside with me."

Her body screamed at her to do it. He stepped closer, tilted her head back. She exhaled as he pressed kisses into first one side of her neck, then the other.

"My parents saw me leave with you," she warned him.

"Please," he whispered. "I don't want to wait anymore."

She looked up at him, into his eyes. "Okay."

He took her hand and led her right to the front door. The house was dark and he unlocked the door as quietly as possible. They tiptoed through the shadowy entrance and he led her quickly, quietly through the in-law unit to his bedroom in the back.

Somehow, she was surprised to find it precisely matched her idea of a typical teenage guy's room. A stereo in one corner. A guitar case leaning up against one wall. Led Zeppelin and Pink Floyd posters. A single twin bed, just like in her own room.

He locked the door and came to kiss her. Took her hands in his, and led her straight to the bed. Kissed her deeply now.

She began to lift his sweater. He helped her, pulled it off over his head. She reciprocated, leaving her bra on for the moment.

He spent a while touching and looking at her face, drinking it in. She was beginning to fear that he was changing his mind, when he said, "I have a condom."

She smiled. "Have you ever done this before?"

He shook his head.

"Me neither," she whispered. "And I've been on birth control pills since the first time you took me on your motorcycle."

His eyes widened, and she laughed softly. He pulled her onto his lap, straddling him. His mouth hovered just over hers, his breath on her lips, and she felt a tugging sensation at the clasp on the back of her bra. Felt the unmistakable sensation of it popping open.

She lifted her eyes to his and held them there, giving him permission. With a sweep of his hands, the bra tumbled down the front of her body.

She felt his breath coming faster now against her lips, and he kissed her softly. Opened her mouth with his, and kissed her with his tongue. His hands swept up the subtle ridges of her ribcage to touch her breasts, and his voice made a little inarticulate sound.

He pushed her down on the bed. Pulled off her pants and underwear and took in the sight of her naked body, lying on his bed. Shed the rest of his clothes and came to lie beside her.

After a while, she pulled him on top of her. Felt the pain her sister had warned her about.

She was grateful it was him, and not anyone else. Grateful that he didn't try to rush things, that he didn't make her feel bad when she asked him repeatedly to stop, to wait. That he didn't freak out when she bled. That he still came back and wanted to try again.

He grasped her hands in his, laced his fingers through hers and looked into her eyes, watching her reaction. She pulled his face down into her hair, muffling the sound of his voice as he came.

Afterward, he lay on his stomach and she saw his caged albatross for only the second time ever. She draped herself halfway over him and ran her hand across it, looking.

He said, "You know what I was trying to say earlier, behind the restaurant."

"What?"

He lifted his head, looked into her eyes. "I love you."

"I love you, too," she whispered.

He rolled over, nuzzled her hair. "What did I do?"

"How's that?"

"When did you decide you loved me?"

"I always liked you, from the very beginning. But I think I really fell for you around the time you thought to take me on your uncle's boat for my birthday."

He tucked a lock of hair behind her ear. "I always liked you, too. But you had me from your conversion to Islam."

They both laughed, remembering. Julia said, "If only I had known how easy it was to turn you on. Just tell you all the details about me that send rational guys fleeing for their lives."

"I'm going with you."

"What?"

"To Santa Barbara."

She propped herself up against him to look in his face. "You'll get a scholarship somewhere. You can't give that up."

"I don't know what I'm doing with my life, except I want to be with you."

"We can still be together, even if we go to different schools."

He shook his head. "I don't believe in long-distance relationships. You'll forget about me."

"I could never forget about you." She kissed him. "Don't make any decisions right now. Especially since I haven't even been accepted yet to UCSB."

"You will be."

"Let's see how you feel after next summer."

He looked uneasy, but let her reassure him with her kisses. After a while, he said, "Are you ready to face the music?"

"What music?"

"Your dad."

Her stomach churned at the prospect. "You'd better not come with me."

"There's no way I'd let you walk all the way home by yourself at this time of night."

"Then you'd better pray he's not waiting on the front step when we get there."

"I haven't done anything I'm ashamed of."

"He doesn't share your liberal sensibilities."

She stayed with him as long as she dared, and then let him walk her the three blocks home. He stopped her in front of a neighbor's house, in case anyone was watching out her window, and kissed her goodnight.

"When can we do this again?" he whispered.

"Pretty much anytime, at my house. My parents don't get home until eleven at night, at the earliest. The only person who's ever home is Alison, and she'll leave us alone."

He looked skeptical at the idea, but kissed her goodnight once more.

After he left, Julia tiptoed into the house and upstairs, dreading what waited for her there. But to her surprise, though the lights were on in the living room, her parents had gone to bed. At least she thought they had. She heard no noise emanating from their bedroom – not even their snoring.

Julia sought refuge in her own room, and switched on the aquarium light after shutting her door.

"It'll probably hurt the first time," Alison had said. Understatement of the year. Though he had been as gentle as possible, Julia felt torn open, shredded. She lowered herself gingerly onto the edge of her bed and sat gazing at her fish for a long time, turning her uncle's watermelon tourmaline over and over in her hand. After a while, she heard a tap on the door.

"Julie," Alison whispered from the other side.

"Come in."

Alison came in and closed the door after her. She came to sit beside Julia on the edge of the bed, and put her arm around Julia's shoulders. The eyes she turned on Julia were serious, for once. Julia grasped the hand on her shoulder, and they gazed in silence at the aquarium.

The day before Thanksgiving, Julia walked the pier to Cardone's to pick up the daily order for the restaurant, tugging the hood of her raincoat to shield her face from the cold rain beginning to fall. She slowed to watch the deckhands tie a boat to the pile with their load of Dungeness crab on board.

The fisherman disembarked, climbing the ladder onto the pier to operate the hoist. The two deckhands hooked their totes of crab to the hoist, which lifted it onto the pier. They all wore head-to-toe yellow foul weather gear, obscuring their faces. One of the deckhands turned to face her, and finally Julia recognized him.

She waved to William and picked up her pace. He climbed the ladder to the pier to join her.

"I didn't know you were going out on your uncle's boat today," she said.

He gestured to the nearest tote, alive with wriggling crab. "Does your family do crab for Thanksgiving?"

"Oh yes. Some years we don't even bother with the turkey."

"Wait here," he said, and disappeared into the plant. When he emerged, he added a bucket of water to the bottom of her cart. Then he reached into the large tote of crab, pulled one out, and held it up for her to see.

"Happy Thanksgiving," he said, dropping the crab into her bucket. To that he added three more, one for each member of her family.

"Why don't you add one more for yourself?" she suggested.

"What?"

"Come over for Thanksgiving tomorrow."

His eyebrows raised. "Is this with your parents' blessing?"

"It will be."

He shrugged. "Go ahead and ask them. Let me know."

She returned with her cartload of crab to the restaurant and wheeled it into the office to show her parents.

"What's that for?" her mother asked.

"This is for our Thanksgiving dinner tomorrow," replied Julia. "William figured it was the least he could do, in exchange for being one of the party."

Julia's father turned to peer sharply at her over the rim of his glasses. "Are you telling me that William is coming to our house tomorrow for Thanksgiving dinner?"

Julia nodded.

Her father turned to his wife. "Did you know about this?"

Her mother hesitated. "Yes," she lied.

Julia's father turned away from them, clearly finished with the conversation. Julia smiled privately to herself, then caught her mother's eye and shared it with her.

Later that evening, her mother came to the hostess' station and touched Julia on the shoulder.

"Your father would never admit this," she whispered, "but he's always liked William a lot. So you can tell William to relax now."

After the semester ended, William did something unprecedented and requested an entire week of winter break off of work. Julia followed suit, and they had the whole week to spend together.

One morning, Julia propped herself up in his bed and looked at him. "Every time I come here, that guitar case is sitting in the same spot against the wall, looking all shut up and forlorn."

"Oh, no you don't."

"Oh, yes I do. Can you play it?"

"No."

"Liar."

He laughed a bit. "Mike taught himself to play when we were kids, and then he taught me. We used to think we were going to have a band one day, Mike and me. Actually, come to think of it, I think that was mostly Mike's dream."

"Well, I can't picture you as a rock star. But I can picture you playing it for me."

He shook his head. "I want to get you back in my bed again someday."

She sat upright. "Oh, see, you have it all wrong. You won't get me back in this bed again if you *don't* play for me."

"You are a vicious tyrant." But he grinned and got out of bed to retrieve the guitar. He spent a few minutes tuning it, then began strumming. A Pink Floyd tune emerged.

"You forget, your brother told me all your secrets," interrupted Julia. "I know you can sing."

He put his hand on the strings. "Oh no, I only agreed to play."

"You have nothing in writing."

He shook his head. "Please don't make me."

She grabbed his hand. "I have a confession to make. I'm getting back in your bed again, no matter what you sound like."

He grinned and began strumming the guitar again. Played the intro to Wish You Were Here. Paused just before he was about to start singing, reddened and laughed nervously. Started over again, and sang.

He was nervous to be sure, and his voice cracked a bit in the beginning. He avoided her eyes throughout, looked down at the guitar or across at the wall. But after a while, his voice gained strength, he played competently, and in short, Mike had been right. He had a very nice voice.

When he finished, he lifted his eyes to hers with a little smile. Her own bright smile, applause and cheers were sincere.

"Now I know the real reason you're such a Pink Floyd fan. You sound just like what's-his-name, minus the British accent."

"Don't insult him."

"Your modesty and hero worship are cute. But why such a sad song?"

"It's a beautiful song. Rips my heart out more than almost anything else I've ever heard."

"Exactly. I demand cheering up after that."

He put the guitar back in its case. "I'll have to find some other way to cheer you up, then."

"Oh, promises, promises," she said as he came to lie next to her.

He draped himself halfway over her and held her face in his hands, inches away from his own.

"How do you do this?" he said.

"Do what?"

"Make me wonder why I would ever want to be sad in the first place. Make me feel more like my own self than I have in years."

"In years? You're eighteen and a half, old man." She brushed the hair back off of his forehead. "Just be yourself. You don't need me or anyone else to give you permission."

He poked her in the shoulder. "Let's go get breakfast. There's somewhere I want to take you after that."

"Where?"

"It's a surprise."

They got dressed and went to eat at the 46th Avenue diner. Afterward, he drove her to a residential area of the Inner Sunset and parked.

"This is obviously not where I was planning to take you," he said. "But it's not far away from here, if you want to walk."

"How far?"

"Just over there," he said, pointing up a hill. "I think you'll like it."

"Okay."

He led her to a large hill with a long set of stairs ascending it. He took her hand, and together they climbed the stairs to the top of the hill. He helped her gingerly down a narrow path and across treacherous, uneven ground scattered with tree roots and rocks.

Finally, he tapped her on the shoulder and pointed.

"Look."

She caught her breath in a gasp. It was a clear winter morning, and the city spread out before them, with downtown to their right, Golden Gate Park and the bridge in front of them, and the Pacific Ocean to their left. He led her to a bench to sit beside him. There was nobody else there, no one else crazy enough to brave that spot at that time. It was cold and windy, but it was beautiful.

He pulled her close beside him and put his arm around her shoulders to keep her warm. "I didn't just bring you up here to show you the view and freeze your ass off. I wanted to give you a Christmas present. But I'm warning you, please don't get too excited."

"You can't give it to me now," she protested. "I don't have your present here with me."

"That doesn't matter."

He reached into the inside pocket of his coat and pulled out a box that was too big to be a ring box. He opened it, and held up a silver chain with a pendant on it.

"This is lame, I know, but it's just a promise," he said, fastening the chain around her neck. "I promise I'll never stop loving you, no matter what."

She lifted the pendant to take a closer look, and smiled. "A mermaid. Now why on earth would that make you think of me?"

He squeezed her around the shoulders. "I'll never forget that night as long as I live. I was so in love with you, and when I saw you, I really thought I could have died a happy man, right then and there."

Her chest flooded with a familiar warmth. She laced her fingers through his and kissed him.

"You make me so happy," she whispered.

"Good," he said, touching the pendant. "Wear it as long as you still feel that way."

She wrapped him in her arms. Held him there for a long time, the world spread out before them.

January, February, and March flew by in a frenzy of work and school. On their rare days off together, Julia and William explored the city and beyond on his motorcycle, finding every scenic point and secluded spot along the way. Julia ate dinner with him and his family at their house, or brought him to dinner at her grandmother's.

One day in late March, Julia put her hand on William's arm as he cleaned his station at the end of a busy shift at the restaurant.

"I got the fat packet," she said.

He looked up without pausing from his work. "What?"

"The fat packet. From UCSB. I got it."

He wiped his hands on a towel and wrapped her in a hug.

"Of course you did. Congratulations."

She pulled away from him, held him by the arms and beamed up at him. After a moment, he took her by the hand and led her out the back door and onto the pier. Turned her face up to his. Put his hand in her hair on the nape of her neck, and kissed her.

Afterward, he rested his forehead on hers and just looked into her eyes. She listened to the sound of his breath as he caressed her hands and fingers with his.

"Shouldn't you have heard back from USF by now?" she murmured after a while.

Silence. He brushed the hair back away from her face, and her heart sank for him.

"You didn't get in."

"No, I did."

"What? When did you find out?"

"The beginning of the month."

"Will! Why didn't you tell me?" He continued silent. "Did you get the scholarship?"

He nodded.

"Full ride?"

Again, he nodded, and she kissed him in congratulations.

"But you don't seem happy about it."

He still wouldn't answer her. She asked again, "Why didn't you tell me when you found out?"

"I don't know if I'll take it or not."

"Of course you will. Why wouldn't you?"

"Well, for one thing, I have no idea what I'll study."

"I told you – photography. See? I have your future all mapped out for you. Aren't I helpful?"

"They don't have a photography program."

"You're not a one-trick pony, like me. You could do any number of things. You have a couple of years to decide."

"I can do a lot of things, but none of them very well."

"You do all of them very well. You take amazing photos of me."

"You're beautiful. No one could take a bad photo of you."

She frowned. "Is this low self-esteem, or just false modesty?"

The hand stroking her hair froze. "What?"

"Your bias is sweet and flattering, but I know for a fact that not everyone makes me look beautiful in photos like you do. You are brilliant at just about everything you try. There's a difference between healthy pride and arrogance."

He gathered her against his chest and held her there. "I wish I had applied to Santa Barbara instead."

She spent a while holding him. Imprinting the long, lean lines of his body on her memory.

"How would you like to go with me to prom?" he asked after a while.

She gave a short laugh. "That's kind of random. Are you sure a prom is really your thing?"

"I want to claim you before anyone else does."

"Like I'd go with anyone else."

He smiled warmly at her. "I can't afford a limo."

"I don't need a limo. In fact, I don't need a prom. Screw prom."

"Are you sure?"

"You know you have to dance at a prom." She tried to picture it, and laughed out loud. "No, you have no business at a prom, and I definitely don't have my heart set on it. Let's do something else that day. Something better."

"Like what?"

"I think it's high time you broke the fifty-mile barrier."

He raised an eyebrow. "The fifty-mile barrier?"

"On your motorcycle."

He laughed. "Where will we go?" After a moment's consideration, he said, "Point Reyes."

"No. That was my uncle's thing. I want to do our own thing. If you've never seen Big Sur, then you haven't lived yet. And bring your camera. You're going to get the best shots of your life."

He touched her face. "You're too good to be true."

She pinched herself. "Yep, I'm still real."

"Will you come home with me now?"

Her heart gave a lurch, and she went back inside the restaurant to retrieve her things.

On the last day of April, William brought Julia on his motorcycle to Año Nuevo State Reserve, near the fifty-mile mark. He took a photo of them there, wrapping his arms around her shoulders, holding the camera in front of him and shooting blindly.

"Save your film," she advised as he snapped away at the elephant seals. "It doesn't get really good until after we get past Carmel."

So they plowed ahead, past Santa Cruz, past Monterey, and into Carmel. Still, she pushed him onward, saying, "Trust me on this."

Soon enough, he saw for himself what she meant as the road cut its tortuous path along the coastline, skimming cliffs that sliced into the intense blue water. He pulled off the road at every opportunity to snap photos, until she said, "We'd better keep moving if we ever want to get there."

"Where am I going?"

"Julia Pfeiffer Burns State Park."

"What's there?"

"You'll see."

After parking and following her down the trail, he saw the eighty foot waterfall plunging onto the sandy beach and said, "The only thing that would improve this view is you in front of it."

"That's very flattering. But it's your turn now."

She reached for his camera, but he resisted. "Oh, no."

"Oh, yes."

"I told you, I make it a point to never be on the other side of the camera."

"Why?"

"I'm not photogenic."

"That's a load of bull. You're just shy." She touched his face, leaned into him. "You're the most beautiful thing I've ever seen. The world deserves a photo of you. *I* deserve a photo of you."

It was just the trick; he handed her the camera.

"I won't smile," he said.

"Yes you will."

She peered through the viewfinder and snapped one photo of him not smiling, just looking at her shyly.

She lowered the camera. "Do you want to hear a really bad joke?"

"Okay."

"I'm warning you, it's really bad."

"Bring it on."

"A baby seal walks into a bar. The bartender asks, 'What'll it be?' The baby seal says, 'Anything but Canadian club on the rocks.'"

He only laughed because it was so outrageous coming from her, of all people. But it served its purpose; she snapped the picture.

"Oh, no fair!" he protested, putting his hands in front of his face. "You're a con artist."

"Takes one to know one."

He laughed some more, and gave up trying to hide himself from her. She snapped as many pictures as she could get before he regained his composure.

"There. I know exactly how many photos I just took. Six. So don't try to hide any of them from me."

"Okay," he said, taking the camera back. "Now it really is your turn."

She submitted to a couple of photos, until he lowered his camera again and just gazed at her.

"Hungry?" she guessed.

He came forward and touched her on the arm. "I had a feeling this road trip might give me a good opportunity."

"What?"

He glanced around to make sure they were really alone, then reached into his pocket and pulled out a diamond ring.

"Oh my God," said Julia.

"I've been saving all winter and spring for this."

Julia stared in disbelief at it. "Is this really happening?"

He slipped the ring onto her left hand. "I'm coming with you to Santa Barbara. I'm not going to USF. And I'd like you to marry me."

He held her hand in both of his, and she spent a while looking at the diamond sparkling on her finger, still in shock. The diamond was modest, and it was clearly a new ring. She looked up at him and brushed back the bit of hair falling over his forehead.

"I'll wear your ring, and I'll marry you someday. But I won't let you give up your scholarship."

"I won't change my mind. I'm going with you."

"No," she said gently. "I told you, I won't forget about you."

"I know you won't, because I'll be there with you."

She touched his face, made him look her in the eye. "I love you. We'll have a good life together. But you need to get your degree."

"I can be a cook."

"I know that's not what you really want."

With a note of desperation, he said, "Why won't you believe me when I tell you I don't know what I want to do with my life, except to love you until the day I die? I'm not going to give up a sure thing for an unsure thing."

His words moved her deeply. She took his hands in hers. "You're right, this *is* a sure thing. We'll see each other once a month, at least. At holidays, during breaks. I'll call you every single week, maybe every day. Write you letters. And, you'll figure out what you want to do and get your degree."

She watched his face, watched him look out on the vista. Touched his forehead to smooth the worried furrows from his brow. Held up her hand for him to see.

"I'm wearing your ring. I'm never taking it off. You'll never get rid of me now."

He smiled halfheartedly.

"Listen to me." She made him wrap his arms around her waist. "I'll never forget this day as long as I live."

His expression softened. "Me neither."

One afternoon in the summer, Julia's father appeared on the pier where Julia and William were taking their break.

"William, can I speak with you in my office when you have a minute?"

William stiffened. "Is there a problem?"

"Problem? No, not at all. Sorry if I alarmed you. Actually, I hope you'll like what I have to say. Julia may as well come, too."

With that, Julia's father turned and headed back toward the restaurant. Julia and William exchanged baffled looks, but followed her father back inside.

Julia's father closed the door behind them and said, "I know you're going to USF, William. Julia tells me you're majoring in Hospitality Management?"

"Yes, I've thought about it. I was thinking I could use it in the restaurant industry somehow."

Julia's father took a seat at his desk and folded his arms across his chest. "If you major in Hospitality Management, you can complete the required work hours here, as a line cook. The hours would be flexible with your school schedule, of course. I'll give you a raise, as well. How does that sound?"

Slowly, William nodded.

"What do you want?"

"Sorry?"

Julia's father waved his hand impatiently. "Wage."

William swallowed. "I don't think I could do it for less than thirteen dollars per hour."

"That's more than what my top line cooks make, William."

"There are a lot of expenses my scholarship doesn't cover, and I was wondering how I was going to cover them while still working here."

Julia's father leaned back in his chair, and a trace of a smile played at his lips. "Nine."

"Ten."

Julia's father held out his hand. Slowly, William took it, and they shook.

"I'll have my wife draw up the paperwork."

William nodded. Julia's father turned away from them, clearly finished with the conversation. William rose, and Julia followed him back to his station.

William gripped the counter for a moment, paralyzed. "What the hell was that all about?"

"I think you just got a promotion."

"Yeah, but why did you have to be there at the same time?"

"I think he wanted me to know he was taking care of you. I think that was his stamp of approval." When William still leaned against the counter for support, Julia prompted, "What's the matter?"

William turned a somber look on her. "I have a strange feeling, like I just signed my life away."

"Where are you calling from?" William asked after Julia's first week of classes.

"My dorm room. I used one of the calling cards my parents gave me. My roommate's not here, so we can talk as dirty as we want."

"How's your roommate?"

"She's about what you'd expect from a girl named Tiffany. Bleach blonde, surgically enhanced, and fake-baked."

"What did you expect? It's SoCal."

"I guess I expected a university full of people who had to get straight A's in order to get in. I didn't expect to suffer social death if I didn't join a sorority."

"You mean you're not joining one?"

Julia scoffed. "Seriously?"

"Well, if nothing else, it might give you some connections. Internships, or job opportunities after college."

"The only thing a sorority will connect me with is a keg stand at a frat house. Oh! Speak of the devil. Did I ever tell you how I practically taught that marine biology summer camp that I went to when you first met me?"

"No."

"Yeah, the guy who was teaching us how to set up saltwater aquariums didn't know the first thing about them."

"I bet you were his favorite person after that."

"Actually, I kind of was. On the last day of camp, Kevin told me to look him up if I ever got into UCSB. He said he'd try to hook me up with an internship."

"Okay. So how is all that speaking of the devil?"

"Because Kevin is now the T.A. for my marine ecology class. I might actually get an internship this year, after all. It's not usually something freshmen are chosen for. But I AP-tested out of all my introductory science courses, so I'm a bit ahead of the game. And with a connection like Kevin, I might pull it off."

"So you might not have to rely so much on your sorority sisters, after all."

Julia laughed. "Tiffany's off the hook."

When Julia sought out Kevin during his office hours a couple of weeks later, he turned from his computer screen and gave a start to see her.

"Julia."

"Hi Kevin," she said, sweeping into the room and drawing up an empty chair. "Sorry if I startled you."

"No, not at all," he said, his eyes wide, swiveling around in his own chair to face her. "What brings you here?"

"I have a question about the mock exam you gave us."

"Oh yeah," he said after a missed beat, as if he had forgotten that she was his student. "The funny thing is, I've been meaning to ask you a question, too. I'm having a problem with the aquarium at my apartment."

Julia smiled. "So you're still doing the aquarium thing."

"Well, yeah. I've been keeping aquariums since I was a kid. But my question can wait. How can I help you?"

Julia opened her backpack and pulled the mock exam out of her binder. "It's this question right here. 'What factor most determines the upper limit of species boundaries in the rocky intertidal zone?'"

"Right."

"The other people in my study group think the most important factor is interactions between species, like competition. But I think it's physiological tolerances."

"Okay. And why do you think that?"

His question made her doubt herself, but she plunged ahead anyway. "Because few species can tolerate the conditions higher in the intertidal zone."

"Conditions? What conditions?"

"Well… like heat, and dessication. Marine organisms aren't well-adapted to those conditions, so they're not likely to be abundant enough to compete with each other, anyway."

He leaned back in his chair and smiled. "I think you've answered your own question."

"Great," she said, filing the mock exam back in her binder. "My study group already thinks I'm a dork and a misfit. Now they can add know-it-all to the list."

"It seems we're both a bit out of place here," he observed.

"Sorry?"

"NorCal types having an out-of-body experience in SoCal."

Of course. Now that he mentioned it, nothing could be more obvious – he was as much an alien in this land as she was. He was one of her kind.

"Where in NorCal are you from?" she asked.

"The Bay Area."

She held up a hand in solidarity. "San Francisco."

"Where in the city?"

"The Sunset."

He smiled, and it was an easy, genuine smile. She found herself returning it more readily than she meant to. He said, "What are you hoping to do with your degree?"

"I'm hoping to go to grad school and get my doctorate."

"Is there a particular area of marine biology you're most interested in?"

"I've always wanted to focus on marine mammals."

His eyebrows lifted. "Really? I would have pegged you as more of a fish kind of girl."

"Well, fish are great, too. I enjoy looking at them in an aquarium; I just don't want to study them. On the other hand, I want to study whales, but it'd be kind of hard to keep one in an aquarium, even if I wanted to." She zipped her backpack and added, "Speaking of aquariums, how can I help with yours?"

"My fish are looking peaked, and I can't figure out what I'm doing wrong. It's almost like the skin around their eyes and the pores of the lateral line is eroding away."

"Sounds like lateral line disease."

"Lateral line disease?" Kevin seized the notepad and pen on his desktop. "What causes that?"

"It could be any number of things. If you're maintaining your tank properly and giving it adequate light, it could be a problem with their diet. Are you feeding them food with stabilized vitamin C?"

"I think so." He scribbeled furiously on his pad.

"You might try adding some vitamin B and E. Also, some people think that stray voltage causes it by stressing them out.

He peered over the rim of his glasses at her. "Stray voltage?"

Julia nodded. "Even a small amount of it can wreak havoc on your aquarium."

He set his pen down and cleared his throat. She realized that he had no idea what she was talking about.

"When appliances around your tank fail – like your pumps, or your lights, or whatever – they can leak stray voltage," she explained.

"And that can cause lateral line disease?"

"Among other problems. Make sure you're using a grounding probe in your aquarium."

"It sounds like science fiction," he laughed, scrawling on his pad again. "I should have you come over to my apartment and take a look at my tank."

Julia's face burned. She felt ashamed, wondering if she had unintentionally led him on. And then she was angry at herself for feeling ashamed. She *hadn't* led him on. She had only come to him with a question about an assignment. Couldn't he see the ring on her finger?

She decided that the best way to sidestep his invitation was to teach him how to do things for himself. "Just get a voltage meter from the hardware store. If there's any needle movement when you put the probe in the water, you've got stray voltage."

"Okay, so then what?"

"Well, you'll have to unplug each appliance associated with your aquarium one at a time and retest until you figure out which one is causing the problem. And from now on, check for stray voltage as part of your routine maintenance."

As she watched him take notes, she wondered if she had been presumptuous before. He might have been as much as ten years older than her. She was struck again by how strongly he resembled Tim in that old photo, before Tim had grown fat and bald. Taken separately, none of the fleshy features of his moon-like face was very handsome at all. His pasty skin contrasted starkly against his black hair and beard.

Yet somehow the sum was greater than its parts. His heavy round shoulders tapered down to a narrower waist. Now that she sat so close to him, the light caught patches of red in his beard. She found the way his dark curls defied structure to be vaguely appealing. He wore black Ray-Ban eyeglasses and a plaid button-down shirt with the sleeves rolled up to the elbows.

He looked like a beatnik, thirty-five years too late.

Finally he tossed the notepad aside, flipped the lid of an oversized travel mug, and took a giant swig of coffee. He leaned back, crossed his ankle over his knee. Held her gaze a moment, then smiled. And though his beard and his pronounced canine teeth gave him the appearance of a yeti, his smile was open and contagious. She once again found herself returning it more encouragingly than she meant to.

He said, "I envy you. You already know exactly what you want to do." He lifted his travel mug, as if toasting her. "Stay the course."

"What about you?" she prompted. "Have you always stayed the course?"

"Not always. My first degree was in Finance, which was my dad's idea. After that, I took two years off to work for the Peace Corps in Brazil, among the Ticuna Indians. It had me re-evaluating everything. I knew I didn't need to be working in finance, for one thing."

"Why not?"

He shrugged. "Money for its own sake isn't something that interests me. It's what you do with it that matters."

"What would you do with it, then?"

"Well… something like the organization my fiancée works for. They do grantmaking for ecological restoration, among lots of other things."

His fiancée. Julia felt chastened. Now she knew for sure that Kevin hadn't been hitting on her earlier. "Really? What organization does she work for?"

"The DeSmet Family Foundation. Have you heard of it?"

"You mean the one that does all that underwriting for NPR?"

"That's the one. They're providing a huge grant for our internship program this year on the Channel Islands."

Julia felt her pulse quicken. "I'd like to apply for that. When does the application period begin?"

"In January. But I have to tell you, the last time a freshman got in was seven years ago." He peered at her a moment, then added, "Put your application in anyway. I think you stand as good a chance as anyone, or better. And since I got them the hook-up on that grant, I'm hoping they'll let me coordinate the internship program this year. Otherwise, I might have to fall back on what my dad wanted me to do for a living."

Julia laughed. "Well, at least you *can* fall back on what your dad wanted you to do. Unfortunately I'm a terrible cook, so I don't think that plan will work for me."

"Your dad wanted you to be a cook?"

"He's a chef."

"Really? Where?"

"Do you know Dunphy's Restaurant on Fisherman's Wharf?"

He looked surprised. "Your dad is the Dunphy of Dunphy's?"

"I'm afraid so. Have you ever been there?"

"No, I don't think so, but my parents have."

"Sounds about right. Nobody our age goes there anymore. And since there are no young Dunphys to take up the chef's mantle, I'm afraid Dunphy's will pass from this life along with my father." Julia rose then from her seat and slung her backpack over her shoulders. "Well, thank you for your help."

"Thanks for yours." Gathering papers into his own bag, he added, "Where are you headed after this?"

"Back to Anacapa. Lots of studying to catch up on."

"I'll walk with you. I'm headed that way, anyway."

As they spilled out of the Life Sciences Building into the bright sunshine, Kevin remarked, "I still can't believe your dad owns Dunphy's."

"What about yours? Why did he want you to go into finance?"

Kevin cast her a sharp look, and for a moment she worried she had said something to offend him. But then he smiled at her as if he thought she were quaint. "My dad is from New York. His family are all in the banking industry."

As they crossed the street, Julia spotted Tiffany waving at her from the front entrance of Anacapa Hall. When they all converged, Tiffany cast a significant look at Julia.

"Hey!" she chirped, before aiming a megawatt smile at Kevin.

Kevin, suddenly awkward, turned pointedly away from Tiffany. To Julia he said, "Listen, you can probably tell that I need as much help as I can get with my aquarium. If you don't mind, I'd like to ask you when I have questions about it. You probably know more than the goons at the fish store I've been going to. I promise, I'll keep the pestering to a minimum."

"Of course," Julia said.

"Great. See you in class tomorrow," he said, and nodded briefly at Tiffany before turning to go. When he was out of earshot, Tiffany pounced on Julia.

"Oh my God. What did he say to you?"

Julia raised an eyebrow at her. "Lots of things. Why are you freaking out?"

Tiffany gaped incredulously. "Julia, do you know who that was?"

"Yeah. Kevin. The T.A. for my marine ecology class."

"Julia. That's Kevin Beale. As in, Beale Partners. His dad is John Beale."

"Okay. Who the hell is John Beale?"

Tiffany looked nearly apoplectic at Julia's stupidity. "Beale Partners. The Silicon Valley venture capital firm. He has forty million dollars, or something like that."

Julia looked in the direction that Kevin had gone. "Okay, so his dad is loaded. I've never heard of him before."

"No, Julia," said Tiffany. "*Kevin* has forty million dollars. In trust. Just waiting for him."

In truth, Tiffany had stunned Julia to silence. But as soon as she recovered, she said casually, "I don't see what the big deal is."

"Julia! Out of this whole university of women shamelessly throwing themselves at him, he's walking around with *you*."

"You're right, that is shameless. He's engaged."

"So what? His fiancée is in New York."

"So you knew he was engaged?"

"Of course I did. Everybody knows that."

"Well I'm engaged too, you know."

"And your fiancé is in San Francisco. Meanwhile, you're here. Kevin's here. And you do seem like his type."

Julia laughed. "What type is that?"

"You know… the brainy type."

Julia sensed that Tiffany did not consider "brainy" to be a compliment. "Tiffany, he wasn't 'walking around with me.' I was only asking him a question during his office hours. And I'm not into wrecking another woman's life."

"Oh, don't worry; he's not going to dump her for you. I'm just talking about having a little fun."

In spite of herself, Julia felt offended. Was it really so impossible that Kevin might seriously consider her?

Tiffany must have read the look on Julia's face, because she said, "You do know who his fiancée is, don't you?"

Julia shrugged. "I know she works for the DeSmet Family Foundation in New York."

Once again, Tiffany looked at her cross-eyed. "Babe, she doesn't work for the DeSmet Family Foundation. She *is* the DeSmet Family Foundation." When Julia still drew a blank, she prompted, "Nicole DeSmet? Banking heiress? Trustee of the whole freaking thing?"

"Well, I guess that settles it, then. He's not ditching the heiress for some trash from the Sunset. And if it turns out he's not in love with her, he can just drown his sorrows in all that money."

At first, everything went according to plan. William exhausted the phone cards Julia gave him, and she sent him letters each week. She came up for her birthday and the holidays, since William couldn't get away from work, and they spent as much of that time together as they could.

After the holidays were over, their parents balked at the credit card bills, and they had to call each other less frequently. The demands of their coursework intensified. Her letters became more sporadic. Sometimes she forgot when it was her turn to call him. And when he called, she let it ring if she was studying or asleep.

On the rare occasions that they did connect, her talk was full of the work she was doing and the people she was meeting down there. She found herself telling him more and more frequently about Kevin.

"I'm going to help him introduce an anemone into his tank," she told William one afternoon in February.

There was a long pause. "At his apartment?"

"No, in the men's restroom of the Life Sciences building."

Julia's laughter caught in her throat when William didn't laugh along with her. He said, "Are you sure that's a good idea?"

"What?"

"Going to his apartment."

"You're not jealous, are you?"

"No," he said slowly, "but how well do you know this guy?"

"Good God, I'm not as stupid as I look. I wouldn't go there if I didn't know him really well by now. Besides, I've been there before."

Another two-beat rest. "You've been to his apartment before?"

"Yeah, many times. At first it was because his fish were sick, and none of the suggestions I made were helping. So I went to check it out for myself, and it turned out it was the activated carbon he was using." When William still said nothing, she added, "Look, maybe if I help this guy with his fish, he'll help me get into that internship I've been wanting. It turns out he's going to be the coordinator this year. Besides, he's really very nice. He's pretty much the only friend I have down here."

William said nothing more, so she decided to change the subject. "What about you?"

"What about me?"

These days it felt like pulling teeth, trying to get him to tell her anything about himself. "How's school? How's the restaurant?"

"Fine."

She considered prompting him for more information, but by now she knew that if he had anything to tell, he would. Going to school for Hospitality Management just wasn't his passion. Working at the restaurant wasn't, either. He was perfectly content to be good enough at something, and to be with Julia. He didn't seem to want anything more out of life.

Julia came home for spring break. After a hike to the top of the hill where he had given her the mermaid necklace, William stood behind her, his arms clasped around her waist, looking out over the city.

"I have to tell you something," she began. Steeling her nerves, she turned to face him and clasped his hands. "Kevin came through for me. I got an internship off the Channel Islands this summer. It's so competitive that I really didn't think I was going to get it. It's almost unheard of for an underclassman."

"That's great news," he murmured. "But how many weeks will you be there?"

Her expression changed. "The whole summer."

He dropped her hands, turned and strode away from her a few feet, his hands in his pockets.

She waited, butterflies in her stomach, then said gently, "Will."

He turned to face her now. "I should have listened to my gut. I'm coming down there this summer."

She shook her head. "I'll be staying on the islands."

He gave a little huff of frustration, and frowned off into the distance.

She moved toward him, touched his arm. "It's three months out of our whole lives. Please don't ask me not to do it."

His expression softened. "I would never do that." He picked up her hand, touched the ring on her finger. "I don't care how long I have to wait."

She left him expecting to see her in mid-June before she started her internship. Then she called one afternoon after her finals were over.

The first question out of his mouth was, "When will you be in town?"

Her stomach tied itself in knots. "Will, there's something I have to tell you. I'm afraid you're not going to like it."

"Okay?"

"Kevin wants me to stay and help with the preparations for the internship on the Channel Islands."

A long pause. "You're not coming home."

"I would be an idiot to say no."

With forced composure, he said, "Do you know what this means? By the time the middle of September rolls around, it will have been six months since we've seen each other."

"Did you really mean it when you said you didn't care how long you would have to wait? Because this opportunity won't wait."

He said nothing for a while, and she wondered if he had really been honest with her. Finally, he said, "I did mean that. But I thought we would at least see each other from time to time. That's what you said when you told me not to come with you to Santa Barbara." He hesitated, then added, "I miss you."

"It's not like this is any easier for me."

"You'll have something to occupy your mind," he said bitterly.

"Yes, I will. Am I supposed to apologize for that? I know you don't know what you want to do with your life and you don't love working in the restaurant. But please don't take your frustration out on me!"

Her sharp tone stunned him to silence. With a pang of guilt, she tried to calm the storm rising in herself and added, "I'm sorry. But I don't like feeling like I have to choose between you and my lifelong dreams."

"I'm not asking you to."

"It sure feels like you are. And I won't do it."

They sat in silence for a while, widening the gulf between their opposite ends of the phone line.

Finally, he said, "I'll come down for a few days before you start your internship. I just want to see you once between now and September."

She sighed. "Even if you come down, I'll be working all day. We'd only have a couple of hours per day to spend together."

"That's fine with me."

She hesitated. "Okay."

So in mid-June, he took his first-ever road trip, solo on his motorcycle, all the way to Santa Barbara. He rented the cheapest motel room he could find, and waited all day until she finally finished her work.

He brought her back straightaway to the motel. Closed and locked the door behind them, then went to stand in front of her. Lifted her face to his.

She couldn't hide her uneasiness from him. He let his eyes do the apologizing. Then he put his hands on her, and in spite of herself, she felt the tension drain from her body.

The next day, he brought her straight to the motel again. But this time, the tension didn't leave her body when he touched her.

She looked up at him. "Is this all we're ever going to do? Is this the only reason you came down here?"

Reluctantly, he let go of her and stepped back. "What do you want to do?"

"Does it matter? I'll know it's not what *you* really want to do."

"That's not true. I want to do whatever will make you happy."

She thought about it for a moment. To her dismay, she had no better idea of how they should spend their time together. She reached up, pulled his face down aggressively to hers in a kiss. Unbuttoned his shirt halfway, then ripped it the rest of the way off of him.

"Wow. What was that?" he asked afterward when he could talk again.

She swung herself off of him, retrieved her bra from the floor. "One more for the road."

"I'll be here one more night."

She shook her head. "I'm going to have to work very late tomorrow."

He was still panting from the sex, and the smile left his face. "So this is it, then? Until September?"

She nodded.

He sat up and looked at her, considering. "Can't you ask for a little time tomorrow? I'll take you out somewhere."

She shook her head. Wriggled herself into her bra, and fastened the clasp at the front. She knew from the look on his face that he knew – she didn't really have to work tomorrow. She was just ready for him to leave.

But he didn't ask any more questions. "I wish I had known that this would be the last time I would see you for three months."

She reached for her T-shirt, pulled it on over her head. Stepped into her jeans.

She felt his hand on her arm and turned to meet his sober gaze. Touching the ring on her finger, he said, "It isn't just about sex, for me. Remember?"

She looked down at the ring, her eyebrows knitting together. A look of horror swept over his face.

"Do you still want to wear it?"

"Of course," she said immediately. "But I need you to understand how important all of this is to me. The work I'm doing here, as well as you."

"Is that what this is about?" He pulled her to him in a hug. "I *do* understand. I promise."

She slept with him that night, and he dropped her off early the next morning at her dorm.

"I guess I'll see you in September, then," he said.

"Yes," she said vaguely.

"I love you," he added.

She hesitated. "I love you, too."

But as he drove away, she turned in the direction of the laboratory. She hoped Kevin would be there so she could get back to work. He would be pleasantly surprised to see her.

"I seem to be always making mistakes," Julia confessed over the phone to William one day in August. "Recently, I almost put a specimen into the wrong holding tank. Kevin caught me just at the last minute; otherwise, the specimen would have contaminated the entire tank. He saved my ass completely."

William pointedly didn't respond to the part about the heroic Kevin. Slowly, carefully, he said, "You always used to say that what you really enjoyed was just going out and looking at the wildlife."

She could feel the annoyance welling in her chest. "Okay."

"Have you ever considered changing your focus just a little bit? Maybe away from strict science, and more toward something like being a naturalist? You know, like being the person who talks to people on board whale-watching expeditions?"

The annoyance overflowed its confines and spilled out through her mouth. "Okay, I get it. You're a guy. You have to try to fix things."

"What does that mean?"

"It means I was really just wanting someone to listen. Maybe reassure me a little bit."

"Well... I am trying to reassure you. Maybe scientist isn't in the cards for you, but naturalist is." When she didn't respond, he added, "I mean, since you said yourself once that what you really enjoy is looking at the animals."

"I don't want to be a naturalist. I want to be a marine biologist."

"Okay. I'm sorry. I shouldn't have opened my big mouth."

"I don't want to sit around talking to people all day about animals. I want to get out there, touch them, get my hands dirty. Help save them."

"That's very noble. I think you should do that."

"Don't patronize me."

He laughed ruefully.

She said, "You just want me to drop out so I'll come home."

"No. I want you to be happy."

She felt her chest deflate. "I'm sorry."

To her own shock, her voice was breaking. Except for when her uncle died, she had never cried in front of him before.

Gently, he said, "Hey. What's the matter?"

"Nothing. I'm just afraid you're right. This has been my dream since I was twelve years old. I'm not the kind of person to just give up on my dreams without a fight. But no matter how hard I try, no matter how hard I work at it, I'm just failing."

There was a long pause. "I don't know what to say to help you. I just really wish I could hug you right now."

But he had hit on exactly the right thing to say. "I wish you could too."

He thought for a moment. "When's the very first day that you're getting back to Santa Barbara?"

"September 15th. Why?"

"Oh, no reason."

"I can't wait to see you."

"Who says I'm coming?"

She laughed. "Okay. I won't see you on September 15th, then."

Late on the afternoon of September 15th, Kevin escorted Julia back to her dorm. As they approached Anacapa Hall, she smiled brightly and said with forced cheerfulness, "Well, it's been great working with you!"

But Kevin read between the lines. "Don't worry about it, Julia. You did fine. And you're only a freshman. There's always next year."

"The way this year went, I'm not sure there's going to be a next year. And if I can't get any more internships or a good recommendation, I'm not sure I'll be going to grad school."

"But you have to," he said with a vehemence that startled her. "You can't let yourself give up that easily."

She considered a moment. "I'm going to stay the course. If it doesn't work out here, I can always apply to another marine biology program."

"Good for you. Don't second guess yourself."

They stood on the sidewalk in front of Anacapa Hall now, and Kevin startled her again by gathering her into a long hug. When he pulled away, he held her by the shoulders a moment. He had a strange look on his face, but he only said, "See you tonight at dinner."

A sudden loud roar assailed them. From the opposite curb, a motorcycle spun around in a U-turn and screeched to a halt right beside them. Julia jumped backward, and then the driver lifted the helmet from his head.

"Will!" Julia's face lit up at the sight of him, but he didn't notice because he was too busy glaring at Kevin.

William swung off the motorcycle and came to stand in front of Kevin, a little too close for comfort. At the look on William's face, Kevin shrank back a bit, glancing back and forth between Julia and William. People walking nearby stopped to stare, anticipating a fight.

"Um... I think I'd better go now," said Kevin.

"Yeah. That would be a good idea," William replied.

With one last wary look at William, Kevin walked as fast as he could in the other direction. Slowly, their disappointed spectators dispersed.

Only then did William turn to glare at Julia. "Where have you been?" he demanded.

"What are you talking about?"

"You told me you were getting back to your dorm at noon. It's four o'clock. I've been waiting here since 11:30."

"How was I supposed to know that? I thought you were coming tomorrow. That's what you told me when we talked last weekend."

"So," he said, ignoring her answer. "Who was that?"

"That was Kevin," she replied, a note of strain in her voice.

William was shaking now. "I knew I should have trusted my instincts. But I didn't want you to think I was a jealous prick."

Julia scowled at him, and refused to answer.

"So it's dinner with Kevin tonight?" He nodded down at her ring. "Why are you even wearing that thing anymore?"

"Will." Her voice trembled with barely-contained fury. "I'm late because I was at the bank, trying to get the ring back from the safe deposit box. I didn't want to damage or lose it during my internship. Oh, and by the way – when we disembarked, we got a visit from Kevin's fiancée, Nicole. Trustee of a little affair out of New York called the De Smet Family Foundation. It was a grant of theirs that made our research possible this season, so we all figured the least we could do was have dinner with her tonight."

She waited until it sank in. Waited for the evidence to show on his face. Then she turned and ran into the dorm. Too late, he ran after her. The door locked behind her.

She froze in horror, watching through the glass as he pounded on the door and shouted her name. A small crowd assembled behind her, staring, whispering. Julia jumped as a resident assistant put a hand on her shoulder.

"Do you want me to call the campus police?"

Panic squeezed the breath right out of Julia's lungs, like a bellows. She ran to her dorm room and locked the door behind her. But she could still hear him banging on the entrance to Anacapa Hall, until a campus police officer made him leave.

A few minutes later, the phone in her dorm room rang. She snatched the cord out of the wall.

Unable to eat or sleep, afraid to even plug the phone back in and call Kevin, she lay in bed and stared at the ceiling.

Finally, at midnight, she reached into the drawer of her dorm room desk. Inside, wrapped in a handkerchief, she found the smooth, flat circle of stone. It had a pink inner section, surrounded by a circle of white, surrounded in turn by an outer ring of green. Just like a slice of watermelon.

"I don't ever want to see you settle for anything less than everything," Uncle Rob had told her. "Just do me a favor, and believe that you deserve it."

At ten o'clock the next morning, she went outside and froze when she saw him waiting there on his motorcycle. When he saw her, he tentatively clambered down from the seat and came halfway up the walkway toward her. He looked as if he hadn't slept much more than she had.

"I just want to talk," he pleaded.

"Then you're going to have to do it right here, in a public place."

He looked aghast. "I would never hurt you."

"I don't know. They say it only keeps on escalating."

"I would never, ever hurt you."

"You looked pretty hell-bent on hurting someone yesterday."

"I could have hurt him, if I had wanted to. But I didn't."

She had no response for that. After a moment, she came down the walkway toward him. "How am I supposed to face Kevin or anyone at my dorm again, after the way you embarrassed me yesterday?"

"I'm sorry."

"Kevin is one of the best friends I've ever had. He's the only person down here who gets me, who likes me exactly the way I am. All these people down here? I'll never fit in with them. The other people in my internship? They think the only reason I lasted at all is because I'm sleeping with Kevin. Which I'm not, by the way, so don't even start."

"I know that."

"You need to get a life."

His brows knit together. "What?"

"You always have some excuse for why you can't do the things you want to do. You can't make a living as a fisherman. You don't have the personality to be a photographer. You're not good enough to be a poet or a songwriter. All just excuses, so you don't have to try and then maybe fail."

"What does this have to do with anything?"

"I don't know. Maybe if you found something besides another person for your life to revolve around, you wouldn't freak out when you see me with someone who happens to have a Y chromosome."

She could tell that she had smitten his pride. That it wanted him to be angry, to tell her how presumptuous she was, assuming that his life revolved around her. That he wasn't sure whether to let his pride or his humility win, until he saw her coming toward him, wrestling the ring off of her finger.

"No," he said, springing forward, trying to stop her from taking it off. She wrenched herself away from him. Glared at him, and took it the rest of the way off. Held it out to him.

"Please, let's go someplace private to talk," he whispered, conscious of the people walking past who either stared or tried not to stare. "We can't talk about this here."

"What's the matter, too proud to say it in front of everyone? You didn't have too high an opinion of my pride yesterday."

"Please," he begged her. "Just come with me. You have to know I would never hurt you."

She said nothing, just held out the ring.

"I'll take it, but only if you come with me and let me talk to you. If you still want me to keep it after I talk to you, I will."

Anger, fear, and compassion waged battle within her as he continued to beg her, "Please." Finally, reluctantly, she nodded. He took the ring, put it in his pocket, and led her to his motorcycle. She put on her own helmet and refused to let him help her onto the back.

He drove her to the motel. Let them both inside his room and invited her to sit in a chair. Knelt in front of her on the floor, and put his head in her lap.

"My life doesn't revolve around you," he said, "but you're the most important part of it."

"Stand up."

He didn't stand, but he lifted his head. "I know you're afraid I'm going to hurt you. But it's not in my nature to hurt people. Think about Kevin yesterday. Why in God's name would I ever hurt you when I wouldn't touch him?"

"No, you don't hurt people. You just bully them with your six feet four inches and your big loud macho motorcycle."

He seized her hands. "When we shared those two classes together in our freshman and sophomore years, I always loved the spunky way you shut down those assholes. The ones who called you Horsey Face, and Mosquito Bites. 'You really can't take your eyes off me, can you?' 'I hate to break your heart, but don't start picking out curtains yet.' The whole class would laugh, and sometimes the guys would talk a little more smack just to save face, but then they usually moved on to someone else."

"What does this have to do with anything?" she interrupted.

"Because at first, that was the only thing I admired about you. But then there was your smile. I never noticed until you started coming in to Cardone's. You kept turning that smile on me even though I did absolutely nothing to encourage it. In fact, I think I did everything in my power to discourage it. But that smile… You just never gave up on me. And then there you were, turning that smile on some Cat Stevens doppelganger with glasses."

In spite of herself, she could feel her anger circling the drain. She knew he could see it happening. He squeezed her hands, his eyes intense and earnest.

"Please don't let this be it. You have to know how wrong that would be. Think of everything we've been through the past two years."

He put his head back in her lap. After a minute, she put her fingertips in his hair, caressing his scalp. He looked up, his forehead creased with anguish. The eyes that met his were grave now, with no trace left of anger.

He reached into his back pocket, pulled out the ring. Grabbed her hand, slipped it onto her finger again and held it there, as if to keep it from coming off again. He scooted forward and pulled her forehead down to touch his. Laced his fingers through hers.

She listened to his breath coming quick. Felt her body responding to it. It was an exquisite contrast, the almost transcendent joy of her forgiveness, coming so close on the heels of her anger.

He waited for her to lift his mouth to hers before he moved up to her, gathered her up. He helped her undress, taking time to kiss every little part of her body that he uncovered, until she stood before him in nothing but the mermaid necklace and her ring. Then he snatched his clothes off as fast as he could. The endorphins surging through both of them made her weigh nothing at all. He lifted her like a feather, wrapped her legs around his hips. Moaned with the sheer joy of being inside of her. The sounds he made when she thrust back against him sent lights flickering through her field of vision.

He spun her around, laid her down on the bed. He stayed on top, delaying the inevitable as long as he could, and then flipped her around on top of him. Held her hands, let her push back against them. Watched her body as she moved fast on him, breathing raggedly, until she sensed his explosion coming and jammed her hips down to meet it.

Completely immobilized, he watched her lay alongside him, run her fingers down his torso and back up again. She kissed him on the mouth, more and more insistently. As soon as he could, he pulled her up onto his mouth. Slipped his fingertips inside of her at the same time, and the sweat beaded up on her skin. She stiffened, bore down on him and forgot to mind what she said or what sounds she made.

But the tension in her body told him that she was far from done, so he flipped her down onto her back, draped her legs across his shoulders. She dropped her head back onto the pillow, gripped by wave after wave, until her body had nothing left to give up.

By then he was already hard again, but he let her float for a while in the haze. As soon as he dared, he climbed on top of her and let her rest while he tried to satisfy his seemingly insatiable need.

Food became a secondary concern. When low blood sugar made it unavoidable, he ordered a pizza so they wouldn't have to leave. He sat her in his lap, both of them stark naked, and she laughed with him at their attempts to feed each other pizza. They lost patience after one slice apiece, and made love right there in the chair.

When the sun went down, and their bodies were tapped out, he held her against his side, kissing her mouth, massaging her hair.

He whispered, "You have every part of me. My heart, my body and my soul. And you always will."

"I love you so much," she murmured, and it gave her pain to say it because she had a feeling it would be the last time she would.

A week later, William called to make plans for Julia's birthday.

"I'm not going to be able to get away for my birthday," she said. "I have too much work to do if I ever want to recover from this."

"From what?"

"I got bad feedback from my internship."

"Oh, Julie. I'm so sorry." When Julia said nothing more, he added, "If you want to get together another weekend, we can."

"Will."

Her stomach was churning, nauseous. This was it – she was going to have to make up her mind. Even at this very moment, she wasn't sure it was the right thing to do. What she said in the next few moments could alter the entire direction of her life. Of his life.

"Will," she said. "It was a mistake."

After a long pause, William said, "What?"

"I'm sorry."

Another long pause ensued. "Julie, *what* was a mistake?"

"You know what I'm talking about."

"I want to hear you say it." When she still said nothing, he prompted, "Is it Kevin?"

"It's not Kevin." Drawing a deep breath, she added, "I told you already. I need to focus on school if I ever want to recover from this."

"And I told you already, I won't get in your way."

"My uncle once talked to me about you," she said gently. "He told me that if it's meant to be, the details will work themselves out. Well, the details aren't working themselves out. I can't offer you the time and attention you deserve and still do what I need to do. Not without completely losing the person I am apart from you."

A couple of minutes of silence ensued. Julia did not try to interrupt it. She knew he needed that time to absorb the truth of what she had said.

Eventually, he asked, "Are you still wearing the ring?"

"No."

There was a puff of air on the other end of the line, as if her words had taken his breath away, and his voice along with it. Eventually, she added, "I'll give it back."

"I don't want it. Do whatever you want with it." After another long silence, he added, "I'm not going to stalk you, Julie. If you want me, I'm here. If you want me to come to you, just say the word."

Her voice cracked. "Okay."

Even so, before giving up completely, he mailed a package to her dorm in Santa Barbara.

Julia's father updated her sporadically on what William was doing.

"Remember your old boyfriend, William?" he asked her not long after they broke up. As if she could ever forget. "He dropped out of college, and now he's working here full-time as a line cook."

Julia's heart sank at the news. But not as much as it did a year later, when her father told her he had moved to Alaska to work on the crab boats.

"Isn't that dangerous?" Julia asked, careful not to let her voice betray too much of the terror she truly felt.

"Very. But the risk to reward ratio is very high. If he doesn't get himself killed, he could make himself a ton of money in a very short time."

She heard nothing more about him for five years after that. Then one day, out of the blue, her father said to her again, "Remember your old boyfriend William?"

Her heart skipped a beat, in spite of the fact that she was married to Kevin by then.

"Yeah?"

"He's back from Alaska now."

"Oh. What's he up to nowadays?"

"Working in my kitchen again."

"What?" Julia could not hide her astonishment. "Why?"

"I don't know, because I'm sure he made himself a fortune up there, but I'm glad to have him. He's the only white guy I've ever seen who works harder than a spic. Of course after the Alaska crab boats, my kitchen must seem like a vacation to him."

And a year or so before Kevin left her for the first time, her father casually said, "Remember William? He's still here."

"Really? What's he doing?"

"Working grill now, or sometimes rounds cook. He's the best damn line cook I've got."

"Then why is he still a line cook?"

"Because he's a soldier, not a general. And because I pay to keep him there."

For some reason, it made Julia sad that he was still trapped there when, as she told herself, she had moved on so thoroughly.

Every once in a while over the years, she heard the song Wish You Were Here on the radio, and then she thought of him. It meant something completely different to her now than it did back then, when he sang it to her in his room. Now, it felt more like an indictment. She imagined him working in her father's restaurant as she pulled into the garage of her house in Menlo Park, and quickly changed the station.

2012, PART II

Julia lugged two suitcases upstairs to her old bedroom in her parents' house. In a way, it was comforting to be back here in these somewhat shabby, close quarters. All the clean space on the Peninsula had always made her nervous.

Through the bedroom window, Julia caught sight of her son Robert playing alone on the back patio with his new remote-controlled car. She found her daughter's backpack already on one of the twin beds, but no sign of Paige herself. With her pulse pounding in her throat, she dropped the suitcases on the floor and ran to the living room.

Her mother came upstairs then, and Julia croaked, "Mom—"

"She's downstairs, watching TV."

Relief made Julia weak, and she flopped onto the sofa. Her mother emerged a moment later from the kitchen with a cup of tea, which Julia accepted.

"You look terrible," her mother said, taking a seat alongside Julia.

Julia absently swirled the tea bag in the cup. "Thanks."

"Cioppino and bread for dinner, once you all get settled in," her mother offered gently. "I brought some home from the restaurant last night."

Cioppino. Had she really forgotten? She must have; Julia knew her mother could not have been so insensitive at a time like this on purpose.

Julia must not have had her poker face on, because her mother said, "Between the church rummage sale and getting the house ready for you guys, I didn't have time to go to the store."

"Of course not," said Julia, patting her mother's knee with a pang of guilt. "You and Dad are so good to put us up here while my house sells."

Her mother waved her hand, as if it were nothing. "You can stay here forever, as far as I'm concerned."

"The least I can do for you guys is make a run to the grocery store, so we're not eating you out of house and home. I'll pick up something for dinner."

"Can you get my Metoprolol from the pharmacy while you're there?"

"Anything you need, Mom. Just make a list."

After finishing her tea, Julia rose from the couch to go unpack her suitcase, and her mother said, "I forgot to tell you that Alison is coming for dinner tonight."

Julia felt some of the weight lift from her shoulders, and smiled. It would give her something to look forward to. She didn't dread talks with her sister the way she did with her mother.

While her mother drew up a shopping list, Julia returned to the bedroom to unpack her suitcase. She could never trust Paige to stay at home with her mother while she went to the grocery store. And Paige would put up even more of a fuss if Julia singled her out but allowed Robert to stay home. There was no way around it – she'd have to bring both of them with her.

As she laid the folded clothes in the dresser, she caught sight of herself in the mirror. Her cheeks were hollow gorges. Dark smudges ringed her eyes, and her scalp had sprouted three gray hairs. But there was nothing she could do about it right now. Dinner was only a couple of hours away.

After her mother handed her the shopping list, Julia dragged herself downstairs to the in-law unit. It was as musty as ever, and the only light came from the TV screen, where scantily-clad female backsides gyrated to a skull-throbbing beat. Paige slouched in front of it on the old sofa that had once lived upstairs when Julia was a kid.

"Grandma needs her medicine and some groceries for dinner," Julia began wearily. When Paige said nothing, she added, "We're all going together."

"*I'm* not," Paige replied, scowling at the TV screen. The dark hair she had pulled back into a ponytail still bore traces of the magenta dye that Julia had made her wash out.

Julia snatched the remote and switched off the TV. "I'm afraid you are."

Paige sucked her teeth and threw herself back against the sofa cushions. "Why can't you just let me stay here by myself?"

"We discussed this after the last time you ran away."

"I told you, I'll never do it again."

"I know you won't, because you're coming with us. Besides, this way you can pick what you want from the grocery store. Otherwise you'll have to put up with what I buy for you."

Julia guessed, correctly for once, that such an argument might hold some sway with a thirteen-year-old. But that didn't stop Paige from grousing the whole way over the indignity of having to accompany her family.

And she was in rare form that day. Four-year-old Robert was more than happy to practice reading labels, pull items off the shelf, and drop them into the shopping cart. But Paige spent the entire time complaining about everything from the temperature in the store, to the paleness of the strawberries, to the fact that the milk did not expire late enough for her.

In line at the pharmacy, Paige shoved a six pack of silver and red cans in Julia's face. "Mom, can I get some of these energy drinks?"

"Is that a joke?"

"All the kids at school drink it."

"If ever there was an argument for you not to, that's it."

"Why not?" Paige demanded.

"If all the kids are drinking it, then I feel very sorry for the teachers who have to try to teach them something."

"Jesus, Mom; I thought you said I should come with you so I could pick whatever I want. Are you just going to say no to every fucking thing?"

"Watch your mouth! Where did you pick up language like that?" hissed Julia, glancing around to see if anyone else had heard them.

But unfortunately, someone *had* heard them. Someone who was almost the last person Julia would ever have wanted to hear them.

Ann Quinn stood in the antacid aisle, gaping in disgust at Paige. She looked up, searching for the mother of this profane creature. When she spotted Julia, her mouth snapped shut and her eyes narrowed.

Julia drew herself up and swallowed the lump rising in her throat. And then Robert ran up to Julia, waving a small box with colorful fruit pictured all over it. "Mommy, can I have these candies?"

Before Julia had time to register Robert's mistake, Paige startled her with a loud guffaw. "I'd check that word again if I were you, Robert. Those aren't candies – they're flavored condoms!"

While Paige convulsed in laughter, Ann's eyes locked on Robert in surprise. More than surprise – shock, really. Julia had just a moment to wonder – did Ann know that she now had a son? Ann's jaw tightened, and her grim eyes met Julia's again.

Well, thought Julia. Now she knows.

Julia snatched the condoms from Robert and recovered enough of her voice to say, "Put those energy drinks away, Paige." She fled the line at the pharmacy and was useless for the rest of the shopping trip, unable to find anything on the shelves. As her children sensed weakness, their unruly behavior escalated. Finally, only part of the way through her mother's shopping list, she gave up and steered the cart into the checkout line, training her gaze to the ground, determined to avoid any further contact with Ann or anyone else in the store.

As usual, Julia heard her sister before she saw her. Loud indie rock blared through the open window of Alison's car as she parked. She slammed the door, clip-clopped up the walkway and burst into their parents' house, bellowing, "Where's my baby sister? I come bearing fat, sugar, and booze."

Julia left Robert with his remote-controlled car on the back patio and made her way inside to the entry hall. Alison carried a pastry box and a paper bag from a liquor store in one arm, kicked off her shoes, and flung the other arm around Julia's shoulders.

"How are you holding up?" Alison whispered into her ear.

Julia shrugged. "I hope you brought gin."

Their mother appeared then at the top of the stairs. "No booze talk, please. The neighbors might hear you."

"Oh, stop the presses! I can see the headlines about you now, Mom: 'Karen Dunphy – head of an Irish family that drinks!'" retorted Alison. She gave Julia's arm one supportive squeeze before springing upstairs to suffocate their mother in a bear hug. Robert bounded inside from the back garden to clamor around Alison for the pastry box, and Julia's mother whisked Alison's mystery bottle off to the kitchen.

Amidst the din, Alison said to Julia, "Paige is hiding?"

"Downstairs, with her easel."

"Should I even try?"

"I don't think even you can breach that armor tonight. You're welcome to try, though."

"Give me a job," Alison insisted. "Anything."

Julia considered. "Help Mom make dinner, and put the kids to bed for me?"

Alison contemplated this for a moment, then threw back her shoulders with a plucky grin and called, "Mother, drinking alone is a sign of a problem!"

She swept into the kitchen, a nose-pierced, pixie-cut amalgam of punk rock and hipster. A welcome chaos to distract everyone from Julia and her problems.

It was Alison who rounded up her niece and nephew and shuttled them off to bed early, with only a few under-the-breath mutterings from Paige. She installed Julia on the back patio to nurse a gimlet, only permitting her inside to kiss Robert goodnight. Julia dared not open the door to the darkened room she shared with Paige.

When Julia returned to the patio, Alison clinked her glass against Julia's and declared, "I deserve a 'Cheers' for a job well done."

Once Julia settled into her chair, Alison did not beat around the bush. "Now, Julie. Tell me everything I don't already know. Where's Kevin?"

"Ecuador, this time."

Alison shook her head in dismay. "Why can't he just leave you for another woman, like a normal man? Was he going to sneak off and put you in a bind, like last time?"

"No, this time he had the decency to let me know he was leaving."

"Christ, Julie. Why am I only hearing about this now? Why did I have to hear about it from Mom?"

Julia swirled the drink around in her glass, but said nothing.

"You thought I'd say, 'I told you so,'" Alison ventured. "I gave you a hard time when you reconciled with him. I guess I can't blame you for not confiding in me."

"You were right, though."

"No. You had reasons for doing what you did, and you had every right to expect it to go the way you thought it would. So then tell me – how exactly did all of this go down?"

"After he started writing his dissertation, he got a chance to do some more field studies in the Galapagos. He saw it as a once-in-a-lifetime opportunity, but it was going to take at least a year. There was no way me and the kids could come with him."

"A year," Alison echoed.

"Or more, maybe." Julia took a sip from her glass. "You know that was just the final straw in a tall heap of straws. After we reconciled, he actually believed that having another baby would make everything better. But of course we've been pulling away from each other at least since Robert was born, if not before."

"But how are you going to handle the divorce paperwork with him being in the Galapagos?"

"Already taken care of. With the postnup we signed, it's pretty straightforward."

"Thank God." Alison swigged her gimlet and ventured, "What are your plans? Please tell me you're not living with Mom and Dad forever."

"No; I'm just here while the house is being staged and sold." A motorcycle blasted down the street, drowning Julia's voice. After it passed, she added, "I may just leave the Bay Area completely."

"Why? Your house will sell quickly. Between that and the investments, you can set up right here in the city."

"I know. I have other reasons for wanting to make a fresh start."

Alison was silent a moment, and Julia knew that she knew the one reason to whom she was referring.

"He doesn't work at the restaurant anymore, Julie. He doesn't even work at the processing plant. You're not likely to see him."

Julia did not know where to look or how to feel. Was she glad, or sorry? And – did she want to know where he was?

Reading her mind as usual, Alison said, "He's doing that whale-watching thing." When Julia continued silent, Alison added, "It worked out."

Julia's mind and heart were a riot of conflicting feelings which all settled on bittersweet. He made a go of it, and it worked out after all.

Alison seemed to sense that Julia needed a few moments. After gulping the last of her drink, Julia cleared her throat.

"I saw his mother in the grocery store today."

Alison sat up straighter. "For real? How did *that* go down?"

Julia filled her in on all the gory details.

"Okay, that does sound brutal," Alison acknowledged. "But why do you care what Ann Quinn thinks?"

"I don't care so much what she thinks. It's what *he* will think that bothers me."

"Do you really think Ann would tell him?"

"I don't know. Probably not. But if she does, I'm sure he'll feel plenty of relief that he escaped being the stepfather of such a brat."

Alison gave her an incredulous look. "That would be the last thought to cross his mind."

"That's right. Depending on what else she tells him, let's consider everything from his perspective. Not only did I hurt him, but I then went on to have another child with my husband."

"Julie, why don't you let me talk to him?"

"About what?"

Alison put her hand over Julia's. "Believe it or not, I'm still in touch with Mike from time to time. I can get to him through Mike. I can get him to talk to you."

But Julia shook her head. "He told me never to come back. He said he'd never believe another word I said."

Alison looked pained. "Let me tell him everything."

"No. I won't put him on the spot like that. Especially not after all this time has passed. He has every right to hate me. I should leave him alone."

Alison released Julia's hand and leaned back in her seat. "As usual, I don't understand your refusal to even consider the possibility of happiness. But hey, if that's your choice, just don't sit around pining for him for the next twenty years. You've got to live your life. And this time, make it *your* life."

Julia frowned. "What are you talking about?"

"I'm talking about doing something for yourself, for a change. You have the freedom to do whatever you want in life, Julia. You owe it to the universe to do it."

After her disastrous outing to the grocery store with the kids – after Alison delivered her admonishment, and went home – Julia had started the next morning with two open browser windows. One contained a search for "Castro Aquarium Service," the other a search for "How to write a business plan."

Soon, she had the barest skeleton of a business plan for a revived Castro Aquarium Service.

Julia wasn't sure where her next act in life would play out. She didn't want to take another paralegal position in the city, only to have to quit a short time later when she opened her aquarium business. Working at Dunphy's had never been much more than a way to fill her time, feel useful, and earn a nominal wage. She certainly didn't need the money anymore. But at a time like this, she desperately needed something to keep her mind off of herself, and her regrets.

Her father was always grateful for the help, so she didn't anticipate any objection from him. But when she approached him that Monday morning on the subject, he gave her a quizzical look.

"As long as you're prepared to steer clear of Cardone's for a while," he said. "Though I'm not sure how much help you'll be to me if you can't go over there."

"For a while?"

"I can't be sure how long it will last."

"How long *what* will last?"

He looked at her like she was an idiot. "William working there."

Julia's jaw dropped. "Alison said he doesn't work there anymore!"

He blinked. "I'm sorry, but I thought you knew."

"Knew what?"

"Jim Quinn has esophageal cancer. He can't work. Ann is out, too, taking care of him. William and Kelly are holding down the fort over there."

"How long has this been going on?"

"Well, Jim was diagnosed about four months ago, but he really took a turn for the worse a couple of weeks ago. That's when Ann took a leave of absence too, and William and Kelly took over."

Julia tossed her hands in frustration. "Why would I have known about this?"

"I'm surprised your mother didn't tell you. Is this going to be a problem?"

"Yes! I can't work there if I'm going to bump into him every day."

He lifted his newspaper again. "Whatever you think is best."

Julia gaped at the crown of his head, visible over the top of the newspaper. "I'm sorry to hear about Jim."

"So am I," he replied without lowering the paper. "He's going to die, you know."

"He is?"

"Esophageal cancer has one of the worst prognoses. And then nobody knows what will become of the business. It might have to be sold. It doesn't seem likely that Mike or William would want it. Maybe Ann and Kelly could keep it afloat."

"That really makes me sad."

Julia's father nodded. "The end of an era."

There didn't seem to be anything left to say. Julia left him alone then, but as she considered what to do, she realized she didn't know what was best.

She decided that, for now, she would go ahead and work at the restaurant. If she bumped into William by chance, so be it. She would not let him drive her away before she was good and ready to go, but she would not engineer any meetings between them.

Yet throughout her first two weeks at the restaurant, she found herself wandering out the back door and onto the pier. It was the spot where they had stood almost nineteen years ago, each of them courting the other, but neither of them really sure what was happening.

It was the same spot where they sat once again, nearly six years ago, the first time Kevin left. Gazing together across the water at a catamaran. Hinting at possibilities. It felt like it had happened moments ago, and yet she had no idea if the catamaran she saw now was the same one they had looked at then, or even whether she was looking for it in the correct slip. With a pang of grief, she realized that she had tried so hard to forget that she had actually succeeded.

2006

After Kevin left her the first time, Julia could not stand to remain in that echoing house in Menlo Park, with all its attendant responsibilities, in that neighborhood that had always felt alien to her. And with Paige unable to sleep at night, crying for her father, Julia wondered if they all needed a change of scenery.

"Why don't you move in with us for a while?" her mother suggested. "The only thing I'm doing since my heart attack is volunteering at the church, and I'm bored out of my mind. I can help you with Paige."

So Julia covered the furniture, turned off the lights, and arranged for someone to care for her fish while she was away. She packed up the few belongings she and Paige could bring with them, and moved into her parents' house.

After settling in, Julia brought Paige straight to the downstairs addition.

"You brought that?" Paige said with a faint smile, gesturing to the painting Julia had hung on the wall. Julia had framed it together with the purple "Grand Prize" ribbon Paige had won at her school's cultural arts contest.

"Youngest winner in school history," Julia reminded her, rumpling her hair. "Look what else I brought."

"My easel," Paige murmured.

"The walls in my old bedroom are looking pretty bare. Will you paint me something to fill them?"

Paige got right down to work, and Julia left her smiling. She returned upstairs to the kitchen, where she found her mother chopping onions for dinner.

"Can I help you with that, Mom?"

"No thanks," her mother replied, setting the knife down and moving to the tea kettle on the stove. Casting a wry smile at Julia, she added, "Though maybe I should let you get some practice, if you're really serious about going back to work at the restaurant."

Julia laughed. "Don't worry; I won't be doing any cooking. I'm just helping Dad with all the stuff you used to do. And that's only until I can get a proper job and my own place to live."

Handing Julia a cup of tea, her mother asked, "What kind of a job are you going to look for?"

"I have no idea."

"Well, I do. I have a very obvious idea. Why don't you start an aquarium service company?"

Julia dismissed it with a wave of her hand.

"Why not? You have two amazing aquariums in that house of yours. You and Kevin practically made a full-time job out of it already. You have connections from all the societies you belong to and all the conferences you go to. And you have some experience from your time working with Rob and Tim when you were in high school."

"Yeah, but Mom, starting a business like that takes a lot of time and money. I don't have either of those things right now."

"Why don't you rent the house out while you're not living in it?"

"Because I'd have to either put all our stuff in storage, or rent it furnished and let a tenant trash it. And on top of that, I'd probably have to get rid of my aquariums. Find new homes for all my fish and animals. And I still have no idea where Kevin is or what his plans are. He could show up any day, and then I would have gone to all that trouble for nothing."

"Can't Kevin's family help you in some way?"

"I won't take charity from those people. As far as they're concerned, I'm the prole who ensnared their golden boy."

"That's ridiculous. Don't they know how hard he worked to ensnare you?"

"No. They still blame me for Kevin breaking it off with the heiress."

"But it took him two years after that to finally win you over!"

Julia shrugged. "They have a blind spot, where he's concerned."

Her mother reached across the table and took Julia's hand. "Maybe he fooled us all."

"What do you mean?"

"I don't know. He seemed so down to earth for someone with his background. You were both so passionate about marine biology and saltwater aquariums." Her mother shook her head in dismay. "It really seemed like it was meant to be. I just pray there turns out to be some perfectly good explanation."

"Unless he was kidnapped, what excuse can there be?"

"Julia," her mother said gently, "do you think he's gotten himself in some kind of trouble? With his business dealings?"

"If so, I haven't found out about it yet."

"Then what do you think he was running away from?"

Julia sighed. "I think he was just miserable. He was under a lot of pressure to go into venture capital with his dad when that was never what he wanted to do with his life. I think what he really wanted was to go back to school for marine biology or rejoin the Peace Corps, or something like that."

After a moment's hesitation, her mother asked, "How is Paige holding up?"

"Terrible. She cries every night, and every night I explain it to her all over again."

"Explain what?"

"That it wasn't her fault. That she didn't do anything wrong to make him leave. But you know what a daddy's girl she is."

They sipped their tea in silence for a minute, until they heard the door downstairs open.

"Mom, Grandma, come look!" called Paige.

Julia and her mother filed downstairs. Julia had hung a clothesline on the wall where Paige could clip her paintings while they dried, and three already hung there.

"I know how much you love them," Paige said to Julia, gesturing to an orange sea star hanging on the line, complete with bumps and ridges.

"That's right!" exclaimed Julia, squeezing her around the shoulders. "This is going to make me feel right at home once it's hanging in my room."

"I hear your teacher kept some of your paintings because she's sure you're going to be a famous artist one day," her mother said to Paige.

Julia added, "Her teacher's not going to bother saving for retirement anymore."

Beaming, Paige pointed to another painting hanging on the line. "This is for you, Grandma."

Her grandmother gripped the paper by the corners. "This is the hyacinth growing in my garden, isn't it?"

"I don't know what it's called. I just saw it and I liked it."

"Were you working from a photograph?"

Julia tapped her head. "Her photograph is up here."

"That's amazing, honey," her mother said to Paige. "Thank you."

"And this one," Paige continued, pointing to the juvenile emperor angel fish hanging next to her grandmother's hyacinth, "is for Daddy when he comes home. It's his favorite."

Julia's heart sank. "That's sweet, Paige. Would you like me to keep it in my room for now?"

"Yeah," Paige said, still beaming. "Hang it on your wall, so he'll see it when he comes home."

On Julia's first day at the restaurant, her mother showed her around the kitchen to re-familiarize her with it.

"A lot has changed since you've been here," she pointed out. As they progressed toward the walk-in, she looked suddenly awkward. "Here's an old holdout you might remember."

Julia looked, and saw him. Moving quickly by instinct and reflex, shouting back and forth in both Spanish and English with the other staff.

"He's busy, Mom. Let's keep moving."

Her mother looked relieved, and nodded. She pressed her lips together grimly, and led Julia away to the walk-in.

After the walk-in, there was no avoiding it. Julia had to pass by his station again. But he was gone, replaced by someone else, at least for the time being. She only saw him one other time that night out of the corner of her eye, back at his station, his eyes trained down at the work before him.

The next day, while updating the work schedule, she stood half-hidden where she could watch him as he worked. He was more or less the same William she remembered. The same tousled hair somewhere between blond and brown. The same intense blue eyes, of course. Certainly he was not quite as slim at thirty as he was at twenty. Though he was still lean, his body had filled out to the proportions of a grown man.

He worked with his sleeves rolled up. As he moved, a flash of black on the underside of his forearms caught her eye. Two new tattoos. Between the distance and his quick movements, she could not make them out.

A prep cook walked past, and he called out, "Amanda."

Amanda stopped right in front of him and touched his arm. He leaned into her ear and said something to her that Julia couldn't hear over all the noise in the kitchen. Amanda stepped back, reached into her coat pocket, and pulled out a hair elastic. Began gathering her loose blond hair into a ponytail. His hands never stopped working, but he watched as she took her time, twisting it around and around itself into a knot, tying it in place. It was obvious what she was doing. Playing with her hair showed off her cleavage to advantage. When she was done, she flashed him a flirtatious grin before strutting off.

He watched her go until she was out of sight, a slight smile on his face. Clearly, he had become much more comfortable with flirting in the intervening years.

His eyes abruptly locked on Julia. He held them there in an icy way that he had never directed at her in the past. And he wasn't smiling anymore.

She flinched and ducked around the corner, out of sight.

She spent as much of the rest of the afternoon as possible in the pantries, refrigerators, and freezers, catching up on inventory. At the end of the night, on her way toward the back door, she found William approaching from the opposite direction, loosening the buttons of his white chef's jacket. Interaction was impossible to avoid now.

He slowed his approach and stopped a few feet in front of her. "How are you doing?"

"Okay."

"What are you doing here?"

He really didn't know. She said, "I could ask you the same thing."

There was no reply, no smile. Only that relentless stare.

"I needed a job," she answered.

"Aren't you a marine biologist?"

He really, really didn't know. "Oh, that. Turns out I wasn't much of a scientist, after all. But you probably could have told me that."

Still, he stared. She knew he had a thousand questions, but that he dared not ask any of them. She felt oddly terrified at the sound of her own rambling voice.

"It turns out I was mostly interested in watching marine life, not studying it. So I set myself a new goal. My new goal was to squeeze out a kid, let my husband skip out to a foreign country, and come home to live with my parents and work for my dad. So you see, all my dreams came true, and I have nowhere to go from here but down."

After the initial shock wore off, she saw the corners of his mouth lift a bit. "You haven't changed much."

Her expression hardened, thinking of his interaction with Amanda the prep cook. "You have."

Once again, his expression became as hard as hers. Slowly, he peeled off his coat. The shirt underneath his coat had short sleeves, and she saw the flash of black on the underside of his forearms again. He held the coat in his right hand, down by his side, and she could see the compass tattoo on that arm.

"How long are you staying here?" he asked. Clearly wondering how soon she would clear the hell out of there.

"Only until I can get another job."

Slowly, he switched hands and held the coat in his left hand now, giving her a clear view of that arm.

She felt herself reeling, and forced herself to look away from it. Without another word, he slowly pushed past her, into the break room.

It has nothing to do with me, she told herself repeatedly as she burst out the back door, allowing the tangy air to revive her senses. Really, what are the odds that it actually has anything to do with me?

It had been one of the defining moments of their relationship, the night she showed up in the mermaid costume. But his topless mermaid had her back turned, distinguishing her from the typical pornographic mermaid tattoo, but also obscuring most of her face. It could have been any face. There was no call for Julia to infer that it was some reference to herself. Especially not after the scene she had just witnessed between him and Amanda. Clearly, they had been flirting for a while. Hell, he was probably already fucking her.

He was not the same William of eleven years ago. That William was long gone, and it was her own fault. She had thrown him away with both hands.

That night, Julia stopped into Paige's room to kiss her as she slept. Paige stirred, and mumbled, "Daddy?"

Julia's stomach clenched. "No, honey, it's Mommy."

Even in the dark, Julia saw Paige's eyes open. "Where am I?"

"Grandma and Grandpa's house, remember?"

Paige looked around. "Where's Daddy?"

"He's not here, sweetie. Mommy's here."

Julia watched Paige's expression change as she remembered. "Can we find him?" Paige asked.

"I'm trying."

Julia gathered Paige up as the tears started. She rocked her, stroked her hair, and sang to her until she dropped back to sleep again.

Then she shut herself up in her own room and sat on the edge of the bed a few minutes. She didn't feel good about not kissing Paige when she came home, but maybe it wasn't worth it, risking the waking and the tears.

She felt herself frowning, and wished to God that Kevin could see the grief he had brought down upon his special pet.

On the other hand, she wished he would just stay the hell away. For good.

She looked toward the closet. Considering. Resisting. Finally, she got up and opened the closet door. Pulled out an old shoe box, bound around and around with packing tape. Set it on the bed beside her, and stared at it a while.

She found a pair of scissors. Cut open the tape, and slowly lifted the lid.

She hadn't looked in here for years. Not since shortly after he mailed it to her in Santa Barbara.

She reached inside. Pulled them out, one at a time. Poems and songs that he had written about her, chronicling his growing feelings over the course of two years, the entire time they had known each other. In all that time, she had never even known he was still writing poems and songs, until he mailed them to her.

One after another, she read them. There was no sap or sentimentality to them. An outsider reading them might never have guessed what they were about. But she knew.

Beneath the poems and songs were the photos. Copies of the ones he had given her when they were together, and new ones that she had never seen until he mailed them to her. The one he had taken of them together at Año Nuevo. The ones she had snapped of him alone at Julia Burns State Park. The ones he had taken of her, just before he proposed.

She knew what lay underneath that – a box containing a silver chain with a mermaid pendant. And finally, carefully preserved in a black velvet ring box, his diamond ring.

She had not had the heart to throw it all away. She had sealed it all up and kept it hidden all of these years. Taken it with her, from one home to another.

She had convinced herself that she was in love with Kevin. That yes, William was her first love and would always have a tender place in her heart. But that she was over him, and had moved on with her life.

Except she hadn't. Which was why she still kept this box.

She spent the next several days talking to the lawyers. Enrolling Paige in school. Driving back and forth between the house in Menlo Park and the city, retrieving more things that they needed. Maintaining and enjoying the fish tanks in the house – her one bit of solace in the past couple of months.

When she brought Paige home from school one afternoon, she said, "I have a surprise for you."

She brought her downstairs. As soon as Paige spotted the twenty-gallon fish tank, she squealed and said, "I thought we wouldn't get one until we moved into our new place."

"I decided I just couldn't do without. Besides, I thought this could serve as inspiration for your art," Julia explained.

"Can I help you?" asked Paige.

"Of course. The first thing we need to do is add the live rock."

"What's that?"

"It's coral skeleton. It makes the aquarium look nice, but it also puts in lots of bacteria and other stuff to keep the water nice for the fish. Ready to help me put it in?"

She let Paige put the live rock on the bottom of the tank and add a layer of live sand. "Why are we putting a dinner plate over the sand?" Paige wondered.

"When we pour our saltwater in, the plate will keep the sand from getting all stirred up."

Then Julia directed Paige to a garbage can in the corner of the room, where she had already mixed up a batch of saltwater and tested it. She showed Paige how to slowly pour the saltwater over the dinner plate to fill the tank, and then they hooked up their pumps and filters.

"Now what?" asked Paige.

"Now we have to wait for about a week before we can add any fish."

"Why?"

"Because you have to let the tank cycle. All the bacteria from the live rock have to grow in the water and make it safe for the fish." At the look of disappointment on Paige's face, she added, "Hey, you know what? You're lucky. When I was a kid, we didn't have live rock, and we'd have to wait weeks before we could put any fish into our aquariums."

"Can we bring a sea star from home?"

"Oh no," Julia laughed, rumpling her hair, "this is just a very small tank. Fish only."

"Oh. Well, can I pick the fish then?"

"Sure, but we have to make sure they're the right fish for this tank. We might start with a damselfish; they're pretty strong." Julia peered at her a moment. "Would you like to be in charge of taking care of this tank?"

"Really?"

"It's a lot of work. You'll have to feed the fish twice a day, and help me keep it clean and safe for the fish."

"I can do it," Paige insisted. "I'm going to do this when I grow up."

Julia felt a little pang. "I've told you about my Uncle Rob, haven't I? He was Grandpa's youngest brother."

Paige nodded. "He raised you."

"He and Tim. They used to design and take care of aquariums for other people. I used to work for them, and I just kept on learning over the years."

"That would be fun."

"You think so? Because I've been thinking about starting my own aquarium company."

"Yeah! Then, when I grow up, we can work together."

Julia laughed and kissed her on the forehead. "Another family business. Well, you can't say it doesn't run in our blood."

That night, after Paige went to bed, Julia sat a while at the kitchen table, nursing a cup of chamomile tea. Contemplating.

Eventually, she picked up the phone in the kitchen and dialed her sister's number.

"You had to make a business plan for your bakery, didn't you?"

"Yeah," said Alison. "Why?"

"Teach me everything you know about business plans."

When Julia came back to the restaurant the next week, she studiously avoided seeing William. She trained her eyes to the ground any time she had to pass his station, and escaped out the back door when it was time for her break.

But to her chagrin he was standing there, looking out on the water as he used to do all those years ago. He hadn't seen her yet, so she turned to flee.

"What kind of a job are you looking for?"

Damn it. She faced him, and forced a chipper smile. "Whatever I can get that's legal and requires clothing. I have no work experience."

His eyebrows raised. "Really?"

"Yeah. I've been doing the whole mommy thing all these years."

She searched his eyes for some sign of triumph, mocking, or insincerity of any kind. But she found none.

"I'm sorry the marine biology thing didn't work out for you," he said.

"Well, it's like I told you the other day. Working for my dad became my new lifelong dream, so I forbid you to feel sorry for me. What about you? Did you finish your degree?"

"No." He hesitated. "I worked here for a while, and then I went up to work on the salmon boats in Alaska the next summer. Then, in the winter, I worked on the crab boats."

"My dad told me you had gone to do that."

"He did?"

Julia nodded. "How long did you do that for?"

"A little over five years."

"Why did you come back?"

"Because I finally got hurt. I bought myself a flight on a Coast Guard helicopter to Anchorage, and a week's stay in the hospital. I took it as a sign that it was time to come home."

"A week. How badly were you hurt?"

"Well, I got whacked in the head by a crab pot. It fractured my skull. I had to have surgery, but I was lucky – it didn't do any more damage than that, and a concussion."

Julia felt alarmed by his account. But she said, "And you decided to go back to work as a cook?"

"I came back to work here, since I can pretty much do this job in my sleep."

"You know, you just insulted line cooks everywhere. That's not an easy job."

He looked sheepish. "You're right. But the job does come naturally to me."

"Do you enjoy it?"

"Yes. I've always liked cooking, as you know."

"But it's not this," she replied, gesturing out to the fishing boats.

"No, that's over now. There's even less future in that around here than there was back then." After a moment, he asked, "Did you ever finish your degree?"

"Yes, I finished it. But I never went on to grad school." She didn't bother adding the part about how she found herself pregnant, and got married instead. "And there was no way for me to really use just a Bachelor's degree."

"I can think of one thing you can do with it."

Julia heard a shuffling behind her. Amanda's scowl traveled the length of Julia's body as she passed her by, slinking up to William.

"Hey, Will, I wondered where you disappeared to."

Will. That's when she knew – they really were fucking each other.

William's eyes lingered on Julia a moment longer. Julia retreated back inside the restaurant and didn't hear what he said in response to Amanda.

Jealousy. The very emotion that had driven Julia from William in the first place. Oh, how the tables had turned.

She thought she had exorcised it from her mind, this idea, this smallest hope that William might ever begin to think of her again. But it was now official – there was no hope.

Julia had the next day off of work and spent it moping around the house and snapping at Paige, much to her mother's chagrin. Alison observed this state of affairs when she came over that evening. After dinner, as Paige ran off to play, Alison said, "I think you can put Paige to bed tonight, can't you, Ma?"

Their mother smiled knowingly at Alison. "I sure can."

Julia peered quizzically at her sister.

"You, my dear, are depressed," explained Alison. "It's a state I've seen you in far too much recently. Well, no more. Tonight you're going to get away from it all."

"No, I don't think so."

"Yes, I do think so. Now come on. I'll help you get dressed. You're gonna look like a star."

"I can dress myself, thanks."

"Very well, but I will be inspecting afterward, so don't disappoint me."

Julia donned the only dress she owned anymore that seemed to say "night on the town." She slipped on a pair of heels and, true to her own sense of style, topped it off with a scarf and a hat.

Alison knocked on the bedroom door and entered when bidden. She flicked a critical eye over Julia and said, "Love the jaunty hat and scarf. Hate the dress. Is that really the best you've got?"

"I'm not trying to look like a cougar."

"You're thirty years old; you're not a cougar." Alison went to the closet and rifled through Julia's clothes. "Hmm. That really is the best you've got. Time to go shopping."

"Thanks."

"Hey! Guess who's going to meet us at the pub?"

"The pub?"

"Yeah, of course! We're going to MacGowan's to listen to some live music. So guess who?"

Julia shrugged. "The Queen of England."

"That would be a laugh, this close to St. Paddy's Day. No. Holly."

"Oh, no. Please tell me you didn't."

"Come on! I thought surely of all the people on the planet, she was a safe bet. How long has it been since you've seen her?"

"Not since Gran passed away. Look, I just don't feel like detailing my personal failures to anyone, but especially not to someone who graduated magna cum laude from Stanford Law School. What did you do, tell her my sob story and get her to come out of pity?"

"No, she's totally psyched to see you! Dropped everything to come do it. And she's Holly, for Christ's sake; she's not going to judge you, especially when there's nothing to judge. Now get your coat and purse; we're out of here."

Since MacGowan's was within walking distance, they were there in no time. They went through the front, blooming green with St. Patrick's Day decorations, to the back room so that they could eat and have a little more quiet. They found a seat, ordered some pub grub and were knocking back their pints of stout when Julia heard a voice behind her say, "Holy crap, I can't believe it's really you!"

Julia clambered to her feet and forced a smile as she turned to hug Holly. Holly held Julia by the shoulders and looked her up and down.

"You look exactly the same."

Julia couldn't say the same for her. Her formerly gargantuan, frizzy mane was now smooth and sleek. She had traded her nerdy glasses for a set of contact lenses, and apparently had a wardrobe consultant.

"You look great," Julia said.

Holly waved her hand modestly and pulled up a seat next to Julia. "How are you doing? Alison told me you're living in the city now."

"Living at home with my parents, yeah," Julia replied. Eager to divert the conversation away from herself, she said, "So how is your non-profit going these days? I forget what you do."

"I help immigrants seeking asylum in the United States. I specialize in women who are victims of violence in their home countries." She pulled out her business card and handed it to Julia.

How illustrious, Julia grumbled inwardly. "That's so amazing!"

"It's a lot of hard work, is what it is. What about you? What are you doing?"

"Oh, my sister didn't tell you? Well, let's just say I'm in between jobs."

At that moment, the waitress came to take Holly's order. While she gave it, Julia stared off into space, fuming. The band had arrived and Julia heard them setting up in the next room. She prayed for them to hurry up and start playing already.

When she finished ordering, Holly turned back to Julia. "You know, we've got more work than we can handle at our office. We really need a receptionist and a legal secretary. You could start off in reception, and my paralegal and I could train you on the secretarial aspects of the job over time. It would only be on a part-time basis, but it would get your foot in the door in a law office, if that's something you're interested in."

"Right. Alison put you up to this, didn't she?"

"What? No," Holly insisted, taken aback.

"No!" Alison echoed more vehemently.

Julia could tell that they weren't lying. "Oh, Jesus. I'm sorry, you guys. It's been a rough couple of weeks, and I'm really out of sorts."

Holly squeezed Julia's arm and smiled. "Well, that's what we're here for." She picked up her glass, held it up. "Sláinte."

Julia and Alison clinked their glasses against hers. "Sláinte."

The band began tuning their instruments in the other room. Their food arrived, and while they ate, Alison caught Holly up on her baking business and everything else she was doing. Julia was happy to let them dominate the conversation for a while. Finally the band began playing and conversation became difficult.

It was Irish pub rock, raucous and rollicking, with lyrics celebrating drinking, women, the working class, and Irish nationalism. But it was also practically an orchestra. Julia counted a mandolin, tin whistle, concertina, banjo, and bodhrán amid the usual guitars and drums. After a while, she felt her spirits lifting and ordered another pint of beer.

Alison and Holly followed suit, and after a while even Julia laughed and joined in the conversation with them, shouting above the noise to be heard.

There was a pause in the set. "I'd like to let my brother do the honors for this next song, since he wrote it," the lead singer said in a low voice, as if to bring things down a notch.

They played the intro to the song, more of a ballad than anything they had played previously, and a new voice piped up with the lyrics. A voice she knew like her own, singing lyrics she had just pulled out of a shoebox a few days ago. Lyrics she had read and re-read until she knew them by heart.

"Julie, are you okay?"

Julia heard her sister's voice, and sprang to her feet. She wove her way through the room, through the wide doorway and into the front room, and around the corner of the stage to stand in front of it.

Unless she was hallucinating, it really was him in center stage, playing the guitar and singing the lyrics he had written for her all those years ago. Around him stood Mike, who she now realized had been singing lead all this time, as well as bunch of other guys she didn't know.

Next to the ever-colorful Mike, William looked positively sedate, quietly playing and singing in a black Guinness T-shirt, with only his two black tattoos showing on his forearms. As she gazed entranced, he instinctively looked up and locked eyes with her.

The guitar screeched.

Hardly missing a beat, Mike stepped up and took over the vocals. William stepped back, stared down at the stage, and resumed strumming the melody, but did not try to sing again.

Mortified, Julia bolted back to the other room and snatched up her purse.

"Julie, what's the matter?" Alison said.

"I have to leave. Please meet me outside. I don't want to walk home by myself."

She stumbled out the back door of the pub, emergency exit be damned. Ran around to the front of the building. Trembled uncontrollably as she waited for her sister.

Moments later, Alison burst through the front door. "I saw," she said, gripping Julia's arms to steady her.

"He wrote that song for me."

"He did?"

Julia nodded.

"Wow. Julie, if ever there was a sign of something that was meant to be, this is it. 'Of all the gin joints in all the towns in all the world.'"

"Alison, Casablanca ended sadly."

"Oh, hell, Julie. You have to come inside. Talk to him."

"I'm not going to make him mess up again."

"Oh, that was you, huh?" Damn Alison's cheeky grin. "Fine, I'll hide you from view. Holly's still in there; we can't leave her alone.

When the show is over, we'll go talk to them. I'd love to catch up with Mike, anyway."

"I bet you would." But Julia shook her head. "Look, Alison, what's the point? He's a thirty year old who plays in a rock band. I'm a single mom. Actually, I'm still married, remember?"

"You still love him. And he's still singing about you. You're getting a divorce. What's the problem?"

Julia groaned in exasperation. "I'll come back in, for Holly. But I won't talk to him."

"Fine. Walk behind me. You don't want to make him fall off the stage."

Julia complied, hiding behind her sister as best as she could as she passed through the front room. When they got back to their table, Holly said, "Is everything okay?"

"Julia had a bit of a shock. It's okay now," said Alison.

But it wasn't okay. Julia twisted her glass in circles on the table top, blind and deaf to everything except the band playing in the next room. Knowing that their set would end at any moment, and her sister would try to make her go talk to him.

When it finally did end, and Mike made his plug to the audience, Alison rose from the table and said, "Shall we greet the band, ladies?"

"Oh," said Holly, "do you know them?"

"In a manner of speaking."

Julia followed Alison and Holly reluctantly into the bar area. Alison led them quite deliberately in front of the stage, where the guys were packing up. She said something to Mike, whose face lit up in recognition.

"Holy shit!" he cried, leaping off the stage and wrapping Alison in a hug. "Long time no see!"

"You remember my sister?"

Mike turned to Julia with wide eyes. "Oh, wow. Hey, Julia." He glanced back apprehensively at William, who occupied himself with wrapping up cords.

"And this is Holly," added Alison.

Mike shook Holly's hand, then turned back to Alison with a big smile. Here he was, approaching his mid-thirties, wearing his hair in liberty spikes. If anything, he had only added to his collection of facial piercings over the years. He positively glinted with silver rings, studs, and bars.

"Hey, let me get finished up here and then I'll come have a drink with you guys at the bar," he said to Alison.

"Oh, well, you can't very well leave the rest of the guys out of the fun. Let me buy you all a drink," offered Alison.

"Um – okay, let me see what they want to do."

"Great! See you at the bar."

Alison led Julia and Holly over to the bar. While she ordered them all another round of drinks, Holly leaned closer to Julia and said in a low voice, "That was your shock, wasn't it?"

Holly turned toward William, still standing on the stage. Julia saw Mike whisper something, and William nodded.

When the band finished greeting their fans, signing autographs, and selling CDs, they packed their equipment and hauled it out of the pub. Then they all filed back inside, straight for the bar.

Mike introduced Alison to the group, and she announced, "Drinks are on me, guys."

After the cries of appreciation, most of the band hovered around Alison. The drummer came to talk to Holly. William took the empty seat beside Julia.

He did not talk to her, or even look at her. He leaned against the bar and watched the bartender work.

After a while, Julia said the only thing she could think of. "So you're in a rock band with your brother, after all."

He gave a single silent laugh, but still didn't look at her. Peeking out from underneath his collar, a thin gold chain caught her eye. If there was anything at the end of it, it was hidden inside of his shirt, below his collarbone. A collarbone that her fingertips recalled the sensation of with a twinge of muscle memory.

Screw this, thought Julia, starting to climb down from her barstool.

"I can't play with them too often, but I do two or three shows a month." He turned to look at her finally.

Julia slowly twisted herself back into her seat. "And you overcame your fear of public singing, I see."

"With a few exceptions, apparently."

Her face burned, and she looked away. Luckily, the bartender pushed their drinks across the counter. She took hers up, and took a big swig.

"I also sell some of my photographs now," he said after a moment. "At art shows, and on postcards, and things like that."

She wondered what his point was. Then she remembered one of the last times she had talked to him, when she told him to get a life, to stop inventing reasons why he couldn't do the things he loved to do.

She stared down at her drink and said awkwardly, "I think that's great."

Another nerve-wracking silence ensued. Finally, she began twisting out of her seat again and said, "Well, I better –"

"Do you want to hear my idea?"

"What?"

"My idea. The other day, when I told you that I had one idea of something you could do with your degree."

Julia wasn't really sure she wanted to hear his idea of what she should do with her life, but she said, "Amaze me."

He twisted his glass around on the bar. "Whale-watching tours."

She smirked. "That again?"

He knocked back half of his drink, and said nothing more.

"Oh, shit," she said. "It's a good idea. It always was. I'm just not sure I have the personality for it."

He turned a wry smile on her. She reddened and said, "What a hypocrite I am."

He gave another little silent laugh. "You have more personality than I do. But I still get up on stage and sing."

She held up her hands in mock surrender. "You're right. I just don't think anyone's going to hire me to be their naturalist with an eight-year-old marine biology degree and no work experience."

"What if someone would hire you? Would you do it?"

"I don't know. I do have to earn a living and support my daughter. That's a legitimate concern, more than the one about my personality."

She felt irritable, having to explain this to him. She wanted to snap at him that this was all a pipe dream. That the most she could hope for was to live to see her daughter make happier choices for herself. That not only did she not have the career she had always imagined, but she didn't have the man she loved, either. She was worse off even than her uncle had been.

I didn't come here to wallow in self-pity, she told herself. She got down from her chair for real now and turned a halfhearted smile on William.

"Thanks for your concern."

She pulled on her coat as she pushed through the door, burst out into the cold air, and stormed down the sidewalk.

Then she heard the footsteps running behind her. Heard Holly's voice cry, "Julia!"

Julia spun to face her cousin. "I'll take your job, sight-unseen. When do I start?"

She began in the mornings, Monday through Thursday. Learning to answer phones, to take messages. Getting drinks for clients in the waiting room. Ordering supplies. Assembling and binding petition packages for court. Making copies. Word processing documents. Nothing special, for a not-special salary.

Still, it kept her busy and, along with the evening job she continued at Dunphy's, it took her mind off of her problems. And after her abortive culinary and marine biology careers, it was gratifying to know that she could be good at something, for a change.

It was also nice to socialize each day with people who were bright and a little quirky, like herself. They were all about the same age, and Holly's paralegal, a Salvadoran woman named Graciela, took to Julia right away.

"You know, I started right where you are today. As a receptionist," Graciela told her one day while training her on the formatting of legal petitions.

"You went to school though, didn't you?"

"Not at all."

"Really?"

"Someone smart and hard-working like you can work your way up to paralegal in a few years, and you can make a decent living, too."

Julia's conversation with Graciela opened her eyes for the first time to the possibility of supporting her family on her own. She might have to move to the East Bay, or out of the Bay Area altogether, but the fact that it was within the realm of possibility gave her spirits an infusion of hope for the first time since Kevin's departure.

One afternoon at the end of Julia's shift, Holly stopped by Julia's desk.

"How's everything going for you, Julia? Personally, I mean."

"Oh, you know. It's going."

"Are you happy with the legal help you're getting?"

"I guess so."

"How long will the divorce process take?"

Julia hole-punched some pages of the petition she was working on. "I haven't filed for divorce yet."

"What?"

Julia sighed. "I know."

With an effort, Holly closed her jaw, straightened herself. "It's none of my business."

"The lawyer told me that as long as I haven't filed for divorce yet, I can be selling things from the house to meet our living expenses. But if I try to sell anything after filing for divorce, it could be construed the wrong way, like I'm trying to abscond with the money or hide assets. And regardless, I'll have to hold on to half the proceeds of anything I sell, because he's legally entitled to half of it if he comes home."

"But surely you can demonstrate that you needed to sell them in order to support Paige."

Julia shrugged. "It's complicated. I just don't know what to do."

"Well, if he ever does come home, do you have any intention of going back to him?"

Julia considered. "I can't say I'd take him back out of love."

"Then why would you go back to him?"

"Paige, I guess. She cries for him every day. I don't know what the effect is going to be on her long term if he doesn't come back."

"Julia. What if he comes back, and then he leaves you all again? What will the effect be on Paige then?"

Julia nodded. "I know. You're right."

"Well, like I said, it's none of my business. But listen, if you want a second legal opinion, our cousin Erin specializes in family law."

"You mean crazy Aunt Brigid's daughter Erin?"

Holly laughed. "I know there was some sort of beef between Rob and Aunt Brigid. But being a militant feminist hardly makes her crazy. And she raised a hella good family law attorney. Was this lawyer you consulted a man or a woman, by the way?"

"A man."

Holly's jaw tightened. "You need a woman. Let me give you Erin's number."

That evening, her spirits lifted, Julia began thinking about her behavior toward William at the pub. She approached him in the break room at Dunphy's and said, "Can I talk to you for just one minute?"

He looked surprised, but said, "Sure."

She beckoned him out the back door, to their old meeting spot on the pier, overlooking the boats.

"I won't keep you long," she said. "I just wanted to apologize."

"For what?"

"For being so rude the other day at the pub. I know you were just trying to help, and I like your idea about the naturalist thing. I'll add that to my list of long-term possibilities. But right now I have to focus on more immediate prospects."

"Do you have any leads?"

"Actually, I started a job already. It's just a part time receptionist and legal secretary job with my cousin Holly, but it's a place to start. Now if I could just get a job with a good family law attorney. Then maybe I could get free legal advice."

At Cardone's, workers hoisted totes of Dungeness crab from the boats and upended them into boiling tanks, right there on the pier. Julia ventured to ask, "How is your family doing these days?"

"Same as ever. Kelly works over there now with them. She's a single mom now. She still lives at home, with her kids."

"What about Mike?"

"Still Mike. We're roommates, believe it or not."

She couldn't resist asking, "Where do you live?"

"Mission."

"Oh. Very hip."

"Don't say that to Mike. No worse insult, in his opinion." After a moment's hesitation, he asked, "What's your last name now?"

Startled somehow that he didn't already know, she replied, "Beale."

He processed it. Julia Beale. Quietly, he said, "I knew you were married to Kevin and had a daughter, because I saw the photos on the wall in your dad's office."

She could not maintain eye contact with him. What used to be a happy memory of that time of her life seemed so incongruous with the present. And his subdued tone of voice left little doubt as to how he had felt about it.

"There really wasn't anything going on back then," Julia blurted, then flushed when William held her gaze unflinchingly. "I mean... we didn't start dating until two years later. I don't know why I'm telling you this, except..." She folded her arms across her chest, shifted her weight. "I couldn't stand it if you thought I was dishonest with you back then."

The hardness in his eyes softened somewhat. Quietly, he said, "Is he ever coming back?"

Her stomach lurched. "I don't know."

A long pause. Then, "Where is he?"

"I don't know." She wondered how much detail to share with him. "They traced him as far as Brazil. We got a postcard from him, postmarked in São Paulo, saying that he just needed to get away. It was in his handwriting. Then it's like he just disappeared."

"Could he have been kidnapped?"

"We wondered about that, but no one has demanded a ransom. His family certainly has the money to pay it, so we figure we would have heard from someone by now."

After a minute, he said, "I'm sorry."

"I'm sorry that I can't sell the house or anything else while he's missing. And that he hurt my daughter so much."

There didn't seem to be anything left to discuss. It was such a surreal conversation, she was happy to be done with it, anyway. After a moment, she said, "I'd better go inside."

"Julia."

His voice was unsteady, his face warped with apprehension. Finally, he pointed to the slips across the water.

"Do you see that boat docked over there?"

"Yeah?"

"That's a catamaran. It has a double-hull, so it's more stable and smooth out on the open ocean. Good for carrying passengers."

"Okay," she said, unsure why he was telling her this.

He looked out at it and said quietly, "It's for sale."

"Are you thinking of buying it?"

He shrugged. "Or something like it."

"What are you going to use it for?" she asked, and instantly knew the answer. "Whale watching."

He turned to her now, his face sphinx-like.

"William. Is that what all your questions were about in the pub? Asking me whether or not I would do it if someone would hire me?"

He shifted his weight and looked back out at the catamaran.

"Oh," she said. "*Oh*."

Against her better judgment, against her will even, her spirits soared. He was thinking of her. Making plans that involved her.

"It will take a lot of time," he said so quietly that she almost couldn't hear him. "I would have to get a license. I'd have to actually buy the thing. We'd have to make a business plan."

"We." She reddened, realizing she had said it out loud.

He turned a piercing gaze on her.

"Give me a minute," she said, sitting down right there on the pier.

To her further amazement, he sat down next to her. "If you'll do it with me, you'll be my business partner."

She took a few deep breaths. Collected herself. "Forgive me, but – how are you going to buy a boat like that?"

"I saved most of the money I made in Alaska."

Had he really made that much money? "William. Like I told you, I don't know if I have the time or the luxury to work on this.

Also, my future is a bit uncertain right now. I'm still married. I don't know what will happen if he ever comes back."

"Will you go back to him?"

She saw the pain in his eyes, the creases in his forehead. She drew her knees up to her chest, wrapping her arms around them.

"This is all so sudden," she murmured. "I need a little time. I'm not saying no. To any of it. I just need time."

He nodded his understanding. After sitting together with him for another minute, she stood up, and he stood as well. Then she turned to go back inside.

The first thing she did was pull out her cell phone, retrieve the slip of paper with Holly's handwriting from her wallet, and dial their cousin Erin's number.

About a week later, Julia realized that she hadn't seen Amanda at Dunphy's in a while. She approached Carla, one of the other prep cooks, and said quietly, "Where is Amanda these days?"

"Quit about a week ago. I wouldn't be surprised if it had something to do with him," Carla whispered, nodding toward William passing by. "If there's a heart anywhere in there, no one has seen it."

An involuntary smile spread itself across Julia's face as she returned to her work. During William's break, Julia came out to meet him.

"What do you have in mind for this business?" Her voice made him jump. "Weekends only?"

He considered a moment. "We could also do private charters during the week. Sport fishing. That kind of thing."

There was that word "we" again. "What about private charters for photography?"

"Yes, that too. But since I have to run the boat, I wouldn't be able to come out and interact much."

"You could also offer private charters during the week for birthdays and office parties, and things like that."

He smiled faintly. "I see you haven't given this any thought."

"It just so happens I've been learning a bit about business plans lately, for another reason. You know we'd have to come up with financials. I don't know the first thing about that, do you?"

"Not particularly."

"What about the present state of the industry? How saturated the market already is? Stuff like that?"

"I have a vague idea, but we'd need specifics."

Her head spun. "This could take months."

"So? Those months will go by anyway."

"I haven't said I'd do it," she reminded him.

"I know."

The boats across the water bobbed in their slips, including the catamaran he had pointed out to her a week ago. "What about Amanda?"

"Amanda?"

"How will she feel about you working on this with me?"

"There's no Amanda. Not anymore." She met his gaze, and he said, "Listen, Julia, I'm not going to kid you. I haven't been a monk all this time. But as far as love…" He shook his head.

She drew her breath in a quick gasp, her heart leaping into her throat, but also hurting on some level because it was past denial. Of course he had been in relationships with other women. She always knew he must have. But some tiny, desperate part of herself had hoped that maybe, just maybe, he hadn't.

"I hope you know I didn't mean to rush you," he said after a minute. "But if there was any chance at all, I had to take it while I still could."

Julia nodded. "It won't be long."

The next day, Julia did not see William at his station. He was on the schedule, and her father had once told her that he never, ever called in sick. Against her better judgment, she approached her father and asked after him.

Her father didn't look up from his work. "His brother Mike is in the ICU at General."

"What?"

He waved his hand impatiently at her. "Some kind of overdose."

Julia knew that, as much as he admired most of the Quinns for their work ethic and down-to-earth demeanor, he wholly dismissed Jimmy and Mike as the bad apples of the family. Clearly, he was annoyed by the inconvenience of William's absence, not at all concerned for Mike, and much too busy to be bothered.

Julia stumbled to the front of the restaurant in a fog. She did not know what replies she gave to the inquiries of patrons and other employees. She looked out the window, saw the closed and locked door of the plant. Thought of a time, long ago, when William had rushed her to the hospital to be at the side of her dying uncle.

She ran out the front door, all the way around the shed to her car. Jumped in and sped to San Francisco General.

Ran up the flights of stairs to the locked door of the ICU. Banged on it, then noticed the waiting room to the side. She found him there, by himself, hunched in his chair, waiting for something to happen.

He looked up when she entered, and his eyes flew open wide.

"Julia," he said in a voice that didn't sound like his own. He seemed to lose all powers of speech after that.

"I came here as soon as I heard," she said, taking a chair next to him. "My dad told me."

He stared at her, his mouth open in shock. Totally mute.

Damn her impulsiveness. "I didn't even think about it until just now. I just came here as fast as I could. I know how much he means to you."

Still, he gaped. Desperately, she tried humor. "I thought I would carry on our old tradition of meeting in hospitals under catastrophic circumstances."

His look of shock gave way abruptly to a short laugh. "My family will be here any minute. They had all gone to Livermore after the plant closed to visit my Uncle Will, and they had to drive back."

"What happened? If you want to tell me."

"I don't know everything yet. They're still stabilizing him. They said he overdosed on heroin and alcohol."

"Heroin," Julia repeated with horror.

"I didn't even know he was using it. I lived with him. Played in a band with him. And I had no idea."

Well, now that she was here, she'd better think of something to say or do. Some way to help.

"My sister," she said.

"What?"

"They reconnected at the pub, you know. I should call and ask her what she knows."

He considered a moment, then nodded. She stepped out into the hallway, opened her cell phone and dialed her sister's number. Told her what was happening.

"Oh no," Alison wailed.

"Alison. Did you know about this?"

"Yes," she admitted. "I hooked up with him once or twice after the pub. The first time he pulled out the kit and offered it to me, I bounced."

"Do you know anything else? How much he was doing? Who he did it with, or where he got it from?"

"Not a clue. I've told you everything I know. It killed me to see him using it, but I can't be around that shit." She hesitated a moment. "I'm coming down there."

"No, Alison, I think you're right. You'd better not get involved."

"God, I'm sorry to hear this. He's such a good guy." After a moment's pause, she said, "Hey. What are *you* doing there?"

Julia debated whether or not to tell her. "I've got to go."

"Julia? It's William, isn't it?"

"Goodbye, Alison."

She hung up. Held the phone in her hand a moment. Turned to go back into the waiting room, and was just beginning to relay her sister's information when William's parents came in, followed by someone Julia was startled to recognize as his sister. Far from her old athletic self, Kelly bore a striking resemblance to Ann now. Eleven years and single parenthood had not been kind to her; she had put on a lot of weight, and she looked much older than her twenty-seven years.

They all looked confused to find Julia there, but of course the first thing out of Ann's mouth was, "What's going on? How is Mike?"

"They're still stabilizing him," William replied. "I don't know anything more than that yet."

154

"When's the last time you heard anything?"

"About thirty minutes ago."

"I'm going to check for any updates." She went to pick up the phone next to the ICU entrance. Jim followed her, and Kelly turned to peer at Julia, bewildered.

"She has some information for us," William tried. "From her sister."

Julia nodded in conspiracy. "Yes. Alison says she spent a little time recently with Mike."

Kelly raised an eyebrow. "She did?"

"She said he offered her heroin, and she said no and left. That's really all she knows, though."

"And you came all this way just to tell us that?"

Julia and William were both silent. Kelly looked suspiciously at her, and then turned angry eyes on William.

"So what you're telling me is that Julia's sister knew all about his heroin problem, but his own brother, who lives with him, who's supposed to keep an eye on him, had no idea?"

William sprang to his feet and left the waiting room. His sister watched him go, then turned to glare at Julia.

Well, I didn't very well come here to hang out with her, Julia thought, and ran after him without another word.

She found him at the end of the hallway, turning into another unit with his hands shoved into his pockets. She fell in step beside him and took the tour of the floor with him. After a while he stopped to look out of a window.

"You should probably go now. It's going to get worse with my sister, and my mom too."

"If that's what you want me to do."

He looked at her, exquisitely conflicted. "You don't want to hear this stuff."

"You don't have to hear it, either, if you don't want to."

"I have to go back in there sometime. I need to see Mike, and hear the updates."

She nodded. After a moment's hesitation, she added, "Your sister doesn't like me very much, does she?"

"Don't take it too personally. She holds some tenacious grudges. It's a Cardone family trait."

"Grudges? Why does she hold a grudge against me?"

William reddened slightly. "She and my mom are very protective of all the people they love."

Now Julia understood. She had hurt him once, and they had very long memories. She had a bit of work to do to get back into their good graces.

"I'll be hanging around," she said. She glanced around, pointed to the nearest waiting room. "Right here. Come find me if you need anything. If you don't – if you're too busy with your brother – then don't worry about it."

A couple of hours passed before he reappeared, looking haggard. She set aside her magazine and stood up.

"Can I get you anything?"

He shook his head and took the seat next to hers. She resumed her seat, and turned to look at him. He slouched in his chair, staring down at the floor.

"Do you want to tell me what's happening?" she prompted gently.

Her voice roused him. He straightened a bit. "He has pulmonary edema – fluid in his lungs. He's sedated and on a ventilator. Hooked up to a ton of IVs and monitors. They say he stopped breathing and his heart stopped beating, and they had to resuscitate him. They don't know how much damage it did to his brain or what the effects are going to be long-term."

"Oh no." She reached for his hand, with no other thought, initially, than to comfort him. After a while, she ventured, "Where was he when this happened?"

"Just some shooting gallery in the Tenderloin, from what I can gather."

Julia shook her head in dismay. "William, when was the last time you had anything to eat?"

"I don't know."

"You wait here." She rose to look for a patient kitchen, but he squeezed her hand to stop her from going.

"I can't eat anything."

"Yes you can. You will." She wriggled her hand free. "I'll be right back."

She found the nearest patient kitchen and gathered up some pudding and a spoon, crackers, and juice. Approached the nurse at the nearest station to beg for coffee, and the nurse went to the break room to retrieve some.

Juggling everything, Julia returned to the waiting room to find him still there, in exactly the same position she had left him. She handed him the coffee, which he gladly accepted. Peeled open the pudding, and tore open the package of crackers.

"Eat this. Don't just drink coffee or you'll puke."

He devoured it quickly. Took the crackers when she held them out and ate those too. Drank the entire container of juice and gulped down the coffee.

"I'll get more," she said.

But he shook his head, and took her hand again.

"Do you know," he said, "that even after all these years, I still felt like I had to protect him from himself. Babysit him like a child. Make sure he took his Lithium every day. And I was happy to do it, because of how he protected me a long time ago."

After a moment, it occurred to Julia to wonder, "Whatever happened to Jimmy?"

He looked at her as if he were surprised that she didn't already know. "Dead."

"What? When did that happen?"

"A couple of years after we broke up, when I was in Alaska."

"Did he get killed in prison?"

He shook his head. "He was paroled."

"Then how?"

With a grim look, he said, "Overdose."

She sat with him in silence for a long time, holding his hand and staring blankly at the TV. The longer she sat, the harder it became to face to prospect of letting go of his hand.

Finally, after ten or fifteen minutes, he looked at her and said, "You should probably go home. Your daughter."

"My mom is with her. I would have been at work right now, anyway. But I am going to go out for a while. I'm going to get some food for you and your family."

He shook his head. "Don't do that."

"Why not?" He had no reply, so she said, "I'll be back in a little while. I'll deliver myself."

He smiled tenderly at her, and she felt the warmth flooding her chest. She squeezed his hand, and reluctantly let it go. He followed her out of the waiting room, back toward the ICU. As she went the opposite direction, she couldn't resist looking back, and saw him do the same.

She drove back to the restaurant as fast as she could. Came into the kitchen and said to her father, "I'm taking some food to the Quinns at the hospital."

"Where have you been?" he demanded.

"At the hospital," she replied calmly.

"You just skip out on work and go to the hospital to be with the Quinns?"

"It was something I needed to do."

He looked at her now, and she watched him making the connection.

"You know that's coming out of your wages," he said.

This gave her pause, but she said, "Whatever you think is best."

He looked annoyed at her for calling his bluff. She knew he would eat the cost, for Jim and Ann.

Back at the hospital, she found them still in the waiting room. They looked just as surprised to see her this time as they had before, except for William.

She held up her sack. "Food from the restaurant."

They murmured their surprise and pleasure. She unpacked the boxes of food, one for each of them, as well as the napkins and silverware. One at a time, they opened the boxes, exclaimed at the bounty.

"Any new updates?" asked Julia.

Ann shook her head. "He's stable. It'll take twenty-four to forty-eight hours before we have a clearer picture."

Julia nodded. "I'll leave you now, but if you need anything, feel free to give me a call."

"It was very kind of you to bring the food," said Ann.

"My pleasure."

Julia turned to go, but not before casting a long look at William. Moments later, he joined her in the hallway and walked around the corner with her, into the other unit. Then he took her hand, and stopped.

She turned to face him, and saw the same gold chain peeking from underneath his collar that she had noticed for the first time at the pub. He lifted her hand and held it in both of his. He looked at it, touched it with his fingertips. Only then did she notice the condition of his hands, scattered here and there with burn and knife scars from his years in the kitchen.

She thought her heart would overflow. "I'll call you as soon as I can tomorrow morning."

He nodded and reluctantly let go of her hand. Put his hands in his pockets as she backed away. Slowly, she turned and made her way down the hallway, toward the staircase. She felt his eyes following her the whole way, until she was out of sight.

She called him on the way to work the next morning after dropping Paige off at school.

"How is he?"

"Still stable. If he stays that way, they might try to wean him off the ventilator today."

"That's good. Did you get any sleep last night?"

"Not much."

She knew he would be back at work that night, regardless. There was no point arguing with him about that.

"Listen, Julia, my brother isn't the only reason I didn't get much sleep last night."

He paused, waiting, she imagined, for some kind of reaction from her. She struggled with what to say, with the right combination of caution and encouragement.

"I didn't sleep too well last night, either."

He hesitated a moment. "Are you working tonight?"

"Yeah. It's Friday."

"I'll see you later."

"Okay."

Breaks were impossible that night, so she had no chance to talk to him until after work, when he leaned against the lockers, looking exhausted.

"I hope you're not going back to the hospital," she said.

To her surprise, he shook his head. "I can't. I have to function tomorrow."

"Good."

"I did call just now. They weaned him, and he's awake. Mom is there; that should be enough for now."

"Good for you," she said emphatically.

He pulled his jacket on and turned to go.

"You're not driving home, are you?" she said.

"I have to. I drove here."

She put her hand on his arm. "Friends don't let friends drive exhausted. Let me take you home." His eyes widened, and she added, "Don't get any ideas. I'm only driving you home. You'd be a lousy screw, in your condition."

He smiled wider than she had seen him do since knowing him again. She gathered up her belongings and he followed her out the back door, which did not go unnoticed by the staff they passed along the way.

She cranked the car engine. "Okay, fare's running. Where to?"

"Go to Van Ness, and then just keep going."

She set out in that direction. Once she had turned onto Van Ness, she said, "When's my next turn?"

She got no response, and turned to find him asleep, leaning against the window.

"Hey." She shook him awake.

He looked disoriented. "Where are we?"

"Van Ness. You're gonna have to find a way to stay awake."

He rolled down the window and turned on the stereo. A Pink Floyd song cut through the quiet.

Frantically, Julia jabbed at the button and missed several times before successfully shutting it off again. But not before several lines of the albatross song drifted into his ears.

"Hey," he said. "Was that actually on the radio?"

She said nothing, just looked straight ahead, her face and ears burning.

How the hell could I have forgotten about that? Damn, damn, damn.

She could not remember the last time she had ever felt so embarrassed. Now she was in worse shape to drive than he was.

Though he seemed pretty wide awake by now. He stared straight ahead, as well. He didn't embarrass her further by pointing out the obvious. She had been listening to a CD. His CD. The one he had given her long ago.

"I'm sorry," she practically wailed.

"What in God's name do you have to be sorry for?"

She let herself peek, just out of the corner of her eye. He was smiling now, almost giddy. He said, "Turn here."

He said it almost too late, as if he had been distracted. And no wonder. She slammed on the brakes, skidded around the corner.

"Sorry," she said again.

Still, he grinned. A minute later, he said, "Turn here."

She turned again, and then he pointed up the street, past the next intersection. "Pull up here. This is it."

She stopped in front of his building in an up-and-coming but still gritty neighborhood, surrounded by corner markets, liquor stores, and taquerías. She gripped the steering wheel and stared straight ahead.

"Hey," he said softly. He reached across, grasped both of her forearms. Tried unsuccessfully to loosen her grip. "Hey. Relax."

She let go of the steering wheel. He turned her anguished face toward his. Made her look at him.

"It's okay," he said.

But the shame was still too palpable. She turned away, faced forward.

He put his hand on hers. "Remember when you heard me singing that song at the pub?"

She smiled at him now. They had never acknowledged it before.

She picked up his arm. Pushed his sleeve back and ran her fingers back and forth across the mermaid. After a moment, he touched her chin. Lifted her face to his, and whispered, "I still love you."

"I still love you, too."

He held her hand against his heart, wove his fingers through hers. Brushed his other hand across her cheek, and kissed her lips.

"I can't believe this is happening," he said.

"Me neither."

"Park your car."

"Aren't you tired?"

"I'm wide awake. I won't get any sleep without you."

Her pulse stampeded out of control. "Okay."

She parked where he directed her to. He took her hand and led her around the corner, down the street to his building, up the stairs.

He let her inside the apartment and closed and locked the door behind him. There was no need to pretend about what they were there for; he took her straight to the bedroom. He lifted the hat off of her head and set it aside. Put his hands all through her hair, and kissed her mouth.

He untied her scarf and pulled it off of her. Lifted the sweater off over her head, opened her bra, and let it fall to the floor. Then he lifted the shirt off of himself so she could feel her skin against his.

She reached up and touched the chain at the back of his neck. Traced it down to the small pendant just below his collarbone. Some patron saint. Then she took his finger and traced it down the silver chain around her own neck, to the mermaid pendant lying against her chest.

Her senses blurred into one another. She had forgotten the way every nerve ending in her body could scintillate; that even her salivary glands responded. The way his eyes locked on hers as she rose over him, reached down between their bodies, and helped him inside of her. The way his hands felt, kneading her breasts, sliding over her torso, resting in the space between her rib cage and her hips while he moved inside of her. She was only sorry that, as ever, he could not last long in that way, but it was gratifying to remember how her body responded in turn to his hands, his fingers, his tongue. How his little involuntary vocalizations tipped her so effortlessly over the edge. The fact that he was the one who could do this to her made sleep fitful, interrupted repeatedly by his body pressing for more.

At four o'clock in the morning, Julia said, "I need to go soon."

He flipped her around onto her back and pinned her arms to the bed. "I won't let you."

She smiled. "Paige is going to wake up in a few hours."

"You need your own place."

"That won't happen any time soon."

"Why not?"

"Kevin's name is on the deed to the house. I can't sell it without his signature."

He touched the mermaid pendant lying against her skin. "Move in with me."

"I can't do that."

"I don't care what anyone thinks."

"It's more than that. I have a daughter, and she just lost her father. It's way too soon."

He looked sober. He let go of her arms and lay alongside her, propping himself up on one elbow. "How much longer until you're divorced?"

She shook her head. "It's hard to say. Since he's missing, the lawyer has to show that we've conducted a diligent search for him. If they still don't find him, we get an Order of Publication and publish a legal notice in the newspaper. We publish it three times, then wait for thirty days. If there's no response, then I get my divorce."

William frowned and shook his head in disbelief. "What kind of a man would do this to you? To his child?" At the look on Julia's face, he said, "I'm sorry."

"It's a fair question."

After a moment's hesitation, he said, "Did you never see this coming? You saw no signs that he was capable of something like this?"

She rolled onto her side, touched the chain around his neck. "Kevin was the shoulder I leaned on after you and I broke up. He didn't tell me right away that he had feelings for me, but he broke it off with his fiancée. And even though we bonded over our aquariums, we still didn't start dating until my grandmother died two years later. He drove me all the way up to San Francisco and came with me to the funeral. He was so kind to me. And when I found myself pregnant, he was so excited. He said he would quit working on his PhD and go to work at his dad's firm. And I had lost my passion for marine biology. It was too easy to let myself just get married, and have a baby, and do that with my life. It made him so happy, so no – I didn't see any of it coming before we got married."

"But afterward?"

"Afterward, yeah; I could see him becoming disillusioned. I admit it – I was never quite as invested in the relationship in the first place. Having Paige shifted my priorities even further away. And Kevin - he hated his work, but once we had Paige, he felt trapped there. His parents looked down their noses at me, and they never tried to hide it. But I still never imagined he'd do something like this."

He tucked a lock of hair behind her ear, but said nothing more. She still touched his chain, and fingered the pendant at the end of it. He looked down at it and said, "Saint Peter. Patron saint of fishermen. My mother gave it to me when I went to Alaska. It kept me safe for five years, so I just kept wearing it."

"But you got hurt in the end."

"Hurt, yes, but I'm here."

"I lost a lot of sleep after I heard you'd gone up there."

"Why didn't you try to reach me?"

"I did." At the look of shock on his face, she explained, "After my dad told me that you'd gone to Alaska, I asked your mother for your contact information there. I sent a letter to you at some processing plant in a town called Unalaska, but it came back saying 'Return to Sender.'"

"When did you mail it?"

"December 1996."

He considered a moment. "I think I know why I didn't get it. King crab season was really short that year. I ended up going caribou hunting with a group of other guys."

"You went caribou hunting?"

He looked sharply at her. "Yeah?"

"You shot a caribou?"

"Uh oh. Am I in trouble?"

"Jesus. You're Ernest Hemingway."

He smiled. "Let's not get carried away."

"We'll come back to this later. So you were caribou hunting?"

"Yeah, and when I got back to Dutch Harbor, I found my boat had gone back south because they closed tanner crab season that year, too. So then I took a berth on a trawler, fishing pollock. But the trawler picked up its mail from a different processing plant than the crab boat did."

"So you think I sent the letter to the wrong processing plant?"

"That's my guess." He looked sadly at her. "I wish you had just tried again."

"I thought surely you must have gotten over me."

He took her hand and kissed it. "I told you you'd always have my heart."

She peered at him. "What would you have done?"

"I would have come straight home."

She touched her forehead to his hand and shook her head in dismay. He lifted her face to his and kissed her. Pulled away again, and smiled tenderly at her. "Do you want to see the pictures I took while I was in Alaska?"

Her eyes widened. "You brought your camera there with you?"

"Of course I did. That thing's like an extra limb."

"Where are they?"

He got up and put on his boxers and pants. She got dressed and followed him into the living room. He rifled through a bookshelf and retrieved a couple of photo albums. "I got these developed whenever I could, and mailed them home to my mom. She stuck them all in albums for me and gave them to me when I came home."

He brought them to the couch and she sat down next to him. He opened them and pointed to the town pictures on the first page.

"This is Dutch Harbor. Ground zero for much of the Alaska fishing industry."

"It looks like a beautiful place."

"This was a very rare clear day. But it is kind of beautiful. I especially liked the Russian Orthodox church in town."

He flipped through some more shots of just the church, then moved on to photos of the boats he worked on, the characters who populated those boats, and the wildlife he saw.

"I've kept the negatives for all of these. I've actually managed to sell some of them at art shows. Blown up and framed, of course. And while I was still in Alaska, I got some of them made into postcards, which were sold at tourist traps."

"Where are you in all this?"

He smiled. "My mom had the same question after a while. So I had some buddies take one or two pictures of me."

"Let me see."

Sheepishly, he flipped to the end of the first album. Pointed to a picture of himself aboard a crab boat, in full foul-weather gear, next to a full crab pot he had just pulled.

"You had a beard!" she exclaimed.

"It helped keep me warm up there. Plus, I didn't have a lot of time for shaving."

"It looks like you had just pulled up a fortune in crab. Why aren't you smiling?"

"I am."

"Barely." She rubbed him on the back, where his caged albatross still was. "What year would this have been?"

"I guess that was around December of '98."

She tried to think of what she was doing around that time in her life, and realized with a poignant twinge that she would have been nine months pregnant in Menlo Park while he was off slinging crab pots in the Bering Sea.

"Did you say there were a couple?" she asked after a moment.

"You don't want to see the other one."

"You don't get to say that and then not show it to me."

"It was while I was caribou hunting."

"Let me guess. Animal carnage is involved." She waved it over. "Bring it on."

He opened the other album and flipped through it until he came to the caribou hunt. Showed her the pictures of the wilderness and of the animals that he hadn't slaughtered.

"Please tell me this is the only shooting you did on that trip," she said.

"I'm afraid not. But this is how I learned that I'm actually a terrible marksman. The guys kindly let me pose with one of the animals they shot."

He pointed to a picture of himself next to a dead, hanging caribou.

"Kind indeed," she said. "But I don't believe you. I think you really shot that thing, and you're just telling me you didn't so I won't hate you."

"Well, I'm happy to let you believe that if you want."

"Bad answer. Now I *will* hate you."

"You won't hate me," he said, setting the albums aside and lifting her into his lap, facing him. "I'm the guy who's going to make you breakfast."

"Oh, very well then. That's worth at least one dead caribou."

"Don't get too excited. It'll probably just be an omelet. Breakfast is not my forte."

"What, a couple of bachelors don't keep fresh fruit and yogurt around?"

He kissed her and said, "I'd rather have you again for breakfast."

"I'd love to lay the buffet out for you, but Father Time has other ideas."

He laughed and stood up with her then, lowering her feet to the floor. She followed him into the kitchen and stood behind him, putting her hands on his waist as he diced vegetables and ham. With a sidelong smile at her, he reached into the refrigerator and pulled out some fruit.

"You *do* have fruit!" she exclaimed, then looked suspiciously at him. "Do you eat like this every day?"

"Out of an abundance of optimism, I made a run to the grocery store yesterday."

She laughed, and watched him chop the fruit. He broke eggs into a bowl and whisked them. Sautéed the vegetables, and cooked the omelet. Served her at the little table in the living room.

After a while, she said, "I'll drive you back to your – what are you driving these days?"

He smiled, shoveled a bite of food in his mouth and chewed it, but said nothing.

After breakfast, he finished getting dressed. From the clothes he put on, she knew he must still have a motorcycle. She followed him downstairs and back to her car, then drove him back to the pier.

"Right over here," he said, pointing.

She knew it as soon as she saw it. "You've got to be kidding me. Is that the same exact one?"

"The very same," he said, rather proudly.

"How is that thing even still running after all these years?"

"My brother kept it for me while I was in Alaska. He's kept it running for me all these years. Best mechanic in the city."

She looked around to make sure no one was watching, then leaned over and kissed him.

He said, "I don't know how I'm going to wait until I can see you again."

She didn't try to tease him, for once. "Me neither."

He put his forehead on hers. "Hurry up and get that new place, okay?"

She kissed him again. "See you later at work."

She watched him go and made up her mind then and there what she was going to do.

Julia unlocked the front door as quietly as possible. The whole house was still quiet, the morning sunlight just beginning to stream through the curtains.

She made her way up the stairs and opened the door to Paige's room just a crack. Peeked through, and opened it wider.

Paige was gone.

She ran downstairs. "Paige?" No response.

She threw open the door and found the light already on.

"Paige?"

"Hi, Mom!"

Julia felt weak with relief as she saw her daughter's face smiling up at her. Paige still wore her pajamas, but she was standing on a chair, feeding the fish.

"Not too much!" Julia warned her. "Remember, only as much as they can eat in five minutes. Overfeeding is worse than underfeeding."

"I know," Paige replied cheerfully.

"Paige, why are you down here at this time of the morning?"

"I couldn't sleep."

"Why not?"

"I was too excited about getting our clownfish today. I went to your room to wake you up, but I couldn't find you. Where were you?"

Julia's heart sank. She had completely forgotten about their planned trip to the local fish store. She decided to sidestep Paige's question.

"Before we get any new fish, we should test the water to make sure it's safe. Would you like me to show you how?"

Paige beamed and nodded, and Julia showed Paige how to perform the pH test and hydrometer check.

"I know it's your aquarium," said Julia, "but you should never do this without either me or Grandma here to watch you."

"I know. One day, when I'm working for your aquarium company, I can do it myself."

Again, Julia's heart sank. And again, rather than dash Paige's dreams, she decided to change the subject.

"Instead of going to the fish store, how about we bring one of our clownfish back with us from the house in Menlo Park?"

"Can I go say hi to Emily while I'm there?"

Julia looked apprehensively at her. Saying hi to Emily meant saying hi to Emily's mom, and Julia felt so far removed from everyone and everything in that neighborhood by now. But as she thought about it, she realized that she had not heard Paige mention any new friends in the city.

"Do you have any friends around here that you like to play with? We could go say hi to them after we get home."

Paige's smile faded a bit, and she turned toward her tank. "Not really."

With a pang of guilt, Julia said, "If Emily's home, then yes, we can say hi."

Paige hopped down from her chair in front of the tank. "Oh, I almost forgot!"

"What?"

Paige ran to the clothesline that Julia had strung along the wall, pulled down a sheet of easel paper that she had hung there, and brought it for Julia to see.

"Another painting for your room," Paige explained. "Can you tell what they are?"

"Of course I can! Clownfish, pseudochromis, goby, firefish," Julia said, pointing to each one in turn. She hugged Paige around the shoulders. "This is perfect. It's just like having an aquarium in my room again."

"You're both up early," came a voice from the door. They looked up to find Julia's mother making her way into the in-law unit.

"It's clownfish day," explained Julia.

"Oh, right," said her mother, smiling. "This calls for a special breakfast. French toast?"

Paige actually jumped up and down for joy, a sight Julia hadn't seen in a very long time. Her mother's eyes widened at Julia as Paige pushed past them up the stairs.

But while Paige watched cartoons and Julia helped her mother in the kitchen, Julia said, "Mom, does Paige ever play with any of the kids around here?"

"Who would she play with?"

"What do you mean? There's plenty of kids around here."

"Julia, I don't even recognize this neighborhood anymore. All the Irish families have moved away or died. For that matter, all the white families of any stripe are gone. There's nothing but Chinese people around here now."

"So? Chinese kids play, too."

Her mother cast her a bemused look. "Half of them don't even speak English. Besides, they keep themselves to themselves. When you and Alison were kids, everyone on this block used to leave their doors open. You kids would run in and out of each other's houses."

"So Paige has no friends around here?"

Her mother shrugged. "We're a bit isolated here. I tried to warn you. Even the school is mostly Chinese now."

Julia frowned and peered out at Paige in the living room. Paige looked content enough, planted in front of the TV with her cartoons. But Julia made a mental note to herself to check in with Paige's teacher the next week and see if she had made any friends there.

Julia really meant to be as discreet as possible at work. But to her dismay, William took every opportunity of falling in step behind her and whispering, "How much longer until your break?"

She found herself watching him work that night, the sleeves of his white jacket rolled up, the black on his forearms flashing as he deftly managed six things on the grill at the same time. The Saint Peter chain peeking out from underneath his collar. Shouting in Spanish with the other cooks, the sweat glowing on all of his exposed skin.

If Carla is right and he has a reputation, she thought, then *this* is how he got the opportunity.

The next day as she passed his station on the way in to work, William took her hand and pulled her into the corridor that led out back.

"Come with me into the alley," he pleaded.

"I'm not going anywhere with you. I see that look on your face, and I know what it means."

"I'll keep my hands to myself. Scout's honor."

"You're no Boy Scout."

He groaned in frustration. "I'm going to rent you an apartment."

"Calm down. No you're not."

"Yes I am."

"How?"

"Don't worry about that. I'm going to do it."

She touched him on the arm. "I won't take a dime of your money. But I am going to rent an apartment."

"Really? How are you going to pay for it?"

"I'll rent out my house."

His forehead creased with concern. "Are you sure this is the right thing to do?"

"No. But I'm sure I want you in my bed every night."

His expression softened. "Me too."

"You wouldn't be able to come over until after Paige is asleep."

"With work, I wouldn't be able to come over until long after then, anyway."

"And you'd have to clear out before she wakes up in the morning. Either that, or lock the bedroom door and don't make a sound until we leave."

"I'll take whatever I can get." He kissed her for a minute, then pulled away and looked seriously at her. "Tuesday is my next day off. Do you think we can start looking then?"

"I'll ask my mom if she can watch Paige that afternoon."

"Plan to spend the night."

At the grim look on her face, he took her hands in his.

"Hey. Look at me." He turned her face up to his. "I'll never give you a reason to regret this. Ever."

"I need to go see a friend tomorrow after work," Julia told her mother on Monday evening. "Do you think you can pick Paige up from school and put her to bed? I'll be home before she wakes up."

Her mother looked startled. "What kind of a friend would ask you to spend all night with her when you have to work the next day?"

"Don't worry about me."

Her mother peered at her. "You didn't come home the other night, either. Is everything okay? Are you doing drugs?"

Julia laughed. "No, Mom, I swear to you I am not using drugs. Everything is okay. And I'm not away that much."

Julia watched with dread as her mother's expression changed. As suspicion crept over her face.

"Julia," her mother said slowly. "Is there something you would like to tell me?"

"Not really, Mom," she replied, as nonchalantly as possible. But she could not meet her mother's relentless gaze. "I'll have my cell phone on me all night, if you need anything."

Julia wished her mother would look angry, reproachful. Anything but the sad expression she gave her now as she watched her leave the room.

Better than an apartment, they found a furnished house that the landlord was willing to rent cheap because it had sat vacant. It had nine hundred square feet and no dishwasher. But though cosmetically everything was badly in need of updating, it was all in working order, and it was only blocks from both Julia's parents and Paige's school.

She broke the news to her parents in the living room on Sunday night, when they were both home.

"Why?" said her mother. "If there's something we've done to make you uncomfortable here, please tell us. It wasn't on purpose."

"No," Julia said, taking her mother's hands. "You've both been so lovely. I just think it's time that you had your house back."

"We don't want our house back. We love having you guys here."

Julia's father, who had been staring suspiciously at Julia during this whole exchange, now said, "They require some proof of income."

Julia played dumb. "Huh?"

Her father's jaw tightened. "Proof of income. You can't prove that you have a sufficient monthly income stream."

Her mother looked at him, slack-jawed, then turned back to Julia. "Oh, no, Julia. Don't."

Julia's stomach dropped. "Don't what?"

"Don't do this. Don't move in with him. Not with Paige."

Julia glared at her father. "Dad, what is she talking about?"

"I made him tell me," her mother said. "I guessed you were having an affair. He told me about William."

"It's not an affair, for the love of God."

"You're still married," her father said calmly.

"I wouldn't be, if Kevin hadn't left the country. I've filed for divorce. It's inevitable. But let's set all that aside for the moment. I'm not renting the apartment with William. I've rented out my house in Menlo Park, and I'm using that income. It's my own place."

"But no doubt, he'll be visiting you there," said her father.

"Julia, think of your daughter," implored her mother.

"I'm not letting him meet Paige. Not yet."

"Then you're getting yourself deeply entangled with him, and you have no idea how well he's going to interact with Paige," said her mother. "What happens if it turns out it's a bad combination?"

"He has no kids of his own," her father pointed out.

Julia clutched her head in her hands. "It's done. The lease is already signed."

"Julia," her mother said gently. "You made vows."

"A lot of consideration Kevin gave to that."

"That doesn't mean you have to throw yours overboard."

"Mom, you know I only got married in the church because both of our families insisted on it. It's the same reason I went through catechism and confirmation. My heart has never been in any of this stuff."

Her mother began to cry silently, and her father glared at Julia.

"Mom," Julia said gently, going to put her hands on her mother's shoulders. "I don't love Kevin. He abandoned me and Paige in a way that has caused us hardship of every kind. Paige cries every day because of him. The sooner we move on, the sooner she can heal."

"Not if you move on just to jump into bed with the next man," said her father.

"Once again, Paige won't know about William for a long time."

"Forgive me, but from what I know about your discretion, I'm finding that hard to believe."

Julia heard her mouth take off like a runaway train. She sensed the danger of it, but couldn't stop herself. "I love William. We've loved each other since we were teenagers. Did you know he gave me an engagement ring back then? We're not going to tiptoe around like we have something to be ashamed of."

Her father glared right back at her. "Grow up."

Julia felt the sting of his words. It was only after she went to bed that night that she realized why it hurt so much. She was afraid he was right. She was traipsing around, indulging her passion for all the world to see, with no thought for the consequences on her divorce proceedings or her daughter. Telling her parents off like an overgrown adolescent, with no consideration for the effect it might have on others. William still worked for her father, after all.

She looked at the clock on her bedside table. It was a little after midnight. William would just be getting home.

She picked up the phone, dialed his number. Told him everything.

"I'm sorry. I'm so sorry," she said. "I don't know what he's going to do."

"You say he already knew about our relationship. I doubt if this will change things much. Besides, by now I can get a job somewhere else if I need to. There's enough people who've worked with me in the past who can vouch for me. A couple of them are sous-chefs now." He paused a minute. "Listen, Julie, don't let the stuff your parents said give you cold feet. I told you, I won't give you any reason to regret this. And when the time is right, I'll take care of Paige like she's my own."

Julia let herself believe him. Let the weight of the night's events lift from her shoulders. Let her spirits soar again.

At work, Holly said, "How is Cousin Erin working out for you?"

"Great," said Julia. "We're almost done with the process of searching for him."

"I'm so glad you decided to give her a call. And to file for divorce, finally."

"Me too."

"You know, you should ask Erin if she has any work for you. Actually, forget that. I'll call her up myself and tell her to hire you."

Julia wondered why she hadn't thought of it, herself. Erin knew that she worked for Holly.

"Would you? I really need to quit working for my dad, anyway."

"Are you kidding? It'll be my first phone call after this."

Julia felt giddy. "I have an appointment with her this Friday."

"Then plan on interviewing at the same time."

Julia sprang to her feet and threw her arms around Holly. "The universe is falling into alignment. Everything's going so great."

Holly's eyebrows rose. "Everything?"

"Oh yes."

At the look on Julia's face, Holly smiled slightly. "My God, it must be *really* great. I'm sure Erin is advising you about that."

Julia's heart sank. "Actually, I haven't told her."

"Julia. You have to tell her. It's attorney-client privilege, so she'll keep it to herself. But she has to know so she can advise and represent you properly."

Julia sighed. "I know."

After a moment, the corners of Holly's mouth lifted slightly. "Is it William?"

Julia nodded, glowing.

"I never thought I'd see you so happy again. And I always loved his rakish hair. Tell me, does he actually style it or does he just roll out of bed looking like that?"

Julia grinned. "He's a thing of beauty, isn't he?"

"If I agreed, would you hold it against me?"

❖

That Friday, Erin reviewed with Julia the progress they had made on her case. "Now all that remains is to wrap up our last bit of business in Brazil. But since he disappeared in São Paulo, I don't think we have much hope of finding him."

Julia nodded, and Erin set aside her briefs. "Now. Holly tells me you're looking for an additional part-time job in a law office."

"Yes, but I'm not sure you'll want to hire me after what I'm about to tell you."

Erin looked startled. "Okay."

"I need you to know that I've been having a relationship with another man."

Erin stirred in her chair. "How long?"

"About three weeks now."

"Are you living with him?"

"Technically, no. He's not on my lease. But he spends every night with me."

"I call that living together."

"Paige hasn't met him yet. He doesn't come over until after she's asleep."

"I'd keep it that way. In fact, I wouldn't have him spending the night in the first place."

Julia's heart sank. "Is this going to cause problems with the divorce?"

"Not unless Kevin is down there in Brazil creating some asset of value even as we speak. Then that asset would be considered separate property, and you would get no share of it."

"Okay; that seems unlikely. Anything else?"

"The other way I can think of is if Kevin or his lawyers could show that Paige's safety or emotional well-being is threatened."

Julia shook her head. "That's definitely not the case."

"Even so, it would have been much better if you had waited until after you're divorced."

"I know."

"Then why are you doing it? Couldn't you have waited a little while longer?"

"No, I couldn't. We were engaged a long time ago, right after high school. Then we tried to do the long-distance relationship thing during college, and it didn't work out. But I always regretted it. He's the one, and I won't wait anymore."

"Okay," she said, but her tone was skeptical. "How many other people know?"

"A lot. My parents. My sister. Holly. Probably his brother. Pretty much everyone we work with at the restaurant. I'm pretty sure his parents suspect."

Erin shook her head in dismay, and Julia said, "I'll understand if you don't want to represent me anymore."

"Don't be so melodramatic."

"Would you still consider hiring someone so irresponsible?"

"You come with a glowing recommendation from Holly, and I trust her judgment more than God Herself. Our receptionist is going on maternity leave soon. She performs a lot of secretarial duties too, just like you do for Holly. I can start training you with her the week after next, and part-time will be fine for now if you want to stay on with Holly in the mornings."

Julia rummaged through her briefcase. "Here's my resume, if you want it."

Erin accepted it, but didn't bother looking at it. "The job pays eleven dollars an hour."

Julia reached out her hand to shake, but Erin said, "You should really learn to negotiate."

Julia laughed. "Thirteen?"

"Monday after next?"

Julia held out her hand again, and this time Erin shook it. "Thanks, for everything."

Life settled into a groove. Julia woke at six o'clock with William beside her in bed. She got up and dressed for work. Woke Paige, made her breakfast, ring mastered the circus that was their morning routine, and took Paige to school. Drove to work for Holly, then ate lunch in the car on the way to work for Erin. Got off work again at five-thirty and went to pick up Paige from her mother. Made dinner and got Paige in bed by eight o'clock. Worked on her portion of the business plan until she dropped from exhaustion at ten-thirty.

Sometimes when William came home after work, they were both too exhausted to do more than hold each other for a few minutes before falling asleep. Other times they lay awake a while, talking about their day and their steady progress with the business plan.

After one busy Friday night at work, William told her, "Mike is coming home from rehab next week."

"Oh. I guess you'll want to spend the night at home a while."

But he shook his head. "I'm done babysitting him. My mother can do that, if it's that important to her. He's going to spend the first week at home with my parents before trying his first night alone at our apartment. But my life is here now."

She reached for him, pulled his face down to hers. After kissing him for a while, she sat up, lifted the nightgown off of herself. He looked at her skin draped in light from the window, at the mermaid pendant glinting against her chest. He put his lips to her ear and whispered, "Come lay down with me."

He leaned back, pulled her on top of him. Touched and kissed her face and her lips. Pulled her up a little further and kissed her breasts. His mouth circled around to her nipples, and he kissed and sucked them gently.

"I can't believe you still want to do this, after the day you've had," she whispered.

He pulled down her underwear, stroked her bare bottom. Slipped his fingers inside of her.

"I see you do, too."

She gave a long exhale of pleasure. He pulled her up even further, made love to her with his mouth and his fingers. Brought her to the edge and pulled her back mercilessly, again and again.

She looked down at him and begged him, "Please."

His eyes flitted up to her face, laughing at her. He shifted his fingers a little, and her body wrenched itself inside-out in wave after endless screaming wave.

When the waves finally subsided, he slid her down onto him and rolled her onto her back. Made love to her that way for a while, then flipped her onto her hands and knees. Gathered up her hair in his hands and held it behind her head as he rode her from behind. Though she tried, she had no way to reach up and muffle the sound of his voice as he came. And he had never been one to be quiet about that.

Afterward, he collapsed on top of her. She let him lay there and listened to his breath lengthen, felt his body sink into hers as sleep overtook him.

"Daddy!"

Julia reacted before she knew what happened, and she practically threw William off of her. She did not know where he landed or what he did. She only knew she was out of the bed, standing on the bedroom floor, stark naked before her daughter.

"Daddy!" Paige shrieked. "You're here!"

Julia snatched her robe off the hook on her bedroom door, spun her daughter around by the shoulders and shuttled her out of the room. After closing the door, she heard it lock behind her.

"No, honey, Daddy's not here," she murmured, scrambling into her robe and tying it around her waist.

"Yes he is! I saw him!"

"No, Paige," said Julia, practically shoving her into the living room, "you didn't."

"I did! I heard a noise, and I came in and I saw him!"

"Paige. Daddy is not here." She didn't know what else to say.

"Yes he is!" Paige shrieked. "What, do you think I'm stupid? Let me see him!"

Julia knelt on the floor and grasped Paige by the shoulders. "I promise you. I would not lie to you. Daddy is not here."

Paige lashed out, smacked her across the face. Screamed, "Then who was it?"

Julia grabbed her around the waist, pinned her arms to her side as she kicked, flailed, and screamed like a being possessed. She contained her until her body unclenched and her rage subsided to a whimper.

"Mommy," Paige sniffled after a while. "Who was that?"

Julia wracked her brain for an answer. She didn't want to lie and say, "No one." Paige knew what she saw. But she certainly wasn't ready to tell her the truth. Not at this time, not in this way.

At a complete loss, she sighed and repeated, "It wasn't Daddy."

"Mommy," whimpered Paige. "Where is he?"

"I don't know."

After a moment, Paige said, "Why won't he come home?"

"I don't know that either, Paige. But it's not your fault. You didn't do anything wrong. He didn't leave because of you."

"Then why?"

"I don't know. I wish I had a better answer for you." She squeezed her around the shoulders. "But I do know that I love you. And no matter what your father did, I promise you that I will never, ever leave you. Ever."

They held each other there for a long time before Julia gently suggested, "Now let's go back to bed."

They stood up and returned to Paige's room. Julia helped Paige into her bed, rubbed her back and sang her a few songs.

"I love you," she whispered at last. "Sweet dreams."

She closed the door, and tiptoed back to her own door. Tapped it lightly, and heard it unlock. Went to sit on the side of the bed.

He sat beside her, grasped her arm. "I'm so sorry."

"It's okay."

"Should I go?"

She buried her face in his shoulder. "If I were a good mom, I would probably tell you to go. But I don't want you to."

"You are a good mom."

"No. Did you hear her? Have you ever heard such rage in a seven year old?"

"That's not your fault."

"I should have been focusing more on her, and not on my own selfish needs."

He touched her chin, lifted her face to his. Stroked her chin with his thumb.

"Are you happier now than you were when you first came back to the city?"

She nodded.

"An unhappy mother can't take care of an unhappy child. Now you can do whatever you think you need to do for her."

She rested her forehead against his. "My God, what have I done to deserve you?"

He pulled her down onto the bed and laid her head on his chest. Stroked her hair until she fell asleep.

The Sunday before William's birthday, Julia called her sister.

"I need a huge favor," she said. "Help me bake and decorate a cake."

"Sure, but what kind of cake are we talking about here?"

"Just a normal birthday cake."

"Whose birthday?"

"William's."

"Oh! Well, for a cause like that…"

Alison came over that night after Paige went to bed but before William came home from work.

"It seems pretty serious between you two," Alison ventured while the cake finished cooling and they mixed the icing. "Forgive me, but I couldn't help noticing the extra adult toothbrush in the bathroom and the home-cooked leftovers in the fridge. I know that's not you, making pasta alla norma."

Julia laughed. "He makes stuff in the mornings occasionally so we have something to eat for dinner."

"Jesus Christ. Has Paige met him yet?"

"No."

"I understand why you're holding off. But I want you to know that I support you one hundred percent, even if no one else does. I've always liked William."

"No you haven't. You once called him a stick-in-the-mud."

Alison frowned. "Really? I'm an idiot. Why do you ever listen to me?"

Julia laughed. After a while, Alison asked, "What about your business plan? How's that coming along?"

"We finished it."

"We? William is helping you with the aquarium business?"

Julia felt her face burning. "Oh, that business plan. That one got shelved in favor of a new one."

"Okay. What's the new plan?"

"Whale-watching tours."

Alison looked almost alarmed. "That sounds ambitious."

Julia shrugged. "You only live once."

"Don't you need some kind of license to run a boat like that?"

"William needs a license to run the boat, but he qualifies for it. He's racked up plenty of hours on his uncle's boat over the years."

"And so where do you fit in with all of this?"

"I would be the naturalist on board, and I'd help with all the other aspects of running the business, too."

Alison peered sharply at her. "Julie, this is *his* dream, not yours."

Julia found herself feeling annoyed. "Don't you think it's a good fit for me? I wanted to be a marine biologist once."

"Yes, but all the hassle of running that business, in exchange for just a few hours a week of talking to strangers about whales?"

Julia frowned down at the icing, turning crumbly in the bowl. "Should I add more milk now?"

Alison gave a start and turned to look. "Oh, yes. Good catch."

After Julia rescued the icing, Alison put a hand on her shoulder. "Look, Julie, I'm sorry. I told you, don't listen to me. It's sweet that you and William are working together on something. And if anyone can make that business work, you two can."

Monday night, William came over after Paige went to bed, and Julia met him at the door.

"I have a surprise for you." She planted him on the sofa and said, "Wait here."

She went to the kitchen to retrieve the cake. Since she couldn't fit thirty-one candles on his cake, she stuck in three, lit them, and carried the cake into the living room.

She set the cake on the coffee table in front of him. "I know your birthday's not until Friday, but I wanted to celebrate on your day off."

"This looks homemade."

"I had a lot of guidance from Alison," she admitted, sitting beside him. "But it's all my own handiwork."

He squeezed her hand and blew out the candles, and Julia cut pieces for both of them.

"This is really good," he remarked after the first bite.

"Don't look so surprised," she laughed. "I have to admit, it turned out way better than I expected. But just like with our business plan, I had the right inspiration."

He leaned over to kiss her, and she let him finish his piece of cake before saying, "Are you ready for the icing on the cake?"

He smiled, no doubt anticipating something entirely different than she had in mind. But she went to open the drawer of her little desk and pulled out a flat, rectangular package, wrapped in paper and tied with a ribbon. She brought it to him on the sofa and sat down beside him.

He took it and peered quizzically at her. "What is this, a magazine?"

"Just open it."

He untied the ribbon and carefully tore open the paper. Pulled out a folder and scanned the contents.

"Is this what I think it is?"

"One completed and typed business plan."

He flipped through the pages. "My God. When have you had time to type all this up?"

"I had plenty of inspiration. I made the time."

He swung her legs across his lap and stroked them with his fingers. "It won't be much longer now. I won't have to work as a cook, and you won't have to work as a secretary."

"It won't take off right away. We'll still need something to pay the bills."

She realized she had said "we." As if it were a given that they would be in it together, this business of paying the rent, keeping the lights on.

"But you don't like that work," he said.

"I do like it okay, and I'm good at it. Just like you and cooking. In time, I can work my way up to being a paralegal."

"By then, you won't need to."

She smiled warmly up at him. "When you say it, I believe it. There's not a doubt in your mind, is there?"

His fingertips nuzzled the hair at the nape of her neck. He drew her face closer and whispered, "Not one."

With one hand, she began lazily undoing the buttons on his shirt. He watched her fingers work for a while, then said, "Icing?"

She answered him by opening his shirt, peeling it back off his shoulders. He lifted her chin, opened her mouth and kissed her. Lifted her whole body off the couch and carried her into the bedroom.

Afterward, facing each other in bed on their sides, he twisted a section of her hair through his fingers. They gazed in silence at each other for a long time, taking in each other's faces.

"My God, you rock my world," he said finally.

She laughed, and he smiled softly in return, but the smile was thoughtful.

"What happens after this?" he asked.

She considered a moment. "Make a sandwich?"

He smiled, but his eyes were serious. "You said 'we' earlier. I want to make that official."

She rubbed his shoulder. "What are we talking about here?"

"Whatever I can get."

"We already live together."

"If you call this living together. I have to sneak in and out of here, and your daughter doesn't know me."

Her stomach tightened. "Maybe this sounds strangely old-fashioned considering what we're already doing, but it doesn't feel right."

"What doesn't?"

She considered her words carefully. "Letting my daughter see you share a bed with me. Letting you openly live with us, in the same house. Certainly not until…" She did not know how to talk about this. Not here, not now. "I have a signed Order of Publication. It should only be another couple of months. But even after the divorce, I'm not sure it would be right to just move you right in, not with my daughter."

He propped himself up on one elbow, fingered the mermaid pendant at the end of her chain. "I would marry you today if I could. If it's not you, it's no one." He cupped her chin in his hand, made her look him in the eye. "You're the love of my life. I've loved you since we were seventeen years old."

She took his hand and put it between her breasts so he could feel her heartbeat. The look on his face told her that he had received the message loud and clear.

"There's something I want to show you," she murmured.

She got up, opened the closet door, and pulled out the shoe box. He recognized it instantly.

"Oh my God."

"I've kept it all these years." She set it on the bed and opened it. "I did a bang-up job of convincing myself that I didn't love you anymore. But here lies the evidence that I always did."

He reached in, pulled out the poems and the songs. Flipped through the photos. "I had forgotten about some of these." Holding up the ones of her, he said, "Not these, of course. I kept copies of them for myself. I wish I could transport us to my apartment right now. I'd show you where I still have them."

She reached for his hand. "I'm sorry for everything back then. I was confused, and scared. But I could never get you out of my heart, no matter how hard I tried."

He put her hand to his lips. Then he reached down into the box again, and froze. Slowly, he opened the black velvet box and pulled out the diamond ring inside.

He picked up her hand, and slid the ring on her finger. "It still fits you perfectly."

"Will," she said.

"It's what I always wanted."

"I swear to you, I'd wear the ring if it weren't for one thing – Paige would ask about it."

He looked soberly at her. "I really think it's time for her to meet me."

She shook her head. "I'm not sure about that."

"I am. You don't have to introduce me yet as what I am to you. You can just introduce me as William. But it's time for her to start getting used to me being around."

She peered at him a moment, considering. "When?"

"Let me take us all out to the Farallones Saturday on my Uncle Frank's boat."

Her eyebrows lifted. "Would he let you do that?"

"I've been running Frank's boat since I was a teenager. I go out there with him once a week during crab and herring seasons, and as much as possible the rest of the year. I know what I'm doing, and he knows it."

"Wow," said Julia.

At the look on her face, he laughed and said, "You don't believe me, do you?"

"Of course I do," she said unconvincingly.

"If you don't believe me, then how can you believe that I can run the boat of a whale-watching business?" She had no answer for him, so he said, "I'm calling Frank right now. I'll let him tell you himself."

"What? No." She tried to stop him, but he laughed and shrugged her off. He reached for the phone on the bedside table.

"You can't call him this late at night," she protested.

"He's an old insomniac. Besides, Italians keep late hours."

"He's Italian-American. Not the same thing."

"Close enough." He dialed the number, and after the initial greeting and explanation for the call, he said, "Tell her honestly what you think."

A moment later, he handed the phone to Julia. She accepted it, and awkwardly said, "Hello?"

"Will is the finest skipper this side of the United States Naval Academy, and I'll fight anyone to the death who wants to argue the point with me."

"Jesus. Okay," she said, and handed the phone back to William.

He took it. "What did you say to her?" After a moment, he laughed, and said, "Thanks."

He hung up again and turned to her with a grin. "Now do you believe me?"

"I think you two colluded on this beforehand."

He laughed, picked up her hand with the ring and kissed it. "I'm taking you and Paige Saturday morning. We'll make an early start of it, and it'll be a very short trip because I have to go to work at three. But it's happening."

"Aye aye, captain."

He looked down at the ring now. "Wear it tonight, at least. And promise me one thing."

"What's that?"

"Marry me within the next year."

"If it's what's right for Paige too, then I will."

"Of course it will be. She'll get to see what it looks like when a man really loves her mother. How can that not be what's right for her?"

She picked up his arm and turned it over. Ran her fingers over the mermaid tattoo, watching the ring pass back and forth over it. Her eyes flitted up to find him watching her with a significant smile.

By way of beginning the subject, she reached for the other arm with the compass tattoo. "How long have you had this?"

"I got it just before I left for Alaska."

"What was happening in your life when you got this one?"

His smile faded a bit. "To be honest with you, I had been leading a pretty debauched existence for a long time, and I was very burned out. I needed a little direction in life."

Her eyebrows lifted. "What do you mean, leading a debauched existence?"

"I was drinking a bit too much. Smoking a bit too much weed. And…" He seemed to be struggling for the right words. "Having a few too many meaningless relationships."

He waited to see how she would react to this last bit of information. She touched the compass, allowing the full meaning of his revelation to sink in.

"That explains the compass," she said softly after a moment, picking up his other arm again. "What about the mermaid?"

"I got that when I came back from Alaska." She saw the pain in his eyes, and he didn't seem to be able to speak of it anymore. She lifted his arm to her lips, and kissed it.

Frank's boat still docked at the same slip where Julia had last seen it eleven years ago. Though she could see the lights on in the cabin, there was no sign of William yet.

"Mommy, who's the captain?" Paige finally thought to ask.

"You'll meet him in just a second." Julia tried in vain to settle the butterflies in her stomach. She called out, "Hello? Anyone home?"

A moment later, William appeared on the deck, waved, and climbed up the ladder to the pier.

"Paige, this is William," said Julia. "He's the captain today."

Paige looked up at him, a bit awe-struck. William squatted down and shook her hand. "Nice to meet you," he said.

"You don't look like much of a captain to me," said Paige.

"I forgot my hook and my eye patch," William replied, which earned smiles from both Paige and Julia. "I have something for you. I'll be right back."

He descended the ladder again and went back into the cabin. When he emerged, he carried a child-size life jacket. Paige groaned, and William explained, "In case I have to make you walk the plank."

"Then wouldn't you want us *not* to wear them?" Paige pointed out.

William's eyes widened at Julia. "She's a precocious one, isn't she?"

Nevertheless, the pirate theme was working well. Paige suffered the indignity of putting on her life jacket.

"Now come on board. I have something else for you. Something better than a life jacket," William said.

He descended the ladder first, then helped Paige. Once Julia joined them, he led them into the cabin, where he had a pan of something waiting on the stove. Paige realized what it was when he poured it into her mug and opened a bag of miniature marshmallows.

"Hot chocolate!" she cried.

"Have a seat," William said. She sat on the bench, and he served her.

With Paige happily engrossed, William turned to Julia. "Coffee?"

"Nice," Julia said with a grin. "Load her up with sugar and keep her in a confined space for several hours."

"It's pure bribery," William confessed, handing her a mug of coffee.

After the hot chocolate, William set the course on the plotter, and then Paige wanted nothing more than to stand at his shoulder and ask him about every piece of equipment as William steered the boat out of the harbor.

"Paige, he needs to concentrate on what he's doing."

"No, it's okay," said William.

Julia had another idea. "You know what? We should go out on the deck. We're going to sail right underneath the bridge soon."

That got Paige's attention, and Julia led her onto the bow to watch the bridge sail right over their heads, as she had all those years ago with William. It impressed Paige so much that she actually shouted, "Whoooaa!"

"Now come around to the stern," said Julia.

"I can see the cars on the bridge!" shouted Paige when they got there.

They saw porpoises during the journey out to the islands, and of course they saw sea lions and birds on the islands, once they anchored.

"Where are the whales?" demanded Paige when they went inside for lunch.

"I sent an invitation, but the postal service must run slow in the ocean," replied William.

"How did you become a boat captain?"

"Well, you don't really need a license or anything to run a small fishing boat like this. I learned how from my uncle, who owns it."

"So you're a fisherman?"

"Only sometimes. Most of the time, I'm a cook."

Paige looked askance at him. "Are you sure you know how to run this thing?"

William turned to Julia and feigned confusion. "Do I know how to run this thing?"

"According to your Uncle Frank, you do." Julia looked at Paige. "He got us here safely, didn't he?"

Paige looked unimpressed. "Well, just don't sink it on the way back."

"Paige," Julia said sharply.

Unfazed, William said to Paige, "I think I'm going to need your help getting this thing safely back to port. Are you up for the job? Will you be first mate?"

Paige tried and failed to look disinterested. She glanced at Julia for permission.

"Go ahead, if you dare," said Julia.

After lunch, William let Paige help him crank the winch to raise the anchor, though in truth, he did most of the work. He let her steer the boat and help with every aspect of running the boat that he could.

A little distance away from the islands, Julia cried out, "Look!"

A gray whale appeared fairly close to their boat. Paige ran to the port side of the boat to watch it dive a few times and send up its distinctive V-shaped spout. William came out with his camera and took a few photos of the whale, then said, "How about a family photo?"

"Hurry up, Paige, before the whale disappears." Julia gathered her up against her side, and William took several photos of them with the whale in the background.

"I don't know if the whale will come out in the photo, but you'll at least have a souvenir of the trip," said William.

After they went back underneath the bridge again, William let Paige come up to the top drive with him and steer the boat back into the harbor, and finally into the slip. As Paige descended to the deck, her only complaint was that the trip was over.

In fact, she clamored around him now, demanding to know when they could do it again.

"Paige, give him room to breathe," laughed Julia. "This is a very special thing William did for us, and it's not likely to happen again soon. But maybe we can do something else with him sometime soon."

"We can go crabbing," suggested William.

"Crabbing?" echoed Paige.

William looked incredulously at Julia. "You mean to tell me you've never taken this kid crabbing?"

"No one ever took *me* crabbing," replied Julia.

William shook his head. "That is criminal. We're going to have to do something about that. Next Saturday, at the municipal pier, you and Paige are going to catch yourselves a crab dinner."

Paige looked skeptical. "I don't know if I like crab."

"Well, you're going to love catching them, and then you can throw them back if you want," replied William.

"Paige," Julia said, "William's got to finish up with the boat and then go to his other job. What do you say to him for the fun day?"

"Thank you," she piped.

William helped them all back onto the pier and took the life jacket back from Paige. "See you two next Saturday," he said.

Over Paige's head, Julia caught his eye and exchanged a warm smile with him as she turned to go.

The following Wednesday night, after tucking Paige into bed, the doorbell rang. Cursing whoever it was, praying that it didn't wake Paige, she walked down the stairs and looked through the peep hole.

She did not recognize the male figure on the doorstep. "Who is it?"

"Julia."

Her heart stopped. She looked through the peep hole again. She recognized the voice, but the face did not match it.

"Kevin?"

"It's me."

Julia debated whether or not to even open the door. Finally she did, but only to step out onto the doorstep and close the door behind her.

It was him, all right, his face altered by drastic weight loss and too much sun, his eyes bloodshot, his bushy dark hair and beard overgrown and a bit disheveled.

She crossed her arms and glared at him. "How dare you come here?"

He blinked. "Your mother told me where you live."

"My *mother*?"

"I called your parents' house first, when I found strangers living in our house." He peered somberly at her. "May I come in?"

"No, you may not."

"Is Paige in there?"

"She's sleeping, so you can just go."

Kevin shifted his weight and stared down at the ground. Cleared his throat. "Julia —"

"Where the hell have you been?"

"Brazil."

"I know that. They traced you there."

"Who did?"

Julia scowled at him. "Where in Brazil?"

"Very, very far in the interior."

"And what have you been doing there for the past six months?"

"Staying with an old friend of mine from the Peace Corps who's an ethnographer, studying a tribe in the Amazon."

"Seriously?"

"Julia, I'd really like to come in and just talk to you for a second."

"Absolutely not." She considered for a moment, then carefully said, "Where are you staying?"

He shrugged. "I guess I'm staying at my parents' house."

"Go there, and stay there. Don't leave. We'll talk tomorrow as soon as I'm able."

With that, she went back inside and closed the door in his face.

The first thing she did when she got back upstairs was to dial Erin's cell phone.

"He came to my front doorstep just now."

"Who did?"

"Kevin."

"What?"

"Out of the blue. He said he'd been spending the past months in the Amazon rain forest."

"Is he still there?"

"No. I have no idea what condition he's in, mentally or physically. But I got an assurance from him that he'll be at his parents' house in Atherton tomorrow. Can we serve the papers on him there tomorrow?"

"Yes. Let me get started on that right away. And don't try to talk to him yourself. Under any circumstances."

"Don't worry, I won't."

"And Julia. You'd better tell William to lay low for a while. In fact, I wouldn't let him come around at all until further notice."

Julia contemplated this with a sinking feeling. "Why?"

"For one thing, if you're concerned about Kevin's mental state, then you should worry about what he would do if he found William hanging around, particularly with Paige in the house. And secondly, let's not give Kevin any more ammunition to use against us in court."

"All right." But privately Julia was not sure how long she'd be able to adhere to Erin's advice.

The first call Julia made after hanging up with Erin was to her mother.

"You gave him my address?!" she yelled as soon as her mother picked up the phone.

Her mother's voice on the other end of the line was maddeningly calm. "He's your husband. He's entitled to give his account to you."

"Really? A man leaves his family for no good reason, with no warning, casting serious doubt on his mental well-being; and then he comes back from the middle of the Amazon, looking sickly for all the world, carrying God knows what; and the first place you send him to is the house where his child lives?"

The line was silent. After a moment, her mother said, "If you're that worried about your safety, your father can come stay at your house tonight."

"No, I don't need any more interference from him or you. You've done quite enough as it is. Stop talking to Kevin, and refrain from sharing your thoughts on my marriage from this point forward."

Julia jabbed the button on the phone, hanging up. She held it in her hand a moment, taking deep breaths to calm herself. Then she pushed the button again and dialed William's cell phone. But of course he was in the middle of dinner service, so she left him a voice mail with the details.

He called her back at the end of his shift.

"I'm still coming over tonight."

"Erin strongly advised against that, for Paige's safety."

"If you think he could hurt you and Paige, then that's all the more reason for me to be there."

"I don't really think he's capable of that. But I don't want him to see you and use that against me in the divorce." Julia's tone softened. "Are you worried that he's going to steal me away from you?"

"No," he said a little too defensively. "You'd be crazy to take him back."

"That's right. I swear, you're never going to lose me again. Please, let's follow the attorney's advice on this point. If only for a little while. Then we can go right back to flipping her the bird and throwing all caution to the wind."

He considered for a long time. Finally, he said, "Make sure all your doors and windows are locked and the blinds are closed. And I'm calling you first thing in the morning."

"Fine, but don't worry about us. We'll be safe."

The next day at work, Erin said, "The deed is done."

"Marvelous," replied Julia. "Now how do we start working with him to sell the house?"

"I'm sure we'll be hearing from his attorney sometime very soon."

That night, as Julia walked into her parents' house, Paige ran down the stairs and cried, "Mommy! Daddy came back!"

Paige grabbed her hand and dragged her up the stairs into the living room. Sure enough, there on the living room sofa sat Kevin, beside her mother.

Julia's jaw dropped, and she glared at her mother, who gazed back at her with maddening serenity.

Rage swelled in her chest. "How dare you come around here like this?" she shouted at Kevin. "This child has cried almost every night since you left, and you just come waltzing back, giving me no chance to prepare her?"

"Calm down," her mother said, grabbing Paige and shielding her, which only infuriated Julia further. As if Julia was the one that Paige needed protecting from.

Paige looked up at Julia in shock. "Mommy, why are you yelling at Daddy? He came home!"

"Much better that you'd kept on playing Indiana Jones in the jungle," Julia sniped at Kevin in response.

To Julia's horror, Paige whimpered and sniffled at her grandmother's side. Shaking with adrenaline as the rage drained from her body, Julia gathered her up and went to sit with her on the love seat.

"Julia," Kevin said quietly after a moment. "There are a lot of things I need to explain to you. So many different things I have to say. Isn't there some way we could go back to your house and talk?"

"Paige can spend the night here," Julia's mother offered.

Julia scowled at them both, and said nothing. After a moment, Paige whimpered, "Mommy, please don't make Daddy leave again."

"Perfect," Julia seethed at Kevin. "You've made me out to be the bad guy."

Kevin knelt in front of Paige and took her by the shoulders. "Paige, sweetie, your mommy has done nothing wrong. There's a very good reason why she's angry at me. Don't blame Mommy for any of this."

Paige looked as stunned by his confession as Julia felt, but she said nothing. Then Kevin turned to Julia, waiting for her answer.

"You have thirty minutes," Julia said through gritted teeth. To her mother, she added, "I'm picking her up after."

Julia and Kevin walked the entire way to Julia's house in silence. She glowered at him as she passed him by, opened the door, and let him inside.

He glanced around himself as he went up the stairs and ascended into the living room. For a moment, she imagined he was passing judgment on the humble surroundings, until he said, "You've done well for yourself."

"No thanks to you."

Kevin turned to face her. "I deserve that."

"You're damn right you do."

"But I'd like for you to hear me out."

"What do you think we're here for?"

Kevin spotted Paige's aquarium. He went to peer at it a moment.

"You've really made it a home," he remarked.

Julia glanced at the clock on the wall. "Now you have twenty-eight minutes."

Kevin sat on the couch. Julia took a seat in the armchair and waited.

"I have no excuse for what I did," he began. "It was selfishness of the highest order. It was so far beyond the pale that it deserves no forgiveness."

"I still want some explanation of what you were thinking when you did it."

"I panicked," he said. After a moment of struggling to find words, he added, "I guess I was having some sort of a mid-life crisis. To be honest, the thoughts that were running through my mind sound insane to me now. I was thinking that my life was over. That I had sacrificed my ideals and dreams to the whims of another person."

"Don't you dare try to blame me."

"No, not you. My father. I was following his dream for my life, not my own. Going to work for his firm. Buying a house in west Menlo and living that lifestyle."

"Oh, you poor little rich kid."

"No, you don't understand."

"No, *you* don't understand. You have no idea what it's like to wonder if you'll have enough money at the end of the bills to buy groceries for your child. To wonder how you'll ever afford to put a roof over her head. These are all real problems that real people have. Real people would kill to have problems like you had."

Sheepishly, he said, "You're right. You're absolutely right. I saw first-hand what it means to struggle for survival. I saw things that would break most people in our part of the world. They couldn't just run away, like I did. They had to endure."

"Paige and I are not something to be endured."

"No, I didn't mean that you and Paige were the problem. The problem was me. I didn't have the courage to continue the life I had started, and I didn't have the courage to change it. I didn't even give you and Paige the chance to either accept the changes, or not."

"I've always told you that if studying marine biology or joining the Foreign Service was what you wanted to do with your life, then that's what you should do."

"Yes, but the more entrenched we became in our lifestyle, the less chance I saw of disentangling us all from it. I felt like it was too late."

"Well, I'm sorry you didn't believe me when I told you otherwise. But you were wrong."

He shifted in his seat, grasping for the right words. "Julia, I'll do whatever it takes to make it up to you and Paige. Please don't tell me it's too late."

"It absolutely is too late. There is a less than zero percent chance of me taking you back. And you have no concept of how badly you've hurt Paige. It has taken months of therapy for her to stop crying for you on a daily basis. There's no way I'm letting you back in."

His eyebrows knit together. "Julia, I know you find this hard to believe, given the way I treated you. But I love you. I really, truly do. And I always have, ever since that marine biology summer camp. You're such a unique spirit. When I think of how I've failed you and Paige, I don't know how I'll ever forgive myself if you don't give me a chance to make it right. Because I can promise you, I can swear to you now that I will."

Julia scowled at him. "I don't love you anymore. I'd like you to leave now, and never come back."

He looked stricken, but he said, "I will leave, for now. But I'm entitled to see Paige."

"Don't threaten me."

"I'm not threatening you, Julia. It's a simple fact. I want to rebuild my relationship with her, even if I can't with you."

"We'll see about that."

He dragged himself to his feet. She followed him out the door, closed and locked it behind her. Turned to him and said, "Go back to Atherton. You'll be hearing from my lawyer this week. Don't call me or come by here again."

She watched him get in his car and drive away. Then she set off in the direction of her parents' house. The walk would clear her head and calm her spirits. When she finally got to the house and found Paige in the living room with her mother, she had enough peace of mind to calmly answer Paige's inquiries after her father.

"Paige, Mom, I want you all to listen to me." She sat down in the middle of the living room floor and waved Paige over to her.

"Paige, there's something you need to understand. Your daddy will not be living with us anymore."

"Julia," said her mother.

"I'm telling her the facts."

"But Mommy," said Paige, "won't I get to see him again?"

Julia softened. "Yes, Paige, you will see him again. But he won't be living with us."

Paige looked stricken. Then she slowly buried her face in Julia's shoulder and began to cry. Julia wrapped her arm around her, stroked and patted her back. She turned to her mother. "I'll say it again. The sooner we can move forward from here, the sooner we can all begin to heal."

Her mother looked chastened, and said nothing more. Then Julia took Paige home, fed her dinner, and put her to bed.

That night, after his shift, she updated William over the phone on the day's events. He seemed satisfied by her account of everything she had said to both Kevin and her mother.

"Can I come home?" he asked after a while.

She realized that by home, he meant her place. Slowly, she said, "I guess you should go to your apartment. That's what Erin would tell me to say, at least until we see what Kevin's lawyer comes up with. I really don't want them finding a way to involve you in all this nastiness."

"I think that's unavoidable." He hesitated, then said, "I really want to come home. Please say I can."

"Oh, God. Okay."

At the municipal pier on Saturday, as Julia watched William show Paige how to assemble the crabbing rig, bait the cage with chicken pieces, and pick up the crabs without getting pinched, she wondered if one year was really too long to wait.

When they had filled their catch bucket with as many crabs as they thought they could cook, William said, "Can you drive me over to the restaurant now? There's something I want to show you while we're down there. It's very close."

"What is it?"

"It's a secret."

They loaded the spoils of the day into her trunk and drove the short distance to the restaurant. When they got out, he brought them right across the pier to a lovely little brown wood-framed building she had known all her life.

"The Fisherman's Chapel? This is what you wanted to show me?"

"But have you ever been inside it?"

"Well, a long time ago, when I was a kid. But I didn't pay much attention to it then."

"Come inside. Let me show you."

"You're taking us to a church?" Paige said, giving William the stink eye.

"Not a church. A chapel. There's something inside I want to show you both."

Just above the double doors of the entrance was a stained glass window bearing the image of a nautical steering wheel. The sunlight streamed into the chapel through that window.

"It's beautiful," Julia murmured. "I never got to see the colors properly before."

"Over here is what I wanted to show you."

He led them over to a wall bearing plaques with scores of names on them. Most of the names were Italian.

"Fishermen lost at sea," he explained. He pointed to some of the names. "Including Cardones. My mother's family."

Paige was thoroughly unimpressed, but Julia knew this hadn't been intended for her. She looked around at the interior of the chapel. At the front, a picture window overlooked the water. The altar that sat before it was a simple affair draped in green, adorned with plain white candles. Underneath a peaked brown wooden beam ceiling, wooden pews lined the sides of the chapel, divided by a center aisle. It was simple, unpretentious, and poetic.

"We should do it here," she said.

He turned to look at her with wide eyes. "Do what?"

So that Paige wouldn't hear, she whispered, "Get married."

He almost grabbed her before remembering Paige. "That's exactly what I was hoping you would say."

"It's perfect."

"Yes." She could tell it was killing him that he couldn't touch her.

At that moment, Paige tugged on Julia's arm. "Mommy, this is boring. Let's go."

Julia smiled at William, and as they exited the chapel, she said, "William has to go to work now, Paige. What do you say to him for the fun day?"

"Thank you," Paige said.

"You're welcome," he replied. To Julia's surprise, he leaned into her ear and whispered, "I've never been so happy in my entire life as I am right now."

He drew back again, and smiled at her with his eyes crinkled up in their distinctive way. He turned to go, his gaze lingering on her a moment longer.

"What did he say, Mommy?" Paige asked.

"He said he was happy." And Julia, watching him go, knew she was too.

When he crawled in bed that night and wrapped his arms around her, she woke up just enough to mumble, "I'll marry you in six months."

He squeezed her, but said nothing. Just let her drift back to sleep as he touched the mermaid pendant around her neck.

The next night, William said, "The band has a gig this Tuesday, at MacGowan's again. Do you think your sister can babysit that night, so you can come?"

"I don't know. I'd have to check."

He brushed the hair out of her face. "I'd love for you to come. Hear me sing properly this time."

She laughed a little bit at the memory of that. "I'd love that, too. Let me call my sister tomorrow."

Alison was available for babysitting, and on Monday, Julia asked Holly if she'd like to accompany her.

"Only if you promise to hook me up with the drummer."

Tuesday night found them at the pub, sitting in the front room this time, watching the band set up for their show and enjoying a pint of Guinness.

"You know, I talked to the drummer the last time we were here, and he's actually Irish," said Holly. "As in, from Ireland. Unlike that wannabe Irish brother of William's."

"Well, they are Irish-American."

"Separated by what, five generations?" Holly shook her head. "Wearing those political T-shirts like he has a freaking clue what it's all about."

Julia smiled. "Well, you don't want to get involved with a musician, anyway. They're a complicated lot."

"Is that supposed to discourage me? Because it failed epically."

Julia laughed, and a moment later Mike introduced the band. Since his stint in rehab he had put on some weight, cropped his black hair close to his head, and removed most of his facial piercings.

The band started in on their set, rendering conversation impossible. William sang back-up vocals, a point Julia hadn't picked up on during the last show she heard. He also played lead guitar remarkably well, and Julia marveled again at his self-effacing assessment of his own talents.

At one point in the show, Mike stepped back and let William take center stage in front of the microphone.

"Every time I play with these guys, I sing one particular song," William said quietly, almost whispering. "What I've never said before is that I wrote that song twelve years ago for one particular girl."

"Oh, no," said Julia, leaning back in her chair and covering her mouth with her hands. Holly laughed and patted Julia on the shoulder for support.

"Well, I can still hardly believe it," William continued, "but that girl is back in my life and sitting here right now. So I get to sing it to her tonight. Julie, I love you so much."

To Julia's dismay, most of the eyes in the audience followed his gaze to her. She felt flattered, yes, but also keenly embarrassed by all the unexpected attention. Her face and her ears burned fiercely.

With that, the band launched into the song. Mike grinned briefly out at her, the rest of the band members smirked down at their instruments, and the eyes of the audience lingered on her.

Julia knew it had taken him a lot of courage to do that, so she somehow found the courage to lower her hands from her face, to beam up at William as he sang his ballad to her. She had never heard the lyrics paired with a melody before, and it was much more of an indie-folk song than anything else that the band played. Like all of his songs and poems, it would not have been obvious that it was about his feelings for her, had he not just informed the entire audience. Sometimes he had to drop his eyes down to his guitar to steel his nerves, but he made it all the way through, and the audience cheered enthusiastically at the end for both of them.

The band launched into their next song, and the eyes of the audience drifted away from her finally. When the band took a break in its set, she touched Holly on the arm.

"I've got to go make a pit stop."

"I'm gonna go hit on the drummer," said Holly.

Julia grinned and found her way to the ladies' room. She found an open spot in front of the mirror, pulled a tube of lip gloss out of her purse, and began re-applying it.

A moment later, the restroom door opened. The woman who passed through it locked eyes on Julia's reflection in the mirror. Julia smiled sheepishly back at the woman's reflection, attributing the attention to the recent serenade she had received.

But the woman did not smile back. She was slim and very tall, with sleek dark hair pulled back into a ponytail and large, dark eyes. Her face would have been very pretty, if it hadn't been for the scowl it wore at the moment.

"So you're the flavor of the month," she said.

The hand applying Julia's lip gloss suddenly felt very heavy. She stared back at the woman's reflection in the mirror. "What?"

"Do you think you're the only woman he's written a song for?"

In the mirror, Julia saw her own jaw slackening. She turned to face the woman and said, "What are you talking about?"

She sneered. "Has he moved in with you yet?"

The whole world reeled. Noise rushed around inside of her head as if she were standing inside of a tin can.

"He has, hasn't he?" She shook her head. "Just don't let him get you pregnant. He's not the marrying type."

The woman turned. Walked out of the restroom. Vanished back into the nowhere she came out of.

"I have to go now."

Julia snatched Holly's hand, jerking her away from her tête-à-tête with the drummer.

"What?" sputtered Holly. "What's the matter?"

"I'll tell you and Alison at the same time when I get home. I don't want to have to tell this twice."

Julia didn't even look at William as she made a beeline out of the pub. On the sidewalk, Holly said, "Can you even give me a little hint?"

"No."

Holly followed her silently all the way back to her house. When they unlocked the front door and clambered up the stairs to the living room, Alison sprang to her feet.

"Why are you home so early?"

Julia collapsed on the sofa, speechless. Alison looked to Holly, who said, "I don't know yet."

Alison sat down next to Julia, snatched her hands. "Julie, tell me what's wrong."

Julia told them everything.

Alison looked sober. "She's a bitter ex-girlfriend."

"What about the part where he got her pregnant and wouldn't marry her?"

"We probably only have part of the story. She's trying to sabotage you and William. Let him tell you his side."

Holly shook her head. "I knew he was too good to be true. They always are."

Alison glared at her. "Thank you, Holly. I can take it from here, if you'd like to go home now."

Holly came to hug Julia around the shoulders. "I'm sorry. Call me later if you want."

"With comfort like yours, I'm sure she won't," Alison replied curtly.

Holly looked chastened, and left the house. Once she was gone, Alison grasped Julia by the arms and made her look in her eyes.

"I know how naïve and inexperienced you are, so let me just tell you right now – do not jump to conclusions here. It may be that little or none of this is true. But most importantly, remember that he's only human. We can't all be as saintly and virginal as you."

"I'm not saintly or virginal."

"Compared to me, you are."

"Oh, that's a high bar."

"Compared to *most* people, you are. How many men have you been with?"

"Two."

"That's what I thought. Many of us have been around the block a bit more. It doesn't have to mean he's a scumbag."

"Well, what if it turns out he *is* a scumbag? What if he has a kid out there that he's never told me about?"

"Then I'll cut his balls off personally and feed them to my cat."

Alison grinned, and Julia couldn't help giving her a halfhearted smile in return.

"Can I get you a glass of wine or something?"

Julia nodded and Alison went to the kitchen. When she returned, she carried a glass for each of them. She sat next to Julia on the couch, turned on the TV, and let Julia rest her head on her shoulder while they tried to watch.

All too soon, they heard the tell-tale rumble of motorcycle pipes. Julia sat up, her stomach churning with so many butterflies that she felt nauseous. Alison squeezed her hand for support.

"Do you want me to stay or go?"

"Go," said Julia. "Thank you."

William appeared then in the living room, and Alison practically sprinted out the door.

"I was just leaving," she called over her shoulder.

After watching her go, William said, "What was that about?"

Julia stared grimly at him. He sat next to her on the couch.

"What happened tonight? Why did you leave?"

Julia sprang to her feet, moved across the room from him.

"Hey," he said. "What's the matter?"

"I had an interesting conversation in the ladies' room. A woman I've never seen before in my life came up to me out of the blue. Would you like to hear a more or less exact transcript of the conversation we had?"

"If it's going to shed some light on what's going on, then yeah."

Julia ran down the conversation with him, except for the worst part, hoping he would be forthcoming with that information himself. "It was actually more of a monologue on her part, since I was too stunned to reply much."

William sat rooted to his spot on the couch, looking for all the world like a deer in the headlights.

"Then it's true," she said.

"Yes."

"You've lived with other women?"

"Yes, two. At different times, of course. Never for more than a year."

"Why didn't you tell me?"

"It never came up in conversation. You never asked."

"But you wrote her a song?"

"You once told me that you did a bang-up job of convincing yourself that you were over me, and that you were in love with someone else. Well, that's what I tried to do, too. I told you that I had not been celibate all this time, but that I was never in love."

"How many women have you been with?"

For a moment, he looked like a deer in the headlights again. Then, steeling himself, he said quietly, "I don't know."

"Oh, Jesus."

"Less than fifteen, for sure," he added quickly.

"Jesus Christ. Did you try to convince yourself that you were in love with all of them, too?"

"No."

"That woman in the bathroom. How long ago was that?"

He blinked, and looked flustered a moment. "I think it was three years ago."

"You think?"

He shook his head, as if to clear it. "I – I'm not sure which one it was. I told you I lived with two women. But the one I wrote the song for was three years ago."

Julia shifted her weight, crossed her arms. "She said, 'Don't let him get you pregnant. He's not the marrying type.'"

William put his hand to his mouth. "Oh, shit."

"It's true?"

He came over to Julia and tried to grab her hands, but she flinched backward. She could see his hands shaking. After collecting himself, he said, "She did get pregnant. I swear to you, I told her that I would help take care of the baby if she wanted to have it. But I wouldn't marry her because I didn't love her. If a kid's parents are married, they should love each other. In the end, she decided to have an abortion." He peered intently at her. "You know how much I love you and want to marry you. Of course I would marry you if you were pregnant. Of course I would take care of you both."

"Will, why was she there tonight? Is she stalking you or something?"

"No. I don't think so." After a moment's hesitation, he explained, "I'm guessing it's just a coincidence she was there tonight. She's from this neighborhood."

"Like I said, I've never seen her before in my life."

"She's… younger than us. She went to Lincoln with Kelly."

He watched her keenly as the knife twisted itself in her heart. After a while, he said gently, "What's going through your mind right now?"

"To be honest, I don't know what to think or believe."

"I never lied to you. If you had ever asked me about my past relationships, I would have told you. But really, how helpful or relevant would that have been? Please tell me you understand."

"I'm trying to understand. I want to believe you."

"I don't think I've done anything wrong, except to lead someone to believe that I loved them when I didn't."

"Maybe not. But to be honest, I'm thinking of all the times we've made love. Then I'm picturing you doing all those things to her, and to a dozen other women. And I'm having a really hard time with that."

He reached for her, but still she resisted. He said, "I've flailed around in life, looking for some way to forget about you. But I love you. I've never loved anyone else."

"See, now I'm thinking that sounds an awful lot like a line. You've had plenty of practice."

"Do you really think that's what I've been doing all this time? Feeding you lines?"

"That's a very skillful response. It gives an answer, without really answering anything."

"Jesus, Julie, what do you want me to say? I still don't think I've been so very bad."

Julia glowered at him, but said nothing.

"Julie, my jealousy once broke us up. Please, let's not do this again."

"Can you just give me a while to process all this?"

"How long is this going to take?"

"I can't give you a time frame on a thing like that."

He looked defeated. "I'll go to my apartment now. But can I call you tomorrow?"

Julia hesitated. "Okay."

He walked to the staircase that led down to the front door. Gave her one somber look before turning to go down the stairs.

She waited until she heard his motorcycle fade into the distance before calling her sister's cell phone.

"What's the story?" Alison said the moment she answered.

Julia ran down the conversation with her.

"Julie," said Alison. "Fifteen women in eleven years is *nothing*. That's like, one or two per year."

"It seems like a lot for someone who claims he loved only me this whole time."

"Julie. He's a horny single guy. What do you expect him to do, jerk off to your memory every day for eleven years?" Alison snorted at her own joke, then cleared her throat when she realized Julia wasn't laughing. "Julie, men are different. Actually, no, they're not different; they're just more comfortable with the truth. There's a big difference between sex and love. You can have sex with one person while you still love another one."

Julia was skeptical, until she remembered her own relationship with Kevin. Then she said, "What about his explanation of that woman's pregnancy?"

"Assuming he's not lying, I think it redeems him. He says he was willing to take responsibility, and I couldn't agree more with his reasoning about not getting married just because you're pregnant."

"Do you think he's lying?"

"That's not for me to answer. Has he given you any reason to think he's a liar?"

Julia considered. "No."

"Then maybe you should give him the benefit of the doubt."

Julia could think of nothing else to say. "I'm going to try to get some sleep now."

"Yes. Sleep on it. You'll think more clearly in the morning."

But predictably, sleep eluded her.

Why does this bother me now? she asked herself as she lay awake, fingering the mermaid pendant around her neck. She always knew he had been with other women, plural. And frankly, it was hard to mind too much when she was the beneficiary of his experience. So why did it make a difference now to have a more precise number?

Julia sensed the truth of her sister's counsel. She knew that if she couldn't take William's word for it, their relationship was doomed, anyway. She knew that, if he was telling the truth, then he had really done nothing so reprehensible. She would just have to align her previous concept of him with the new one.

The next night, her cell phone rang at the end of William's shift. Groggy, Julia fumbled for it in the dark and answered it.

"Hey."

"Hey," said William.

Neither of them said anything for a few moments. Finally, William murmured, "Jesus Christ, Julie. Please let me come home."

It tore Julia's heart, but she said, "There's a few more things I need to know."

"Like what?"

"You once told me you had led a debauched existence for a while. That you'd had a lot of meaningless relationships."

She waited to see how he would respond. Slowly, he said, "I was very depressed for a while. It's why I dropped out of school. Why I started drinking and smoking pot so much. And yes, I slept around a lot."

After a long pause to consider his response, she said, "I know you're a guy, and maybe this is a stupid question. But why did you feel the need to sleep around like that?"

"Julie..."

"No. I really need to know."

"The truth is, I don't really know how to answer that question." He considered for a moment. "It was one thing that made me feel better for a short time."

"And has that really changed since then?"

"Well, obviously I never took a vow of chastity. But I haven't been reckless about it, the way I was back then. I tried to take the first two relationships seriously, but like I told you, I realized I wasn't being honest."

"So what did you say to the other girls, like Amanda?"

"Jesus, Julie. They knew what they were getting from the very beginning. That's all I think I should say about it."

She considered his answer for a while. "Is there anything else I need to know about that time in your life? Or any time, for that matter?"

"No."

After a while, she said, "I need a little more time."

He sighed. "I'll call again tomorrow."

But less than a minute after she hung up, her cell phone rang again.

"Yes?"

There was a pause. "Hi, Julia. I have to admit, I'm surprised you answered."

"Kevin." If she hung up on him, he would know she had expected him to be someone else.

"I'm sorry if I woke you up. I was going to leave you a voice mail."

"Well, what were you going to say?"

"I wanted to let you know that, against my lawyer's strenuous objections, I'm willing to sign a postnuptial agreement. The house and all of our community property since our marriage would be legally yours as much as possible, and I would have no future claim on them."

Julia sat stunned for a moment. "Okay."

"But Julia. This is only if we stay married, and we live together as a family. I've told you that I'll never abandon you and Paige again, but I know you have no way of knowing that for sure. I want you to feel confident that, if you come back to me, you and Paige will always be safe and financially secure."

"Then don't waste your time, Kevin."

"Julia, if I go through with this, and later you decide to leave me anyway, I'll have no claim to any of those assets. You'll take all of it with you. But I'm willing to take that risk, because that's how important you and Paige are to me."

"Kevin, I'm telling you for the last time, it's not happening."

There was a long pause. "If you're determined to go through with this, I won't do anything to hurt you in the divorce. I'll make sure you and Paige get everything that you deserve. But Julia – I know you've been in a relationship with someone else. I know he's the one you were still with when I first met you. The one who nearly jumped me when he saw me with you." He waited to see if she would respond to this. When she did not, he added, "He's not going to take my place with Paige. And I'm going to make very sure Paige is safe with him."

"Please contact me through my attorney from now on." She hung up, and blocked his number.

On Friday afternoon, Erin approached Julia at her desk and said, "Do you have a minute to talk?"

"Sure."

Julia followed Erin into her office, and Erin closed the door behind them. "I'm afraid I have some bad news."

Julia's eyebrows lifted. "Okay."

"Kevin's lawyer has been hard at work. They've dug up some dirt on William from a long time ago, and I'm not sure how much of it you were already aware of. You might want to prepare yourself for a bit of a shock."

Julia felt her head spinning. "Okay."

Erin handed the brief across the desk to her. Julia took it up. Flipped through it. Felt her stomach churning with every item she read.

"How much did you know?" asked Erin after a few minutes.

"I knew about the girlfriend with the abortion," Julia admitted. "I knew the gist of the earlier stuff, but not the specifics. How could they dig up so many details from such a long time ago?"

"It's not that hard. A criminal background check and a private investigator. Interviewing old coworkers, and that kind of thing."

"Most of this was ten years ago," Julia protested. "Doesn't it count for anything that my dad later hired him back?"

"They can still use all of this against you. Bringing a man like this into your home with your children. Stuff like that."

Julia threw the brief down on the table. "So now what?"

"I suggest you talk to him tonight. On the phone, not in person. See how much of it he says is true."

That night, when William called her after work, she said, "We need to talk."

The tone of her voice gave him pause. "Okay."

"I'm afraid Kevin's lawyer has found out about you. All about you."

"What does that mean?"

"It means that I'm sitting here with a rather impressive list of dirt he dug up on you from the time before you went to Alaska."

There was a long pause. "I told you how I was living at that time in my life."

"Yes, Will. But now I have plenty of specifics. I see, as just one example, that Alison wasn't exaggerating about the kinds of high jinks that go on in the alley behind Dunphy's. Is that why you wanted to take me out there that time? To carve another notch into the wall?"

"Julie –"

"And you neglected to mention that you got yourself fired for that, and for showing up drunk and high. Or that you got your license suspended for DUI. Should I go on?"

There was another long, sickening pause. He said, "I had completely lost my way."

"Lost your way? That's your euphemism for it?"

"I'm sorry."

"You told me you didn't think you had done anything so very bad. Maybe I'm a total prude, but I think this is pretty bad. You also told me there was nothing else I needed to know from that time in your life. You've been disingenuous at best, and at worst, you outright lied to me."

"But why did I have to go into so much detail? The person I was then is not even someone I recognize anymore, so how could knowing all those details have possibly helped?"

"Don't you think I deserve to know this stuff? If nothing else, I'm wondering now if I need to get tested for anything."

"No," he said a bit breathlessly, as if mortified. "Of course I've been to a doctor since then."

"What about since Amanda?" There was no response. "I can't believe how stupid I've been."

"I made a lot of mistakes back then. But I am not that person anymore."

"Yes, you are. The fact is, you were and always will be capable of that stuff. I know for a fact, from firsthand experience, that taking risks still turns you on."

"Yes, and that's always turned you on about me. Don't try to tell me it doesn't."

She had no response for that. After a while, he continued, "That drunk driving thing was a wake-up call. That's when I went to Alaska. Working the boats there didn't leave me any time for that kind of shit. I know you haven't made anything close to the kinds of mistakes I've made. But I'd like to ask you to forgive me for what I did for a few months, over ten years ago, when I was so unhappy."

"Listen, Will, if you had just told me up front, it might not have been so bad. Waiting until I found out this way was just plain cowardly, and you know it."

After a moment, he said, "I'm sorry. Can I please come over, and let's talk about this?"

"No. I know how that's going to turn out. You're going to look at me with those sad eyes of yours, and I'm going to wind up in bed with you. I need some time to think rationally."

"Please don't push me away again," he said so quietly it was almost a whisper.

"I'm not pushing you away."

"Then let me call you tomorrow."

She hesitated. "Okay."

Very early the next morning, Julia's mother called her.

"Can you come over here this morning for a little while? There's something I'd like to talk to you about. Paige can watch a movie while we chat."

Julia glanced at the clock, not sure what time William was going to call. Not sure if she really wanted to talk to him yet, anyway. "We'll be over as soon as we can."

At her parents' house, Julia sat Paige down in front of Mary Poppins while her mother made them both a cup of coffee. At the kitchen table, her mother said, "Do you know why it took your father and me so long to get around to having Alison and you?"

"You always said it was because you were both too busy with the restaurant."

Her mother shook her head. "That's not the real reason. I was in and out of psychiatric hospitals for years before you two were born."

Julia's eyebrows lifted, but she could find nothing to say.

"They could never seem to get the right combination of medication. Eventually I had to undergo electroconvulsive therapy. That helped for a while, but it had some horrible side effects on my memory, so then I couldn't work for a while after each session. And eventually the benefits would wear off, anyway."

"Why didn't you ever tell us about this?"

"There was always such a stigma attached to it."

"So what finally helped?"

"They finally decided to try something different. Medication for manic depression – what they call bipolar disorder now. They had always diagnosed me with plain old depression, you see. I was never manic enough."

Julia allowed this to sink in for a few moments. Then she said, "Why are you telling me about this now?"

Her mother sipped her coffee. "I didn't struggle with depression until after my parents divorced."

Now Julia understood. "So divorcing Kevin will drive Paige to insanity."

"Will you just hear me out." It was a command, not a question, and delivered in a tone strained with frustration.

Julia sat back in her chair and waited.

"They divorced when I was eight," her mother continued, her voice placid again. "I came home one day from school, and he was gone, with no warning. I just withdrew. I was angry all the time. My grades in school plummeted. I had no more friends. I was the target of bullies."

"I'm sorry, Mom. It sounds like it was so hard on you. But what does this have to do with us?"

"I cried every night for my father. Begged my mother to let him come back home, even after my mother remarried. Oh sure, I saw him every once in a while. But I missed his daily presence, his constant influence on my life. Surely you know."

"What do you mean?"

"You had your grandmother and your Uncle Rob and Tim. But do you think that was any substitute for having your parents around?"

The stinging in Julia's eyes, the catch in her throat were ominous. She did not dare to meet her mother's eyes, for fear of what it would set off.

Her mother reached for Julia's hand. "I'm not saying that Paige is doomed to the same fate as me. But I am saying that the parallels between my experience and hers frighten me."

"You're right. She's not doomed to the same fate."

"She's a sensitive girl who loves both of her parents very much. I'm not making excuses for what Kevin did, but it seems like he's really trying to make amends." Her mother hesitated. "Julia, how much do you really know about William?"

With that, her mother stopped talking. The kitchen clock ticked loudly. Refrains of Mary Poppins drifted in from the living room.

"Are you hungry?" her mother asked eventually.

"No."

"Would you like to leave Paige here today and let her spend the night? Give yourself some time to think without any interruptions?"

Julia nodded. "Thank you."

When she got home that afternoon, she found a message from William waiting for her on the answering machine. Nothing much, just asking her to call him when she got the chance. She pulled her cell phone out of her purse, and found one there from him as well, saying the same thing.

It was one o'clock. Two hours until he started his shift. But she decided not to call him just yet. She would give herself the night to think.

When William called her after his shift, he waited for her to do the talking.

"Are you really sure this is what you want?" she said after a while.

"What do you mean?"

"Being a father figure to a kid who isn't yours? Putting up with her resentment because she thinks you're trying to take her father's place? Not being able to do whatever you want, whenever you want?" He said nothing for a moment, so she continued, "Are you really going to be happy limiting yourself to only one woman, for the rest of your life? Because I'm not going to want to share."

"If everything I've said and done hasn't reassured you by now, I'm not sure what will."

"I know your feelings are intense right now. But I'm afraid it's the kind of intensity that burns out quickly. We haven't been back together very long at all."

"You think I'm shallow."

"I'm just afraid you haven't thought everything through. I'm afraid we're letting our bodies run away with our brains."

"There you go with that again. Why can't it be both ways? Why can't we be great in bed and also genuinely in love?"

She considered a moment. "I think we should go back to our original plan – wait a year before getting married. At least. We all need to be sure this is the right thing."

"Whatever you need," he said, but she did not miss the note of resentment in his voice.

"Are you sure about that?"

"Julie, if it's time you want, then time is all I've got, because I'm never going to love anyone else."

Julia felt her heart ache, but forced herself to remember that it was the wise thing to do.

"Julie," he said. "Can I please come home now?"

"Will, you lied to me."

"I did not lie," he snapped.

"It was lying by omission."

"Tell me, Julie, at what point was I supposed to just work that stuff into the conversation? 'Hey, Julie, I love you so much, and by the way, I've slept with a dozen women, had two DUIs, and my ex-girlfriend aborted my child.' How do you suppose that would have gone over?"

"Let me remind you, I came right out and asked you if there was anything else you needed to tell me about your past."

He had no response for this.

"I've had a few shocks recently. I need more time," she said.

"How much longer are you going to keep on punishing me?"

"This is not about punishment. I'll take the time I need to work through it."

"Fine," he said petulantly. "Call me when you want to talk."

To her dismay, he hung up on her. She jammed the button on her cell phone and threw it across the room. Drew her knees up to her chest and stared out into the darkness of her bedroom.

Before Paige woke up the next morning, Julia guzzled a pot of coffee and surfed the internet for fresh ideas of what to do on a Sunday that wouldn't cost any money. She checked her e-mail.

A message waited there for her from Kevin.

She stared at it a moment. Against her better judgment, she clicked on it.

> Dear Julia,
>
> I'm e-mailing you because it looks as if you've blocked my number. I know you can't forgive me. I accept that you don't want to be married to me anymore. I'm still prepared to give you the full value of our house and all of our community property, with no strings attached. It's the least I can do for you and Paige. The money is of

no use to me. I hope one day, you
can bring yourself to forgive me. I
wish you all the happiness in the
world.

Love,
Kevin

After a moment's hesitation, Julia ran to the phone and dialed his number.

"Julia?" Apparently, he had caller ID.

She had a moment of relief. "I just read your e-mail."

"Oh."

"Are you okay?"

He hesitated. "Aside from facing the end of our marriage?"

"Well, yeah. I mean – to be honest, for a second I thought it was a suicide note."

"Oh. I'm sorry I alarmed you. Though I'm pleased that you cared."

"Kevin, I may not love you anymore, but I don't want to see you dead."

"I can see how it might have sounded that way, and I'm sorry."

A long pause ensued. Then Julia said, "I don't need all of that, Kevin. I just want my half."

"I don't need much to do the things I want to do with my life. I'm thinking maybe I'll go back to school and finish my doctorate in marine biology or something like that. Beyond that, I know how to live simply, believe it or not. I know there are things you'd like to do besides being a secretary, and the money will let you do them. It'll be legally yours and I'll have no further claim on it. And don't rely on another person to pay for your dreams, either."

In spite of herself, Julia felt her heart aching. "We don't have to talk about this right now."

"It may be the only time that we can, since you've blocked my number."

"That can be changed."

There was another long pause. "Julia, I have only one question. I hope you'll forgive me; I ask only out of concern for Paige."

Julia hesitated. "Okay."

"Are you really sure about this man? William? Will you marry him?"

"Eventually."

"Will he be good to Paige?"

"I'm not marrying him until I'm certain of that."

"But you're not certain yet?"

Carefully, she said, "I haven't wanted to throw him into her life too soon. I'll have to see him together with her many times before I can be sure of that."

"That's good. Of course you would have put so much thought into it." After a long hesitation, he added, "I wish you every happiness. But you know if it doesn't work out with him, I'll still be here. Don't worry about what the rest of the world will say or think."

Monday was William's day off work. After Paige went to bed, Julia called him.

"Hello," he said, without the question mark, and with a note of surprise.

"Hi. I'm ready to talk now."

"Should I come over?"

"Yes."

He was there within a short time. He searched her face for clues to her thoughts and feelings, but said nothing. He went to sit on the couch, and waited.

Julia found herself squirming, even though she had planned what she was going to say. "Okay. I'd like you to admit that you should at least have told me about the DUI when I asked you if there was anything else from your past."

"Is that all? I should have told you about that. I'm sorry."

Julia frowned. "That doesn't sound very sincere."

William laughed ruefully. "I don't know what else to say. I still think that when I told you I had been leading a debauched existence, it encompassed all of that. It honestly didn't occur to me that the DUI needed to be mentioned separately. But I can see it was important to you, so I'm sorry I couldn't read your mind. Now, would you like me to tell you the specifics of every single sexual encounter I've had since we broke up in 1995, even the ones Kevin's lawyer didn't find out about?"

Julia recoiled. "No."

"Good. Because I don't see what purpose that could possibly serve. What's done is done. What's important is that I love you, I've always loved you, and I always will."

Julia gaped at him. After a moment, she said, "How do you do this?"

"Do what?"

"Erase all of my doubts in less than one minute?"

"I know – you were so determined to stay mad at me. But don't worry, I won't touch you. We're just here to talk, remember?"

She couldn't help smiling a little, and at the sight of it, he relaxed and broke into a wide smile as well. They sat in silence for a while. Then Julia said, "I have some news."

"Okay."

"Kevin's not going to fight me in the divorce. In fact, he's going to sign a postnuptial agreement. Once it's all said and done, I'll be able to sell the house and keep all the proceeds for myself. Same with all of our investment accounts, 401K, everything."

William's eyebrows raised. "Why the hell is he doing that?"

"Because he's sorry for what he did. And because he still has his trust fund money."

"Wow. Are you sure there's not some catch in there?"

"No, but that's what my lawyer is for." After a while, she added, "You know what this means."

"What?"

"I'll be able to help with our business venture now."

"What do you mean, help with it?"

"Financially, of course."

William's expression hardened. "No."

"What?"

"We're not using his money for our business."

"What are you talking about? It's my money. Even now, half of it is mine. By the time he signs it all over to me, it's one hundred percent mine."

Still, he shook his head. "I've got it covered."

"Will. You can't possibly have it covered. I'm sorry to prick your pride, but I'm not stupid."

"Don't forget, I have three hundred and thirty thousand dollars in my savings account from my time in Alaska."

"Yes, but the boat alone will cost at least that much."

"I can get a fifty foot sport fishing catamaran for between three and four hundred thousand. We'll get loans if we need more."

"Will, I have a five bedroom, three thousand square foot house in west Menlo Park. I expect to get at least two point six million for it. I could get a place like this for six or seven hundred thousand. You do the math; that's leaves a huge chunk of change for the business. And that doesn't include my savings and investment accounts."

"I won't take that money."

"And I won't let you go it alone. That's final."

He frowned, rose to his feet. Walked across the room and stared at the aquarium.

"What is the big deal?" she demanded. "Is this an ego thing? The Italian side of you coming out? Women pay for things nowadays."

"No, of course that's not it."

"Then do you still imagine it's dirty money somehow?"

William turned to look at her now. "It might be your money, in name. But it originally came from him. You didn't earn that money yourself."

"What do you think I've been doing all these years, sitting around getting pedicures? Raising a kid is a hell of a lot harder work than my receptionist job. For that and for all the hardship Kevin has put me and Paige through these past months, I think I've earned that money."

"I want a clean break from your ex."

"So it *is* an ego thing. Somehow you've got this delusion that if you take that money, you owe him something. At what point and in what way would he come claiming some obligation from you?"

"I won't take the money. Save it for a rainy day."

"That would have to be a hell of a rainy day. Don't be so damn stubborn."

William shrugged. "I warned you, it's a Quinn family trait."

"Will, it's for my peace of mind. I've lived almost my entire adult life in a state of dependency on one man. I'm not going to do that again. We either go fifty-fifty on this, or I'm out."

"Then I guess you're out."

"If you form this business alone before we're married, then I may have no claim to it after we're married, because it might be considered separate property. I'm not sure; I'd have to ask Erin."

"Then marry me before we start the business."

"No! Why are you trying to rush me? For my daughter's sake, I won't make hasty decisions. Why can't you look beyond your own selfish desires and see that?"

The moment she said it, she regretted it. The look on his face told her she had crossed the line.

"I've thought of nothing but you for the past several months," he began with forced calmness. "I was prepared to co-sign a lease with you, if you needed it. I'm putting my entire savings on the line to start a business with you. I want to help you raise your daughter. And you call me selfish because I can't wait to start doing all this with you?"

Julia put her head in her hands. "I can't think clearly. All I know is, I need to have my own, independent stake in this. Even Kevin told me not to let you pay for it all."

William's eyes flew open wide. "What?"

Oh, shit. "Kevin. Told me not to let you pay for it all."

"When have you been talking to Kevin?"

Julia avoided his gaze. "We've talked once."

"About our business?"

"No! Not exactly. He told me to take the money and use it to follow my dreams. And then he said not to let anyone else pay for them."

"It sounds like a pretty in-depth conversation. I thought you weren't going to speak to him at all, except through your lawyers."

Julia said nothing.

"Julie. When have you been talking to him?"

"Just once."

"You're being evasive."

Julia sighed. "He sent me an e-mail yesterday, letting me know he was going to give me all the assets, even if I still divorced him. He said he had no more use for the money. I thought it was a suicide note. I panicked, and I called him."

"Well, it sounds as if the conversation went a little further than, 'Just checking to make sure you didn't off yourself.'"

"I told him in no uncertain terms that it's over between him and me and that I'm planning to marry you."

When Julia finally worked up enough courage to look him in the eye, he said, "You know, I'm starting to agree that it would be a good idea if we wait at least a year to get married. We both need to be sure this is really what you want."

Julia nodded. He gathered up his jacket, and moved toward the stairs.

"Where are you going?" she asked.

"Home."

"This is home."

His face was sober. "My home."

She watched in dismay as he turned and went down the stairs. She heard the front door open and close. Heard his key locking it behind him. Listened to his motorcycle roar away into the distance.

Julia went through the next day in a fog. While driving to Erin's office, her cell phone rang twice, but she waited until she parked the car to check the message. She hoped it was from William, and was disappointed to see two numbers she didn't recognize on her screen.

She listened to the first voice mail. "This message is for Julia Beale. This is the principal of Paige's school. Please call me as soon as you get this message. I'm afraid it's urgent."

Alarmed, Julia listened to the second message. "Yes, I'm trying to reach the mother of Paige Beale, and I was given this number. This is the Emergency Department at the children's hospital. Please call as soon as possible."

Frantically, Julia dialed the number that was left for her. "Please hold a moment, Mrs. Beale," said the receptionist who answered.

After several agonizing minutes, a doctor came on the line. "Hello, Mrs. Beale. My name is Dr. Albanez. I'm sorry to have alarmed you. Paige is going to be fine, but I'm afraid she did need to come here today."

"What happened?"

"I'm afraid she cut her wrists pretty badly."

"How?" asked Julia, imagining some kind of accident.

"She cut them herself."

Julia felt her world reeling. "What?"

"From what we've been able to gather, she got upset at school and got a hold of a sharp object of some kind."

"Do you mean she was trying to hurt herself?"

"It sounds that way, from the account we received."

"But..." Julia didn't even know where to begin. "She's seven years old!"

"Mrs. Beale, it is unusual, but we've seen this is in even younger children."

Julia pressed her hand to her mouth, shaking. "Is she okay?"

"Yes. We've had to put in a few stitches, but she'll be okay, from a physical standpoint. However, we may have to transfer her to our inpatient psychiatric unit for further evaluation."

"What?"

"Mrs. Beale, your daughter tried to harm herself. We have to ensure that she's no longer a danger to herself before we release her from the hospital. If it really comes down to it, this is a dedicated pediatric unit, and everyone there is highly skilled in the care of children. I'm sure you'll see that it's not the nightmare that you're imagining."

But Julia could not refrain from sobbing into the phone. "Oh, no."

"Mrs. Beale, can you please find someone to bring you safely to the hospital?"

Julia nodded, then remembered that he couldn't see her. "Yes."

"Please don't try to drive yourself."

"I won't."

"We'll keep her in the ER until you get here."

After bumming a ride to the hospital with another secretary, Julia found her daughter's hands and wrists bandaged, with just the fingertips poking out. Since Paige was still too sedated to talk to her, she pieced together from the doctors and the school that somehow, Paige had found a craft knife in her teacher's desk and slashed her wrists.

Julia stayed with her while they waited for a bed in the psychiatric unit. Yearning for some support, she picked up her cell phone and looked at the time. It was after three o'clock; William would have just started his shift.

If she called him now, what would he do? Would he drop everything and come running? Probably.

I can't do that to him, she thought. It can wait until after he gets off work.

Who else could she turn to right now for comfort? Not Kevin. She didn't care if Paige was his daughter, too.

Her mother.

"Oh no," Julia said out loud.

At that very moment, her mother would be at the school to pick up Paige. And she didn't have a cell phone.

Julia opened her cell phone to call the school, but she didn't get any reception inside the hospital. She bolted outside as fast as she could, and opened her cell phone again. At that moment, it rang.

"Hello?" she gasped.

"It's Mom."

Weak with relief, Julia said, "Mom, Paige is not at school."

"I already know. I'm here at the school. The principal told me. I've been trying to call you."

"I couldn't get any reception in the hospital."

"What's going on?"

Julia updated her, and then her mother said, "Kevin is on his way."

Julia's stomach dropped. "What?"

"I couldn't get a hold of you, so I called Kevin. I needed to know what was going on, but he was just as much in the dark as I was. More, actually. He hadn't even heard."

"That's because I didn't call him."

224

"Julia, he's her father."

"And he's also the cause of all this."

There was a long pause. "Well, he's on his way."

Exasperated, Julia hung up. She went back to Paige's room and paced the floor, anticipating Kevin's arrival at any moment.

All too soon, he burst into the room, then reeled at the sight of Paige, drugged and bandaged. Julia grasped him by the arm and steered him into the hallway.

"What happened?" he demanded.

He listened gravely as Julia filled him in. After a moment to digest it all, he said, "I'm guessing this is not a total bolt out of the blue."

She glared at him, but said nothing.

"You once told me she had cried every day since I left."

"She did, until we started going to therapy together once per week. The crying stopped for a while, but I'm sure you can guess when it started up again." He looked away uneasily, and she added, "Does it make you uncomfortable to see your handiwork?"

"I deserve that. And I'll do anything to make it better."

"Then get out of our life, and stay out."

But he still refused to let her bait him. "I know you're angry right now. But I think we both know that Paige is going to have to see me. Ask your therapist what she thinks. Don't take my word for it."

In spite of herself, she felt the anger slowly draining. She gazed at him a moment. "Maybe you should start coming to therapy with us."

Kevin brightened. "That's a good idea."

"I'll check with the therapist. Make sure it's okay."

"I know it's inadequate, but I'm so sorry. I pay for it every single day when I see the pain I've caused."

The rest of the anger drained from Julia's body, leaving her exhausted and beyond speech. She turned back into Paige's room, and together she and Kevin waited until a transporter came to move Paige upstairs to the psychiatric unit.

After the admissions process, there was nothing left to do but leave Paige in the hands of strangers and go home. Julia put on a brave face until they were out of the unit and the nurse closed and locked the door behind them. Then she allowed the tears to come.

Kevin put his arm around her shoulders. "I hope you didn't drive here."

Julia shook her head.

"Well, I did. Will you let me drive you home?"

She nodded, and he led her out to his car. Driving down the road, he looked over at her, slumped in his passenger seat, and said, "Is anybody going to be there when you get home?"

Julia shook her head.

"Will anybody be there eventually?"

She turned to look out the window and decided not to answer.

Parked in front of the house, Kevin said, "Maybe you should spend the night at your parents' house. You shouldn't be alone."

"I'll be okay."

He didn't press the point any further. "I'll see you back at the hospital tomorrow, then?"

"Yes."

He peered at her intently a moment. She had caught a glimpse of herself in the side view mirror, so she knew she looked frail. Her shoulders slumped, and her eyes were puffy and rimmed with shadows.

He reached for her, enfolded her in a hug. For once, she did not try to resist. After a moment's hesitation, she even put her arms gingerly around him.

He stroked her hair, and she let her head sink into his shoulder. He felt so much thinner and bonier than she remembered, but his warmth and gentle touch were hard to resist. She wrapped her arms all the way around him, and he drew her in closer. Rubbed her back. Kissed the hair on the top of her head.

When she didn't draw away from this, he turned her face up to his. Looked into her eyes a moment.

"I think this is about where this should stop," she said.

Kevin shifted in his seat. "I'm sorry," he said, not convincingly.

"I'm going now."

She unbuckled her seat belt and opened the car door. He stopped her with a hand on her arm.

"I know how it looks – like I'm trying to take advantage. But I really do still love you."

She shrugged off his hand and stepped out of the car. Slammed the door behind her, and walked stiffly up the front steps into her house. His engine revved, then faded into the distance.

She went straight to the bathroom. Splashed cold water on her face, held on to the rim of the sink, and let the tears come.

Midnight came and went with no appearance from William and no phone call. At a quarter past, she picked up her cell phone and called him.

"Hello?" His greeting was subdued.

"I thought you might like to know that Paige is in the hospital."

"What?"

"She slashed her own wrists at school and is in the psychiatric unit. I get to see her for ninety minutes each day."

"Oh my God. Where are you?"

"At home."

"I'm coming over."

"Is that what it takes?"

He paused. "What?"

"To overcome your pride? My daughter has to be in the hospital?"

"What are you talking about?"

"You accused me of punishing you after you lied to me. All I did was talk to Kevin, and you punish me by not calling and not coming home. Telling me it's not even your home anymore."

He said nothing.

"You might like to know that, in spite of all this, I still told Kevin to leave tonight when he was the only person on earth willing to offer me any comfort. It's the worst day of my life, and I'm lying here by myself, in an empty house, out of loyalty to you. You, who don't even think I'm worthy of a phone call."

"Julie —"

"Don't come over, William. Just stay home."

She hung up.

The next night at the hospital, Julia and Kevin sat on a sofa on either side of Paige, touching her fingertips, careful to avoid the bandages around her wrists and hands.

Gently, Julia prompted, "Do you want to talk about what happened?"

Paige stared down at the floor. "Not really."

"Was somebody teasing you?"

Still, Paige stared.

"Paige, honey," said Kevin, "we love you more than anything. Nothing you tell us can change that."

"They call me stupid all day," she said.

"Who does?" asked Julia.

"The other kids. And these girls were pulling out the waist band of my pants, letting the other kids look down them at my underwear. And then on the way back from lunch, I heard someone say something funny in the hall, and I turned around to laugh. The boy behind me thought I was laughing at him, and he punched me hard in the shoulder."

"Did you hit him back?" asked Kevin.

"Yeah, but then the teacher punished me, not him."

She stopped talking. Julia said, "Is that when you hurt yourself?"

Paige nodded. "I found some kind of a knife in the teacher's desk."

Julia gathered Paige up in her arms, and gently rocked her. "You're not stupid, Paige, no matter what those kids say. You're having a hard time, and it's hard to think about anything else when you're having a hard time."

"Mommy, I don't want to go back to school anymore."

"Let's worry about one thing at a time. You're here to feel better, and that's enough for now. But I can promise you one thing." She pulled Paige back so she could look her in the eye. "It's not going to be as hard for you anymore."

Paige looked back and forth between Julia and Kevin, and rested her head on Julia's shoulder. They sat quietly together for the rest of the visiting hours, watching the TV in the recreation room, or playing board games.

After visiting hours, Kevin brought Julia to an Italian restaurant in North Beach, where she picked at a Caesar salad.

"You need to eat," Kevin said.

But Julia pushed her plate back. "It's like there's a big rock sitting in my stomach."

"You're putting too much on your own shoulders. You need to let someone help you carry this burden, even if that someone isn't me."

She knew he was wondering where William was during all of this. She stole a glance at him. Though he was still painfully thin, he was looking better. Clearly he had benefited from his parents' personal chef. His mother had probably badgered him into trimming his beard and cutting his hair, and he was looking more like his old self. Like the proto-hipster he was when she first met him.

"Why don't you talk to me about it?" he offered. "It's just talking."

Julia set her fork down and leaned back in her seat. "It's like my mother, all over again."

"What?"

"My mother told me recently that she has struggled with depression all of her life. That she's been hospitalized for it several times, even. Undergone shock therapy. She said that it all began when her parents divorced. That the other kids in school would tease her mercilessly."

Kevin reached for her hand, and she let him hold it. "This is a different time. They know more now about depression. Treatments are better."

Julia straightened again. "I just remembered something. Mom told me that nothing helped her until they tried bipolar medication."

"Your mom is bipolar?"

"Well, I'm not sure she was ever really diagnosed with it. But she said they finally tried bipolar medication as a last resort, and it worked."

"Can a kid Paige's age have bipolar disorder?"

"I'm not sure, but I think it's worth mentioning to the psychiatrist. I'll do anything to save her from the kind of life my mom described. From the kind of horrors you see on the streets every day. How many of the homeless people in this city have mental illness underneath everything else? Probably close to one hundred percent."

Kevin squeezed her hand. "With a mother like you, she's not going to suffer anything near that fate."

"I'm sure plenty of those people had better mothers than I am."

"You don't give yourself enough credit. Take it one day at a time, Julia. Just like you told Paige. That's all we can do."

Julia gazed down at their hands, clasped together on the table. "My mother told me that she never got over the absence of her father. And she reminded me of all the ways I've suffered from the absence of my parents over the years. There are ways in which their regular presence in my life might have made a difference."

His dark eyes peered keenly at her. "We can downsize. Sell the house, and move somewhere much smaller, in a much more humble neighborhood. Until I finish my doctorate, we can live off the proceeds from the house. It wouldn't take anywhere near that much money. You can forget about your secretary job and do whatever your heart desires."

Julia shook her head. "I would keep working toward becoming a paralegal. It's not that bad. I'm good at this work, and I'll always have a way of supporting Paige and myself if I need to."

"You didn't shoot down my idea altogether, though. Does that mean you're considering it?"

"Considering what?"

He smiled and enclosed her hand with both of his now. "You'll never be sorry, I promise."

Julia felt a pang, remembering the last time someone said more or less the same thing to her. She withdrew her hand.

"I've not agreed to anything yet. And I may never. I need a little time."

Some of the giddiness drained from his face, but he still smiled. "I'm happy you're even considering it."

Julia lay awake in her empty bed, staring up at the ceiling. Near midnight, her cell phone rang.

"Hello?"

After a pause, William said, "Do you want to talk to me?"

"Yes."

"Can I come over?"

"Okay."

He was there within thirty minutes. After taking a shower, he went to sit beside her on the sofa and took her hands in his.

"You have no idea what I felt when I realized what you had been going through all day, and all the while I had been too proud to even call you. I'm so sorry."

Julia lifted his hands and pressed her forehead against them. "I'm sorry too. I've been so on edge lately."

"You've had a lot of stress."

"Every day I feel like I'm going to be the next one going to the hospital. But I don't have the luxury of losing it, because I still have to be a mom."

He gathered her up and held her there for a while. After a while, he asked for the details of what happened, and she told him the whole story.

"Should I take off work for a while?" he asked.

"No, there's no sense in that. Just come home at night and be with me."

"Of course," he said, stroking her hair. Kissing the top of her head, as Kevin had done just the night before.

There was nothing more to say and no energy left for conversation, anyway. They went to bed, and he held her all night.

The next day, with Kevin at her side, Julia informed Paige's psychiatrist of her mother's history with depression.

"I think it might be worthwhile to try a mood stabilizer for a while, and see how she does with that," he replied.

"What if that doesn't work?"

"There's a lot of different mood stabilizers we can try, and if none of those work, we'll go back to square one with traditional antidepressants. It could also be that your daughter will end up needing more than one medication; that's not uncommon in children."

"It kind of feels like Paige is going to be a lab rat for a while," said Kevin.

"Well, there probably is going to be a trial and error period. The brain is very complex, and I'm afraid the treatment of psychiatric disorders is as much of an art as it is a science."

"What else should we be doing to help her?" asked Julia.

"Just keep doing exactly what you're doing – showing up for these family conferences, sharing with us any insights you can think of, and keeping an open mind. The good news is that Paige has two parents who love her very much. I know what you two have been going through personally, but it's good that you can come together for her sake."

Over dinner that night, Kevin said, "Have you given any more thought to what we talked about last night?"

"Yes, and I owe you a big apology. I spoke in a moment of weakness last night, and I gave you false hope. But I haven't changed my mind."

Kevin looked crestfallen. "Julia, where is William right now?"

"It's Friday night. He works the dinner shift at the restaurant."

"But where has he been all along? I don't get the impression he's really been there for you during this crisis."

"He works different hours than I do."

"So when do you see him?"

Julia stabbed her salad with her fork. "I don't have to talk about this with you."

"Julia, you need someone who's really going to support you through these next few years with Paige. You shouldn't have to do it alone."

"You're still planning on helping out, aren't you?"

"Yes, but think of what the psychiatrist said. How lucky Paige is to have two parents who can come together for her sake. You want her to have every possible advantage, don't you?"

"Jesus, Kevin, of course I do," snapped Julia. "But hopefully not at the expense of my self-respect."

Kevin looked stricken. "Why should you have to respect yourself any less? Everything we own will be in your name from now on. There's no risk to take. I'll be home when you're home. I'll be home when Paige is home. I'm her own father. What's not to respect about that?"

"The fact that I don't love you."

"Can you really tell me that you were just kidding yourself these past ten years when you thought you loved me? We've had our ups and downs, but you seemed content enough until I left you. Then this man came along, reminding you of the people you both used to be but aren't anymore, and offering you comfort and sex and whatever else at a time when you really needed it. How much can you really know about him based on one or two hours a day, at most? You know what I think? I think he's got you wrapped around his finger, but when it comes down to it, it's infatuation on both sides."

Shaking, Julia reached into her wallet, put some cash on the table, and stood to leave. He stood as well, and put his hand on her arm.

"Don't go," he whispered. "Let's talk calmly about this."

"I've heard about all I care to hear," she said, and left the restaurant.

When Julia opened her eyes the next morning at the usual time, she found William already awake and looking at her.

She said, "I must have sensed I was being watched. Like an animal."

He smiled. "Sorry. I couldn't sleep."

She reached out and stroked his shoulder. "Why not?"

He shrugged. "I don't know. I'm used to waking up at this time."

"I wish I could say we can sleep in for once, but my mom and I are going to have breakfast and then I'm going to head over to the hospital. I can visit Paige all day today."

She got up, stripped out of her nightgown and started putting her clothes on. He got up as well, opened the jewelry box and brought the ring over to her. Swallowed nervously as he slipped it on her finger.

"I really do still want this, no matter how long it takes," he said.

"Me too."

"Then wear it. All the time."

"You've forgotten Paige."

"What about her?"

"She'll see it and ask about it."

"Do you really think she's going to notice?"

"She's a kid; she's not an idiot."

He considered a moment. "Then tell her it's a gift from somebody."

"And what if she asks what the gift was for, or who it's from? I'm not going to lie to her, Will. I'll wear it someday, after we tell her about us. But in the meantime, we don't need a ring to know we're engaged."

He frowned. "Won't you accept anything from me?"

"Will, this isn't about *you*. If Paige sees this ring, she's going to think her father and I are back together. Then, when I have to explain to her that we're not, it's going to set off another whole meltdown."

"I'm not just talking about the ring. I've barely seen you at all in nearly two weeks. I'm here with you now, but you're rushing out the door."

"My seven-year-old daughter is in the psych ward of the hospital."

"I know that. I know," he said in a conciliatory tone, squeezing her hands in his. "But are you really going to spend all seven hours in there with her? Don't you need some time to recharge your own batteries?"

"If your idea of recharging my batteries is to relieve your pent-up urges when my daughter is surrounded by strange adults and crazy teenagers – then no!"

Why am I practically shrieking? she had the presence of mind to ask herself. And yet she couldn't contain the monster welling up inside of her. Maybe she really did belong in the psych ward, alongside her daughter.

William slowly dropped her hands. He backed away and pulled his jeans on over his boxers.

"Christ, Will, I'm sorry," she said, alarmed to discover that she was on the verge of tears. "I told you before, I feel like I'm coming unhinged."

She dissolved into tears now, and sat down on the bed. He came over to her and touched her shoulder.

"You're going to have to start trusting me. Otherwise, this is never going to work."

He finished dressing and left her alone to gather up her last shreds of dignity.

When Julia arrived at her parents' house, her mother took one look at her and said, "Sit down, honey. Let me bring you a cup of tea."

Julia flopped into a chair and stared listlessly at the table top while her mother put a kettle on the stove. Then her mother joined her at the table.

"You've been crying."

Julia looked away and covered her face with her hand.

"Julia, I assumed you were getting some support at home. But maybe you should spend your nights here for the time being. I can take a load off for the next couple of weeks. Make you dinner and breakfast each day, so at least you get something to eat. I would have hoped that William would be seeing to that, but you're thinner than ever."

"I've been trying to eat dinner out with Kevin after visiting hours. My stomach is just twisted in knots these days."

Her mother looked surprised, and pleased. "I'm glad somebody is trying to take care of you. But men don't really know how to do these things. From now on, come here instead of your place. You won't be shut up in that house all alone."

Julia knew that William wouldn't like it, but the idea of being around other people at the end of the day did appeal to her. And this way, she wouldn't be even more tempted to let that other person be Kevin.

After a few minutes, the kettle whistled. Her mother poured the tea and brought the cups over to the table. "You like it plain, right?"

Julia nodded and dipped the tea bag in and out of the water pensively.

"Julia, is anything else the matter besides the obvious issues with Paige?"

To Julia's dismay, she felt tears stinging her eyes again, and covered her face with her hand. "What is wrong with me?" she said out loud.

"Oh, honey," said her mother, reaching for her hand. "Please tell me."

"I can't."

"You have to talk to someone."

"I already know what your opinion is." To Julia's own astonishment, she cried uncontrollably. Her mother squeezed her hands.

"Honey, I'm done lecturing you on all that. I just want you to be happy. And it sure looks to me like whatever you're doing right now is not making you happy."

"Mom," she said after a while, "no matter what happens, I love William with all my heart. But I'm just not sure anymore. I want to do the right thing, for everyone."

Her mother got up and went around to Julia. She knelt on the floor and drew Julia's head down to touch hers.

"I know what it's like to love someone with total abandon," she said gently. "How else could I have put up with your father all these years?"

In spite of herself, Julia laughed raggedly.

"William is not a bad person; I know he's not," her mother continued. "I've seen and heard just as many good things about him as otherwise. If you didn't have Paige to worry about, I probably never would have objected to him. Maybe I shouldn't have opened my big mouth, anyway, but there it is. I just want you to be really sure, and that's all I'm going to say about it."

Julia took another sip of tea. Her mother left her to herself while she finished making breakfast.

Then, before leaving for the hospital, she called William on his cell phone.

"I'm sorry about the way I acted this morning," she said, "and I'm sorry for what I'm about to say."

He hesitated. "Okay."

"I'm going to spend the next few nights, at least, at my parents' house. I just really need the support of my family right now."

There was a long pause. "Julie, I asked you if you wanted me to take off work for a while."

"I know, but you can't really afford to do that."

"Have you forgotten about my savings?"

"You shouldn't have to dip into that."

"It's a week or two. I can afford it."

Julia hesitated. "Will –"

"Damn it, Julie." She had never heard him speak so angrily to her before. "You've always run hot and cold on me. Decide what you want from me, and let me know."

He hung up.

When Julia walked into Paige's unit, she found Kevin already there with her. They hadn't spotted her yet, so she hung back a while and watched them read a book together. She seemed so much perkier there with her father, so much like her old self, before Kevin abandoned them. To Julia's astonishment, when she finally approached them, Paige broke into a wide smile that Julia hadn't seen since Kevin came back from Brazil.

Julia kissed Paige on the cheek. "You look happy."

"I'm happy because you and Daddy are together again."

Alarmed, Julia turned to Kevin for some explanation, but he shook his head and looked just as alarmed. Julia decided not to contradict Paige. Not just yet, anyway.

But Julia was unable to shake her discomfort. Throughout the day, it was clear that Paige had gotten it into her head that her parents were back together. And it was even clearer that this idea gave her more comfort than anything had in weeks, if not months.

At the first opportunity, Julia pulled Kevin aside and said, "Where did she get this idea from?"

"I don't know, but I swear to you I didn't give it to her. The only thing I can figure is that she's seen us together, and you told her things would be easier for her from now on. Maybe in her mind, that means us being together." He rubbed his jaw thoughtfully. "How are we going to explain this to her?"

Her stomach churned. "Maybe it's what's best."

Cautiously, he said, "What's best?"

Julia picked at her fingernails. "She seems so much better."

He said nothing for such a long time that she finally looked up again, to find him staring keenly at her.

"Julia, what are you saying?"

"I'm saying give me a day or two to think really hard about what's best for Paige before we tell her one way or the other."

Kevin looked as if he might fall over. "Of course."

"If this is really what you want, we'll have to pay off my lease. And I intend to keep working full-time from now on."

"I understand."

"And Kevin. I won't do it unless you follow through with the postnuptial agreement first."

"Of course. It can be done Monday. I'll make it happen."

She touched his arm. "Don't get your hopes up again like you did last time, Kevin. I have a lot of thinking to do."

He nodded. "I know."

She fidgeted with her fingernails again, not really aware of anything happening around her until she felt his hand slide across hers and close around it.

"This would make everybody so happy," he whispered.

Not me, she thought. And certainly not William.

But maybe it didn't matter anymore. Paige had made it clear that it was what would make her happiest. Somehow, in time, she could learn to be happy with her decision. She knew all of her reasons, and she would repeat them to herself over and over again.

That night at her parents' house, the first phone call Julia made was to Alison.

"I really need to talk to someone."

"Oh, Julie… can it wait until tomorrow night? I have a big order to deliver tomorrow. A wedding. I'm going to be working on it all night."

Julia hesitated. "Sure. Good luck with the order."

"I'm sorry, Julie. Hang in there one more day."

After Julia hung up, she considered a moment, then dialed Holly's number.

"I desperately need to talk to someone. I don't suppose you'd be up for a drink tonight?"

"What's the matter?"

"I'll tell you about it over drinks, if you'll meet me at MacGowan's."

"Julia... I'm so sorry, but I'm giving a huge talk about violence against women at Stanford on Monday evening. I'm in over my head, preparing for this thing. Can it wait until Tuesday, or is it really an emergency?"

Julia felt her heart sinking. "Sure, it can wait. That's very cool that Stanford invited you to give a talk. Good luck."

"Thanks; I'm pretty psyched about it."

After they hung up, she tried to think of someone, anyone over the years that she could talk to, but she knew that none of the friends she had made on the Peninsula during the past ten years would understand.

Once she found her way upstairs to her old bedroom, she looked at the clock on the bedside table. Just after midnight. She pulled out her cell phone and found no message waiting for her.

She reached around behind her neck, unfastened the mermaid necklace, and closed it away inside the drawer of her bedside table.

On Monday night, after spending the day with the lawyers and getting back to her own house from the hospital, she made the call.

"Can you come over for a little while? I'd like to talk."

"Okay," said William coldly. "What about?"

"We can talk about it when you get here."

When he arrived, he sat down in the armchair instead of on the sofa beside her. The icy look in his eyes told her he was still angry.

It's just as well, reflected Julia. Maybe it will make it easier.

"Listen, Will, this is the hardest thing I've ever had to do in my entire life."

She watched the alarm, the suspicion, the disbelief cycle across his face, each in turn. He said, "Okay."

"We're going to have to go our separate ways."

He stared at her as if she had slapped him across the face. "Are you breaking up with me?"

She forced herself to hold his gaze. "Yes."

He sat frozen. After a moment, he said slowly, "Okay, I'm sorry. I shouldn't have yelled at you like that the other day. I was really angry, and... but I shouldn't have done it. I'm sorry."

"I understand why you were angry. That's not why I have to do this."

"Then why?"

"This is what I think is best for Paige."

"Why?" he demanded, frowning. "I think I deserve an explanation."

"Will." She drew a deep breath. Steeled herself. "She needs her own father."

If it was possible for him to look any more incredulous, he did. He tapped his foot on the floor, clearly growing more agitated by the moment.

"Julie, I'm starting to believe you when you say you're losing your mind."

"Since he first came back, he's made some good faith gestures to make amends for what he did. And most importantly, Paige seems much happier now that he's back in her life."

"Please tell me you're joking."

"No."

"Julie, how can you honestly believe this is what's best for Paige? Have you forgotten what he put you through? That he abandoned you and Paige out of the blue and left you to fend for yourselves with no resources? He did it once without warning; you know he'll do it again."

"No, I don't know that. But if he did, everything would be in my name."

"But what if he does do it again? What effect do you think that would have on Paige?"

She had no response for this.

"And besides that, you led me to believe that you loved me, and that you don't love Kevin anymore. Has that changed?"

"I don't see how this is helpful."

"It's helpful because if you do love me, then Paige will be happiest when she sees her mother happy, as I've said before." He crossed his arms over his chest and leaned back in his seat. "But maybe you don't love me. Maybe you never really did."

Her heart contorted with pain, but she said, "You have no idea how good it is to see Paige smiling again, and it's only because she believes that Kevin and I have reconciled. I couldn't cope with it if she ever does something to hurt herself again. If she grows up unhappy and out of control when I could have done something to make it better."

"You didn't answer me."

"Answer what?"

"You know what." He fixed a piercing gaze on her, but she refused to let it rattle her. He gave a short, rueful laugh. "I don't think it's too far of a stretch to assume that you lied about loving me in the first place. You swore I would never lose you again, but you lied about that, too."

"I did love you. I still love you."

"Well then how can you do this to someone you love?"

"Because I love my daughter more."

"Bullshit. If you did, you wouldn't lie to her and let her believe you love her father when you don't. Don't you think the best gift you can give your daughter is to let her see what a loving relationship looks like?"

"Do you think what we've had in the past couple of weeks can be called a loving relationship?"

Her words stunned him to silence. After a moment, his expression softened. "You're right. We've been arguing too much lately about stupid things. Is that what this is really all about?" He came to sit beside her and took her hand in his. "I've been thinking about changing shifts at work, to the lunch shift. If your dad won't let me do that, then I'll get a new job. Something to give us more time together."

"Why, so we'll have more time to argue?" It grieved her to see him grasping desperately for something, anything. She drew her hand away. "That's not what this is about, Will. I gave you my honest reason up front."

The incredulous look returned to his face. He seemed to be waiting for her to say it was all a big joke. Waiting for her to say anything.

She said, "I've gathered up your stuff and put it in a bag on the bed."

She watched with dread as the storm clouds gathered across his face. After a moment he sprang to his feet and crossed the floor to the bedroom. She heard before she saw him rifling through her jewelry box, and she ran to stop him, but not in time. He pushed past her to the bathroom and slammed the door in her face. By the time she got it open and reached frantically into the toilet, the ring was already gone.

"Why did you do that?" she screamed.

"You have no problem throwing me away, so what difference could a little diamond ring make to you? Unless that's all you care about. Is that why you're going back to him? Because of his money?"

"No! If all I cared about was money, I could have it without him. I wouldn't take your money when you offered it."

"Then what? Why are you doing this to me?" he shouted, his face reddening, his voice acquiring a peculiar note of strain she had never heard there before. To her horror, she realized that he was fighting back tears. Never in all their time together had she seen or even imagined him crying. The sight of it terrified her more than his anger did.

But just as quickly, his lifelong training took over. She watched him choke back the tears, and anger darkened his face again.

"I'm not going to beg you," he said quietly, his voice shaking. "If you're looking for someone to come chasing after you, I'm not that guy. And don't ever come back saying you're sorry, because I won't believe you. I'm not giving you a third chance to break my heart."

He bolted into the bedroom and snatched up his meager bundle of belongings. She ran after him, put her hand on his arm.

"Will, don't leave yet. Wait until you calm down."

He snatched his arm away and started toward the front door. Desperately, she grabbed at his shirt, at his collar. At anything she could get a hold of.

"Will, you're going to hurt yourself," she pleaded. "You'll hurt someone else."

But he wrenched himself from her grasp and stormed across the living room, down the stairs, out the front door. A moment later, she heard the motorcycle roar to life and peel violently away from the curb. Within seconds, even the sound of the pipes was gone.

She stood frozen in place for at least a minute afterward, paralyzed by a growing sense of dread. Then she spotted it, on the living room floor.

She went to pick it up. The chain had snapped, but the patron saint that had protected him all those years was still attached to it.

She bolted for the bathroom, knelt over the toilet just in time to watch the contents of her stomach spray into the bowl. There wasn't much in there to begin with, but her body didn't seem to realize that. She vomited green bile, and when that was all gone, she clenched the toilet bowl and dry heaved until faintness overcame the waves of nausea. She fell back against the opposite wall, her ears buzzing, her field of vision dimming, clammy sweat beading on her forehead.

But she didn't pass out. No, that would have been too welcome of a release. Instead, consciousness taunted her. She lay down on the cold tile of the floor and clutched his chain, too spent even to cry.

2012, PART III

On a Wednesday two weeks after Julia started back to work at the restaurant, someone came onto the pier while she was taking her break and said, "Julia, there you are. There's a call for you."

Julia's eyes swept from the catamaran in its slip, to Cardone's across the pier. He might only be a few steps away from her, but a gulf of silence more than five years wide felt unnavigable.

She tore herself away from her solitary brooding and returned inside to pick up the extension.

"This is Julia."

"Julia Beale? Paige's mom?"

Oh, no. "Yes?"

"Mrs. Beale, this is Mary Jenkins, the principal at her school. First of all, Paige is safe and well, but we do need you to come pick her up."

"Can you tell me what's going on?"

"I'd rather discuss it with you in person, if possible."

"I'm at work right now. I really need to know what this is about."

The principal heaved a sigh. "Then I'm very sorry to have to tell you in this way. Paige was found in the boy's restroom, with a boy."

Julia caught herself against the wall. "What?"

"I'm afraid so."

"What do you mean, 'with a boy'?"

A pause. "Well, they were smoking marijuana. We're not sure what else they had been up to."

Still in denial, Julia said, "Mrs. Jenkins, she's a thirteen year old girl. Are you sure there wasn't some misunderstanding?"

"I think it would be better if we could discuss this more in person."

It was just as well. Julia wasn't sure she could stand still anymore. She needed to put the adrenaline to some use.

"I'll be there as soon as I can."

Julia slammed down the receiver, and ran straight to her father.

"Dad, I've got to go pick up Paige. She's gotten herself into some kind of trouble at school."

"Is she okay?"

"I'm not sure. I've got to go."

Her father nodded, and she ran to gather her belongings from the break room. Then she ran out the back door to her car.

When she finally arrived at Paige's school, the secretary immediately ushered her into the principal's office. There, she learned that a teacher walking past the boy's restroom detected the unmistakable odor of pot, and found Paige and an eighth grade boy together in a bathroom stall. Paige would be suspended for a few days, and she was waiting in the counselor's office, swearing she didn't give a shit what her mother thought about any of this.

Julia put her hand over her mouth. "I wish I could say I can't believe this, but I can. I can't imagine what you must think of me."

"I don't judge you," the principal replied. "All of the kids in this school are coming in here with some unique challenges. We want to work with her and you so she can come back and be successful here."

"You're very kind. Thank you."

"There are plenty of resources available to families when a situation like this occurs. We don't just suspend kids and expect everything to resolve itself. We really want to help."

With that, the principal pushed a ton of brochures for health clinics and counseling services and paperwork for Paige's suspension across the desk to Julia. She tried to explain everything, but Julia was too distressed to absorb any of it.

When the principal had finished, she smiled reassuringly. "Will you follow me, please?"

After that, there was nothing left but for Julia to retrieve Paige from the counselor's office, and for them to leave together. They walked in stony silence back to the car. Once Julia unlocked the door and they were both inside, she said, "I had to leave a lot of work behind in order to come here. I'm going to have to go back to the restaurant for a little while to wrap some things up before we can go home."

"That's bullshit," Paige stormed.

"Watch your mouth," snapped Julia, before drawing a deep breath and biting her tongue. Luckily, Paige turned to look out the window and said nothing more.

Julia drove back to work as quickly as possible. She installed Paige in the office, and ordered her not to move until she had finished shelving all the items in the walk-in.

To Julia's dismay, once she got to the walk-in, she discovered that more deliveries had arrived during her absence. It would take hours to catch up. She frantically stocked items, trying her best not to make any mistakes on her inventory chart as she did so, but nevertheless discovering some mistakes along the way, and then having to go back and re-count all over again. Every fifteen minutes or so, she went back to the office to check on Paige, and was alarmed to find her using the office computer to entertain herself. But there was no remedy for it now; something needed to occupy her while Julia worked.

Yet another delivery arrived. Julia allowed forty-five minutes to pass until she checked on Paige again, and found the office empty.

Julia gasped, and ran in search of her.

"Have you seen my daughter?" she asked everyone she passed in the kitchen. "About this tall, with long dark hair?"

But no one had seen her recently. She ran to her father, busy filleting fish due to a short-staffed kitchen, and said, "Dad, I can't find Paige anywhere. Have you seen her recently?"

Her father scowled. "Of course not. It's not my job to keep an eye on her."

Julia frantically searched the dining rooms and the lobby. Once it was clear that Paige had left the building, she ran to the back again, snatched her belongings out of her locker, and prepared to search outside.

She ran up and down the pier, stopping in every processing plant along the shed except one. Searched every other nearby shed as well. Scoured every store and gift shop along Jefferson Street, ripe for the picking from Paige's experienced sticky fingers. Checked every bus stop along the way, describing her to the waiting tourists and commuters. Finally made her way back to the pier.

She was gone.

Unless.

For some reason, Julia had not been able to bring herself to go in there. Why not? She couldn't be sure Paige was gone until she checked there.

Her stomach churned at the prospect of seeing him. Of having to explain to him why she was there.

This is ridiculous, she scolded herself. Seriously, what's the worst that could happen?

She somehow propelled herself into Cardone's. Thankfully, the first person she saw was Kelly, behind the counter of the little storefront, serving some customers. Julia waited as patiently as she possibly could. Finally, Kelly spotted her and, after an initial look of surprise, pressed her lips together in a scowl.

They ought to give a prize for holding the longest grudge, Julia reflected.

Once the customers left, Kelly said, as if Julia were just another customer, "Can I help you?"

"I'm looking for my daughter."

Kelly blinked. "Here?"

"Yes. She was with me at the restaurant, and now I can't find her. I've checked everywhere else around here. I just need to rule this place out before I call the police."

"Why would she be here?"

Julia frowned. "May I please take a look around?"

Julia thought she saw Kelly roll her eyes as she turned unceremoniously toward the door leading into the plant. "What does she look like?"

Julia followed her. "She's thirteen. Long dark hair; about five-three. Her name is Paige."

Kelly gestured to the interior of the plant, then crossed her arms over her chest. "Feel free to take a look around."

Julia had never been back here before. It was a vast, open space, piled high with totes. Workers, mostly Hispanic, shucked Dungeness crab, dropped it by twenty-five pound units into the brine tank, and glazed it.

"I don't know where to begin," admitted Julia.

"Like I said, I don't know why she'd even be in here."

Julia considered. "Where would you keep anything of value?"

"Everything in here is of value."

Julia forced herself to remain civil. "Small things that could be easily carried off. Cash. Wallets. Things like that."

"The office." Kelly gestured for Julia to follow her all the way to the back of the plant where the bays were, around a corner, and into yet another section of the plant. Here, workers dropped boxes over wire baskets of processed crab and loaded the boxes into trucks parked in the open bays.

Kelly gestured again, this time to a little door off the main floor. "The office is the one place where she might find valuables. Of course we lock them away, but you're welcome to check in there."

Julia didn't bother to inform Kelly what a skilled pick-lock Paige had become over the years.

"Who the hell do you think you are, acting like you know me?!"

Julia's heart leaped into her throat at the unmistakable sound of her daughter's voice. Before Julia had time to prepare, Paige stumbled out of the office.

The first thing Julia noticed was the defiant look on Paige's face. The second thing she noticed was the way that William gripped the back of Paige's collar, though she almost didn't recognize him because of the beard. And the final thing she noticed was the icy glare William gave her.

He gave Paige a little nudge toward Julia. "Looking for her?" he said coldly.

"Yes," Julia heard herself croak.

"What about these?" He pulled wads of credit cards and cash out of his pockets.

Julia lost her voice again. She accepted the first handful of currency he held out to her and recognized, among it, her own credit cards, and those of her father and the other staff in the restaurant.

He said, "I found her in here, going through the drawers and cabinets."

Still unable to speak, Julia stuffed the first handful of cards and cash into her purse, then accepted the other handful from him and stashed that as well. Then she seized Paige by the arm, hard.

Somehow, she brought herself to look William in the eye. Fixed him with an earnest gaze and said emphatically, "I am so sorry."

He looked down at her with utter contempt. "Keep her away from now on. Next time, I'm pressing charges."

Shame, hurt, and despair welled in her chest. He watched it all cycle across her face, each in turn. Then he turned stiffly back into the office, closing the door in her face.

He was gone. Completely out of her reach.

Kelly still stood there with her hands on her hips. Julia couldn't bring herself to look her in the eye. She dug her fingertips harder into Paige's arm, until Paige said, "Ow!"

"Let's go," Julia said through clenched teeth. Over Paige's protests, Julia dragged her out of the plant, down the pier.

Not here, she told herself. Just make it back inside the restaurant first.

Julia shoved Paige through the back door, into the corridor, and waited for the door to close behind them. Closed her eyes and counted to ten.

It didn't help.

Paige was already heading back to the office. Julia ran to meet her, seized her arm again, and spun her around. Seized her by the shoulders, and shook her hard.

"What the hell were you doing?!" she screamed.

All the staff nearby froze and turned to stare in shock. Paige gasped, and shrieked. Fought back like a cat, kicking, scratching, and pulling hair. Julia shoved her backward. She reached into her purse and threw the wads of cash and credit cards at Paige.

At that moment, her father seized her, pinning her arms and pulling her away from Paige. "What the hell is going on here?" he roared.

But Julia ignored him. She wrestled an arm loose to point to the pile of currency on the floor and shouted, "It's not enough that you get suspended from school today, but you also have to steal, from me? From your grandpa? From the people who work here? From the Quinns, for God's sake?"

Julia's father looked in shock at Paige, who shook with silent sobs of rage, glaring right back at her mother and her grandfather.

"Get out of here," he ordered Julia after a moment.

"She's coming with me."

"*I'll* deal with her. You get out of here, and get a grip on yourself."

Julia wrenched herself free from his grasp and swooped down to snatch her own credit cards from the floor. She had the satisfaction of watching Paige flinch backward as she did so.

Julia pushed past all the staring eyes, through the kitchen, and out the back door. Stormed across the pier, diverting her eyes at all costs from the plant. Rounded the shed to her car. Started the engine and choked back the tears, determined to make it home before giving way to them.

The next day, Julia stayed home from work with Paige, who took refuge all day in their bedroom. With her mother in the living room, ready to intervene at a moment's notice, Julia steeled herself for the inevitable talk.

She tapped lightly on the bedroom door, but heard no response. Gently, she opened the door and found Paige at the aquarium, earbuds in her ears, listening to loud music and cleaning the protein skimmer. Julia knew that Paige could see her, but Paige made no effort to acknowledge her presence.

Julia made her way to the aquarium and tapped Paige on the shoulder. Only then did Paige remove one earbud, without looking around.

"Can we talk now?" said Julia.

Paige paused the iPod and removed the other earbud. She sat on her bed, but refused to make eye contact with Julia.

Julia sat down on her own bed. "First of all, I owe you an apology for yelling and shaking you like that. There's no excuse for what I did. I'm so very sorry."

Paige said nothing, just stared straight ahead.

"Paige, I was angry at you for stealing, but it wasn't the biggest reason I was angry. I can't go into all the reasons with you because it's very personal, but I want you to know it wasn't because of you. I just took it out on you, and that was wrong."

Paige looked up at her now in some surprise, but still said nothing.

"I'm not going to bother asking how long you've been smoking marijuana, because it doesn't really make any difference," Julia continued. "But are you using any other drugs?"

Paige refused to answer.

"You'll be undergoing a full drug test, so the answer will come out anyway. If you're honest with me now, I'll take that into account later."

"No, I'm not using any other drugs."

Julia felt weak with relief. "Can I ask you – why were you taking all of that money and all of those credit cards? What were you planning to do?"

Still, Paige sat in stony silence.

"Were you going to buy drugs?"

"No."

"Were you going to run away again?"

Paige sighed. "Why does it matter?"

"I just want to understand. Were you going to run away on your own, or were you planning to go with someone else this time?"

Nothing.

"Paige, the only thing I care about is that you're happy. We've been through so much counseling together. If you're angry with me, I hope you know how to tell me by now."

"What's the point? Nothing I say makes any difference."

"I'm going to make a stab in the dark here. I'm guessing you're angry with me because your dad left again. That you think I drove him away."

"Didn't you?"

"It's partially my fault, yes, but I can't take full responsibility. He chose to leave, all by himself. I know you love and miss your dad, and knowing all this doesn't really make it better. But I want you to know that I love you and I'll always be here."

Paige's face remained carved in stone. "So what's my punishment?"

"I'm not ready to talk about that. I still have some more questions." After a moment, Julia ventured, "How long have you been sexually active?"

"Oh God, Mom, I don't want to talk about this."

"Paige, I thought I had always made this clear, but I guess not. I certainly wouldn't want you to have sex when you're still this young, but if you are, it's so important that you're being safe. Have you had vaginal intercourse?"

Paige cringed at her clinical terminology.

"I'm sorry, but I want to be perfectly clear what I'm talking about. Have you? Please, just be honest."

"No."

"Okay. What about oral sex?"

"No."

"Were you thinking about having sex?"

No response.

Julia felt nauseous. "Paige, honey, I don't believe there's anything bad or dirty about sex, but I do think it would be so much better if you wait until you're older."

Before Julia could go into all the reasons again, Paige interrupted her with, "Fine. Is that all?"

Julia's jaw tightened. "No. You're going to the doctor for a check-up, and I'm getting you some condoms. You can get pregnant and you can get diseases. You don't think it will happen, but it will. So you must protect yourself."

"Jesus, I won't have sex with him."

"I'm not taking any chances. And Paige, you're coming with me to work for the next few days. You're going to do some work for your grandpa and for all his employees that you tried to steal from. Then, if I can get them to let you, you'll do some work for the Quinns."

"What if I say no?"

"Well then, you can lose all TV and iPod privileges, and you can sit around your room all day with nothing to do until you're ready to go to work."

Julia stood up to go. Just before she closed the door behind her, Paige crammed the earbuds back in her ears and whispered, "Fuck."

That afternoon, Paige cleaned long-forgotten crevices of the restaurant clogged with grease and cobwebs, and helped cook meals for the employees to take home to their families. During her break, Julia found her father and said, "I may be a bit longer than usual before I get back. I'm going across to the plant to talk to them about letting Paige do some work for them tomorrow."

"Don't bother. I already talked to William about it."

In spite of herself, Julia's heart sank. "He won't let her."

"No, he'll let her. He's got plenty of dirty jobs for her to do over there."

"Really? How did you convince him to let her set foot in there? How did you convince him to let *me* set foot in there?"

Her father shrugged. "He won't see much of either of you. He's swamped over there. He's doing the best he can, but he and his sister just can't hack it."

"I'm sorry to hear that."

"Oh well. Pretty soon the business will be sold, and we'll have to start sourcing our fish from somewhere else."

"What?"

"You didn't hear? They're going to have to sell the business."

"Because Jim can't work anymore?"

"That's not the biggest reason. Jim's health insurance policy was rescinded. Now they owe over a million dollars in medical bills, and counting."

Julia gasped. "What?"

Her father nodded. "They'll have to sell their house, too."

"Oh, no."

"Oh yes. And from what I understand, it was all for some bullshit reason. Some tiny thing they left off their insurance application, or something like that. William's going to sell his boat and his business, too. To help them with all the bills."

Julia lost all powers of speech. At the look on her face, her father said, "Don't worry. He's not coming to work here again."

Ignoring his obtuse remark, Julia said, "Can't they declare bankruptcy?"

"I'm not sure what the story is there, but it wouldn't surprise me if they're just too proud to do it. You know they believe in paying what they owe, and maybe they don't want the stain on their credit, either. William opened up a fund for them at the bank. I've given as much as I can, but they're never going to collect enough to cover everything they owe."

With that, her father walked away, leaving Julia to process the news on her own.

The next morning, Julia gently nudged Paige through the open entrance of the plant, unsure who would meet them there or what reception they would receive.

Kelly stood at the counter, darting back and forth while helping customers and attempting to restock the case. Julia hung back with Paige for a minute, until Kelly finally noticed them standing there.

Her lip curled at the sight of them. But she said, "I'll be with you in a minute."

After a while, Kelly finally emerged from behind the counter and said, "Follow me."

Julia and Paige followed her back onto the pier and around to the other entrance. Julia knew it would have been faster to go through the back. She assumed Kelly was hiding her from William.

Kelly brought them into the office, and said curtly, "I don't really have time to show you around. The cleaning supplies are in this closet. You can put her to work cleaning the office, for starters. It needs it, badly. Don't let her out of your sight."

With that, Kelly unceremoniously left them there to return to the front counter. Julia watched her go, then turned to Paige.

"Well, come on."

They opened the closet door and rummaged through all the cleaning supplies. With a look of resignation, Paige took rags and cleaning products and began dusting the furniture. Julia had to lift piles and piles of paperwork off of every horizontal surface in order to give Paige access to the furniture.

Clearly, they needed a lot of help in there.

She waited an hour for Kelly to return, and when she didn't, she told Paige, "Come with me."

She led Paige back onto the pier, into the other entrance again. She waited for Kelly to finish with a customer, then approached her and said, "I think we're about done with cleaning the office now, and I was wondering if you'd like some help filing paperwork. I'm a paralegal, so I'm pretty much a pro with paperwork."

Kelly's hard expression softened a bit. "I don't know how my parents did it all by themselves. Will and I haven't figured out the division of labor yet."

Julia sensed an opening. "I'd be happy to come in here for a few days and help out with anything you guys need."

But Kelly shook her head. "We can't pay you anything."

"No charge."

Kelly peered suspiciously at her. "Let me think about it. But I'll take you up on your offer for today, at least."

"You'll have to take a little time to show me what everything is and the basics of your system."

Kelly nodded. "Let me get Will up here."

Julia felt her stomach flop. She took Paige, and went back to the office again via the pier.

A few minutes later, Kelly appeared in the office and oriented Julia to the filing system at breakneck speed.

"Invoices. Accounts payable. Accounts receivable. Inventory."

"So this is an unpaid invoice?" asked Julia.

"Yes. Anytime you see one that hasn't been stamped like this one has, then put it in this tray here. It means it still needs to get paid."

After a while, Kelly left them by themselves in the office. Julia found some file folders and turned to Paige.

"You can start labeling these."

She showed Paige how to use the label maker, which Paige actually found rather fun.

"This is better than cleaning," Paige remarked.

Working together, Julia and Paige sorted through the mountains of paperwork and filed it all away within the next couple of hours. Then it was lunch time. Julia and Paige gathered up their belongings, and as they left the office, they almost bumped into William on his way in.

He flinched a bit at the sight of them. Julia put her hand on Paige's back, and nudged her toward the pier.

After lunch, they returned to the plant, and Kelly put Paige to work cleaning out live crab tanks, crab cookers, and fillet tables.

"Oh my God, I think I'm gonna hurl," Paige said as she pulled chunks of fish flesh, skin, and innards from the central floor drain.

Kelly leaned into Julia with a hint of a smile and whispered, "This is the kind of stuff Dad used to make us do when we got in trouble."

Back here, Julia caught sight of William more often as he pitched in at the filleting table and supervised the packaging. Though she was in plain sight, he never looked at her. He was too busy anyway, she reflected, and she would have left him alone even if she had no other incentive to do so.

At two o'clock, the plant began wrapping up operations. Julia took Paige to the restroom to wash up, and together they returned to the office to retrieve their belongings.

They found William and Kelly there, engaged in some earnest conversation which stopped abruptly when Julia and Paige entered. Julia silently gathered up her jacket, hat, and scarf, and waited for Paige to do the same.

"You did good work today," Kelly said finally to Paige.

Julia nudged Paige, who mumbled, "Thanks."

"Thank you, too," Kelly said, lifting her eyes to Julia.

"You're welcome," Julia replied. Taking a deep breath, she added, "I'd be happy to help out here in any way you need for a few days. I know what you and your family are going through right now. I can help you keep on top of your paperwork and your bills."

William turned a solemn gaze on Julia. "I don't think that will be necessary."

In spite of herself, Julia felt her heart sinking. Before he could see the evidence on her face, Julia nudged Paige through the office door.

One final burst of inspiration struck her.

"My dad told me about your dad's health insurance. That your parents are going to have to sell this business, and their house."

William nodded.

"Sometimes these rescissions can be fought in court," Julia continued. "If the insurance company is found to be in the wrong, they can be made to reimburse your parents."

"We're not litigious people, Julia," replied Kelly. "We're not trying to get anything that's not ours."

"No, but if you can save what's already yours, and keep your brother from having to sell his business, too…"

Julia looked pointedly at William. He said, "He's been getting treatment for four months. None of his claims were denied, but the providers weren't getting paid, either. Then, last week, out of the blue, my parents got a letter in the mail from the insurance company, saying boom, we're rescinding your policy. In effect, cancelling it back to the time you first got it. Here's a check, refunding you for all your premiums paid so far, minus the claims we paid for you, and by the way, you still owe a million bucks for your medical care."

Julia shook her head in dismay. "Why did they say they were rescinding it?"

"They said Dad failed to disclose on his application that he had a lung condition, high blood pressure, and a mental disorder."

"But none of that is true?"

"No, but the insurance company says it was in his medical record."

"They should consult an attorney."

Kelly scoffed. "They're already drowning in bills. How are they supposed to pay a lawyer?"

"The initial consultation is free. And if they have a case, they pay the attorney nothing until they win."

"And if they don't win?" William inquired.

"The attorney assumes the risk of the litigation. You won't pay anything if you don't win."

She waited for a response, but William only looked at her in that same piercing way. She turned, and ushered Paige out of the building.

Julia spent the next few days attending counseling sessions with Paige, taking her to the doctor and the psychiatrist, and tending to other business. But the next week, as soon as Julia dropped Paige off at school, she drove to the law library to dig through the books.

That afternoon, she dialed a familiar old number she hadn't dialed in years.

"Hello?"

Julia took a deep breath. "Is this Ann Quinn?"

"Yes."

"Mrs. Quinn, this is Julia Beale. Julia Dunphy, formerly." Quickly, she added, "Before you hang up on me, I may have a way for you to save your house and your business."

There was a long pause on the other end of the line. "Okay."

"I know you don't want to see me or even talk to me, but I think what I have can help you. Can I meet you somewhere, just for a few minutes? Either today, or sometime in the next day or two?"

After another long pause, Ann said, "Can you come over now to the house?"

"Yes."

"Do it, then."

Julia hung up and drove straight to the Quinns' house. Ann scowled from the front door, but opened it wide to admit Julia.

"Come with me in here," said Ann, gesturing toward the in-law unit. "Jim's sleeping upstairs, and I don't want to disturb him."

Julia followed her silently, took a seat on the couch next to Ann, and spread her paperwork on the coffee table. Ann scowled some more at her, and said, "Well?"

Julia considered inquiring after Jim, but judged it best, for now, to get down to the point. "I spoke with William last week, at the plant. He told me that the health insurance company is saying that Jim lied on his insurance application. He also said that's not true."

"Of course it's not true," snapped Ann.

"Here's the point, Mrs. Quinn." Julia held out a photocopy of a page from the code book. "This is a new law that went into effect on January 1, 2010. A health insurance company cannot rescind your policy unless it can prove that you intentionally lied on your application. Have they provided any kind of evidence that Jim intentionally lied on his application?"

Ann frowned thoughtfully a moment. "They said it was in his medical record."

"Mrs. Quinn, I don't mean to pry, but can I ask you exactly what conditions they claim that he lied about? I only ask because I'm hoping I can help you guys in some way."

Ann looked suspiciously at Julia. "Why do you want to help us?"

Julia shifted uncomfortably in her seat. "I hate to see you and Jim lose your business and your home like this. You've been friends of my family for years and years. And I know William is going to sell his business, too. If there's anything I can do to stop all this from happening, I have to try."

Ann shook her head. "We don't need any help from you, Julia."

"Then don't take my help. But please, consult an attorney about your case, if you haven't already. You may or may not know, I'm a paralegal now. And no, I don't specialize in these kinds of cases, so I'm not trying to reap any benefit from this for myself or my employer. But the initial consultation is free, and the attorney can tell you if he thinks you have a case or not." Julia held out another piece of paper. "This is the name and number of an attorney who specializes in these kinds of cases. My cousin Holly, who's an attorney, gave me his name."

Ann sneered. "You're not trying to get any personal benefit from this, eh?"

"No. How would I?"

Ann leaned toward her. "He has a good and loyal heart, and I'll be damned if I'm going to let you anywhere near it again."

Julia felt her pulse quickening and her face burning. But she forced her voice to remain steady. "William has no idea I'm here talking to you, and he never will unless you tell him."

"Good. Because he'll never owe you a damn thing."

"If I had wanted to put him under some obligation to me, don't you think I could have done it by now?"

The sneer on Ann's face vanished. Slowly, she leaned back in her seat again.

Julia said, "If you think I don't know I made the worst mistake of my life, you're wrong. I'll pay for it every single day for the rest of my life, and rightly so. I love William with every fiber of my being, but I know I've lost him. I don't want him to lose his business. I don't want you and Jim to lose your business or your home. It's as simple as that."

Julia and Ann looked at each other for several more moments. Then Julia ventured, "If you have Jim's medical records, and you're willing to share them with me, I may be able to tell whether you have a case. I'll write the case up for you and submit it to this attorney myself to get his attention. It would save him some work and get the ball rolling on your case even faster."

Ann considered a while longer, then got up and went upstairs. She returned carrying a file folder.

"When we got the letter from the insurance company rescinding our policy, we asked Jim's doctor to fax over his records to us so we could see for ourselves," explained Ann. She opened the folder, and pointed to one page. "This here, where it says 'SOB', does not mean Jim is a son of a bitch, though that would be right on the mark. But the doctor says it means 'shortness of breath.' That's what the insurance company calls lung disease."

Julia examined the page more closely. "All it says here is that he had shortness of breath due to nasal allergies."

"Yep, but the insurance company says 'shortness of breath' indicates a lung disease." She turned to another page. "Here's where it says Jim had elevated blood pressure during a couple of visits, five years ago. Jim told the doctor he was feeling nervous, because he was under a lot of financial stress. See, here the doctor wrote 'anxiety.' All of that is what the insurance company calls high blood pressure and a mental disorder. But the next time Jim came into the office, our financial troubles were over, his blood pressure was back to normal, and he wasn't having anxiety anymore."

"Did he ever get any medication or treatment for the elevated blood pressure or the anxiety?"

"No, nothing. It all resolved itself by the next visit."

Julia said, "Would you mind showing me the letter from your insurance company? The one rescinding your policy?"

Ann went to retrieve that from her files. When she returned, Julia looked it over.

"I've never heard of this company before," she said.

"They offer cheaper policies for self-employed people."

"They're out of state. They might be unfamiliar with the law in California regarding rescissions. Listen, I definitely don't want to get your hopes up. But the more I'm looking at this, the more I'm thinking you might have a case. You might even be able to settle with the insurance company fairly quickly."

"And you said you could write it up for us? Submit it to that attorney?"

"Yes, I can. Would you feel comfortable if I took these documents with me right now and made some photocopies to work with? I'll bring the originals right back to you as soon as I'm done."

Ann nodded. Julia gathered up the file folder and the letter from the insurance company. Ann accompanied her silently to the front door. On the front step, Julia faced her and said, "I'll be right back in just a minute."

She drove to the grocery store and made copies of everything. Back on the front step of the Quinns' house, Julia handed the originals to Ann. "I'm going to call Jim's doctor. You'll need to give him permission to speak to me about Jim's medical record."

"How long do you think this will take?"

"It will only take me a couple of days to write up the case for the attorney. If he's willing to take the case, then he can answer your questions about how long the litigation process will take. I imagine it all depends on whether there's a settlement, or whether it goes to trial."

"But are we talking weeks? Months?"

"If it settles, it could be weeks. If it goes to trial, it could even be years, if you include the appeals process."

Ann looked sober. "We don't have years to get these bills paid. We haven't wanted to file bankruptcy, but I guess we'll have to. Then all this is moot, anyway."

"It's not moot, because you'll stop the insurance company from doing this to other people, and you'll receive punitive damages. And bankruptcy may not be good for your case if you decide to litigate, anyway. The bankruptcy trustee may be able to control the litigation. In the meantime, you could try and level with the creditor, or give them liens against the case. That's another thing the attorney can advise you on."

Ann looked thoughtful a moment. Then Julia ventured, "How is Jim?"

Ann shook her head. "It won't be much longer now."

"I'm so sorry."

There didn't seem to be anything left to discuss, so Julia said, "I'll call you as soon as I have anything to tell."

Ann nodded, but could not quite bring herself to say more. Julia turned to go.

A few days later, when Julia's phone rang, the caller ID identified the attorney that Holly had referred her to. Julia scrambled to answer it as quickly as possible.

"This is Julia."

"Hi. Julia Beale?"

"Yes."

"This is Joel Robinson."

"Yes, I know. How are you?"

"Great. Hey, listen, I'm sitting here in front of this remarkable brief you sent me."

Julia felt her pulse racing. "I hope you mean remarkable in a good way."

"Yes, though not good for the insurance company. This company must be either really stupid or… no, I think that about sums it up. They're just really stupid."

Julia laughed.

"I wonder what these people were thinking, or if they were even thinking at all. I thought we'd seen the last of these kinds of cases."

"Oh, really?"

"Well, yeah. This law has been in place for two years now. And now there's a federal statute that covers this, as well. So these people are either really ignorant, or really greedy."

"So you agree they have a case."

"Oh, I think this might be a slam dunk. I'm just eager to discover what their reasoning was on this one."

"So you'll take the case, then?"

"Well, yeah, if they'll let me."

"You mean the family? Yes, I'll let them know you're willing to take it, but I'm not sure whether or not they're ready to go forward with it."

"Well, they ought to be. If they are, put them in touch with me in the next day or so."

"Thank you."

"You're welcome. And good work on this. You should apply here for a paralegal position."

Julia steeled herself. "Thank you; that's very flattering. But right now I'm looking into some other opportunities."

"Okay; well, let me know if you change your mind. And good luck."

"Thank you. And thanks again for being willing to take the case."

"Are you kidding? Easy money."

After hanging up with Joel, the first call that Julia made was to Ann Quinn.

"I have some good news for you. The attorney is going to take your case."

There was a pause on the other end of the line. "I guess that is good news. Though I'm beginning to wonder if I want to drag Jim through this process, or just focus on making his last days comfortable for him."

Julia considered a moment. "That's a tough call. But I do think you should follow through with it in the long run. Holding the insurance company accountable, for one thing."

"Yes, that's the main thing, for us. I wouldn't feel good about it if I heard they'd done the same thing to someone else, and we might have stopped it."

"Do you still have the name and contact information of the attorney?"

"Yes, I do."

"You might consider meeting with him at least once, just for an initial consultation. You don't have to follow through with anything if you don't want to."

Ann considered. "I think I could find time for an initial consultation. I might hold off on the rest for a while. At least until everything is all over. It won't be much longer now, anyway."

"I'm so sorry. May I ask, what is the time frame they've given you at this point?"

"Hard to predict, but it's weeks, at most."

"Well, you have my number if you need anything."

"Yes. And thank you for the work you've done. I really do thank you for trying to help. But Julia... I can't ever forgive you for what you did to Will. I was really afraid for him for a couple of years. You very nearly broke him. But you didn't. He moved on."

Julia felt a crushing sensation in her chest. "Goodbye, Mrs. Quinn."

She hung up the phone.

A few weeks later, while the kids were in school on her day off, Julia worked in the living room on her new saltwater tank. While pouring in the salt mix, she heard her mother coming in with a load of groceries.

"Oh," her mother said upon reaching the top of the staircase. "I didn't know you were here today."

"It's my day off," said Julia, relieving her mother of a bag of groceries and following her into the kitchen. "I didn't know you were out running errands, or I might have asked you to run by the fish store for me. I need a new hydrometer for the aquarium I'm setting up in the living room."

"I wasn't expecting to run errands, but I need to make a casserole for Ann Quinn. Jim passed away today."

Julia put her hand to her mouth. "So soon."

Her mother looked as if she might choke up. "Everyone knew it would be quick, but I don't think we realized just how quick."

Julia tried to think. "Are you taking the casserole to the Quinns yourself?"

"Yes. But Julia, I don't think you'd better come. Everyone will be there."

By everyone, Julia knew she meant William.

If she had not made the choices she had, she could be there now. Part of the family. A hand for him to hold, a shoulder for him to lean on. Instead, she was excluded even from paying her respects.

Julia hid her face from her mother by putting away some cans of soup. Her mother watched her for a moment, and changed the subject.

"I didn't know you were setting up a new aquarium. Can I see?"

"There's nothing to see yet. I'm just getting started."

Her mother filled a bowl with oranges. "It looks like you're settling in for the long haul."

"Hm?"

"Setting up a new aquarium. Looks like you're planning on being here for a while."

Julia placed the bread into the bread box, and avoided her gaze.

"You know we can't take care of that thing ourselves once you move out. I don't imagine you'd be wasting your time setting that thing up if it was only for a short stay."

Julia dropped some onions into the wire basket that hung from the ceiling in the corner of the kitchen. "The truth is, Mom, I've just about made up my mind what I'm going to do. I don't think I'll go back to work as a paralegal at all. I don't even think I'll leave San Francisco."

"Oh? What will you do?"

"I think I'll revive the old aquarium business."

"You mean Rob and Tim's business?"

Julia gave her a wry smile. "Do you think anyone will remember?"

"I don't know. But I know two people who'd be smiling down on you from somewhere." Her mother hesitated a moment. "Is that why you're working on your aquarium right now?"

"That, and I really am going to stick around here for the time being. With you and Dad's blessing, I'd like to put off getting a new place. I want to focus my energy on the business and see how that goes first."

"Don't get me wrong – I'm delighted to have you and the kids here. But I thought you would want your own space. I didn't think sharing a bedroom with Paige was in your long-term plans."

"Long-term, no. But mid-range, yes."

Her mother smirked. "Paige will be thrilled about that."

"I think it'll soften the blow when I explain why."

"Yes, that's probably the only explanation you could give her that *would* soften the blow." Her mother reached out and squeezed Julia's hand. "Yet another family enterprise. I can't believe you're finally doing it."

"Me neither," admitted Julia. "But the stars kept aligning for me. Persistent little buggers."

❖

A couple of months later, the phone rang in the house as Julia gathered up her bag for the day. She answered it in the kitchen.

"Hello?"

After a brief pause, a familiar husky voice said, "Julia?"

"This is she."

"Julia, this is Ann Quinn."

"Oh." Julia went to sit at the kitchen table. "Hi, Mrs. Quinn."

"Ann, please."

Startled, Julia said, "Okay."

Julia could hear the bustle of the processing plant in the background. "Joel Robinson said you'd be interested to hear the update on our case," Ann continued finally.

"Yes, I'd be very interested."

"The insurance company is settling."

Julia beamed. "That's such great news. Can I ask, how did they get them to settle?"

"During the discovery process, they found a couple of memos. Let me see here; I've written it all down somewhere." Julia heard papers shuffling, and after a moment, Ann said, "Yes, here it is. They uncovered a memo from an insurance commissioner to the health insurance company, saying that the laws governing rescission had changed. Then they uncovered a letter from the claims adjustor to the president of the company regarding Jim's specific case. In the letter, the adjustor asks the president if he should still rescind the policy."

Julia's eyes widened. "Wow."

"Joel said it showed the company engaged in — what did he call it? Let me see… 'Malice, oppression, and fraud.'"

266

Julia felt giddy with excitement. "I hope you're getting a nice settlement from the company."

"Enough to reimburse us for the bills we paid and pay the attorney's fees, with something left over so that the kids won't have to pay my bills when I get too decrepit to keep working. And maybe put a little something aside for the kids when I go belly up."

Julia grinned and dared to say, "That'll never happen. You're too stubborn to go belly up."

Ann laughed. "Well, I may not have much say in that. I do have emphysema. Besides, it's the Quinns who are the stubborn ones, not the Cardones."

Julia could not wipe the smile from her face. After a moment, she said, "Congratulations."

"Thanks. And Julia... when I came back to work after Jim passed on, I found the office in much better shape than I left it. When I went on leave, the paperwork was already out of control. Since Jim got sick and went on leave, I hadn't had time to do much with it. And I knew that with Will and Kelly in charge, it could only have gotten worse. So imagine my shock when I came back and found that the pile had actually shrunk."

A long pause ensued, neither of them wishing to be the first to say something. Finally, Ann continued, "Kelly says the paperwork that I did see that morning had piled up since you put everything in order for them."

"I'm glad I could help in some small way."

"It hasn't been small. Thanks for getting the ball rolling on all this. I'm sorry for how rude I was before."

"It's okay. I understand."

After they hung up, Julia sat for as long as she dared at the kitchen table. That might be the last time she would interact with Ann. Which meant it was probably the last time she would interact with any of the family. Any of them.

It seemed impossible that she should just never speak to him again. That maybe she should never even see him again. A gaping chasm of time stretched before her, and it just seemed so vacant and so wrong and so impossible.

But soon, she glanced at the clock and went to gather up her bag. Pulled on her sweater, hat, and scarf, and left the house.

She drove across the city to the Castro and parked near the business district. Walked to the storefront, and gazed up at the sign that said "Castro Aquarium Service – Coming Soon." Put the key in the front door, and turned it.

On a Friday evening in early May, as Julia hung streamers from the dining room ceiling, the phone rang in the house. She got down from the ladder and went to answer it in the kitchen.

"Julia."

She instantly recognized the husky voice. "Hi, Ann."

"I just wanted to see if you were home. I'm sending something over for you."

Julia felt embarrassed, imagining a gift basket of some kind to thank her for the work she had done on the case. She couldn't think of a way to protest without sounding presumptuous, so she said, "I'm getting ready for a birthday party tomorrow, so it may take a minute before I can answer the door."

"Okay. I'll let them know."

After they hung up, Julia returned to the dining room and climbed back on the ladder. After a while, the front doorbell rang. Julia finished pinning the banner on the wall, then climbed down the ladder and went to answer the door. When she opened it, she had to catch herself on the door jamb.

Julia's field of vision reeled, and she couldn't breathe. It occurred to her that she might actually be losing her mind. At the look on her face, William said, "I know what you did for my family."

Her voice managed to come out in a croak. "How?"

"I went with my mom to the attorney's office to receive the check from the settlement. The attorney mentioned the e-mail you sent to him, writing up the case. He didn't know it was supposed to be a secret."

She held the door open. "Would you like to come inside?" He hesitated, and she added, "My dad's at work, and my mom's out with a group of friends from church."

He stepped then into the house, his hands in his jacket pockets. She led him upstairs to the dining room and pulled out a chair for him.

He looked around the room, and spotted the party decorations.

"You're busy. I'll let you go."

"No," she said firmly. There was no way in hell she was going to let him back out that door. "The party isn't until tomorrow."

He looked a bit startled by her tone, but complied, taking a seat in the chair. She took another seat across the table from him. William frowned down at his hands folded on the tabletop. She noticed his hairline was starting to recede from his temples a bit. The only sounds came from the in-law unit, where Robert pestered Paige while she worked on her aquarium.

Finally, he said, "I wanted to thank you."

"That's not necessary."

"Yes, it is. After we left the attorney's office, my mother told me everything."

Everything? "What did she tell you?"

"She told me how you had done all the research and came to her with it. How you found the attorney, and wrote up the case."

He lifted his eyes now to her face. Those same blue eyes; the same solemn gaze as ever. It moved her exquisitely. He held them there for what felt like an eternity, saying nothing, just looking. The expression softened. The creases in his forehead deepened.

"I'm trying to understand," he said quietly.

At that moment, the door to the in-law unit squeaked open downstairs, and Paige barked, "Get out of here, before you break the fish tank with that stupid hook!"

Robert bounded upstairs, wearing the pirate costume Julia had made him, and stopped short when he saw the unfamiliar visitor.

"Arrrrgh! Who goes there?" he demanded, shaking his pirate hook at William.

William looked startled, and Julia knew that Ann hadn't told him. He had no idea that she had a second child, a son.

"This is William," replied Julia. She turned to William and struggled to steady her voice. "This is my son, Robert."

Robert turned to William, the pirate hat askew on his head. "Arrrrre ye coming to me party tomorrow, matey?"

William looked uncomfortable receiving an invitation to a birthday party from the son of his ex-fiancée and her husband. Julia watched Robert pull the wayward pirate hat from his rumpled blond hair. Watched Robert's grave, pale blue eyes gazing at William.

Watched William's world spin.

Watched him look up at the banner on the wall that said, "Happy 5th Birthday, Robert." Watched him doing the math, counting backward five years. Counting back again nine months from there. Turning to her with eyes as wide as any she had ever seen in his face, looking to her for confirmation.

She sprang to her feet and bundled Robert back downstairs. "Paige! Come get your brother and take him outside."

From the in-law unit, Paige shouted, "No, Mom; he's getting on my nerves!"

Julia stepped down the stairs a bit more. "Paige, come get Robert right now, or you'll spend the rest of the day in your room!"

Her sharp tone finally summoned Paige to the bottom of the stairs. "Jesus," she muttered, seizing Robert's hand and leading him outside.

Once Julia was sure they were safely outside, she returned to the dining room, shaking from head to toe. William sat frozen with his elbows on his thighs, his hands covering his mouth and nose. Julia had never seen a person so shocked in her entire life.

She resumed her seat across from him and waited for him to speak, to react in some way. He sat there like that for a full two or three minutes.

"Can I get you a glass of water?" Julia offered gently. "Something stronger?"

Slowly, he took his hands from his face. "Why didn't you tell me?"

"I didn't want you to feel obligated to me. I knew how angry you were."

He frowned. "How could you seriously have thought it was better not to tell me?"

Julia's stomach quivered. "You told me never to come back. That you would never believe another word I said."

"But *this?* It was easy enough to prove."

"You were so angry with me."

"I was angry because I was hurt. But did you seriously think I wouldn't have set all of that aside in a heartbeat if I had known that we were going to have a baby together?"

Julia's pulse raced so quickly that she really worried she might faint.

"I missed the chance to be there when he was born," he persisted, increasingly agitated. "To see him when he was a baby. To teach him about things, and watch him grow. I'll never get that back. He may be the only child I ever have. How could you really believe that's what I would have preferred?"

Impulsively, Julia reached across the table and touched his hand. "I'm sorry. I'm so sorry. I was so confused. I know you don't know all of the stress I was under, but I swear, it was impossible to think clearly. Once I started feeling better, I began to realize that maybe it wasn't right to keep this from you, but by then I worried it was too late. The more time that went by, the harder it became to face you and admit the secret I had kept. Kevin agreed to raise him. As sort of a penance, I suppose."

William looked alarmed. "Who else knows, besides him?"

"It's pretty much an open secret in my family. You saw him. Can it really be ignored?" She hesitated. "Your mom knows."

He looked shocked again. "My *mom?*"

"She saw him once. In the grocery store. Didn't even have to look twice."

He frowned. "Why didn't she tell me?"

"She had a lot of reasons of her own not to tell you. We spoke about it, sort of, when I told her about my research and the attorney I had found to help her. Mainly, she was trying to protect you."

"Protect me? From what?"

"She said you had a good and loyal heart, and she'd be damned if she'd let me anywhere near it again. I pretty well memorized those words, they stung so much. And then another time, she said she really worried about you for a while after we broke up, and she could never forgive me. She must have been really afraid of what would happen to you if you had any contact with me. That's the only reason I can think of why she wouldn't even tell you about your own son; her own grandson."

He seemed to consider something for a long time. "She sent me over here. She practically shoved me out the front door. To thank you, she said." After another moment's contemplation, he added, "She insisted I come with her to the attorney's office. I didn't understand why."

They listened to the tick-tock of the pendulum clock on the mantelpiece. Quietly, Julia said, "He's incredibly bright and imaginative, but very serious. He already has a beautiful singing voice and a talent for music, and he certainly couldn't have gotten those from me or Kevin. And he loves anything to do with boats."

He covered his mouth and nose again with his hands, and really looked as if he might cry.

"Come to the party tomorrow," she suggested. "It starts at eleven."

He swallowed hard, considered for a moment. "Tomorrow is Saturday; we have excursions. And I don't want to be a distraction." Her heart sank, until he added, "But I'd like to come over afterward, if I can."

At that moment, Alison burst into the house with all her noise, already talking non-stop to Julia even though they couldn't even see each other yet.

"I hope your kid appreciates this pirate ship cake because you have no idea how many times it nearly turned into a life raft on the way over here. I was between two homeless guys on Muni who were each arguing with the voices inside their head, and they each thought the other guy was really cursing at them. I had nowhere to move to; I was sure the cake and I would both get squashed flat before I made it halfway here. I was calculating all the different ways I could use a cake as a weapon."

Julia tried to head her off, but once Alison started moving, inertia rendered her unstoppable. Not to mention her mouth would not quit long enough for Julia to get a word in edgewise. Alison barreled upstairs and into the living room like a ten ton truck, but both she and her mouth stopped flat when she saw William sitting there at the dining table.

"William! Long time no see! Now let me see, where did I put the candles?" She shot one quizzical look at Julia before dashing into the kitchen.

Julia followed her. As soon as she came in, Alison snatched her by the arms and whispered fiercely, "What the hell?"

"Help," implored Julia.

"What exactly am I helping with?"

"Go outside and warn Paige. Keep him here while I make dinner."

"What is going on?"

"I can't tell you now. Later." She clutched Alison's hands. "Keep him here. Talk to him. And for God's sake, keep your mouth shut."

Alison smirked at the oxymoronic request. "I got it covered. But I have just one question."

"What?"

"Does he know?"

"Yes."

Alison nodded, and Julia thought she looked pleased. While Alison went outside to prepare Paige, Julia returned to William. She found him looking thoughtfully at a framed photograph of Robert that stood on the mantelpiece.

"Would you like to get to know him?"

He nodded without a moment's hesitation. Julia felt her heart soar with hope, and angrily trampled the dangerous emotion back down. Of course he would want to get to know his own son. In itself, that meant nothing for her and him.

"Stay for dinner."

Again he nodded. She gestured for him to follow her downstairs and outside.

As soon as he caught sight of them, Robert cried, "Mommy, the hoop came off again!"

The basketball hoop dangled precariously from its post. William came forward a bit shyly, and Paige retreated back indoors. Julia cast Alison an anxious glance, and Alison gave her a reassuring nod.

William examined the post and hoop and declared, "I can fix this."

Julia went to the shed and retrieved the toolbox for him. She and Alison hung back, watching him work. Within a few minutes, he successfully screwed the hoop back onto the post and began showing Robert some of his best pick-up basketball moves.

"Go make dinner. I got this," whispered Alison.

While she cooked, Julia occasionally caught sight of them through the kitchen window. They moved on from basketball to T-ball. Alison shouted encouragement to Robert and coaching tips to

William from her seat at the patio table. By the time she was setting the table for dinner, Robert had lost his reserve, and now engaged William in a spirited battle of pirates and hapless ships on the high seas.

"Why is he here, Mom?"

Julia turned to find Paige at her elbow. She set the plates and cups back down and went to sit at the kitchen table. She patted the chair next to her, and Paige took a seat.

"When you were seven years old, this man took you on a boat to see the Farallon Islands," Julia began. "Do you remember that?"

Paige looked surprised. "Yes, I do. That was a lot of fun." She hesitated a moment, then said, "Is he your boyfriend?"

Julia fidgeted, startled by how much her daughter's question discomposed her. "No."

Paige stared at her, and Julia realized that her daughter was old enough to see through the word to the feelings underneath them. But thankfully, Paige said nothing more. She got up and went back to her room.

Julia put the food on the table, reflecting wryly that William would have to endure her cooking, for once. When she came outside to announce dinner, she found Alison and William sitting next to each other at the patio table. Though not out of the ordinary for William, the grave expression on Alison's face alarmed her.

Oh God, Julia thought. What did she tell him?

No time to find out now. "Dinner's ready," she heard herself call.

Robert came sprinting inside. Alison and William were not so spry on their feet, dragging themselves out of their chairs. As Alison brushed past her, Julia shot her a sharp, questioning look, which Alison avoided so studiously that Julia felt more alarmed than ever.

William's expression revealed nothing, and besides, it was time to face Paige's dreaded integration with their little party, her first interaction with William since trying to steal from him.

Alison escorted her from her room, and to Julia's surprise, Paige actually looked William in the eye and said, "Hi," before taking her seat at the table. Julia pointed William to a seat between Robert and Alison, which he accepted.

After dishing some spaghetti onto Robert's plate, Julia passed the bowl to William. He served himself, then passed it across to Paige.

Paige said, "I thought you used to be a cook."

He glanced briefly at Julia and replied, "I did, once."

"But now you work at the plant?"

"I was filling in there for a while. My family owns that place."

"So what do you do now?"

"I run a whale-watching business. I run the boat myself."

Paige nodded. "I remember when you took me to see the whales."

"Will you take me sometime?" Robert asked William.

"Yes, definitely. I can take you all."

"I hope you weren't including me in that invitation," said Alison. "If you were, thanks, but I get seasick."

Julia knew that was a lie, and could not help smirking a bit.

After that, Paige said very little. Occasionally, Julia saw Paige's eyes flit between her and William and drop back down to her plate again. But their expression conveyed only curiosity, with no resentment or sullenness.

"What kind of a boat do you have?" Robert asked William after a while.

"It's a catamaran. Mine was built for sport fishing, and it's only fifty feet long, so it's pretty small. But it gets the job done."

"Do you sail it every day?" asked Robert, still innocent of the distinctions between sailboats and power boats.

"No. On the weekends, I always do whale watching trips. Some weekdays, I do private charters. Groups of people pay me to take them on the boat, either for whale watching or for sport fishing."

"What about photography?" Julia ventured quietly, remembering how they had discussed the possibility once.

"Yes, I do private charters for wildlife photography sometimes, too."

Robert continued to pepper William with questions throughout dinner, and when it was over, Robert looked up at him and said, "When can we go?"

William's expression softened a bit. "I have to reserve my weekend excursions for paying customers. But I'm pretty sure I could do it Tuesday."

"Awesome," said Robert.

Paige looked up at Julia. "Does that mean we get to skip school?"

"Just this once." Julia turned to smile at William, and realized too late that she had lowered her guard. Something in the expression on her face stopped his eyes for a moment, and a full gamut of emotion cycled through them before he quickly turned them back down to his plate.

Once dinner was over and they had all cleared the table, Paige disappeared into her room again, and Robert ran to turn on the TV.

"I have a lot of orders due tomorrow," Alison said to Julia.

"Yes. See you later."

Alison extended her hand to William. "Good to talk to you."

William shook her hand and nodded, but said nothing.

Alison let herself out of the house, leaving Julia momentarily alone in the kitchen with William.

He leaned back against the kitchen table, bracing himself against it with his hands. Julia gestured and said, "Do you want to sit down?"

He took a seat. Julia reached into the refrigerator for a beer, and offered it to him wordlessly. He declined it, but the gesture prompted him to sit up straighter and finally meet her gaze.

"I've missed the first five years of his life."

"You don't have to miss any more time with him. You're welcome here as often as you like."

He raised an eyebrow. "Here? In your parents' house?"

"Yes. They're just going to have to deal with it, until I find my own place."

"Will that be in the city?"

"I'm not sure." Julia fidgeted with her fingernails. "I may move to the East Bay."

He seemed unsure what to say next, so after a while, Julia suggested, "You can have a little time with just Robert. Maybe play a game of Go Fish with him."

He nodded, and she waved him into the living room. She brought the cards out of the cabinet, and the three of them settled in around the coffee table.

When bedtime rolled around, William hung back in the doorway of Robert's room, watching as Julia tucked him into bed. When Julia brought the bedtime book down off the shelf, Robert said, "William, will you read it?"

William looked to Julia, and she nodded her encouragement. He moved forward uneasily and took the book from her. Pulled up a chair at Robert's bedside on the lower bunk. Glanced at the cover and said to Robert, "*Where the Wild Things Are.* That was one of my favorites when I was a kid, too."

Robert smiled at him, and William returned the smile a bit shyly. Then, with an uncertain voice, he began the unfamiliar task of reading his son a bedtime story.

Robert listened attentively as William slowly gained confidence and improvised the sounds and voices of the rumpusing Wild Things, which Robert laughed at.

When the story was over, Robert met William's gaze with the same blue eyes and pleaded, "I want another one!"

"Not tonight," Julia said. "We have to save some of your books for another night."

She stepped forward to kiss Robert goodnight one last time, brushing past William as he retreated back to the open doorway.

After she turned out the light and closed the door, she checked in briefly on Paige. Then by silent agreement, Julia and William resumed their seats at the kitchen table.

"It must be strange for Paige, seeing me here," he finally remarked.

Julia gave an awkward laugh. "I'm sure it was, a little bit. But Alison prepared her, before she saw you." After a moment's hesitation, she added, "I never got the chance to really tell you how sorry I am for what happened with her at the plant that day."

He waved his hand dismissively.

"No, I think you should know this. She's run away from home twice. On the day you found her at the plant, she was stealing

277

because she was planning to run away again. But she's also very intuitive and perceptive, and she's had her artwork featured in galleries already. Sometimes I think she's more Alison's kid than mine. But she inherited my passion for aquariums, and that's the glue that's held us together through the worst times. When her medication works and she takes it, she does pretty well, but it's a constant battle."

"Reminds me of my brother Mike."

"Yes, but I will be dealing with this for the rest of my life. She's my daughter."

He slowly nodded his understanding. They sat in silence while he digested it all.

She watched him quietly a moment, then said, "I didn't know I was pregnant when we broke up. But I knew within days."

He looked up at her sharply. "How?"

"The morning sickness. I had it with Paige, too, but never like this. This came on like a lion, and it lasted all day. I had to be hospitalized for it. I had to receive IV fluid and nutrition. It was impossible to hide from anyone. With the timing, everyone knew he couldn't possibly be Kevin's, including Kevin."

"And he was okay with that?"

"Like I told you, at first he accepted it as a sort of a penance. But within a few months, when I asked him what he thought we should name the baby, he told me it was my decision. That's how I knew his remorse was wearing thin. So I named him Robert, after my uncle. I figured you wouldn't mind, and with you being such a Led Zeppelin fan, the allusion to Robert Plant couldn't hurt."

He couldn't help laughing a little bit at this. Then she said, "His middle name is Patrick." She waited for this to register, and added, "Either Kevin didn't know that's your middle name, or he didn't care."

The look he gave her was pained. "Did he treat Robert well?"

"He was always just as kind and provided just as well for him as he did for Paige. He never blamed Robert directly, but I do think it was the strain that drove him and me apart for good. He could never just accept that I had borne another man's child. And for me, Robert was a permanent bond – a daily reminder of you."

The wariness that had held him back all night came crashing down, and he looked at her with poignancy. After a while, he asked her, "So you only knew when you got morning sickness? Didn't you miss a period or anything?"

"Yes, but I attributed it to all the stress I was going through at the time. I also blamed stress for the way I was coming unhinged and crying all the time, as you may remember. I didn't suspect I was pregnant because I thought I was taking my pills. But clearly, with everything that was distracting me, I messed up somewhere along the way. That's how determined this little life was to burst onto the scene, and he definitely made his presence known."

William opened his mouth once or twice as if he wanted to say something, but just couldn't get it out. Finally, looking resigned, he said, "I can be here by four or five tomorrow afternoon, if that's okay."

"Of course it is." She wondered how much to press the point. Instead, she said, "If you're going to be a part of Robert's life from now on, I think it makes sense for me to get your phone number and your address. In case I ever need to reach you about him for any reason."

He nodded, and she went to retrieve a piece of paper and a pen. He wrote his information down, folded it up, and slid it across the table to her.

He lingered a moment longer. Then, finally, he dragged himself to his feet and gathered up his belongings. She followed him silently to the front door, and held it open for him. As he passed through it, she thought of what to say.

"I'll tell Robert you're coming."

It was manipulative; she knew it was. But he looked at her briefly and nodded, and she thought she saw the corners of his mouth turn up.

She closed the door and ran straight up the stairs to her darkened bedroom. She pulled the curtains aside just a crack, and peered out at the street below. He was heading in the direction of his parents' house, on foot.

"He was the man in the house, wasn't he?"

Julia jumped at her daughter's voice behind her. She dropped the curtain, making it even harder to distinguish Paige's face in the darkness. Carefully, Julia felt her way to her own bed, and sat at the edge of it.

"Paige, honey, why are you awake?"

"I couldn't sleep." Paige sat up and said, "I remember, when Dad left us the first time, I heard a noise one night and saw a man in bed with you. I remember thinking it was Dad, but you said it wasn't."

Julia's heart pounded. "Can I turn on the light?"

Paige reached over and turned it on herself. She shielded her eyes and squinted up at Julia. After a moment, she said, "I knew I wasn't crazy. I knew someone was there."

"You're right," said Julia. "Of course you weren't crazy."

"All these years, I thought you were lying to me. I thought it really was Dad. I thought Dad must have come back, and you didn't want me to know for some reason. But once I was old enough to understand, I realized it must have been someone else." She lowered her hand from her face now, her eyes adjusted to the light. "Was it William?"

Julia didn't know how to lie to her, and didn't want to, anyway. "Yes."

"So that's Robert's real dad."

This rattled Julia to the core. Her mouth opened, and she shifted her weight a bit. Unable to think of a better response, she said, "You think William is Robert's real dad?"

"They look exactly alike. And Grandma Beale told me a couple of years ago that Dad isn't Robert's real dad."

"What?" gasped Julia. "Why would she tell you such a thing?"

"We were having an argument. About you. I defended you, and that's when she told me."

Julia felt the fury rising in her chest, while simultaneously marveling that Paige would ever defend her in any argument. "How old were you at the time?"

"Eleven."

Julia scowled. "It was very wrong of her to tell you such a thing, especially at that age. I wish you had talked to me about it."

"So is he?"

Julia sighed. "Yes."

"So you're going to shack up with him now."

"No! I mean – there's no relationship between us now. There's no reason for me to think there ever would be."

"But you wouldn't mind if there was."

Julia marveled at her daughter's powers of perception, on the cusp of young adulthood. Unsure how else to respond, she said, "You're going to see William a lot more now. He didn't know before about Robert, but now he does, and he wants to be a part of Robert's life. I'd like to ask you to be respectful to him, even if you don't like him."

Paige looked surprised. "He's okay. I mean, I know I didn't like him after he caught me and everything, but I didn't know who he was. I remember him from the whale watching trip. He let me drive the boat. He was the one we went crabbing with, too, wasn't he?"

Julia nodded.

"He was cool," said Paige, and Julia knew that was high praise, coming from her. "He looks different now."

Julia touched her hand to her chin. "The beard."

"Yeah, I think that's it. Because he used to be kind of cute."

Julia couldn't help giving a short laugh. After a moment, she said, "I'm sorry you had to figure things out in this way. I'm afraid this night has been a bit of a shock for us all."

Paige shrugged, and seemed to have nothing more to say.

After a moment, Julia said, "Can I hug you?"

Paige smiled as if a bit embarrassed, but nodded. Julia went over and squeezed her around the shoulders.

"Get some sleep," she said, switching off the lamp once Paige had climbed back in bed.

As for herself, she knew sleep would be impossible for the rest of the night. She went back to the kitchen, switched on the light, and sat down at the table again. Stared at the empty seat where, half an hour earlier, against all odds, William had sat.

She knew how important it was to be complete all by herself, and she had taken that lesson to heart. She had plenty to fill her life, even without him. She did not need him.

But she wanted him. It was as simple as that.

In spite of everything – in spite of all her pep talks to herself, and all her fears, and all her independent accomplishments – she knew that without him, it would always feel like something was missing. And there didn't have to be anything wrong with that.

She saw the piece of paper on the table top and snatched it up. Unfolded it and read his address, still in the Mission. Beneath it, her eyes seized on the words he had written: "I'm by myself."

What in the world did he mean by that? Because she didn't dare trust the hope rising like a phoenix that it was some kind of a message to her. That after all this time, he was still alone, and if she came to him, no one would stand in their way.

With the party over, the mess cleaned up, and her mother out of the house, Julia still had an hour or two of nervous energy to burn before William was due.

At four-thirty, she was beginning to worry that he might have changed his mind, when she heard the doorbell ring.

"I'll get it," she called, and stumbled downstairs.

She opened the front door, and was startled to find him bearing a wrapped gift for Robert.

"Oh, you didn't have to do that," she said breathlessly, reaching for the gift. He started to hand it to her, but she suddenly retracted her hands. "On second thought, you should give it to him yourself."

He smiled, a bit nervously she thought, and she stepped aside to let him in.

"I didn't have time to go shopping for anything," he said. "But I stopped by my parents' house and went digging through the attic for something I've been holding on to since I was a kid."

She smiled, and said, "He's out back, playing. Do you want me to bring him in now?"

"I was thinking it might be best to wait until his bath time to let him open it. But I'll go out and see him now, if that's okay."

"Okay, but the other idea I had was for us all to go down to the beach for a little while, since it's such a warm day."

He nodded his agreement, and she took the gift after all and hid it. Then she led him out back, where Robert was busy playing with his new train set, still clad in his pirate costume from the party.

"Robert, William is here," she called.

"Hi," he chirped, barely looking up from his game.

"Would you like to walk down to the beach?"

"Yeah!" he cried, and while he ran inside to change into his beach clothes and gather his sand toys, Julia poked her head into Paige's room to see if she wanted to come. To Julia's shock, Paige said, "Okay."

Anxious not to leave William a moment's opportunity to escape, Julia returned to the living room. She found him gazing thoughtfully at the framed photograph of Robert on the mantelpiece. He had not yet detected her presence, and she did not know what to say, so she watched him silently. He covered his mouth with his hand as if struggling with some intense emotion.

She heard Robert emerging from his room, and ducked quickly out of sight before William found her spying on him.

They all walked the few blocks to the beach. After a while, Robert, still in full pirate mode, entertained himself with digging for buried treasure in the sand, and Paige strolled thoughtfully at the edge of the water. William joined Julia at her side, his eyes trained on Robert.

They stood that way in silence for a while, until William quietly said, "After I heard what you did – with the research, the lawyer – I wondered why you were still hanging around, living in your parents' house, when you had sold your own house and could go anywhere and do anything with that money." He paused a few moments. "Alison told me you're reviving your uncle's old aquarium business."

She looked straight ahead at the ocean, but said nothing in response. He searched her face for an answer.

"I'm sorry," he said.

"For what?"

"You said it yourself. If I hadn't been so angry, you might have let me know about Robert. I was so hateful. I'm not surprised you were afraid to tell me."

"You have nothing to be sorry for. You had every right to be angry."

The creases in his forehead deepened. "Being angry all this time was the only way I knew how to keep it together."

Her heart leaped. "It's okay."

"I didn't know all the rest of it."

"The rest of what?"

"Well, besides the fact that you were pregnant, I didn't know everything else you had been through. I didn't know all of the details about the pressure you were under from your parents, from Paige, and from Kevin. How sick you got while you were pregnant. The fact that you had nobody to talk to."

Julia's face darkened. "Alison told you."

"Don't hold it against her. I told her I knew about Robert, and I asked her to tell me more about what was going on in your life during that time. I'm glad she was so thorough. I just wish I had known at the time."

"I didn't want you to be angry with my parents and Paige. It was ultimately my decision."

"I'm not blaming you, or anyone else. I only blame myself. If I had been around more – if I had bothered to find out more about what was going on – I might not have missed all this time with Robert." After a moment, he added, "I want you to know I intend to help support him. Financially, I mean."

"No," she said firmly, then quickly added, "I appreciate the offer so much, but the best way you can support him is by being a part of his life."

He looked almost stricken. He hesitated, as if struggling with what to say. "I know you're trying to get your business off the ground. You shouldn't have to live with your parents, if you don't want to. And –" She watched his feelings do battle on his face, his brows knitting together with the effort. Finally, with a look of determination, he said, "You shouldn't have to leave the city."

He looked up at her now, his expression solemn. There was no way to know whether he wanted her to stay too, or if he just didn't want Robert to be so far away.

"I don't want to leave," she said. "I won't need to. I'll eventually find my own place, once I have the time to look."

He looked back at Robert now. After a moment, he went toward him. Helped him build sand castles for a while. She watched them in between keeping an eye on Paige.

William searched with Robert for seashells. Robert's voice drifted back to her. "Mommy loves seashells. She collects them."

"She does?" William handed something to Robert. Leaned down into Robert's ear and whispered something. Robert grinned, and ran back to Julia.

"Here, Mommy. William says you'd like this." He handed her a tiny sand dollar. "He says it's a mermaid coin."

She peered up at William, but he was already digging down through the sand again. Robert ran back to join him, and Julia closed her hand around the little treasure and smiled.

After dinner, William said aside to Julia, "I think now would be a good time to give Robert my present."

She nodded, and he went to retrieve it from the credenza. He brought it into the living room, where Robert sat on the floor, watching TV. William sat down on the floor beside him, and Robert tore into the present with gusto.

Beneath the paper was a plain cardboard box, clearly recycled for this purpose and taped shut. William opened it with his pocket knife, and Robert reached inside. Packed in some tissue paper was a toy boat.

"I used to play with this in the bath tub when I was a kid," William explained, a bit shyly.

Julia came over and examined it. "This is classic Fisher Price."

"It's a houseboat. You can make the people walk the plank." William pulled the plank in and out to demonstrate.

"What people?" Robert wondered.

"Look inside again," said William.

Robert reached inside, and found several Fisher Price Little People.

"I remember these!" exclaimed Julia. "They don't make them this way anymore."

Robert looked up at Julia. "Can I take my bath now?"

"I never thought I'd hear you say that. You go get ready, and I'll be down there in a minute."

He took his boat, filled with the Little People, and carried it downstairs. When he had gone, Julia said to William, "It was really sweet of you to give him that, but are you sure? That's pretty irreplaceable."

"It's not like it's worth any money. I've been saving that all these years, in case I ever had kids of my own. Of course I had pretty much given up on that ever happening, but I'm happy to be able to share it with someone, after all."

She smiled. "I'm going to help him with his bath." Just in case, she added, "Don't go yet. I'm sure he'll want you to read him another bedtime story."

After Robert bathed and dressed in his pajamas, he asked Julia, "Is William still here?"

"Yes. Do you want him to read you another story tonight?"

Robert nodded, and Julia called up to William who, at Robert's request, read Harry the Dirty Dog.

Afterward, while William retreated back into the open doorway, Julia kissed Robert, turned off the light, and said, "Night-night."

"William." Robert's voice summoned William forward again. "Yeah?"

"Are you coming over again tomorrow?"

William glanced sheepishly at Julia.

"We'll have to see," replied Julia, "but you'll see him again on Tuesday, for sure."

"Good night," called Robert, and Julia knew it was meant for William.

"Good night," William answered.

They ducked back into the hallway again, and Julia closed the door. Upstairs again, she turned to look at William.

"I'm going to check on Paige a minute, and I'll be right back."

"Okay."

While he made himself comfortable, she went down the hall and found Paige on her bed, listening to music from her iPod and reading a book.

Paige took the ear buds out of her ears. "Is he still here?"

"William? Yeah."

She curled her lip. "Please don't spend the night with him."

Shocked, Julia came inside the room and closed the door behind her. "What gives you the idea that he's spending the night?"

"I just kind of assumed."

"Why would you assume such a thing?"

"The way you two were acting, I just assumed."

Julia gaped. "What are you talking about?"

"So you're not together?"

"No."

Paige set the iPod aside. "What are you waiting for?"

Julia laughed. "Well, make up your mind. What do you want?"

"It's okay for you to date him. Just don't sleep with him." She grimaced and added, "Gross."

Julia found it reassuring, at least, that her daughter was still innocent enough to find such a scenario likely. "Paige, there's a lot you don't understand."

"Like what?"

"Like old wrongs don't mend overnight."

"Why not?" she demanded. "It's obvious you're both still crazy about each other. He stared at you all night long, any time you weren't looking. And you stared at him."

Julia tried hard to wrestle the hope back into the little spot deep down where she had hidden it. "I don't think so."

Paige laughed. "Mom, I'm not stupid or blind."

"Well, I think it would be a good idea to wait and see how it goes this coming Tuesday, after the whale-watching."

"Why?" When Julia didn't have an answer for her, Paige added, "Mom, do you know what *carpe diem* means?"

Julia laughed. "Of course I do."

"Okay then. Don't be such a wuss. Do something."

Julia gazed helplessly at her daughter. Paige snorted in disgust and put her earbuds back in. She sat back against her pillows, and picked up her book.

After a moment's hesitation, Julia went to the bedside table and opened the drawer. Inside, wrapped in a handkerchief, she found the smooth, flat circle of stone. It had a pink inner section, surrounded by a circle of white, surrounded in turn by an outer ring of green. Just like a slice of watermelon.

"Don't be afraid of love. And don't compromise." She slipped the watermelon tourmaline into the pocket of her sweater.

Finally, she went to the safe in her closet, where she hid her valuables from Paige's sticky fingers. From within the safe she retrieved a small box, slipped it into the other pocket of her sweater, and stumbled out of the room.

William turned off the TV when she appeared in the living room. She sat on the love seat and touched the watermelon tourmaline in the pocket of her sweater.

"If it's meant to be," her uncle had said, "the details will work themselves out."

William reached into his back pocket and pulled out his wallet. Retrieved a photo, and held it out to Julia.

"I found something of yours."

She went to sit beside him on the couch and took it from him. "My God. This is the photo you took of me and Paige when you took us whale watching."

"I think Robert must have been in the picture, too." He waited for her to grasp his meaning. "I knew there had to be a reason I kept this all these years."

She stared down at the photo, blinking, her eyes stinging ominously. After a while, William ventured, "He's so much like me, it's scary. It must have been the worst kept secret on the planet."

"It was," she replied with a shaky laugh. Looking up at him, steeling her resolve, she said, "It's been both a comfort and a torment, having such a big piece of you with me all these years."

He shifted his weight in his seat. Stared down at the floor in front of him.

"From the second he was born, it took my breath away to look at him," she continued quietly. "The way he would look up at me with those big blue eyes while I nursed him. *Your* eyes. You can't imagine the pain I felt, knowing he might never know who his father was."

He put his face in his hands, and she heard him whisper, "Julie."

She took his hands and gently pulled them away from his face. He lifted his eyes to hers, and the creases in his forehead deepened.

"I have something of yours, too," she said.

She reached into her sweater pocket and pulled out the small box. Opened it, and held up the chain with the Saint Peter pendant.

He gaped in disbelief at it.

"I must have snapped the chain when I grabbed at you, trying to stop you from leaving," she explained. "I had it repaired. I was going to mail it to you. But by then I knew I was pregnant. I thought maybe one day Robert would realize Kevin was not his father. I wanted him to have at least one thing that was yours."

She opened the clasp, leaned forward, and put the chain around his neck. After she had closed the clasp again, she leaned back to find him overcome with emotion. He would not look her in the eye.

"Now you can give it to him yourself," she said.

The tears spilled over and he swiped at them with his hand. She swallowed, leaned forward and gently wiped them away with her thumb. He looked her in the eyes then, and she took his hands in hers.

"What I did six years ago, I did when I was not in my right mind," she said. "Not one single day has passed when I haven't asked myself why I did it."

The pain in his eyes was palpable. "I don't know what to say," he whispered.

She squeezed his hands. "You have no reason to trust me. I have no right to make you promises. But if there's even one tiny part of yourself that still cares – that can find some way to forgive me – I will love you and make you happy for the rest of your life."

All the air seemed to leave his lungs, and he looked away from her again. After a while, she took his left arm in her hand and slowly began to push up the sleeve of his sweater.

He snatched his arm away, avoiding her eyes. She said, "Did you cover it, or have it removed?"

He said nothing, and after a while, she gently took his arm again. Pushed the sleeve up.

It was still there.

She gazed in disbelief at the mermaid. Then she picked up his arm, and kissed it.

He watched her for a moment, and said, "I tried so hard to hate you. But as far as I'm concerned, you're all there is. I'm never going to love anyone half as much as I love you."

She touched her hand to his face, nuzzled his beard. Smiled tenderly, and said, "This is going to take some getting used to."

He covered her hand with his. Their foreheads touched, and his face contorted as he looked over the familiar cliff.

"It's okay," she whispered, stroking his hair with her free hand. Then, from beneath the lining of the box where she had stored his St. Peter chain, she lifted the mermaid necklace.

He let her kiss him; let go and let himself love her again.

♥ THE END ♥

AUTHOR'S NOTE

I started writing *The Catch* in 2012. By the time life imitated art in 2013, I had already written the vast majority of the manuscript. I can honestly say, therefore, that any resemblance between *The Catch* and my own life is purely coincidental.

However, as an unexpectedly-single mom to three children under the age of four, it would be another decade before I could return to writing. I also no longer had the time or energy to seek traditional publishers for *The Catch*. Meanwhile, I was sitting on this lovely manuscript, and I didn't want it gathering dust! Still, it would be 2015 before I finally managed to publish *The Catch* as an indie author.

Now that you know my story, let me say this:

NOTHING HELPS INDIE AUTHORS MORE THAN REVIEWS!
And I do mean absolutely nothing – especially reviews on Amazon and Goodreads. Seriously, Dear Reader – reviews are just *so* critical to an author's discoverability and success.

SO PLEASE, I'M BEGGING YOU: LEAVE A REVIEW
on your platform of choice by going to
https://linktr.ee/jennamilesreviews
Or by scanning this QR code.

Thank you so much!

ABOUT THE AUTHOR

An avid writer since she first picked up a crayon, Jenna Miles creates compelling, heartwarming stories that touch on themes of romance, mental health, and feminism. When she isn't working or writing, Jenna loves to tend her garden and cook delicious, healthy meals for her three sassy daughters. Originally from Dallas, Texas, Jenna now resides in the San Francisco Bay Area, where she saves the world one calorie at a time as a Registered Dietitian. Her dream is to one day pursue an MFA in Creative Writing.

LINKTREE:
https://linktr.ee/jennamileswrite

WEBSITE:
www.jennamilesauthor.com

AMAZON:
www.amazon.com/author/jennamiles

GOODREADS:
www.goodreads.com/author/show/14594436.Jenna_Miles

INSTAGRAM:
@jennamilesauthor

FACEBOOK:
www.facebook.com/jennamilesauthor

TWITTER:
@jennamileswrite

TIKTOK:
@jennamilesauthor

Made in the USA
Las Vegas, NV
06 July 2023

74261267R00167